The Story began in...

The Kind of a Girl...

as Lorraine Innis, a man in disguise trying to avenge the death of his girlfriend, accidentally foiled the assassination attempt on Russian president Kropotkin.

It continued in...

The Girl in the Diamond Studded Heels...

as Lorraine, now famous, became an international symbol of peace!

Then came...

The Girl in the Aubergine Sandals...

where we met Lorraine's Aunt Elinor and started to learn about the tragic flaws in Lorraine's past.

Which led to...

The Girl in the Lime Green Wellies...

and the star-crossed love affair with Verity Goodhue.

The Girl in the Saffron Espadrilles...

Where we learned the final pieces of the puzzle that resulted in the creation of Lorraine.

Now get ready as the adventure continues in..

The Girl in the Blood Red Stilettos!

I0653096

ALSO BY G.C. Allen

The Kind of a Girl

The Girl in the Diamond Studded Heels

The Girl in the Aubergine Sandals

The Girl in the Lime Green Wellies

The Girl in the Saffron Espadrilles

Coming Soon...

The Girl in the Sky Blue Plimsolls

Visit www.iLorraine.com

The Girl in the Blood Red Stilettos

G. C. Allen

Daley•into•Print LLC

Mundus Est Vestra Locusta

All characters appearing in this work are fictitious.
Any resemblance to real persons, living or dead,
is purely coincidental.

For All the Valeries:
Ever Reaching
and Never Realizing

I will rise now and go about the city,
     in the streets and in the squares;
I will seek him whom my soul loves.
     I sought him, but found him not.

- Song of Solomon 3:2

The Girl
in the
Blood Red
Stilettos

– 1 –
The Maternal Undertow

P lease, call me Lorraine."

"Really?" The woman asked with her mouth agape.

"That's my name, Sharon."

"Of course, Mrs. Innis," Sharon blushed. "Sorry, I mean, Lorraine."

Just "Lorraine" made her feel closer to real people. Because of her fame, most people were in awe of her. She didn't like that.

"We appreciate your visit today," said Sharon. "It helps raise awareness of everything we're trying to do here."

"It's my pleasure," said Lorraine, "and I'm glad I was able to help with…"

"Another shot, Mrs. Innis," interrupted a photographer.

Sharon stepped aside. Lorraine put her arm around her and pulled her into the picture.

"Really, no, they don't want me…"

"Of course they do. You're the director of the shelter. You have to be in the picture," said Lorraine, holding up the serving spoon that she'd been wielding for the last half-hour.

The woman looked at her own empty hands.

"You'll need one of these," whispered Lorraine as she handed Sharon a spatula. "It makes the photographs more interesting, at least to utensil fans."

The woman looked at Lorraine and smiled.

The photographer's flash went off, and his shutter clicked.

"One more, please, Mrs. Innis…"

After the photographers and reporters hurried off to meet their deadlines, Lorraine looked over her shoulder.

"Well," said Lorraine, walking towards the kitchen, "let's wash up."

"Wash up?" The woman scurried after Lorraine. "You want to wash the dishes?"

Lorraine headed for the large steel sink, turned on the faucet and reached for a bottle of dish soap.

"But Mrs. Innis…"

"Lorraine…" reminded Lorraine, squeezing soap into a washrag.

"No, Mrs. Innis, you can't…"

Lorraine stopped and looked at her.

"I mean, you shouldn't…" said Sharon.

"Don't the dishes need to be done?" asked Lorraine.

"No, I mean, yes, we do the dishes, that is, they need to be done…"

"Well, then," smiled Lorraine and turned back to the sink.

"…but not by you."

Lorraine turned off the water and faced the woman.

"You've heard about the time I broke the gravy boat," said Lorraine. "I was young and reckless. I didn't know that the bottom was attached…"

"Gravy boat? I don't understand."

Lorraine smiled. "I'm kidding. It was a joke."

"Oh," said the woman, and then laughed.

Lorraine wiped her hands on her apron and gave her a hug.

"I came here to help."

"But the reporters and the photographer have gone."

"And the dirty dishes are still here," said Lorraine. "So let's clean them. I'll wash and you dry."

Sharon nodded, and they started on the pots and pans. After a few minutes, Lorraine started to hum.

"Only, I thought…" interrupted Sharon. "I mean, I thought you came to get us some publicity, you know, for the shelter."

"I suppose," said Lorraine, not looking up from her scrubbing. "I actually came to help."

"But, you gave us that check…"

"That was from the foundation," said Lorraine. "It's not my money."

"But it's your foundation."

"It just has my name on it."

She scoured some baked-on macaroni from the bottom of a pot.

"The mayor came by once," said Sharon. "He took some pictures, in the serving line…"

Lorraine kept scrubbing.

"They put his picture in the paper and wrote about his visit to the shelter. But as soon as they took the pictures, he left."

Lorraine looked up. "Do you have any more soap pads?" she asked.

"Um… yes, here…" she handed Lorraine a fresh steel wool pad. "It was good to get the shelter in the paper…"

"Oh, yes…"

"But, we don't really expect politicians to do the actual work."

Lorraine rinsed out the clean pot and handed it to Sharon.

"Good thing I'm not a politician," she said and reached for another dirty pan.

Twenty minutes later, the last of the dishes were put away. Lorraine Innis slipped off her apron. Sharon was just staring at her.

"Is there something wrong?" asked Lorraine touching her face.

The woman shook her head. "Oh, no, it's not you, it's me. I mean, forgive me for… it's just that, well, you're just like you are on television."

Lorraine looked down at her hips. "Are you sure? They usually say that the television camera adds ten pounds."

Sharon smiled. "I mean, you're just like the way you seem on TV."

Lorraine shrugged her shoulders. "That's because I'm me. Who else would I be?"

"No, well, it's not like when other people come here, you know dignitaries and politicians, and big shots. But you're more important than all of them put together."

Lorraine shrugged as if to debate the point.

"When all those other people come for photo opportunities, they smile for the cameras, but when the cameras are turned off…"

"They leave…" said Lorraine.

"Worse, before they leave when they're short-tempered and they act like they're more important than anyone else. And I always figured that was because they were."

"Oh."

"But you didn't act like that," said Sharon. "You were even nicer after the reporters left. I suppose those others come because they want something. But you're here like you wanted to give us something. And I don't just mean the donation."

"I can't claim anything original," said Lorraine. I'm just following some ancient advice: 'Be merciful in action, kindly in heart, humble in mind.' I'm just trying to be consistent."

The woman stared with such reverence that Lorraine felt uncomfortable. She didn't understand why people made such a fuss. After all, she reasoned, she was just being herself. You can't give a person credit for that. It's like admiring them for their height or the color of their eyes.

"Let's see the rest of the center," said Lorraine, changing the subject.

"Oh, yes, of course," said Sharon pointing down the hallway. "We're very proud of these new rooms. And they wouldn't have been possible without your generous donation."

Lorraine reminded her again that she was just the glorified delivery person.

They toured the rooms, as Sharon described the uses of each. Then at the end of the hallway, they came to a room with a large picture window.

"And this is our new daycare," Sharon beamed. "It's been a real blessing for the working mothers in the neighborhood.

Lorraine was introduced to the volunteers and the children in the room. The caregivers appeared awed in her presence, the children much less so.

"And here is our newest arrival," said Sharon reaching into a crib. She lifted a baby no more than one-month-old. "This is Jessica."

"She's beautiful," said Lorraine.

The shelter director offered little Jessica to Lorraine. "Would you like to hold her?"

Lorraine smiled. "Could I?"

She took the baby and cradled it in her arms. "She precious, she's..."

Suddenly, a feeling overspread her. It was a feeling unlike any other she had ever experienced before. It was a feeling of love, but not quite the same as the love she had felt for persons in the past; it was more nurturing. It was maternal.

"Are you okay, Mrs. Innis... Lorraine," she heard a voice ask. The question was repeated, jarring Lorraine out of the emotion that had engulfed her.

"What? Oh, yes, thank you," she said, staring at the child in her arms. "It's just... just..."

Sharon smiled and nodded. "I always get that way, too."

Lorraine looked up. "You do?"

She nodded. "There's something about a baby, especially when they're so small. I remember when I had my first. It was like a miracle, holding a brand new life that hadn't been there before, so tiny, so perfect."

Lorraine sighed.

"Do you have any children?" Sharon asked.

"No," said Lorraine, "but I'd like to someday." Then she stopped. "I mean, no, no, I don't, that is, I can't... I can't have children."

"Oh, I'm sorry."

"So am I," Lorraine whispered. "It's... it's a birth defect."

"What a shame. You'd make such a good mother."

"I would?"

Sharon smiled and nodded at the contented baby in Lorraine's arms. "Of course, you're a natural, and that's not just my opinion."

The baby stirred and then reached out and touched Lorraine's breast.

"At least you can feed her," said Sharon.

Lorraine's mouth dropped open. She couldn't do that either, due to another birth defect. How could she explain that? She didn't have to, for as she turned, Sharon handed her a bottle of formula.

Lorraine breathed an inward sigh of relief and took the bottle. She sat down in a nearby rocking chair and began to feed the baby. A fresh wave of maternal feelings swept over her. A few minutes later, a voice intruded.

"My sister couldn't have children," said Sharon, "or a least that's what she thought."

"Oh?" said Lorraine.

"Yes, and now she has three. It's amazing what modern medicine can do."

"Yes," agreed Lorraine. Modern medicine. She was due to see her doctor next week, Dr. Clott. "Yes," repeated Lorraine, "yes, I'll have to speak with my doctor."

Motherhood: what a wonderful feeling.

- 2 -
Fighting Polonius
with Polonius

M ike Valvano assumed most people had happy memories of their childhood home. No fond memories washed over him as he steered his car through the gates of *Bella Culo*, the family's Pennsylvania estate. He was yanked from his boyhood at the age of eleven because Robert, his brother, was turning thirteen. That's when their training in the family business began.

Now he was summoned home by Robert. It was couched as an invitation, but it was a command all the same. And it didn't even come directly from Robert. He rarely had contact with his brother now.

The Valvano boys were like two branches of the same headwater. They sprang from the same source and traveled together for a time but flowed increasingly apart once they separated. They were now following courses miles away from each other.

Men loitered around the large house as Michael drove up. He never knew what to call them: henchmen; goons; thugs? They worked for Robert in a variety of odd jobs. While they looked menacing, at best, they were gofers. Michael imagined they had all seen too many gangster films for their own good.

Alfonse was another matter. Alfonse was scary and was reputed to have done many violent acts. Alfonse recognized Michael's car and waved him to the front door while waving off the wannabe hoods.

"Mike, *come va?*" asked Alfonse as he reached out for Michael's hand, and once he had it, pulled him into a warm embrace.

"Alfonse, how are you?" said Michael.

"Good," said Alfonse, "indubitably good."

Mike Valvano smiled. "Still listening to your vocabulary tapes."

"Decidedly," replied Alfonse, though in his clumsy manner of speaking.

"I like it," said Mike, "So what else is new?"

Alfonse cast his eyes down. "You heard about Mr. Liverot?"

Mike Valvano nodded. "Yes, I didn't know him very well, but my girlfriend worked for him."

Alfonse's somber expression lightened into a gentle smile. "Yeah, I heard you got a girl. She nice?"

"*Bella!* She's beautiful."

"That's nice," said Alfonse. "You know we was all, uh, nonplussed, yeah, that's a good word, when you gave up the priesthood. But I figured you must have had a real good reason, even one what was, what's the word... compelling."

Michael nodded and thought of Valerie Fierro. "Yeah, Al, compelling is the word."

"Good thing I take them courses," concluded Alfonse, "or else we wouldn't have known why you did what you did. We wouldn't have known you was compelled. And your girl knew Mr. Liverot?"

"At the bank," said Mike, "at least until she went to work with her cousin, Lorraine."

"Yeah, yeah," said Alfonse excitedly, "that's what I heard. She knows Lorraine, *The* Lorraine, huh?"

Mike Valvano gave the brute a sideways glance. Though he had known Alfonse his entire life, he never ceased to be amazed at his childlike streak. "You like Lorraine Innis, huh?"

"Lorraine," said Alfonse, his face lighting up, "oh, yeah, I'm a big fan, she's great, and often she's even peripatetic. Didja know she's Italian, too? Well, a modicum of her is Italian. Her maiden name was Amaccappane."

"I knew she was part Italian," admitted Mike, "but I didn't know her maiden name." He thought it was odd that Valerie had never mentioned much about Lorraine's past, even though they were cousins. If anything, when Mike mentioned Lorraine, Valerie seemed annoyed. He wondered if Valerie was a little jealous of Lorraine.

"Do you think, Mike, that maybe, I mean, peradventure, yeah, peradventure you could get me a picture of Lorraine?"

"Yeah, sure, that's no problem."

"And peradventure," continued Al, lowering his head, "do ya think that she could, you know, autograph it, like personally, to me?"

Mike Valvano suppressed a smile at Alphonse's manner, which had melted from menacing to bashful at the mere mention of Lorraine.

"I'll see what I can do," said Mike.

The hitman's face lit up. "Really? Gee, Mikey, I would be esteemed, and it would make my countenance real salubrious."

Mike patted Alphonse's shoulder and promised that he would do his best. Then he nodded towards the house. "Is my brother waiting for me?"

"Yeah, he's in there. So is Mr. Rosen."

Mike thanked him and started inside. He hadn't been to *Bella Culo* for months, not since he informed his family that he was leaving the priesthood. He made his way to the spacious library just off the entry hall. He was met, not by a family member, not even by an Italian, but by Julius Rosen, the family's attorney.

"Michael," said the lawyer, extending his hand, "good to see you home, again."

Mike shook his hand, which was fleshy on the exterior but concealed a firm grip beneath, much like a white chocolate candy with a hard center. Rosen smiled, though Mike suspected sincerity was merely part of Rosen's legal training.

"I had to come," said Mike, "or was that summons to appear just an informal demand and not a binding request?"

"We just had some business to discuss with you," said Rosen, "family business, of course."

Mike almost reminded Rosen he wasn't family. Still, in business matters, Rosen only took a backseat to Robert and, of course, their grandmother.

"You know, Julius, I always wondered," began Michael, "why you didn't change your name?"

"How so, Michael?"

Michael ran his fingers along the books on the shelf. "Well, I mean, you look Italian. We're all from around the Mediterranean. You could pass for a guinea. I just thought you would have changed your name to Julie Rosselli, or Julie Rossini, you know, something like that."

"I couldn't do that," said Rosen.

Mike turned around and said with mock seriousness: "If you need a lawyer, I'm sure we could find one to do a simple name change."

Rosen smiled without a hint of mirth. "'To thine own self be true,'" said Rosen wagging his finger, "Polonius, in *Hamlet*."

Mike nodded at Rosen's expensive suit. "Polonius also said: 'Clothes make the man.'"

"I didn't ask you here today to listen to two *stunads* swap Shakespeare," barked a voice.

In the doorway stood Robert Valvano. They were obviously brothers; both had the same thin, muscular build, both the same facial features. The main difference was that Robert's hair was dark brown, almost black, while his younger brother's was light brown. Their voices were also different. Michael had a smooth baritone, while Robert spoke in a gravelly bass.

Robert also had a taste for the finer things in life. He stood there in his silk sweater and tailored slacks. Though casual, his imported ensemble was costlier than Julius Rosen's expensive suit.

"Rob," said Michael exchanging a fraternal embrace. Robert added a kiss to his brother's neck before they sat down in facing leather chairs. Julius Rosen sat off to the side.

"So, last we heard from you, you came here to tell us you were quitting the holy orders for your girlfriend."

Michael sat expressionlessly.

"She must be quite the lady, this Miss Fierro," continued Robert.

"I don't recall mentioning her name," said Mike dryly. "You haven't been checking up on me, have you?"

Robert Valvano raised an eyebrow while cocking his head to one side. "Don't flatter yourself, Michael. It's none of my business who you sleep with, whether you dump them or marry them. That's your affair. What is my business are the people I employ, whether directly or indirectly. And in that regard, Valerie Fierro is an asset of the family business. I've made no deeper investigations on her than anyone else who works for me."

Robert would have made a champion chess player, expertly gathering information and plotting moves. Though he had never been the victim of his brother's strategic thinking, Michael had long learned that the best way to play Robert to a stalemate was through distraction.

"How's Nonnia?" asked Mike, though the question was rhetorical. He knew how their grandmother was. He called the old woman weekly. It was his only regular contact with the family.

Without moving his head, Robert's eyes glanced upward toward their grandmother's room as if to confirm it still existed. Then his eyes met his brother's again.

"I want you to go to work for the bank," said Robert cutting to the reason for their meeting.

"The bank?" Michael almost laughed at the notion. "Why would I go to work for the bank?"

"Because I told you to," said Robert.

"But I've got my own business."

Robert Valvano examined his fingernails. "It's doing well," he said, not bothering to look up, "but it's inconsequential. Julius can find someone to tend to it, or we can just liquidate it."

Mike fought to keep his temper in check. The family had bankrolled his venture. Robert had the right to pull the rug out from under him. But while the family had loaned him the funds to start the business, Mike was making it a success.

"Mike," interjected Julius Rosen, "no one wants to shut down your company, not unnecessarily. It's just that this Liverot thing puts us in a bad spot."

"Isn't there anyone at the bank who can run things," said Mike. "I mean, Peter Liverot couldn't have been that indispensable."

A smirk crossed Robert's lips. "You apparently thought he was. Otherwise, why would you call me up and spare his life? Alphonse had the gun to his head. It was only my call, at your request, that saved Liverot's life. Do you know how difficult that was, how that went against my moral code?"

"It goes against your moral code not to execute a man?" asked Mike. He started reaching for his clerical collar before recalling he had left the priesthood.

"It was justice," said Robert. "Liverot betrayed the trust placed in him. I spared his life at the personal request of Father Michael Valvano. You not only parlayed your family relationship, but your church connections, Mikey, and for what?"

Michael looked away. He had no love for Peter Liverot. He still didn't fully understand why he had called his brother that night after seeing Valerie on his regular hospital rounds. She was lying there in a coma. But then he saw the flowers from Liverot at her bedside. He didn't know the connection between the girl in the bed and Liverot, so he called his brother. Robert had told him that Liverot wouldn't matter, not for much longer anyway, and Michael knew that the banker's days were numbered. Not sure of how it would impact Valerie, he interceded for Liverot. At first, Robert was immovable until Michael mentioned Valerie and Lorraine Innis. Suddenly, Robert became interested, pumping his brother for the scant information he had on the two women and their connection to Liverot. Over the phone, Michael could almost hear his brother's mind working out various moves and scenarios.

"Now you're telling me," Robert continued, "that you want to use your family without giving back at all. You use me to save the life of Peter Liverot. You use me to set you up in a nice little business so you can make a good living, but you don't want to pay for what you get, Michael. You're like a shoplifter, but you're stealing from your own family's store. If it wasn't for me, where would you be? You'd still be a priest sitting in some crumby little parish burning for the body of the girl who you wanted but couldn't have. You became a priest, Michael, because you were ashamed of your family's business like we're some sort of hoodlums and thieves. We're 100 percent legitimate, Julius can attest to that..."

Julius Rosen made an expression indicating the number was less than that.

"You're ashamed of your family's power, except when you need it. And now, when I ask you to help me, you act like you don't want to know. If it wasn't for me, you'd be a priest, and Liverot would be dead."

"Liverot is dead," reminded Mike. "You called me here today to take over for him."

"Liverot is dead because of some lunatic," said Robert. "I'm sure Father Valvano could preach a sermon on God's decrees always getting done one way or another."

"So you're the instrument of God now? Is that the choice? You or a lunatic, those are the only options for the Almighty?"

Robert Valvano jerked his head to the side as if to say the conversation had become absurd.

"If God can replace you with a lunatic," asserted Mike, "why can't he replace Liverot with someone other than me? Doesn't the bank have a vice-president?"

Robert rolled his eyes. "That little shit, what's his name?" He snapped his fingers in Rosen's direction.

"Eckner, Albrecht Eckner," said Julius Rosen.

"A disgusting little *disgraziat'*," said Robert, unconsciously wiping his fingers. "No, I don't trust Eckner. Thanks to you, the bank has succeeded far beyond what we had hoped for it."

"Me?"

Robert smiled coldly. "Don't be modest. If it wasn't for you, we'd never have had the pleasure of employing the most beloved person in the world. As long as Lorraine Innis is the face of our little organization, it couldn't be anything but pure. After all, Lorraine Innis wouldn't lend her name to any enterprise that wasn't entirely ethical." Robert laughed. "What was it, Julius? What did Liverot tell us that Mrs. Innis refused to endorse..."

"A brand of soft drink..."

"Some soda," said Robert, "just because she didn't drink it. She preferred the competition. She's turned down millions in endorsements for one reason or another. And she's working for us."

"She has her own charity," cited Mike.

"And I provided the seed money," said Robert. "And she uses the facilities of Fourth Fiduciary, my bank. So let's say Mrs. Innis and I are cozy little bedfellows. And of course, Miss Fierro assists her cousin in the running of the charity. Now, Mikey, why wouldn't you want to associate with such fine, beautiful ladies as Mrs. Innis and Miss Fierro? You're the perfect choice for the job. After all, we wouldn't want someone... heavy-handed... working with such priceless and delicate assets, would we?"

The two brothers locked eyes. Michael searched Robert's steely gaze. Robert neither blinked nor flinched. As he looked into his brother's eyes, Michael couldn't help but think of Alphonse standing watch outside. The self-improving hitman had expressed regret at the passing of Peter Liverot, though he had nearly been Liverot's executioner. Michael recalled Alphonse's fascination with Lorraine Innis. He wondered if he could perform a hit against her or Valerie. He didn't want to know the answer. Nor would he want to test his own brother's resolve in the matter. Though he didn't want to be drawn into his brother's affairs, it would be better for Valerie and her cousin if he was there to insulate them from Robert.

"Yeah, okay," said Michael, blinking first. "I'll do the bank thing for you." He almost gave conditions for his acceptance but realized Robert's promises were only valid as long as they suited him.

Robert smiled and looked at Julius Rosen as if to say: I told you he'd do it.

"Good," said Robert. "This makes me very happy, Mike. And you'll see, it'll be good for you, too. Isn't that right, Julius?"

"Old friends are the best friends," said Rosen, before turning to Michael, "that's *Hamlet*, Polonius again, Michael."

Mike Valvano nodded. He thought of one more quote from Polonius, though this one he kept to himself: "Though this be madness, yet there is method in it."

– 3 –
Photographic Reaction #1: The Removal

E xcuse me, Mr. President?"
Yuri Belikov, the aide to Russian leader Nikolai Kropotkin, gently placed his pudgy hand on the body slumped over the desk. There was no response.

"Mr. President?"

Still no response. Drastic measures were needed.

"Uncle Nikolai? Uncle Nikki?"

Nikolai Kropotkin hated to be reminded he was Yuri's uncle by marriage. He detested Yuri using a diminutive of his name.

Kropotkin barely replied. It was more of a sigh directed toward the framed photograph on his desk. It was of Lorraine Innis.

Since the previous October, Kropotkin, international leader, man of steely resolve, had been a different person. That autumn day, his life was saved, quite accidentally, she insisted, by Lorraine. It wasn't her act of heroism that changed Kropotkin's life. That had only got his attention. It was when he actually met Lorraine that Kropotkin began his extraordinary metamorphosis. From then, Kropotkin started to see the world differently. It was as if a fog had been burned off by the sun. His feelings for Lorraine Innis grew from gratitude to appreciation, to admiration, to infatuation. Finally, he was certain, to love.

Kropotkin fought the emotion. His widower's heart was open to love, but his code of honor refused to consider an affair with a married woman. Then Kropotkin, and the whole world, discovered that Lorraine's husband was a bigamist. Since then, he plighted his troth, though he learned Lorraine was not interested in anyone's troth, plighted or unplighted.

Yuri Belikov reached out and shook Kropotkin's shoulder. Kropotkin glanced up.

"Oh, it is you," said Kropotkin. He sighed and retreated into his melancholy.

Yuri decided even more desperate action was needed. He moved to the front of the desk.

"Forgive me, Uncle President," said Yuri, "but as the Americans say: 'this is for you, for good!'"

With that, Yuri snatched away the photograph of Lorraine Innis. For a moment, Kropotkin continued to stare at the spot where the photo had been. Then the spell was broken. Kropotkin looked up with violence in his eyes.

Yuri stood triumphantly across the desk. He finally succeeded in rousing Kropotkin. However, his victory was fleeting; a moment later, he wished for a return of the love-sick zombie.

"Yuri, what are you doing?!" growled Kropotkin.

"Uncle, I... I... mean, Mr. P-president, sir, I... I...."

Yuri's feeble explanation was cut short as Kropotkin bounded over the desk, fingers splayed for strangling Yuri. Yuri concluded now was the perfect time to run for his life.

"Get back here with that you inflated nincompoop," shouted Kropotkin as he chased Yuri around the office. "Give me that picture, you overstuffed imbecile!"

"Uncle, President," panted Yuri, "calm yourself, you don't know yourself..."

"I know me," bellowed the enraged leader. "I am the man who will commit justifiable homicide as soon as I can beat your tubby little carcass to a gelatinous pulp!"

Yuri grabbed a bottle of Kropotkin's favorite soft drink as he passed the office bar. He held it out with his left hand while cradling the silver frame under his right arm.

"Uncle, please, calm yourself, have a drink..."

Kropotkin came close enough to grab the bottle, but instead of drinking it, he flung it at Yuri's head. Instead of ducking, Yuri reflexively threw up his other arm, the one holding the frame. The bottle smacked straight into the back of the frame. It shot back at Kropotkin, hitting him squarely in the forehead and knocking him to the floor.

Yuri looked back at the motionless figure of his uncle.

"President Uncle?" he mewed, but Kropotkin just lay there with his eyes closed. Yuri approached tentatively. "Are you all right?"

He bit the end of his thumb. Kropotkin looked so still. He couldn't be... dead, could he? People didn't die from being hit in the forehead with a plastic soda bottle, did they? Yuri inched closer still. Kropotkin's breathing was shallow. He picked up the bottle of soda and hefted it in his hand. It was Coca-Cola. Perhaps a Diet Coke would have been less lethal. Leaning over Kropotkin, Yuri noticed a red ring in the center of his forehead, the same shape as the bottle cap. It had been a direct hit.

"Ugggghhhh…"

Nikolai Kropotkin began to stir.

"Oh, good, very good," cried Yuri, "you are not dead!"

Yuri looked around for something to revive Kropotkin and then realized he was holding the Coke. He knelt beside Kropotkin.

"Here, Uncle, here, have a sip of this …"

Yuri opened the bottle. The contents, agitated from being tossed around the room, exploded all over Kropotkin's face.

"You idiot!" bellowed Kropotkin as Yuri struggled to cap the gusher of soda.

"Uncle, I'm sorry, it must have been shaken up…"

"Shaken up? Of course, it was shaken up, you boob. First, you ran around the room with it, and then you bounced it off my head!"

The carbonated drink trickled to an impotent fizz, after which Yuri finally screwed the cap back on the bottle. He looked at Kropotkin, who was now sitting. Kropotkin wiped the liquid from his face then slowly raised his hands towards Yuri. Resigned to his fate, Yuri remained on his knees to receive the retribution he knew he deserved. But instead of choking him, Kropotkin's fingers went limp. The animosity drained from his face, replaced by a look of mourning. Yuri turned to see the object of Kropotkin's sorrow: the silver frame.

Nikolai Kropotkin crawled to the frame, picking it up tenderly and turning it over to examine the front. A single crack ran through the glass, though the picture inside was unharmed.

"Lorruska, my Lorruska," cooed Kropotkin. Then, cradling his treasure, he made his way to the sofa and sat down, never taking his eyes from the photograph.

He's gone again, thought Yuri. He shuffled over and sat beside Kropotkin.

"Lorruska, Lorruska…" Kropotkin muttered, stroking the photograph. "I will get you a new glass, a whole new frame…"

"Uncle…" Yuri tentatively placed his hand on Kropotkin's shoulder. "Uncle, I'm sorry, but…"

"I thought I was getting better…"

"Uncle?"

Kropotkin sighed. "This woman," he said, shaking his head, "I do not understand this woman. This feeling is like nothing else." He was speaking to Yuri but never once took his eyes off of Lorraine Innis. "When first I met her, I was smitten. I did not indulge that feeling, believing that she was married and with child. Then, when she came here to visit last winter, and I knew she was free, I made my proposal. But it was odd, my boy."

"Odd, Uncle?"

"The attraction wasn't the same," said Kropotkin.

"Oh, yes, she pushed you off the parapet into the snowbank," recalled Yuri.

"No, that wasn't it. She was different, somehow. Lorruska didn't... exude."

"Exude, Uncle?"

"She didn't..." Kropotkin waved a hand limply through the air as if to grasp a wisp of meaning. "Before she was so strong, so vital, and yet emanating an intense womanhood."

"Oh," said Yuri.

Kropotkin waggled his head from side to side. "In Delaware, it was very raw, very sensual, very feminine, while at the same time completely pure and virginal."

"But not in Moscow?"

Kropotkin's expression drooped. "Not so much by half. It was the same face, the same voice, the same everything, but not the same, do you understand?"

Yuri scratched his head. "The same, but not the same?"

Kropotkin turned to him. "You do understand! So, I did what any man would do."

"Forget about her?"

"No! Pursue her," said Kropotkin. "I had to find my Lorruska, the woman who so captivated my heart and inspired my soul back in Delaware."

Yuri shrugged. "Maybe she only captivates in Delaware."

"Yes, she only captivates in Delaware, while you are a numbskull worldwide! No, I knew she was there, somewhere with all the passion, the kindness, the wisdom, the..." Kropotkin closed his eyes and clutched his chest as if gathering some primal essence to his bosom. "I tried sending her gifts, writing her notes, anything I could think of to reach out, and rekindle the flame that existed before. I tried for months and months until I despaired that it had all been an illusion, a mirage in the desert of my heart. I watched every interview she gave to see if I could catch a glimpse of the woman I once knew."

"And did you... glimpse, Uncle?"

"Not a bit," he confessed. "If anything, she was fading away. I concluded that it had been a brief vision, a mist within a dream."

"So, now you are feeling sad," said Yuri, "for what was, but then wasn't, and is no more."

Kropotkin shook his head. "No. Just as I was about to give up all that she had been to me, there was that madwoman, the woman at the White House."

"The one that blew up President Merton?"

"After that incident, Lorruska disappeared from public view for several weeks, and then..."

Kropotkin's face shone as if facing the rising sun.

"Then what?" asked Yuri.

"Then," said Kropotkin in a voice barely above a whisper, "then, she was back."

"Back?"

"My Lorruska!" exulted the Russian. "She was back and more magnificent than before. I do not know why. I cannot explain it. Perhaps she rises to the point of a crisis. Perhaps she has that innate greatness that comes along once in a lifetime. All I know is that something in her calls to my soul..." Kropotkin wiped a tear from his eye. "She is my soul, my heart," said Kropotkin, "I do not care what you call it. All I know is that I am in love with Lorraine Innis, and if I cannot have her..."

For the first time in his life, Yuri felt more in control than the mighty Nikolai Kropotkin. He reached out and grabbed Kropotkin's chin.

"Stop this, stop it, now, Nikolai," Yuri paused, shocked by his own affrontery. Kropotkin was also stunned, but he hadn't the resolve to argue in his current emotional state.

"You are the leader of Russia. Your country needs you, Nik... uh, Mr. President. Pull yourself together, for Russia."

Kropotkin wavered as if weighing the choices: Russia or Lorraine Innis. Yuri guessed Russia would lose and made the strongest appeal he could think of.

"Remember Kateryna," said Yuri. "Kateryna needs her father."

Kropotkin nodded. "You are right," said Kropotkin patting his nephew's knee. "Kateryna needs me..." He started to rise to his feet and stopped. "Of course, Kateryna could use a step-mother, too."

Kropotkin returned to his desk with the picture and resumed his original pose.

Yuri flapped his arms against his sides, shook his head, and started from the private office. Upon reaching the door, he turned back for one more look at the strongest man he had ever known. He had tried his best.

Yuri slipped out of the room and started down the hall to his little office. There must be something he could do. He walked into his office. There he found someone sitting in his swivel chair with his back to him.

"Excuse me," he said, "but that is my chair. What do you..."

The chair spun around. Yuri gasped.

"I beg your pardon, my dear Belikov," said the man. His smile contained enough teeth for two men. "But I didn't think you'd deny a seat to your old friend, would you?"

"Comrade Teplov," gasped Yuri. "What are you... I mean..." Yuri reached in his coat pocket for his handkerchief and began to mop his forehead, which was suddenly drenched in sweat. "I mean, what can I do for you?"

Teplov smiled, drawing on a reserve of bicuspids. "Me? No, my dear Yuri, you have it backward. The question is: what can I do for you?"

- 4 -
Photographic Reaction 2: The Revelation

"Will there be anything else, Miss?"

The butler always made her uneasy. And, since learning the truth, she not only disliked him, she distrusted him… intensely. Verity Goodhue looked down at the tea and toast he'd set before her.

"No, that will be all, Towson," she said. "Thank you."

He bowed obsequiously and backed out of the dining room.

Verity hated Bagnall Hall. She preferred the cozy caretaker's cottage, where she had enjoyed so many happy years with her grandfather. The cottage was where she retreated after the death of her beloved Chesney. The death, which she now knew, had been a sham.

Lorraine Innis had revealed the truth last October. She first saw Lorraine one evening on the BBC News.* At first, Verity thought she imagined it. She switched to ITV. Her suspicions were confirmed. The face was the same, though thinner. The hair was the same color, though longer and cut in a feminine style. The voice was similar, though in a woman's register and timbre. But she knew immediately that it was Chesney Potts. Not only would Verity know Chesney in any disguise, but he also was the spitting image of his Aunt Elinor, albeit twenty-five years younger.

But Chesney died in a car crash several years before. It was just three weeks before their wedding. Her father had taken her there. She saw the burnt shell of the car down in the ravine. She saw the rescue crew removing the charred remains of his body. They brought her his scorched license plate: "Potts 7."

Her father, Lord Bagnall, insisted on interring the body on the family estate, claiming he had grown so fond of the son-in-law he would never have. Those days were a blur viewed through a veil of tears. She was out of her mind with grief and was sedated. The funeral was delayed to allow

* The Girl in the Diamond Studded Heels – Ch. 13

Chesney's mother and brother to attend from America. They had seemed oddly detached. Now she realized they were only actors hired to play the parts.

If only she could have retreated behind a role and played a part. Instead, Verity Goodhue was consigned to spending her days reliving regrets. If she hadn't agreed to marry him, her father wouldn't have given them the matching sports cars as a wedding present. If they hadn't set the wedding date when they had, then perhaps it would have worked out differently. Chesney wouldn't have had to drive to London that exact day. Verity wouldn't have had to go for a wedding dress fitting. She relived that day down to the smallest detail. If she had kissed him a few seconds longer, it would have changed the course of everything. If only...

Added to her pain was the news that Chesney's Aunt Elinor died the same day. She had looked forward to Elinor's return from Tibet. If nothing else, Verity could commiserate with Elinor. She was the one person whose grief would approach her own. Then Verity learned Elinor died in hospice, the same day as her beloved nephew. Now she was truly alone. No one understood.

In public, she made a pretense of being cheerful, or at least less depressed. She saved her grief for herself, and as a result, it only deepened. Verity kept waiting for the day that didn't begin and end with tears, but it was always over a distant horizon.

Then came the night when she saw Lorraine Innis. It was as if a new person somehow emerged from the ashes of two. This Lorraine looked like Elinor Potoski while at the same time radiating the essence of Chesney. The person on television was either Aunt Elinor magically rejuvenated or Chesney brought back to life. There was only one way to resolve that question: she would have to raid his grave.

Putting on some old clothes and her wellies, Verity went by night to her beloved's grave. There, stumbling in the darkness, she discovered the truth. Approaching the grave from behind, Verity fell through the shrubbery at the rear of the stone. Putting her hand up to catch herself, she felt carving on the back of the stone. She turned on the torch to read it. The inscription sent a chill up her spine. It was her own gravestone. It read:

> Verity Elizabeth Goodhue
> Beloved Daughter
> You're My Beloved, Too

For a moment, she thought that it had been prepared for a future time, but then she saw the dates. Her birthday was there, and it was correct, but it gave a date of death: the same day that Chesney had died. The inscription also was telling. Beloved Daughter: that was obviously placed there by her father. But the next line, "You're My Beloved, Too," could only have been written by Chesney. But if Chesney wrote the inscription on her tombstone, who was buried in the grave? And why had both sides of the stone been completed and with the same date of death?

In the dark, she went around to the front of the grave and dug down to the coffin. She recalled the day that the coffin had been lowered into the ground. It was a closed casket service, given the horrific incineration of the body. Once she opened the coffin, however, she found the contents perfectly intact: undamaged bricks.

Only one person could be responsible: her father, Lord Bagnall. Why had he done it? She could guess his motives. She reasoned as she sat on the edge of the grave; if her father had faked Chesney's death to her, then the inscription on the back of the tombstone suggested the other half of his plot. Her father must have faked her death to him. Verity recalled adamantly telling her father that Chesney was her love. If Lord Bagnall forced her to choose between them, she would choose Chesney. Though at first Bagnall bristled at her declaration, he seemed to accept it. And now she knew why. He would break them apart in the only way that would be permanent for both. He would make each think the other was dead.

Her first impulse was to take the shovel, march over to Bagnall Hall, and part her father's hair with the same. But that would be too easy. He needed a more painful lesson. She couldn't let him know that she knew the truth. As Verity filled in the grave, she thought how it almost succeeded. It would have worked except for two things. First, her father's stinginess had led him to only buy one headstone and hide the other side with a thick planting of shrubs. Who looked around the back of headstones, especially in a private plot? Verity hadn't. She visited the grave every day and never walked around the back of the stone.

The second factor that unmasked her father's treachery was something he could never have planned against, this person named Lorraine Innis.

Verity finished filling in the grave and scattered fallen leaves over the area to mask her work. Then she made her way back to her cottage.

The question remained: who was Lorraine Innis? Well, that was fairly obvious to her. Lorraine was Chesney.

Perhaps the right question was: why was Lorraine Innis? Verity's grief had nearly driven her mad, but she hadn't adopted the guise of her favorite dead relative: her grandfather. Had Chesney gone mad? No, there was intelligence and rationality behind this "woman" named Lorraine Innis.

But, how deep below the surface was Chesney Potts? Had Chesney made any permanent changes? She didn't ponder these possibilities for very long. For one thing, there was no way of knowing, at least not now. Still, two critical facts remained: Chesney was alive, and that she loved him as desperately as ever.

Her immediate impulse was to hop the first plane to the States, find Lorraine Innis, and reclaim the Chesney beneath the surface. But she needed more information. Lorraine Innis was a popular public figure. If Verity suddenly appeared, would she place Chesney in danger? She would wait until she learned more. Verity sent a simple note to Lorraine Innis as a small concession to her excitement. All it said was: "I love you. Wait for me." She wanted to say so much more, but she dared not. Though it was agonizing, Verity would wait. She wasn't sure what she was waiting for: a signal, a sign, the turning of events, something. Until then, she would rest in the knowledge that her beloved was alive.

Verity's breakfast and pondering were interrupted by the heavy tread of her father. He had been a sergeant major in the army and still entered a room like he was storming a defensive position.

"Morning, muh dear," said Lord Bagnall.

She glanced up. As always, he was impeccably dressed. One could almost believe he was noble from birth and not just a life peer, at least until he opened his mouth.

"Splatterguard been 'round with me kippers, eh?" The question was redundant. He already lifted the silver dome under which his kippers were waiting.

"Good morning, Father," said Verity, careful to smile as a token that everything was just fine.

Bagnall leaned over and kissed Verity atop her head.

"Everything tickety-boo, my dear? Everything Hunky Dunky? Haw!"

Verity smiled indulgently.

Lord Bagnall took his place at the head of the table and ripped off a piece of the kipper with his fork. Only after he had thoroughly masticated the kipper and taken his first gulp of coffee did he look up and smile.

"It don't not 'alf do me 'eart good, my dear," he said, a piece of kipper stuck between his teeth.

"What's that, father? The fish?"

"Fish? Ha! No, not the fish. It does me good to see you out of it."

"Out of what, Father?"

"Out of your funk, your rut, your mélange…"

"Oh, yes, I've left my mélange far behind," agreed Verity, knowing he meant malaise.

"Quite right, too," said Bagnall, reaching for a baguette with his fork and spearing as if it were trying to escape. "Life goes on."

"Like so many things," said Verity.

"Not nothing to get upset about," said Bagnall, but then he caught himself. "No, no, I'd didn't mean it like that. I means to say that it's good to be upset, to what'd ya say…"

"Grieve? Mourn?"

"Yes, if you like. Those is good as any words. It's only natural to pine away and be blue when you suffer a loss, but like I said…"

"Life goes on."

Bagnall slapped his palm against the dining table as if the phrase was just coined at that moment.

"Precisely! I'm just glad that you're starting to live again."

"So many things are alive again, Father," she said, looking down into her teacup.

"Are they?" he said, puzzled by her vague remark. He shrugged. "Oh, well, yes, good to see you, you know... getting over..."

"You miss him, too, don't you, Daddy?"

Bagnall looked stunned for a moment and then caught himself and raised his linen napkin to the corner of his eye.

"There h'ain't not a day goes by," he said, "that I don't not think of... 'im."

"Him?"

Lord Bagnall placed his hand over his heart. "I don't not like to say 'is name. It still hurts."

"Oh, you do miss him," she said. Only two things kept her from throwing her teacup at his head: first, it was very fine china; second was the assurance that she was fomenting greater retribution.

"Miss 'im? Like 'e was me own boy! I treated 'im like what he was me own flesh and blood."

"Yes, Father, I know," said Verity. It was true enough, she thought. The scoundrel had faked the death of his own daughter. That he had done the same for Chesney proved he held them in the same regard.

"Oh, well, that's all done, now, h'ain't it?" said Lord Bagnall. Verity looked up. She wasn't sure if he was referring to the last bite of his breakfast or his supposed end of Chesney, probably both. "I'm very proud of you, my dear," he continued wiping his mouth. "You've been a real soldier through all of this."

"Thank you," she muttered.

"No, no, I admire 'ow you've got back into the swing of life," he said. "'Ow's that sick thingee you're sitting on?"

"Fine," she said. He was referring to the board of a hospital charity upon which she was serving.

"Good, good," he said. "Thanks again. I would have done it myself, but failing that, I'm glad you could step in on my tread."

"Yes, on your tread," she repeated.

"Look to the future," he said. "The future is ahead, and the past is, uh, behind. And now, that the past is past, I've got some news of the future that's quite h'excitin'."

"Oh?"

"Yes, quite h'excitin'," Lord Bagnall coughed into the back of his hand. "I've got a smashin' idea wot to boost sales."

"Oh," muttered Verity. She had never shared her father's enthusiasm for peddling toilet paper.

"Yes, it's super-pendous, absolutely gigantic," he said.

"But Father, you're already the king of paper products in the entire country," noted Verity.

"Like that Greek geezer, I got me bigger worlds to conquer," he said, jabbing his finger in the air. "And I've got the idea that's going to make me the top conveyor of tissue in the entire Earf'."

"Oh?"

"Guess 'ooo I'm going to get to be me new spokesman?"

"The Prince of Wales?" she offered facetiously.

Lord Bagnall curled his lip in upon his neatly trimmed mustache.

"I'm? Not likely. With all dull respect, 'is 'ighness couldn't sell ice to an Eskimo."

Verity almost pointed out that the analogy didn't make sense but just shook her head and sighed. "I'm sorry, Father. Who is your new spokesman?"

A broad grin spread across Lord Bagnall's face as he picked up a manila envelope, undid the clasp, and pulled out a glossy 11 X 14 photograph.

"Me new spokesman is... 'er!"

He turned the photograph around to reveal a beautiful color portrait of Lorraine Innis.

Verity stared at the image for a moment. Behind the soft shag hairdo and the makeup smiled the face of her beloved. How ironic, how deliciously paradoxical. Her father was proudly brandishing a photograph of the "woman" upon whom he was pinning his hopes, the same young man whose death he had faked a few years before. Verity pursed her lips, but the humor of the situation could not be denied. She burst out laughing. What made it even funnier was her father's reaction: he just stood there, bemused. Then, to make it worse, he turned and studied the photograph of Lorraine Innis, as if he were looking for something funny he had missed. He really couldn't see Chesney in Lorraine, could he? No, of course, he couldn't, and that made it all the more hilarious to her.

"I don't not see nothing 'umourous," he said.

"I'm sorry, I'm sorry," said Verity between the laughter.

"I think she's quite nice."

"Oh, I love... I mean, yes, I think she's lovely!"

"Lovely, yes, yes," said Bagnall looking at the photograph afresh. "She's lovely, I'd say she's about the loveliest lady in the 'ole wide world," he beamed at the picture before he caught himself. "I mean, after you, of course, me dear! I didn't not mean no slight upon you."

"Oh, none taken, none taken," said Verity, her laughter starting to ebb.

"But you do think she's okay?" said Bagnall.

"Lorraine Innis? Father, I think Lorraine Innis is wonderful. She's absolutely marvelous. And I think your idea for doing business with her is fantastic."

He eyed her sideways. "You really think so, does you?"

"Of course," said Verity.

"Then why was you taking the mickey when I showed you 'er photograph?"

"Oh, I wasn't making fun of you, Father."

"You was making fun of 'er?" He pointed to Lorraine's photograph.

"Certainly not her," said Verity. "I can honestly say that there's no one in this whole world for whom I have more respect or admiration than the person in that photograph. It was just that it came as such a surprise, such a delightful surprise that I reacted with... unbridled joy."

"Joy, eh?" he said skeptically.

"I'm sorry I laughed. I guess I don't fully have control of my emotions yet. I was so happy that my happiness spun out of control."

Lord Bagnall cocked his head to one side. "Yes, I suppose that makes sense. And it does me 'eart good to see you 'appy again, even if it's a little too 'appy. So, you likes the idea?"

"Of Lorraine Innis? I told you, it's wonderful," said Verity. "Do you really think you can get... her to endorse your products?"

"Oh, I think so," he bragged, and then his face dropped. "Well, at least I 'ope, I can."

"Why, Father, what's wrong?"

"Blast if I can understand it," said Bagnall scratched his head. "But me market research boffins tell me that I don't not have no appeal to the, well, the gentler... feminine... persuasions."

"Really, that's hard to believe," said Verity, though she not only understood, she concurred. "On what do they base that conclusion?"

His Lordship shrugged. "Oh, about eight years ago, I did the commercials, recollect?"

Verity remembered it vividly. Her father had just been made a life peer and made a commercial bragging that the toilet tissue without peer, now was the peer's toilet tissue.

"Any road," continued Bagnall, "them genies in survey research said me personality didn't not score 'igh with women or other females. Sales took an un'ealthy nosedive when we ran the adverts. Spun down the 'opper faster than a one-ply sheet. So they're right about me and women. Sales came back, but now I really want to make a hit with the fairer gender. My advert brains suggest we get a popular woman, the most popular one we could find."

"And you thought of Lorraine Innis?"

"Uh, no," he coughed into the back of his hand, "actually, I thought of 'er Majesty. But she don't not do no ads, 'cepting for 'er Christmas speech and opening Parliament. This Lorraine was the advert boys' idea. They said if I wants my product to have womanly appeal, the kind what will appeal to females, then I need a popular woman to give it that woman's touch. "

"And so you're going to approach Lorraine Innis?"

Lord Bagnall looked down at his feet. "Actually, they said I didn't have the tact needed to woo such an important lady."

This was the opportunity for which she'd been waiting all these excruciating months.

"I'll do it!" she exclaimed. "I'll approach Lorraine Innis. I'll enter into negotiations with her."

His eyebrows shot up. "You? You?"

"Why not? Don't you think I have the necessary tact and refinement?"

He chuckled. "My dear, it h'ain't not that you h'aint got tact and refinement. After all, the h'apple don't not fall far from the tree. But, I mean, you h'ain't never not taken the slightest bit of interest in the business of your ol' Pater."

"Yes, well," said Verity, "I'd like to make amends for my past neglect. A good portion of the business will fall to me someday. Perhaps it's time I should take an interest."

"Hmm, yes, well, if you puts it that way," he said, stroking his chin, "After all the dosh I spent on your posh education it'll at least give me the chance to recoup some of that. Yes, you should go ahead and be the one to negotiate directly with this Lorraine Innis woman, that is, if you think you could. I mean, she's the most famous woman in the world. You wouldn't not be intimidated?"

Verity stared at the photograph of Lorraine Innis and suppressed a smile.

"Intimidated? No, actually, Father, it would be a good experience for me, a very good experience. In fact, I can't wait."

– 5 –
A Woman is Like
a Potato Chip

I'm a right pillock, Miss Patsy."

Patsy Einfalt never saw Purvis Twankey so depressed. In his western-style suit and Stetson hat, she found even his melancholy cute. Still, she wanted to cheer him up, so she invited him for lunch.

"A pillock?" asked Patsy. "If that some sort of a fish?"

"No, it's a twonk, a prat, a berk," he moaned.

"Oh." She still didn't know what a pillock was, but it didn't sound complimentary.

"I've messed it all up, Miss Patsy."

"But Purvis," she said, "you have a top ten album, two top singles, and, well, I... that is, everyone, thinks you're very, very nice."

Purvis grimaced. "Fame t'ain't all it's cracked out to be. I mean, it's nice that everybody knows you, but the flip side of that is that everybody knows you."

Patsy cut the deviled ham sandwich on a diagonal as her mother had taught her and placed it on the kitchen table in front of Purvis.

He thanked her and took a bite.

"I know what you mean," said Patsy, "about fame, that is."

Purvis muttered a sandwich-muffled: "you do?"

"I remember when all I ever wanted was to be on television."

"Aye, I recollect that," said Purvis. "T'was first night I met Miss Lorraine. You were there, too. T'was just before she got famous. And then I got famous." He looked at his sandwich. "And you, not so much."

"I thought it was thrilling to be on television," said Patsy, "but then, I realized there was something more important..."

She tentatively reached out to take his hand but withdrew it.

"Aye," he agreed, looking into the deviled ham, "you can be on telly, you can be on radio, you can even have a string of pop tunes toppin' the charts, but…"

Purvis completed his sentence with a mouthful of sandwich.

"Sorry, what?"

He looked up at her. His eyes seemed even more gentle and tender than when he first lassoed her heart.

"Well, Miss Patsy," he said, shaking his head, "it's all just for now't if you've no one to share it with."

"You're right, Purvis." She clutched her hands under the table to keep them from hugging him.

"Aye," he moaned, "fat lot of good it does me."

Purvis took off his hat and scratched his unruly sandy hair. "I made a hit record album all for her. Seems everybody in the country likes it. But I'd trade all those millions of folks who like it if she'd like it. So, you see fame t'ain't worth a moldy puddin' if it can't get you what you really want."

The "she" to whom Purvis referred was Valerie Fierro. He'd been infatuated with Valerie ever since he'd put her in the hospital. Patsy also knew Valerie couldn't stand the sight of Purvis. Instead, each expression of devotion from Purvis drove Valerie further away. The last straw was his hit album: "To Valerie of Who I Dream." It didn't help that Valerie learned of the album via a poster on the side of a bus, causing her to hit the bus, total her car, and break her arm.

Since then, whenever his name was mentioned, Valerie turned a deep shade of purple and would mutter "Brit-head," her shorthand for "British Shithead."

A moment ago, Patsy wanted to hug him, now she was fighting the urge to throttle his scrawny throat. Didn't he realize that not only couldn't Valerie stand him, but she didn't even like him? Didn't Purvis see that Valerie was in a torrid relationship with Mike Valvano? And most importantly, couldn't Purvis see that Patsy loved him with a passion that was twice as strong as his puppy love for Valerie? No, Purvis was as blind as he was cute. Patsy kept her feelings for the little Brit-head well hidden. One day, she hoped, his eyes would be opened. Until then, Patsy would be as kind as she could be while not strangling him.

"I suppose fame can be disappointing," said Patsy.

"It's nice enough," said Purvis. "And I'm not ungrateful for all that Miss Lorraine and all of you have done for me."

"All of us?"

"Aye," he said, "well, it's plain as the nose on me face what Miss Lorraine has done, and then there's you, Miss Patsy…"

"Me?"

"Aye, well, you were one what called up those TV people. You could say that I rode Miss Lorraine's shirttail to fame, but you put me hands on her shirttail."

Patsy smiled. Perhaps Purvis wasn't completely oblivious.

"And then, of course, there's me inspiration..." Purvis sighed and hung his head. "...Miss Valerie."

Once more, Patsy resisted the urge to scream.

"So you see, fame's nowt enough," said Purvis. "It joost means lots more folk know you." He looked down at his plate. "By itself, it's like a sandwich without..." Purvis raised his head. "Got any crisps?"

"Crisps?" said Patsy. "Oh, you mean potato chips. Yes, I've got some." She fetched a bag from the cupboard and poured some on his plate.

"Back home, we've got smoky bacon crisps," he said, taking a bite.

"I'm sorry, all I have is plain," said Patsy.

Purvis assured her that the chips were "right tasty" but fell into a moody silence as he crunched, interrupted only when he asked for a second helping. Patsy deposited the remainder of the bag on his plate.

"Aren't crisps funny," he said.

Patsy looked at the crumbs on his plate. "I'd never really thought they were particularly amusing."

"No, they're nowt like laugh out loud things," he said. "I mean funny in a pharmacological way."

"Do you mean philosophical?"

He thought a moment. "Well, no, but, yes, maybe in that way too. I meant chemically. You know, to look at them," Purvis turned a chip slowly before his eyes, "you'd think one was the same as the rest."

"Aren't they?"

"No," he said, "they all look similar, but then they're different. Some are just plain, an' some are onion flavored, an' barbeque, an' smoky bacon..." Purvis' voice trailed off.

"I suppose," said Patsy, thinking of her own frustrated yearnings, "I suppose potato chips are like... women."

Purvis looked up as if he were Sir Isaac Newton, and an apple just bonked him on the noggin.

"Y'what?" he said, his mouth agape.

"I, uh, potato chips... um..."

"Like women," said Purvis leaping up from his chair. He started pacing Patsy's kitchen sputtering half-completed thoughts that barely qualified as syllables. Next, he reached down and picked up two chips, one in each hand.

"That's proper champion," he said. "Do you know what this means?"

"Uh, that you've got two potato chips?"

"No, no, well, aye, that an' all," said Purvis. "But if you take a plain chip, and dust it with barbeque, or chive, or smoky bacon, then you've got totally different taste. And they're just like women... or I mean, women are just like crisps!"

"T-they are?" asked Patsy.

"Aye, you said it yourself," said Purvis.

"I did? Well, yes, I did. I meant that one could be as nice as another." She had been hoping that the analogy would make Purvis realize she could be as desirable as Valerie Fierro. For some reason, she didn't think this was what was exciting him.

"Aye, aye," exulted Purvis, "and if you get down to what makes them different, then you've got something there!"

"Y-you do?"

"Aye, well, I've got... I need..." He began to rush from the kitchen, still holding both potato chips high. Then Purvis ran back in and gingerly returned the chips to his plate before starting out again, stopping and looking back at Patsy.

She smiled at him nervously, wondering if his next stop was the potato funny farm.

Purvis Twankey broke into a broad grin, leaned over, kissed Patsy on the forehead, winked at her, and said: "Champion!" Then he rushed out the door.

Patsy looked at the two chips, touched her forehead, and wondered what it all meant.

– 6 –
The Edge of Desire

Valerie Fierro sat in the empty board room and glanced at her Cartier wristwatch.

Stupid Lorraine; it was all her fault.

It was ten minutes before the weekly board meeting of the Cross of Lorraine charity. Why they needed a weekly meeting was beyond her. The board was just Lorraine, Valerie, and the president of Fourth Fiduciary Trust. That had been Peter Liverot. Since he was blown to bits at the White House, Liverot had been absent. Now, Mike Valvano was the president of the bank. That was a surprise.

The greater shock was that Mike's brother, Robert, was the bank's majority silent partner. Valerie knew Mike had a brother. She knew the bank was owned by shadowy partners. That they were one and the same was a stunning revelation.

Mike downplayed it when he told her. He mentioned it casually over dinner – between the salad and the soup - his brother had the controlling interest in Fourth Fiduciary and wanted Mike to take over.

Valerie almost jumped on the table and shouted: "Yahtzee!" Michael controlled the bank. Valerie controlled the charity. But Michael seemed to have little enthusiasm for taking the job. What did this guy want? His brother handed him the world on a silver platter. Michael was reacting like it was a runny dollop of baked beans on a paper plate leaking through onto his white trousers.

Now the only roadblock on Valerie's highway to person fulfillment was Lorraine Innis. By itself, Fourth Fiduciary was a cheesy little operation. The real money, power, and prestige were in the Cross of Lorraine.

Valerie had been in firm control of the charity until that day in Washington. She had just reached a verbal agreement with Peter Liverot.

Valerie would have a free hand in the charity, including a generous percentage of the non-donation revenue. All she had to do was to control Lorraine and keep her from retiring from public life. It was all set. Then Liverot had to go and get himself blown up. Valerie cursed her bad luck.

Valerie didn't really need Liverot, but he told Lorraine something on his deathbed that Lorraine wouldn't share with her. Since then, Lorraine was acting strangely. First, she didn't talk to Valerie for several weeks. Next, when Lorraine did start talking again, she was too, well, Lorraine. She refused to acknowledge, even in private, that there was a person named Chesney Potts and that she was him. Lorraine was so confident, so self-assured, so utterly feminine that Valerie wondered if she had been drugged. Worst of all, this version of Lorraine had none of Chesney's insecurities and was immune to Valerie's control. This Lorraine was a loose cannon and one that might just be pointed at Valerie.

Stupid Lorraine! If only Valerie could…

Her thoughts were interrupted as a gentle pair of hands lifted Valerie's hair, and a soft pair of lips kissed her neck.

"Mmmm, Michael," she purred.

"*Caro mio*," he whispered. She felt herself yielding to his touch, which was both commanding and tender.

"Michael, stop," she exhaled. He stopped and sat down next to her. Valerie was disappointed.

"You're right," said Mike. A playful smirk curled around the corners of his mouth. He was teasing her. She could hate him for that, but she wanted him so much. And now that he was a bank president and wearing even more expensive suits, Valerie wanted him that much more.

"You'd better be careful," he said.

"Me? Why should I be careful?"

"I could charge you with sexual harassment."

She snorted. "You could charge me with sexual harassment? That's a laugh. You were the one who just snuck up on me and started fondling my neck. How would you explain that?"

"Irresistible temptation. No judge would convict me. How could they?" Mike gently pushed aside the edges of her suit jacket. "I mean, when you put these out here like this." With his index finger, he traced around the precise boundaries of her areole. He was good, she thought as her eyelids involuntarily closed halfway. He had memorized every erogenous bit of her body. He knew precisely where to caress. He knew from patient experimentation to keep away from her nipple. If he tightened that swirl by even an eighth of an inch, she would lose control, right there in the conference room. He knew her boundaries, and he was negotiating the border, just close enough to tantalize her. Valerie wanted him as she had wanted no other lover before. Part of her hated him for that.

"You," said Michael looking into her eyes while continuing his tracing, "leave me defenseless."

Valerie could only murmur and exhale.

"You could drive a man wild."

"Mmm...."

"You'd force me to make passionate love to you right now."

"Yes, yes," she purred.

"Right here, on the top of this conference table..."

The image of Mitchell Minear seducing her on the top of a similar table barged into Valerie's mind. She saw the cracked glass top, the pregnancy tests, the borrowing of the credit card from Martina Fergus, the procedure, the death of..."

"NO!" Valerie shouted.

Michael jerked his hand back. "What's wrong?"

"Uh, we, they... they'll be in here any minute," she said.

He looked at his watch, nodded, and moved to a seat out of reach from her. Once seated, he raised his eyebrow, lifted his index finger in a slight twirl, and announced: "to be continued."

"Michael..." said Valerie, sharpening her tone. "Sometimes, I can't figure you out."

He grinned. "What's to figure out? I got a girlfriend with a hot body."

"I'm talking about the bank," she said. "It's like you didn't want to be the president of the bank."

"Really?" he said. "If you get that impression, you're right."

"And that's what I don't understand," she said, lowering her voice. "It's a dream situation, don't you get it?"

"Dreams are funny things, *Caro mio,*" he said enigmatically. "We all have different ones."

"Why did you take the job if you're not going to use it? It's like getting a Maserati and then using it to go to the grocery store."

"Or it's like taking the keys of the car from a drunk," he said.

"I don't get you sometimes," she said, folding her arms across her chest, "you could have so much."

"Trust me, Valerie, trust me," he said with the patience that reminded her of his previous vocation.

Valerie stared at him. How could he be so smart and so blind at the same time? And why did he have to be so sexy?

"All I'm trying to say," began Valerie. The board room door opened, and in glided Lorraine Innis with Patsy Einfalt, the official board secretary, at her heels, scribbling notes on a steno pad.

"Good morning, Valerie, Michael," said Lorraine taking her place at the table opposite Valerie. She exchanged pleasantries about the weather, complimented Valerie on her blouse, and Michael on his tie, as Patsy handed out the reports on the charity's activities.

For Mike's benefit, Lorraine provided a history of the charity: its origins, mission, and initiatives. Mike interrupted from time to time with questions. Lorraine gave detailed answers. Valerie sat there, trying to make sense of it all. Not that anything was wrong. On the surface, it all seemed too right. Mike was asking cogent questions. Lorraine was giving perfect replies. Patsy was jotting down minutes. It was the most professional, dignified business meeting Valerie ever attended. It was all so absurd. Lorraine was behaving like the model businesswoman. She had to know it was all a scam, didn't she? Every so often, Lorraine's eyes would meet Valerie's. Each time they did, Valerie tried to puncture Lorraine's female façade with a piercing stare, one that said: "you may be able to fool them, but I know who you are." And each time Valerie did so, Lorraine would deflect her withering looks. There had to be a way through Lorraine's armor to the soft Chesney underbelly.

"Valerie? Valerie?"

"Huh? What?" said Valerie rousing herself from her thoughts.

"I said, you need to do an audit," said Lorraine.

"An audit?"

"Yes, an internal audit," said Lorraine. "In preparation for our official audit."

"Me? Why me?" Valerie wondered if it was a trap.

"Because you're the one with compliance experience," observed Mike.

Valerie looked from Mike to Lorraine and then back to Mike. What was Michael trying to do to her? She didn't want to poke through the organization's books. She had a good idea of Liverot's shady deals. Or maybe Michael knew. Perhaps he suggested she do it to keep it all hidden.

"Well," said Valerie sharply, "since it's your idea…"

"It wasn't my idea," said Michael.

Valerie looked back to Lorraine, who turned her head to the person on her right.

"Uh, actually, it was my suggestion," said Patsy sheepishly.

Valerie squinted at Patsy.

"And an excellent suggestion it was, too, Patsy," said Lorraine. "Please arrange Valerie's travel plans…"

"Travel plans?" said Valerie. "Where am I going?"

"To Gibraltar, of course," said Lorraine.

"Gibraltar?" While Valerie was never averse to traveling to Europe on the company's dime, Gibraltar conjured up thoughts of that big rock, those ugly apes, and worse of all: Albrecht Eckner.

"Haven't you been listing, Babe," said Mike in an aside. "The charity gets most of its assets through the Gibraltar bank."

"Yes, I know, Michael," snapped Valerie. "I'm not an idiot. I've been here since the start of this whole thing. I have been paying attention."

The room fell silent, and though she was looking at Mike Valvano, Valerie could feel Lorraine's looking at her. Valerie turned. Lorraine was looking at her. Her eyes were kind, almost motherly. Damn Lorraine, thought Valerie, she trying to kill me with love and understanding.

"Fine," said Valerie, "I'll go to Gibraltar." But she wouldn't go meekly. She added: "First-class!"

Patsy's mouth dropped open.

Lorraine cut in. "Yes, of course, first-class."

Valerie smiled. Her triumph was soured though when Lorraine said in an aside to Patsy: "I'll pay the difference, personally."

Damn Lorraine! Still, thought Valerie, it didn't matter who paid. In fact, it was even better that Lorraine would be shelling out of her own modest resources to foot the bill to pamper her dearest friend. Yes, she'd enjoy this trip. She deserved it.

"Thank you all," said Lorraine closing her portfolio. "And I want to thank Michael for assuming the presidency of the bank and taking his place on our board under what must be challenging circumstances."

Mike said he looked forward to working with Lorraine. He even went so far as to ask her to lunch.

Valerie gave him a dirty glance. He was just being nice, but she didn't want the two of them to get too close. Still, it was what happened next that leaped into the realm of impossibility.

"I'd love to join you for lunch," said Lorraine.

"You can't," interrupted Patsy, "not today."

Lorraine looked at her.

"Today is your doctor's appointment," said Patsy.

– 7 –
The Lemmings
Rush Back to Capistrano

D octor's appointment?" Valerie screeched. "YOU?!"
Lorraine looked at her sideways. Valerie was behaving so oddly lately. She had been through so many traumatic events.

"Yes, Valerie," said Lorraine, calmly, "I have a doctor's appointment. It's just a check-up."

"YOU?!" Valerie pointed at her.

Lorraine exchanged glances with Patsy and Mike.

"Yes, it is my doctor's appointment," said Lorraine. "For whom else would I be seeing a doctor?"

Valerie's mouth hung open.

"Babe, what's the matter?" Mike asked. "People go to doctors every day."

"It's nothing serious," said Lorraine. "It's just a routine visit."

"Routine," repeated Valerie.

"She's probably still upset about doctors after the accident," said Mike to Lorraine, as if Valerie wasn't there or worse was an imbecile. Valerie gave him a nasty look.

"I'll be fine," said Lorraine.

Valerie gave her a look of disbelief.

Poor Valerie, though Lorraine. Perhaps she needed a psychiatrist experienced in trauma.

"It's a woman's thing," said Lorraine, softly to ease Valerie's fears.

Valerie burst out laughing. Mike took Valerie by the arm.

"I'll take care of her, she'll be fine, I'm sure…. I hope," he said as he guided his hysterical girlfriend out the door.

After they left, Patsy and Lorraine looked at each other. Neither spoke until the sound of Valerie's hysterics faded down the hallway.

"That was odd," said Lorraine.

"I've never seen her like that," said Patsy. "Did she ever do that when she was a little girl?"

Lorraine began to answer, but, for some odd reason, she couldn't remember Valerie as a little girl.

"Not to the best of my recollection," said Lorraine.

◆

An hour later, Lorraine arrived at the doctor's office. That last statement kept running through her mind. She couldn't remember Valerie as a little girl. Of course, she knew Valerie then, but all her memories were factual in nature, as two dimensional as Columbus discovering America or the Battle of Bosworth Field.

The Battle of Bosworth Field?

Why did she think of an obscure English event? And why, when she thought of it, did Lorraine feel an odd ache in her heart? That battle was hundreds of years ago.

As she stood outside the doctor's door, Lorraine didn't quite know why she was there. She didn't even know the doctor. But something inside her knew she had to be there. It was like the swallows going back to Capistrano, or Lemming rushing to the sea… or the Battle of Bosworth…

No, it couldn't be like the Battle of Bosworth Field, she thought as she rang the doorbell. As she waited, it occurred to her that this doctor had no professional sign. It looked like an ordinary house.

A woman answered. She was around Lorraine's age.

"Right on time," said the woman with a smile. "Come in."

Lorraine did so.

"Doctor Clott?" said Lorraine tentatively.

Doctor Clott turned around and studied Lorraine's face as if she were looking for something in her eyes or her expression.

"You are Doctor Clott, aren't you?" asked Lorraine. She should have felt nervous, but for some reason, she didn't. She had a calm assurance that this place, more than any other, was where she belonged.

"Please, sit down, Lorraine," said Dr. Clott. They entered what appeared to be the woman's living room. It was very welcoming but very odd for a doctor's office. "And, please call me 'Clodagh.'"

Lorraine sat on the settee and smiled. "Yes, Clodagh."

"You remember now?"

The smile fell from Lorraine's face. "No, I don't, Clodagh. But I know that it's good."

"Yes, it is good," said Clodagh Clott, "perhaps a little too good, but it's very effective."

Lorraine around for medical equipment but saw none. She looked at a closed door. That must be the examination room.

"Do you want me to go in there and take off my clothes?" asked Lorraine, nodding toward the door.

Clodagh Clott suppressed a giggle. "I'm sorry, no, that's not necessary. You really don't know why you're here, do you?"

"No, but I do need to be here," said Lorraine. "Don't I?"

"Good, yes," said Clodagh, with a reassuring pat to Lorraine's hand. "Now, I want to say something to you, but I want you to remain calm. Do you understand? You will remain calm and completely in control."

Lorraine's brow furrowed. "Is it bad news? What is it?"

"You'll understand as soon as I say those two words, and you won't get upset, Lorraine."

"I... no, no, you're right, I won't get upset."

"Good," said Clodagh. She held both of Lorraine's hands and then looked into her eyes. She took a breath and then slowly and deliberately said: "Verity..."

Lorraine blinked several times. It was as if something in her was stirring, as if a breeze was blowing across her thoughts.

"Verity Goodhue..." said Clodagh.

The veil that had cloaked her doctor's visit was suddenly removed.

"Clo," said Lorraine with a smile.

Clodagh squeezed Lorraine's hands and then released them.

Lorraine looked around the room. "That went well. Nothing's broken." She reached up and felt her hair. "No hair pulled out either. Not like that other time."

"No, I wasn't expecting that sort of reaction," said Clodagh. "This is a safe, non-threatening environment, but still, you never know. As you know from the past, being yanked out of a personality that you completely believe in can be quite jarring."

"Yes, the doctor's appointment strategy worked very..." Lorraine gasped. "Oh, no, poor Valerie!"

"What?"

Lorraine recounted Valerie's reaction.

"She's the only person who knows about me, aside from you," said Lorraine. "She must have thought I'd lost my mind."

"When actually you were going to retrieve it," observed Clodagh.

"Bosworth Field!" exclaimed Lorraine.

"Pardon?"

"On the way here, I was thinking about the Battle of Bosworth Field, and I didn't understand why. "It was where I proposed to... the other one," said Lorraine.

Clodagh patted her friend's hand and then invited her into the kitchen for a cup of tea.

"I'd ask what you've been doing," said Clodagh, "but all I have to do is read the papers or watch the news."

Lorraine looked into her cup. "Yes, well, I keep expecting to be less popular, but unfortunately, that hasn't happened yet."

"Still, you seem to be dealing with it very well," said Clodagh. "You're always the picture of the perfect person."

"It's not hard creating perfect people when you start with adults without a past," observed Lorraine.

"I suppose not. The more important question is: how is Chesney?"

Lorraine tilted her head to one side. "That's an odd question. The last Chesney Potts knew it was one month ago. It's like asking a person waking from a thirty-day nap what's new. I guess you would say he's dormant."

Clodagh rephrased the question. "I suppose what I want to know is how are you," she poked Lorraine, "you... how are you doing?"

Lorraine thought a moment. "Lorraine Innis seems perfectly happy and contented... most of the time."

There was a thoughtful silence.

"And otherwise?" asked Clodagh.

"Oh, there are times when she's not so contented. Those are the scary times. Oh, they're not scary when they're happening, Clo. They're only scary when I'm fully cognizant of myself, and I realize the things I've been feeling. Looking back on them, they're a little frightening."

"Frightening?"

Lorraine recounted her visit to the community center.

"Holding that baby," said Lorraine, "I just wanted one of my own. I had this feeling that I never had before. I can't explain it."

"It's not unusual," said Clodagh. "You were feeling maternal. You wanted to give life and to nurture it. It's the most normal feeling a woman can have."

"But I'm not a woman!" Protested Lorraine.

Clodagh just looked at her.

"That's the gentlest 'I told you so,' I've ever had," said Lorraine.

Clodagh shrugged. "It's not an 'I told you so.' It's more of a 'what did you expect?' You've been there before when you were first Lorraine, and you forgot your identity. That was an accident. This is on purpose, but the results are the same. When you're one-hundred-percent Lorraine, psychologically, you're a woman. You'll feel all the things that the rest of our sex feels. You'll enjoy our strengths and vulnerabilities. You've bought the ticket for the full ride, well practically the full ride."

"The full ride," she said, nodding her head. "I just didn't know parts of that ride were so scary."

"...like holding a baby," said Clodagh.

"She wanted me to feed her."

"The baby was working off on instinct, too. She didn't know you were just putting up a good front." Clodagh nodded at Lorraine's breasts.

"And the most frightening thing is that I wanted to do something about it, though deep down inside, I knew that I couldn't. Still, I was determined to see my doctor about it."

"Fortunately, in your mind, I'm your doctor," noted Clodagh. "But aside from wanting to be a mommy, are you making progress? Are you finding out who is responsible for Martina's death?"

"I'm not sure. You have to remember, when I'm all Lorraine, I'm not aware of that goal. Lorraine doesn't know about Martina or Chesney." She fell silent and thought for a moment. "There are some encouraging developments. Valerie is going to Gibraltar to do an internal audit."

"What does that have to do with Martina?"

"Nothing, at least not on the surface, but I thought Peter Liverot was responsible for sending Martina to Chicago when she died."

"So?"

"So," said Lorraine, "if Liverot wasn't responsible, that means someone else in the company was. Martina was in charge of regulatory compliance for the bank. If anyone was likely to find out something illegal was taking place, it would be her. After Liverot comes Albrecht Eckner. It's my suspicion that Eckner was double-crossing his double-crossing boss."

"No honor among thieves, huh," said Clodagh.

"There's no honor what so ever in Albrecht Eckner," said Lorraine. "It was just before Martina's death that Eckner was transferred to Gibraltar. Maybe he was afraid of what Martina might discover without him in Delaware to cover his tracks."

"So, couldn't you just do an internal audit in Delaware?"

Lorraine shook her head. "There have been audits since then. I suspect that Eckner must have sent Martina to Chicago to distract her. Between Martina's going to Chicago and then the wedding, Eckner would have had enough time to cover up his dirty deals and move them to the bank's Gibraltar subsidiary."

"And Valerie's going to look over his books?"

"Not directly," said Lorraine. "She works for the charity, now. But there's enough overlap between the bank and the charity that she should be able to spot anything shady."

"Does Valerie know that's what she's looking for?"

Lorraine thought a moment and sighed. "Poor Valerie. As hard as this has been on me, it's probably been worse for Valerie. She can't communicate with me... that is with Chesney. She even tried showing me a picture of me, that is him."

"Interesting," said Clodagh, "and what was your reaction?"

"High marks for you. I didn't recognize myself. In fact, I practically accused Valerie of cheating on her boyfriend with Chesney Potts."

"And what was her reaction to that?"

Lorraine's brow furrowed. "Actually, I think she took it as an insult. Perhaps this is too much for her. After all, I just accused her of being unfaithful to Michael. Maybe we should let her in on what we're doing."

"Why?"

"So she doesn't worry," said Lorraine. "She was also distraught when I said I was going to see a doctor."

Clodagh's expression grew clouded.

"So what do you think?" said Lorraine, "about telling Valerie what we're doing."

Clodagh's expression was kind but also a little patronizing.

"Let's not tell, Valerie, not just yet, at least. I don't know what good it would do."

"It would keep Valerie from worrying about me," interjected Lorraine.

"Yes, but at the same time, it might be counterproductive to your goals."

"Counterproductive, how?"

"And it might put Valerie in danger," said Clodagh ignoring the question. "If she knows why you're all Lorraine, what you're looking for, and that you're sending her to audit Albrecht Eckner, it could be disastrous."

"Then I'll send... someone else."

"Is there anyone else you trust as much as Valerie?"

"There's Patsy," said Lorraine, "but she doesn't have audit experience, and she always thinks the best of everyone."

"Then I think the safest course of action would be to not let Valerie know any more than she knows now. Send her to Gibraltar for what she believes is a routine audit."

Lorraine nodded her head. "I suppose you're right, Clo. But next time, instead of saying I'm going to the doctor, why don't we make you my accountant?"

"Fine, an appointment is an appointment. Just as long as you show up. Now, is there anything else?"

Lorraine looked at her wristwatch. "No, I guess not. I've got to be back at the office in an hour." She laid down on the sofa. "I'll see you next month, Clo. Thank you for everything." Then Lorraine closed her eyes and took a deep breath.

"You're welcome. See you next month, Ches."

Then in steady, calming tones, Clodagh returned Lorraine to her full womanhood. After several minutes, Clodagh awoke her subject.

"All done, doctor?" said Lorraine opening her eyes.

"Yes," said Clodagh, "all done. You're in perfect health."

Lorraine smiled. "That's good to know," she said as she rose to her feet. After adjusting her suit jacket and smoothing her skirt, Lorraine stopped at looked at Clodagh.

"Is there something wrong?" asked Clodagh.

"Wrong? No, not at all," said Lorraine, "in fact, this may seem odd, but I've never felt more right. Does that make sense?"

"Yes, it does," said Clodagh. "I'm glad to be of assistance."

She escorted Lorraine to the front door and extended her hand. Lorraine looked at it and paused.

Did you ever feel," said Lorraine, "like you knew someone before?"

"Of course, that's a fairly common feeling. Do you think we've met before?"

"No, not exactly," she said as she shook Clodagh's hand. She had the strangest desire to give the woman a hug, but Lorraine kept this to herself. It must be, she reasoned, the euphoria she was feeling. Everything was fine.

– 8 –
Filling the Blank Slate

A month ago, Davis Flemming kept people waiting where he now sat. Technically, the Oval Office wasn't his office, but he was President Merton's top advisor. Now he had to wait for permission to enter.

Quinton Merton had two years left in his term when that deranged woman blew him to smithereens, or Kingdom Come, or wherever cardboard politicians went when they died. It only took one lunatic to ruin everything for Davis Flemming.

Still, Merton was becoming unpredictable. At their last meeting, Paul Rocher of the Secret Service told them that Lorraine Innis was a fraud, or at least an enigma. When she burst on to the international stage, Flemming had Rocher and his ex-CIA pal dig for dirt on the woman. They had found nothing; not just any dirt, but nothing. As far as the public or private records were concerned, Lorraine Innis hadn't existed prior to the day she saved Nikolai Kropotkin's life. They had searched all the records, scoured every database, even secret files in other countries. They had checked every missing person report for every woman between the ages of 20 and 50. And they came up empty. They created the record that now existed from Lorraine Innis' own testimony extracted from her one afternoon when they drugged her.

Flemming authorized them to do whatever it took to get the goods on Lorraine Innis. The woman had shown up Flemming in the media, and worse of all, she had appeared sweet and innocent while doing it. Far worse was that the media… his media… took Lorraine Innis' side. It was like having the dog you'd trained, allowing a burglar into your house, and then turning around and biting you!

Flemming was surprised by Quinton Merton's response to it all. Rather than exploit the information, the idiot, rest his soul, ordered Rocher and his operative to forget it all. It was just as well Merton was blown up.

But the death of Merton left Flemming without a horse in the race. Congress and the country's Statehouses were brimming with brainless politicians. They were bargain outlets for pea-brained statesmen. Flemming compiled a list of possible successors. They were all pliable dunces: senators and governors who looked the part but hadn't enough brains to blow their own noses. He reached out to one senator: tall, handsome, vapid, ambitious, and, most importantly, malleable. Lambert Pugh was his name. The name made Flemming wince. He could always build him up as a "Bert." That left the last name; an unfortunate homonym of what most people said when they encountered a malodorous object. Pugh, Phew, PU, it didn't matter now.

The new president, Tom Ottinger, would run for his own term. Though not a skillful politician, Ottinger was likely to be an effective leader. It may wake up the American public to what they had been missing for so long. It was like re-introducing an ex-gourmand to haute cuisine after years of eating Happy Meals. Flemming would just bide his time, find the right candidate, and wait out Ottinger's term.

Flemming glanced at his Rolex. He'd been waiting for more than ten minutes. That had to be a ploy. It's what Flemming would do to a waiting opponent. Ottinger and his chief of staff, Frank Weston, had been together in the Marines. Flemming despised that, especially in Weston. He had enjoyed ordering Weston about and treating him like an inferior. Now, the situation was reversed. A few weeks ago, Ottinger wasn't even among the top ten of the country's most powerful people. Flemming had been number one, though few knew it. The recognition of power didn't matter, just the actual possession of it.

Flemming wracked his brain for instances of mistreatment towards either Ottinger or Wesson. Of course, he had nothing but contempt for either of them. But had he ever actually said what he thought of them? Did they have actual words they could now use against him?

The secretary spoke. Davis was so lost in his spiral of introspection that he didn't hear her the first time.

"I said, 'you can go in now, Mr. Flemming,'" she repeated.

The door opened, and Frank Wesson appeared, still sporting his Marine crew cut.

"Davis, thank you for coming in," said Wesson extending his hand. "Sorry to keep you waiting." He shook Wesson's hand, trying to exert the same amount of pressure the Leatherneck applied and failing by half.

"Come on in; the President's waiting for you," said Wesson.

Though he had been in the room every day for the past six years, Davis Flemming noticed the difference in the atmosphere. And there was a difference in Ottinger. The man seemed presidential; in fact, he seemed more presidential than Quinton Merton had on his best day.

While Merton usually favored casual slacks, open-collar shirts, and sweaters in the office, Ottinger wore a suit and tie. President Ottinger asked

Flemming to sit down on the sofa while he sat in a wing chair catty-corner to him. Frank Wesson sat on another sofa opposite Flemming.

"I want to personally thank you, Davis, for coming in to meet with me," began Ottinger. "I know it must be difficult. The memories of that horrible day still so fresh in your memory." Ottinger nodded over his shoulder towards the South Lawn, where Eugenia Bupp had detonated herself and Merton.

Flemming wasn't on the lawn when the explosion took place. He was around the other side of the building, cursing under his breath because Lorraine Innis, the guest of honor, was late.

"I'm sure," the president continued, "that your days have been consumed with grief and mourning."

Flemming assured him that they were. The grief and mourning were for his own future. As for Quinton Merton: becoming a martyr was an astute career move, the lucky bastard.

"I asked you in here today," said Ottinger, "as the point person for President Merton's staff." Ottinger outlined the accommodations made for the staff's transition, Flemming included. They were more generous than they needed to be, though Davis Flemming wasn't interested in office space or cleaning up any loose ends.

"And you can use Frank's former office over in the Eisenhower building, that is, of course, until my replacement is chosen and confirmed."

Flemming's ears perked up. Flemming assumed that Ottinger would have made a choice for the new vice-president by now. However, protocol dictated that he wait to announce it until after the mourning period for Quinton Merton. Here was his opportunity. If Flemming could get one of his people installed as Vice President, he'd be back in business.

"I appreciate your kindness," said Flemming, "I know President Merton's staff will be grateful. I've been in constant communication with most of them, helping them deal with their grief." Who cared about a bunch of political appointees, he thought. "And of course, my needs are modest. I don't anticipate being in the way for too long."

"You're not in the way," assured the President.

Flemming bowed his head. "That's very kind of the President to say. I'm just grateful that in this national tragedy, we have an experienced hand on the wheel. And I just want you to know that if I can be of any service, in an unofficial capacity, of course, Mr. President, you can rely on me."

"Yes, well, that's gracious of you, Davis," said Frank Wesson, looking down at the President's schedule. Wesson leaned forward, indicating he was about to usher Flemming from the room.

"Hold on, Frank," said Ottinger. "Davis, I'd like to get your opinion on something."

"Me, sir?"

"It's more political in nature," said the President. "I don't have much of a stomach for that game, but I'd like to get your read on a few names that I've been considering for Vice-President."

Flemming suppressed a smile as he glanced over at Frank Wesson. Obviously, Wesson thought the President's discussing the matter with Flemming was ill-advised. But like a good Marine, he kept his mouth shut when his commander was talking.

"Well, sir, I hadn't really thought about it," said Flemming, "given all that's happened. I've been consumed with the tragedy. But, if I could be of any assistance..."

President Ottinger rattled off several names. All of them were thoughtful choices that reflected Ottinger's philosophy of service. All would have made good vice-presidents or good presidents. Consequently, none of them were pliable enough for Flemming's liking.

Deliberately but subtly, Flemming went through each prospective candidate and analyzed their strengths. Actually, he was subtly damning each of them. This one was a consensus builder, oh, but only because he lacked the power of convictions. That candidate was a deep-thinker, but the other party had branded him an intractable ideologue. Ottinger's face sagged as, one-by-one, he saw flaws that had previously gone unnoticed, mainly because they had never existed.

Finally, the President sighed and shook his head. "Well, that's my list. Frank, it looks like all our choices are either unacceptable or wouldn't pass confirmation by the Congress."

"Yes, Mr. President. Unfortunately, the process became more difficult when we lost both the House and the Senate in the mid-term elections. Sorry I couldn't be of more help, sir," said Flemming, placing his hands on his knees as if he was about to stand and leave. Then he paused as if a fresh thought had just occurred to him. "There is, of course, one name that comes to mind that has yet to be mentioned. Someone who is a person of unquestioned integrity, popular, yet still principled. A person who would be a great asset to your administration." Flemming paused for dramatic effect. He was going to mention his candidate: Lambert Pugh.

"Really?" said Ottinger. "We've been through the list of every governor and most members of the Congress. Hell, we even considered the biggest idiot in Washington, Bert Pugh." The President then laughed.

Flemming sat still for a moment, hoping that the shock didn't register on his face. Then, he laughed, mirroring Ottinger's own chuckle at the preposterous notion that Lambert Pugh be considered for such a high office. Inwardly, his mind raced for a substitute.

"I shouldn't laugh," said the President, "but presiding over the Senate these past six years told me more than I ever wanted to know about Bert Pugh. But you were about to say..."

Flemming froze. "Sir?"

"You were about to tell me the man who you thought was qualified."

Flemming looked at him blankly while he wracked his brain. If Ottinger thought Lambert Pugh was an unmitigated pea-brain, then Flemming's other choices would be utterly unacceptable.

"Come, Davis," said Frank Wesson. "The president is waiting. Who is this popular, principled, man?"

"Yes, Flemming," said Ottinger, a tone of impatience rising in his voice, "who is this man?"

"Man..." repeated Davis Flemming as a name rose to his mind. Popular, integrity, principled... all the qualities that got in the way of practical politics... all the qualities he hated. Who personified that more than anyone else? One person. They were intelligent, a political neophyte, but that was an asset. He had gotten off on the wrong foot, but that didn't mean he couldn't insinuate himself with them. It would be a challenge, but...

"Man?" repeated Flemming, this time with confidence. "Gentlemen, you're missing the obvious. The perfect person for the job isn't a man at all. The one person who would receive unanimous support in the Congress, with the media, and with the public is a woman: Lorraine Innis."

Both men stared at him for a moment before broad smiles overspread their faces. Ottinger and Wesson looked at each other and then back at Davis Flemming.

"It's brilliant," said Wesson.

"It's inspired," said Ottinger.

"Will she do it?" asked Wesson.

"She'd be a fool not to," muttered Flemming.

"She's an American, isn't she?" said Ottinger. He wasn't questioning her citizenship, but rather her sense of duty to her country.

This remark caused Flemming to think about Paul Rocher's report stating they didn't know who Lorraine Innis was. Obviously, that information hadn't been passed on to Ottinger. That also worked to Flemming's advantage. He'd have no problem controlling Lorraine Innis. He knew her secret, or at least that she had a secret, and that, in his skillful hands, would be enough. Lorraine Innis was the perfect candidate. A stellar public façade, and enough dirt in private to make her easy to command. Davis Flemming was back in business.

"What a wonderful choice. I met her last fall. She's bright, intelligent, and she'd be a real asset to the country. I can't thank you enough, Davis," said Ottinger rising to shake Flemming's hand.

"Believe me, it's my pleasure, Mr. President."

– 9 –
Let Go and Let Lorraine

Valerie looked down at her plane tickets for Gibraltar and shuddered. Gibraltar meant Albrecht Eckner: he of the doughy physique, the shifty eyes, and the absence of scruples. If only Mike had just ten percent of Albrecht's cunning, there would be no stopping her. Now she had to audit the charity's accounts at Fourth Fiduciary's European subsidiary. She could only imagine the fiscal cesspool Albrecht was happily tending like some wading pool for the dishonorable.

She picked up the ticket and tapped it against her lips. She might be able to have it all. That's all she deserved. Peter Liverot had promised her a line of her own clothing and lingerie; fashions that were sexier than any that could be marketed under Lorraine's chaste banner. With Liverot gone, she would have to find a way to make that promise a reality without looking greedy. Still, it was owed her.

She would go to Gibraltar and examine Albrecht's books. It may be a cesspool, but perhaps it was also filled with the fertilizer for her dreams. In the past, Albrecht always managed to get the best of her. Now she would have the upper hand. This wasn't a prom, and he didn't have disgusting pictures to blackmail her with. This time she would…

"I'm sorry," said a voice jarring Valerie from her thoughts, "am I interrupting?"

Valerie looked up. There in her office doorway stood Lorraine.

"What? Yes, I mean, no, I was just sitting here… and that's all."

She put her airline ticket out of sight and sat up straight. Lorraine smiled and moved gracefully to the chair in front of the desk. How was Lorraine doing it? Fat, lumbering Chesney Potts was now gliding through life. Chesney was either off his rocker or was putting on the act of the century. Lorraine sat down and crossed her legs with the poise of a princess.

The two looked at each other for a second.

"So," said Valerie, "how did your doctor's appointment go?" It was the perfect question, provocative, but innocent-sounding.

Lorraine smiled. "Everything's fine."

Valerie nodded and pushed her tongue against the inside of her cheek. There had to be a way to break through that shell.

"That's good, Chesney."

"Pardon?"

"I said: 'that's good.'"

"But you said 'Chesney,'" said Lorraine.

"Did I?"

"Yes, you did?"

Valerie feigned innocence. "Oh, I must have been thinking about someone else. Sorry, I have so much on my mind. But I'm glad you had a nice doctor's visit. Routine check-up, was it?"

"Yes," said Lorraine, "I suppose."

Valerie nodded and smiled. "Only, you said it was a 'woman's thing.'"

"I suppose I did. But everything is normal."

Valerie nodded. If Chesney was going to play this game, she could too.

"You're not," Valerie leaned forward and whispered, "you're not... pregnant, are you?"

Lorraine's face turned red, and she looked down. That did it, thought Valerie. Personal matters would always make Chesney stammer. She had pierced the armor.

"No, I'm not. Sorry, I don't mean to get so flustered..."

"Oh? What is it?" asked Valerie.

Lorraine sighed and smiled bravely. "You'll have to forgive me. But, it's just, well, if I can't tell you, who could I tell? It's just that, well, I can't have children. I'll never be a mother."

Valerie sat back. Chesney was playing this all the way to the end of the line, even further. He was out of track and still rolling along at full steam. She wanted to shout "no shit" and punch Lorraine but restrained herself.

"And did the doctor tell you that?"

Lorraine nodded.

"Anything else?" Valerie almost asked if the doctor was out of his mind or just legally blind.

Lorraine exhaled. "No, that's it. Aside from that, I'm a perfectly healthy woman."

"Are you?" said Valerie dryly.

"Yes, I suppose that's a great blessing, isn't it? Good health. I won't say I'm not disappointed, but there it is."

"Yes, there it is," said Valerie.

"Thank you for being so supportive."

Valerie waved her hand, dismissively.

"But that's not why I came in," said Lorraine. "Well, I did want to share that with you. After all, we've been through everything together. Without you, well, I would have lost my mind."

Valerie almost began searching the floor for the mind that Lorraine was so positive she still possessed.

"And you're there to help me," continued Lorraine, "to do what I need to do."

"And just what is that?"

"To help others, of course, but I don't need to tell you that. You've always helped others."

Valerie reached up and touch the pendant around her neck.

"What about you?" asked Valerie.

Lorraine lowered her eyes. "I know," said Lorraine, "I need to do more."

"More?" Valerie was incredulous. Lorraine's salary was more like a stipend. For the number of donations and endorsements she raked in, Lorraine could have demanded millions and still only take a fraction of the total.

"But I will do more," said Lorraine looking up, "with help from you and Michael. I'm encouraged. I'm sure Michael will bring a fresh approach." She leaned forward. "I hesitate to tell you this…"

Valerie leaned across her desk to meet Lorraine.

"…but it's about Peter Liverot."

Finally, thought Valerie, she would find out what Liverot had told Lorraine on his deathbed.

"Go on, go on," encouraged Valerie.

Lorraine looked side to side. "Peter Liverot… was not running an entirely honest operation. I don't mean to speak ill of the dead," said Lorraine, "but it's true." She leaned back in her chair again. "I'm sorry. I shouldn't have said that much. I've betrayed his confession."

A confession, thought Valerie. Peter Liverot not being entirely honest? That was the extent of Lorraine's great revelation. That wasn't news. It was like saying a prostitute wasn't entirely virginal.

"Forgive me, forget I said it," said Lorraine.

Valerie nodded. It hadn't been worth hearing, let alone remembering.

"I'm just encouraged that going forward, the charity will be able to accomplish even more thanks to Michael. You know, when I first met Michael, I was a little suspicious of him. I suppose I was being overly protective."

"Of who?"

"Of whom," corrected Lorraine, "of you. The first time I met him, he was standing over your bed when you were in the coma. The way he was looking at you, well, I just wondered about his motives."

Valerie repressed a grin. She had long discovered Mike Valvano's motives, and they were all sensual and delicious.

"Since then," continued Lorraine, "I've learned his intentions are honorable; in fact, they're laudable."

For a second, Valerie thought Lorraine said: "audible," and wondered if their lovemaking had been overheard.

"He's a fine man," said Lorraine, "and he loves you very much. I can tell by the way he looks at you. I mean, the way he looks at you when you're not looking. I'm convinced Michael would suffer any pain, move any mountain, bear any burden for your good. I know, because that's the way I feel, too. You are very precious to us, and we're blessed to have you."

Lorraine lowered her eyes, the way Chesney used to do when making a compliment. Damn them both, thought Valerie. Damn all three of them: Chesney, Lorraine, and Michael. They were making this so difficult. Valerie felt that annoying moistness forming in the corner of her eyes. She bit the inside of her lip to staunch the emotion.

After a few moments of silence, Lorraine continued.

"You're both in my prayers. Perhaps in the not too distant future, well…"

Valerie knew Lorraine was referring to her marrying Michael. It was what she wanted, too, but she certainly wasn't going to swap girlish hopes and aspirations with Lorraine.

"And if there are little ones," said Lorraine, "I want you to know that they'll be cherished by their Aunt Elinor."

"Who?" Valerie looked up.

"What?"

"You said something about little ones being cherished…"

"Yes, by their Aunt Lorraine."

"That's not what you said."

"Yes, I did."

"No," said Valerie. "You said 'Aunt Elinor.'"

For the first time in a month, Valerie saw a look of disorientation cloud Lorraine's eyes. She looked around for a moment as if scanning the air for something elusive. It only lasted a second and then evaporated.

"Oh, well, it doesn't matter, does it?" said Lorraine, her impenetrable poise back in place.

Valerie almost shouted: "Elinor, Elinor, Elinor," but the moment had passed. Whatever portal there had been into the mind of Chesney Potts, it was now closed. If Valerie couldn't pry it open by showing Lorraine photos of her male self, she doubted anything else would work. Then a fresh thought occurred to her. Perhaps she was better off without Chesney Potts. True, she could manipulate Chesney, but he was so exhausting, so fawning. Actually, Lorraine Innis was a better person to have around. Chesney would do anything for her, that was true, but he could be inept at times. Lorraine was smarter, more capable, especially when she really believed she was a woman. And while Chesney was devoted to Valerie, Lorraine also wanted what was best for Valerie, and in a purer way that she couldn't define. Perhaps, thought Valerie, she was working at this too hard. She had Lorraine and Michael both laboring for her best interests. Maybe she just needed to relax and let them take care of her. She'd been struggling to claw her way to the top. She could have it all and let Michael and Lorraine carry her there.

A satisfied smile spread across Valerie's face.

Lorraine returned the smile, but then a quizzical look appeared. "What is it?" she asked. "You just had the oddest little grin," said Lorraine.

"Oh, I just had a happy thought."

"Oh?"

"Yes," said Valerie, "I've been so busy with everything that's been happening that I didn't realize how fortunate I am."

"It's easy," said Lorraine, "to become distracted and lose sight of our blessings. I remind myself every day of how grateful I am for everything and especially for everyone."

Valerie noticed from that last statement the difference between Lorraine and Chesney. Lorraine was content to say "everyone" and know that she meant Valerie. Chesney would have gotten sloppy at this point and then tried to milk reciprocal feelings from her. Yes, thought Valerie, she liked Lorraine a lot more than Chesney. So what if Valerie couldn't control Lorraine? She didn't have to.

"But enough of that," said Lorraine. "I just wanted to make sure that you're ready for your trip to Gibraltar."

"Yes, I'm ready," said Valerie. What she said next astonished even her. "Why don't you come along?"

"Me?" Lorraine laughed. "I don't know anything about auditing or finance."

"It wouldn't all be work. We could do some shopping, go sightseeing, or just lay on the beach." This last suggestion made Valerie think twice. Was Lorraine capable of maintaining her identity in a bathing suit? How quickly Valerie was warming to the idea of a full-time Lorraine!

"That sounds wonderful," said Lorraine, "but I'll be traveling, too. I've got to go to London."

"London?"

"Yes, the largest paper products manufacturer in the UK wants our endorsement. It's quite possibly the most generous offer we've ever received."

"But why do you have to go? Can't someone else negotiate it?"

Lorraine shrugged her shoulders. "They specifically asked for me. I suppose they want me to personally approve all their products. That's a good sign. It probably shows that they're as committed to integrity as we are."

"Yes," said Valerie, slowly, "integrity...:"

– 10 –
The Man with the
Golden Pez Dispenser

Happy Birthday, Uncle President."

Nikolai Kropotkin sighed. "Yuri, this is a family occasion. You can just call me 'Uncle.'"

Kropotkin gave his niece, Yuri's wife, a kiss, and welcomed them into his home. Yuri tried not to appear nervous. He had been to Kropotkin's house many times for such celebrations. The only difference now was the gift.

◆

"What can I do for you?" was what Grigori Teplov, his former KGB boss, asked that day Yuri found him sitting behind Yuri's desk.

"For me? Comrade Teplov?" Yuri said, backing away.

"Please, Yuri, we have known each other so long," said Teplov, his teeth in full display. "And I am no longer your supervisor. And you are no longer a clerk. Please, call me Grigori."

"Grigori?"

"It is my name."

"*Da*, I knew that," gasped Yuri, as if he was being interrogated. "What... what is it that you want? I mean, what can I do for you, uh... Grigori?"

Teplov looked down. "Oh, I'm so sorry Yuri, I'm sitting in your chair."

"Oh, no, it's my chair, but you may sit there, in my chair... you can have it if you like. I can sit somewhere else... or I can stand..."

Teplov came around the desk and guided Yuri into the chair.

"There," said Teplov, moving to the other side of the desk. "May I sit here?"

"P-please d-do."

"So," said Teplov, "I want to do you a favor. Well, not for you directly. Our dear president's birthday is soon, is it not?"

"Yes, it is not," said Yuri, "that is no, it is. I mean, yes, that is correct."

"Good, I want to give dear Nikolai a present."

Yuri took out his wallet. "Do you want to go halfsies?"

"No, nothing like that," said Teplov. "It is just with the recent political reforms I am no longer allowed to give my old friend Nikolai even a simple birthday gift."

"You can," corrected Yuri, "only not over a certain amount."

"And there is my dilemma," said Teplov. "I had something made just for him but then learned that it exceeds the amount allowable. And I would not dream of circumventing the law."

"Can you return the item?"

Teplov shook his head. "As I said, it was made just for him. It is one of a kind. I cannot return it. But even if I could, I would want him to enjoy it. That is where you come in, Yuri."

"Me?" squeaked Yuri.

"As a family member, you would be allowed to give a gift to dear Nikolai," said Teplov. "You are his nephew, by marriage. So I simply have to give the gift to you, and you give it to him."

Yuri chewed on his thumb. "But, it would be from you."

"You would know that, and I would know that..."

"And Uncle... I mean, President Kropotkin?"

Teplov shook his head. "Ah, well, I could not take credit for it, even in a whisper. He must not know it was from me." He shrugged his shoulders. "It is the penalty I must pay for letting my friendship run ahead of my knowledge of the law. Still, it is pleasure enough for me to know that he will enjoy this gift."

Teplov removed a small rectangular box from his jacket pocket and slid it across the table to Yuri.

Yuri opened it and gasped. "May I?"

"Please do," said Teplov, "but be careful. It is one-of-a-kind. I know he will love it. I only wish I could see my friend's face when he opens it."

"You could come to the party," said Yuri.

"I imagine that is just for the family."

"Oh, yes, it is," said Yuri. A suspicious thought crept into Yuri's mind by the side entrance. "I never knew you two were close."

Teplov smiled wistfully. "Our friendship goes way back, Yurivitch. We were both in the army together. We went through training together. Our bunks were across from each other. Deep friendships form when you sleep across from a comrade." Teplov sighed. "Yes, we were together several years, Nikolai and I. Then I was recruited into the KGB, while Nikolai decided to stay in the army; good thing, too."

"Good? How?"

Teplov shrugged. "He was always the best. If he had gone into the KGB with me, he would have been my boss." Teplov stopped, thought a moment, and then laughed. "What am I saying? He is my boss. He is the boss of us all, and that is just as it should be. Yes, the man and the hour have met in my dear friend Nikolai."

Yuri thought he could detect a tear in the corner of the former KGB man's eye.

"I'll do it," blurted Yuri, jarring Teplov from his reverie.

"You'll do what?" He looked down at the little box in front of Yuri. "Oh, the gift! I'm sorry, my boy, I forgot myself for a moment there, forgive me. You'll give it to him, then?"

Yuri nodded.

"That is excellent," said Teplov. shaking Yuri's hand. "Sorry, I got carried away. And you will let him know it is from you, won't you? I wouldn't want to get into trouble over a little birthday present. But there's no fear of that. I know you can keep a secret, our little secret, eh?"

Yuri raised his index finger to his lips and nodded.

"Excellent," said Teplov, as he backed out of the office. "Then, I'll leave it all in your hands."

◆

Yuri placed the package on the sideboard, next to the other gifts, and sat down for dinner. After dinner, the celebration began in earnest.

"Uncle, uncle," cried Svetlana, Kropotkin's niece, "aren't birthdays just the most delightful things?" Svetlana clapped her hands and bellowed as if the room was full of revelers, and she was standing at least ten yards away.

Kropotkin forced an indulgent smile. Kropotkin looked at Yuri as if to thank him for marrying the girl. Yuri smiled back. He knew his wife could be wearing on her uncle. When she was there, Yuri no longer felt like the most annoying person in the room.

Kropotkin's housekeeper carried a cake into the room, which Svetlana quickly took charge of and placed in front of Uncle Nikolai.

"There," she said, "oh, what a lovely cake. I hope it's your favorite. It's made without wheat, Uncle Nikki."

"I'm sure it is good," said Kropotkin.

"Oh, we should have had balloons," said Svetlana. She turned to Katryna. "We should have had balloons, shouldn't we, Katryna?"

Katryna shrugged in a manner reminiscent of her father.

"I think Katryna is too grown up to be fascinated by balloons," noted her father.

"Yes, of course, she is," said Svetlana. A severe look momentarily eclipsed her jollity.

After the cake was cut, it was time for the gifts. Like many men his age, Kropotkin rarely took delight at receiving presents. Still, he made a show of being surprised and pleased for the sake of the givers.

"And what is this?" he said, picking up a flat package and hefting it his outstretched palms.

"That's from me," said Katryna.

"What is it, an automobile?"

"Daddy," she said in exasperation.

He smiled at his daughter, and she smiled back as if to say that she no longer appreciated his silly jokes but still loved him very much.

Kropotkin unwrapped the paper to reveal a framed drawing.

"I made it in art class," said Katryna, almost apologetically.

"If you had told me you bought it in an art gallery, I would have believed it; it's beautiful," he said.

"It's a field of flowers..."

"Like we saw down near the Black Sea," he added. "I can almost smell them and feel the breeze on my face. And I shall put this in my office, so I can tell all my visitors of my precious, talented daughter."

"I had it framed. It's a very good frame," she added.

"Only eclipsed by the beauty of the artwork it displays. Thank you, Katryna."

Katryna hugged her father's neck, and he kissed her cheek.

The warmth of the moment was shoved aside by Svetlana. "And here's another one, Uncle Nikki." She dropped a package in his lap.

"It's a good thing that this was not an automobile," he observed.

Svetlana giggled, proving she had not yet achieved Katryna's level of maturity.

"Shirts," said Kropotkin, opening the gift.

"Now, you will let me know if they are not the right size," said Svetlana. "We had them handmade by your usual haberdasher."

"I'm they will be the right size." Kropotkin thanked his niece and Yuri.

Kropotkin looked at the last package in front of him and paused. For a moment, Yuri thought he could see a look of anticipation in his eyes.

"Well," said Kropotkin slowly, "there seems to be one more gift. Who could this be from?" He smiled as if he thought he knew the answer.

"It's is from... uh, from... me," said Yuri.

Kropotkin's expression fell. "From you?"

"Uh, well, yes..."

Kropotkin looked at the box at his side. "But the shirts, they were from you and Svetlana."

"I... uh," Yuri ran his finger across his collar, "I didn't know about the shirts and bought, that is, I got this for you."

Svetlana's face wore a puzzled expression. "You didn't tell me, Yuri."

"Well, you didn't tell me about the shirts," he said defensively.

"Yes, I did," she said. "You don't listen, Yuri," she said, throwing up her hands.

"I do…"

"Apparently not to me," she pouted.

Kropotkin raised his hands. "I am grateful to you both. Please, do not squabble."

Yuri smiled at his wife and took her hand. Svetlana also smiled, though her eyes promised to continue the debate later.

"For you, Uncle," he said, pushing the small package toward Kropotkin.

Kropotkin unwrapped the paper, opened the lid, and reached inside. For one of the few times Yuri could recall, he seemed genuinely surprised.

"What…" began the President.

"It's a Pez dispenser," said Yuri.

"It's gold!" gasped Svetlana. She gave her husband a look as if to say: you never gave me a gold Pez dispenser.

"It's Mrs. Innis," Katryna was quick to add, pointing at the top of the device.

"It's…" Kropotkin stopped short of saying the name as he stared at the head atop the dispenser. After a moment, he gently prodded the bangs of the hairdo, and the head pivoted back to reveal a tiny brick of candy.

"It's gold," repeated Yuri, before quickly adding, "but not the candy. The candy is not gold. The candy is… candy." He smiled nervously as Kropotkin just looked at him. Perhaps he didn't understand the gift. Perhaps he didn't like it. Suddenly, Yuri felt an explanation was necessary.

"It, uh, President, I mean, Uncle," fumbled Yuri, "it is just a simple little combination of two of your favorite things." He smiled again. Kropotkin continued to look at him. Yuri forged ahead. "Your two favorite… the candy, see it is filled with candy. Those are grape flavored, but we can get another flavor if you prefer. I know it is not the Kit-Kats or the Reesey thingies. Uh, they, they do not make dispensers for Kit-Kats or the Reesey thingies. I… I suppose they could, but they would be very large, certainly too large to fit into one's pocket. Unlike this Pez dispenser, which will fit into your pocket and will dispense, uh, Pez. And it has the second thing, that is a person that you like." Not sure whether Kropotkin liked the gift, Yuri decided not to mention the name of Lorraine Innis. Instead, he merely pointed at the golden head. "That is her. They, the Pez people, uh, not people made of Pez… that would be silly… they would melt in the rain. No, the people who make Pez, and the dispensers, they made her head, that is, the likeness of her. Her head is actually much larger… not that the lady has a large head; it is certainly large than that one. But they made it, the dispenser that is. They are sold all over the world and, as I understand, are very popular. Those ones are plastic. This one is special, in gold. This one is only here, there, in your hand. You alone have that one, and…"

Yuri bit his lower lip, forcing himself to stop.

Kropotkin eyed him somewhat skeptically for a moment until his expression softened. "Yuri, my boy," said Kropotkin, "please, it almost sounds as if you are apologizing for giving me a birthday present. I often seem stern towards you, but I have always tried to treat you as my blood nephew. I wondered if I succeeded, but now, this…" He held up the candy dispenser. "It must have been very costly."

Yuri almost blurted out that it hadn't cost him a single ruble, but then recalled the need for secrecy. "Happy Birthday from all of us… I mean, from us, here, right here, in this room."

Kropotkin looked at Yuri and laughed. It was a hearty laugh. Soon the others joined in, happy to see him so happy. As the joviality petered out, Kropotkin sat at the head of the table, looking at the Pez dispenser with the most curious look on his face. After a moment, that curious look spread into a broad smile.

"What is it, Uncle?" asked Svetlana, staring at the Lorraine Innis Pez dispenser. "Do you wish we had invited someone else?"

He shook his head. "No, my dear," said Kropotkin, "everyone who should be here tonight is here."

"Then what, Uncle?"

Kropotkin winked and tapped the side of his nose. "It is nothing to be concerned about. I will be making a trip soon, rather confidential in nature. But I've said too much already."

"But you haven't said anything, Father," said Katryna.

"True, I haven't," he looked at the table. "Next birthday, we may need a larger cake."

◆

Several miles away, another smile, this one with bared teeth, spread across the face of Grigori Teplov.

"A larger cake?" he chuckled to himself. "Who could you be expected at that party, my dear Kolya? Could it be your little friend Lorraine Innis, or perhaps you're thinking of your old friend Teplov?"

Teplov ran his hand along the edge of his laptop computer. He marveled at the technology that allowed a tiny device hidden in a gold-plated Pez dispenser to transmit the details of an intimate birthday dinner.

– 11 –
Perfect Love and the China Cup

It was confirmed. Chesney was coming, albeit in the form of Lorraine Innis. Lorraine Innis was flying to Britain to negotiate an endorsement deal with Lord Bagnall's consumer conglomerate. His Lordship wanted to attend, but Verity reminded him of his poor record appealing to women. He would stay away, at least until an agreement had been reached.

Agreement? Verity didn't care about contracts, or negotiations, toilet tissue, or charities. She only cared that she and her beloved would know they were both alive. Then they could finally conclude the proposed marriage contract they negotiated years before.

How would she approach him? Did Chesney know she was alive? If he hadn't figured out those vague notes were from her, then her appearance might come as a shock.

She would make sure that their meeting was private. She would meet Lorraine Innis in the board room of her father's London headquarters. The lights would be low to help conceal her identity, and then from across the room, she would slowly approach. Verity thought of various ways she would do this all, the things she would say, and even what she would wear. She didn't want to clash with her fiancée. Lorraine Innis' style was very tasteful. Hopefully, those feminine accoutrements were only on the surface.

Even though their meeting wasn't until the next week, Verity was in London making preparations. After fussing around the office all morning, Verity took a cab from the glistening headquarters tower of Paper House in Canary Wharf to the Marylebone neighbourhood. It was where he first saw her. Marylebone was where Aunt Elinor had lived. And it was where the curious Mr. Postlewaite had his memorabilia shop.

She had avoided the area after the death of Chesney. The whole of London had been too painful to visit. But after she learned he was alive, Verity rushed to Postlewaite's shop, trying to find out additional information about Chesney and Lorraine Innis. The only thing she discovered was that Postlewaite's shop was no more. The new tenant knew nothing of Mr. Postlewaite. Still, Verity often found comfort in visiting the old street, now that she knew her beloved was alive.

"Pardon me," said a voice, as Verity stood in front of the shop.

She stepped to one side, thinking she must be blocking someone's way. Instead, a hand tapped her shoulder.

"Again, I beg your pardon."

Verity turned to see an Asian man of approximately fifty or sixty wearing a leather jacket and a flat cap.

"I didn't mean to startle you," said the man, "and forgive my presumption, but you are Verity?"

Verity nodded.

"I thought so," said the man. "I recognize you from your photograph. It was given to me by a dear friend."

He pulled a photograph from his wallet and handed it to her. It was a picture of Elinor, Chesney, and Verity.

"I thought you bore a remarkable resemblance to this young lady," he continued. He looked down at the photograph again and then up at Verity. "And that is because you are she."

"Yes, but..."

"I am Li Gao, a friend of our dear Elinor," the man bowed his head.

"Yes, Aunt Elinor spoke of you often, as did..." Verity wasn't sure why, but she couldn't bring herself to say his name, least of all not in the street.

Li Gao smiled. "Yes, your Chesney."

She clutched Li's arm. "He's alive."

The man nodded. "Yes, we had assumed you were the one who was deceased." He looked around. "But this is not the place for such a discussion. I feel we have much with which to enlighten each other. Please, let us go somewhere more private."

Several minutes later, they were in the corner of a small tea shop. Li Gao ordered a pot of tea and waited until it was delivered before he began, but not until he served Verity.

"Please, Mr. Li..."

"My dear one, call me 'Gao.'"

"Yes, of course, please, tell me all you can about... my beloved."

The serene countenance of Li Gao grew disturbed.

"He was most hurt," said Gao looking into his teacup. "It was a cruel blow, losing you both the same day."

Verity gasped. "Then he learned about Aunt Elinor that same day?"

Gao nodded and related the events of that afternoon. "After it was my solemn duty to tell him of the passing of his aunt, Chesney's first instinct was to find solace in your arms. But when he called, your father..."

"Father told him I had died," said Verity.

"Just so."

"By that time, I had also been told that my beloved had died. Father staged one accident to convince each of us that the other had perished."

"Clever economizing. Quite a head for finance has your father," conceded Li Gao.

"Yes, quite a head, until I knock it off of his shoulders," vowed Verity. "But how very horrible for Chesney to lose his Aunt and think he lost me the same day. Did he suffer much, Gao?"

"Did you suffer, my dear?"

Verity took a handkerchief from her bag and dabbed her eyes.

"But I only lost him that day," she said. "What... what did he say?"

Gao grew even more thoughtful and nodded. "He was most regretful for what he had done to you."

"To me? But he hadn't done anything."

"He related not allowing you to purchase, what was it? Oh, yes, frozen pizza."

Verity laughed through the tears. "Pizza? Oh, yes, I recall it was at the grocery store; the silly dear. And I was thinking about the meal he wanted. As it turned out, we didn't get either."

Li Gao smiled. "I suspected some circumstances such as that. He just felt that he had denied you."

"I haven't thought of it from that day until now," said Verity. "But I have thought of ways that I had let him down."

"You both affirm your love for each other," said Gao. "You are both blessed, and you will be all the more so when once you reunite."

Verity fell silent for a moment, not sure how to broach the next subject. She swirled the tea in her cup, and without looking up, said: "Have you seen him... lately."

There was a prolonged silence, and she almost thought Li had evaporated from the chair. Finally, he cleared his throat, and she looked up.

"Ah, yes, I have seen Chesney, not in person, but I believe it was either him or an apparition."

Verity whispered: "Lorraine Innis?"

Li Gao nodded. "We have been cautiously stalking the same notion."

"Do you know..."

He shook his head. "I know as little as you, my dear. I do not closely follow the news of the day, but even a hermit would find it difficult to avoid reports of the person of whom we speak."

Verity looked around the café. Although they were alone, she lowered her voice.

"Thank you for not saying that name," she said.

"Discretion is always the wisest course."

"I don't know why he is doing what he is doing, but I trust him," continued Verity. "There must be a good reason for the extremes to which he's gone. I only hope he hasn't been, well, too extreme if you understand my meaning."

"I share your hopes, my dear," said Gao. "I trust he is basically himself and that his current course of action is both purposeful and temporary in nature. Though, I was rather stunned when first I saw... the person."

"Does he look much like her... back then?"

A wistful gaze filled his eyes. "Very much so. Remarkably so. It is like looking through a window thirty-five years into the past. And not only is there the physical resemblance, but they are also very much of the same admirable spirit, though now on a global scale it would seem." He began to lift the cup to his lips and then stopped. "I only pray that it is not my fault."

"Your fault?"

"In consoling him, I mentioned that his present sorrow would help to create character."

"But how would that cause what he's done?"

"I gave the example of his dear aunt," said Gao, "mentioning that, if he allowed it, it would make him more like her."

Verity thought a moment. "So do you think he's..."

"Got bees in his cockpit? Forgive me, that was a euphemism that dear Postlewaite often employed. I would tend to think not. The famous lady of whom we speak comports herself as the very soul of sanity."

"Yes, I agree. I never miss the opportunity to watch... that person on the television. She always seems sharp and lucid. No, I don't think that person is detached from..."

"The moorings of sanity," offered Gao.

Verity smiled. "In fact, in just a few days, I'll be meeting with that person."

She then explained her father's desire to have Lorraine Innis serve as the spokesperson for his products and Verity's insistence that she handle the negotiations.

"Again," said Gao, "I bow to your father's sage business sense."

"And again," said Verity, through bared teeth, "I must express my resolution to knock his business sense senseless."

A concerned look crossed Li Gao's face. "And does your father know of this resolve?"

"Not yet," she said, "I'm planning a surprise for him, almost as pleasant as the one he gave to his daughter and her beloved. I haven't decided what form that surprise will take, but I vow it will be devastating. Though it could never match what he did to us."

For several minutes Gao sat motionlessly. The longer he did so, the more uncomfortable Verity grew. She felt the need to elaborate on the depth of pain she and Chesney had gone through. In some way, Verity felt that her last statement was being judged by Gao, though his face remained imperturbable. Finally, he spoke.

"Your father is a weak man."

"I..." Verity, poised to launch a rationale for her actions, stopped. "My father? Weak? He's one of the most powerful men in Britain. He moves through life as if the Earth were his private China shop, and he's the world's prize bull. Weak? Mr. Li, with all respect, I don't think you understand what my father has done. He's run his personal life with the same disregard that he uses in his business dealings; only in his personal life, he's much more ruthless. He's never faked the death of any business associates or rivals. He's never plunged them into inconsolable darkness. No, I could ascribe a litany of vices and flaws to that man, but weakness? I'm afraid you just don't understand."

Li Gao tilted his head as if to acknowledge the receipt of her feelings. He took another sip of tea.

"Your father loves you."

"He loves himself," said Verity.

"Indisputably so," Li Gao agreed, "and thus, his love for all others is quite imperfect. Imperfect love is motivated by fear, while perfect love triumphs over fear. That is why I called your father weak because he allowed himself to be driven by his fears. He feared losing you, so much so that he would kill you rather than lose you. He killed you to Chesney, and he killed Chesney to you, even though that action nearly crushed you with grief."

Verity pondered this. "So basically, you agree with me."

Gao stayed silent, his passivity speaking volumes of disagreement.

"But you do agree," said Verity, "that he needs a... a..."

"A lesson? A taste of his own medicine? His comeuppance?"

"Yes," she said. At last, he agreed with her.

Again, he sipped his tea. After draining the cup, Gao held it up and examined it.

"So many vessels in life," he said. "So many choices on what to fill those vessels with, and what to do once they are filled. If I were to fill this cup with scalding water and throw it at someone who had wronged me, my own heart would justify my actions. The heart is deceitful that way, deceitful above all things.

"When I was a young man, I wanted justice. My sinews ached for its application, the swifter, the harsher, the better as far as I was concerned. The world needed to be set aright. There are so many wrongs.

"I was quite certain that justice was just what my enemies needed. Then the thought occurred to me that perhaps there was as much justice that needed to be visited upon me. If I were called to account, would I be so zealous to have complete justice applied to myself? I came to the conclusion that the greater needs are for mercy and grace.

"This cup can be filled in many ways. And I had better like what I place in my cup, for in time I will surely drink from it. And the amount I give towards others is the same amount that returns to me, without fail. I can fill this cup with mercy, with grace, and with love and be assured that the same measure I meted out would redound to me. Or I could fill that cup with vengeance and await its dividend in kind."

He spoke all those words without once looking at Verity. Finally, he returned the cup to its saucer and then picked up the teapot.

"Will you join me in another cup of tea, my dear one?" he asked. Verity nodded, and Li Gao poured.

After several sips, Verity spoke.

"So, you don't think I should take revenge on Father?"

He tilted his head to one side. "It is not my choice, dearest. I can only advise that you savor whatever you choose since you will certainly have the opportunity to sample it yourself."

"Like karma, huh?"

Li Gao smiled. "I would select a different word, as I am convinced of a more personal supreme being. But if you mean to apply the principle of 'what goes around, comes around,' yes, that is the general idea."

"Perfect love..." said Verity aloud as she recalled what he had said.

"Just so," said Gao. "I believe the love you both share is purer than the force which tried to drive you apart. Though you were separated, seemingly by death, your love survives, and I believe it will blossom anew. Only do not allow your love to be disfigured by repaying evil for evil. Rather prove your love by practicing love."

They sat quietly, finishing their tea before Verity spoke again.

"I'm meeting that very prominent person next week."

"So you said," said Gao. "You must be fraught with anticipation."

She laughed nervously. "That's one way of putting it, Mr. Li. As much as I can't wait, I'd be lying if I didn't admit that I'm also..."

"A bit scared?"

"Terrified out of my boots," she said. "There are so many questions to which I don't know the answer. But I do know that somewhere in that person is my dearest, my love, my beloved."

"Then all will be well," said Li Gao.

She reached out and took his hand. "Thank you, and if I could ask a great favor: would you be there with me, with us, next week, when we meet? You're the bridge between us now. You know we've both survived. If you could, well..."

"Reintroduce you to one another?"

A tear formed in the corner of her eye, and Verity Goodhue nodded her head.

"It would be my great honor," he said.

– 12 –
How to Make a
Fairy Moan

"Well, I took our girl to the airport," said Mike Valvano, leaning through Lorraine's open office door.

"Michael, please, come in, sit down," said Lorraine.

"I've told you before, it's Mike."

"I've never called a bank president Mike," she said, "of course I've never known any bank presidents named Mike, either."

"Well, I've only been a bank president a little while. Maybe when I've been one longer and grow fat and prosperous, you can go back to calling me: Michael."

"Or, Mr. Valvano," said Lorraine with a laugh.

Mike feigned a frown. "Oh, I don't think I'd ever get fat enough to be called that. But what do I call you?"

"How about 'Lorraine?'"

"Don't you have a nickname? What did Valerie call you when you were kids?"

Lorraine opened her mouth to speak but drew a blank. She couldn't remember Valerie or anyone calling her anything when she was a girl.

"They... well, I guess I've always just been Lorraine."

"No nicknames? No pet names?" He winked at her. "You can tell me. I promise I won't spill any secrets."

Lorraine smiled nervously. "I'm sorry. I never thought about it before, but I don't have any other names other than my middle name: Elizabeth."

Mike smiled. "Well, maybe I'll figure something out."

"Figure out some..." said Lorraine, starting to correct him. "Sorry, never mind, it's a bad habit."

"Did I split an infinitive or step on a defenseless gerund?" He was making fun of her but without a trace of malice. Lorraine felt herself blush, but now it because he was innocently flirting with her.

"No, really, it's fine," said Lorraine. "I can see why Valerie feels the way she does about you."

"I feel that way about Valerie, too," he said. "I hated to say goodbye."

"Yes, and I have to get ready for my trip."

"And," said Mike. "that's what I wanted to see you about."

Lorraine pulled her itinerary from the folder. "It doesn't say with whom I'll be meeting, just a top representative. They're the largest manufacturer of paper products in the UK."

Mike agreed. "They probably want to use your international image to invade Europe."

"Well, that will depend on the quality of their products," said Lorraine. "I still won't endorse anything that I wouldn't use. I suppose that's why they want to meet with me. Alone."

Mike Valvano's eyebrow shot up. "Alone?"

"Yes, why, do you think that's a problem?"

"I'm just considering your safety."

Lorraine laughed. "My safety?"

A grave look shadowed Mike's face. "Yes, sorry, it's just that strange conditions for meetings, such as going alone, raise red flags in my mind. I've seen it before."

"In the priesthood?" asked Lorraine.

"No, uh," he said, "another area that I'm familiar with. Perhaps I'm being paranoid, but a healthy bit of paranoia is often a prudent thing."

Lorraine shrugged. "Why would anyone want to hurt me?"

"Forget I said it. And having said that, it's going to seem even odder to say the other matter I need to discuss: your life insurance."

Lorraine gave him a puzzled look.

"I know," said Mike, "I just said that no one would want to hurt you, but it's standard for heads of large organizations. It basically indemnifies the charity should they lose you. As I said, it's a standard thing."

"Oh," said Lorraine, "if it's routine…"

"Absolutely routine," said Mike, "just a brief medical exam."

A wave of panic rose in Lorraine, though she couldn't understand why.

"But I've just had a visit with my doctor. I'm fine, I don't need an examination. I can't have one." Lorraine wasn't sure why she was protesting so vehemently, but she knew she had to. "I... I can't see a strange doctor."

"No, no," said Mike, his hands outstretched, urging calm, "you won't see a doctor. It's just routine. In fact, there's a nurse from the insurance company waiting. They just take your blood pressure, height, weight, and blood samples."

Lorraine thought for a moment. Again, for reasons she didn't understand, her anxiety lifted. "Yes, I can do that, if that's all."

"That's all," agreed Mike. "I'll go get the nurse."

Fifteen minutes later, Lorraine was stepping on a portable scale.

"One thirty-three," said the nurse, and then realized Mike Valvano was in the room. "Oh, sorry, Mrs. Innis."

Lorraine laughed. "It's not like my weight is a state secret."

"I admire your confidence," said the nurse. "Most women don't like their weight publicized."

"Really?" said Lorraine. Was she normal? Maybe she should be more secret about her weight. She glanced at Mike, sitting on the sofa, reading a magazine. "But, it's just Mr. Valvano."

"Even my husband doesn't know how much I weigh."

"No?"

"No," said the nurse, as if the notion were scandalous.

"Oh," said Lorraine. "I'll remember that. I mean, I'll be a little more circumspect about, you know, weight."

The nurse gave her a curious look and proceeded to measure her height.

"Five foot six," she proclaimed.

Lorraine glanced over at Mike and then back at the nurse. "Is that okay to say?"

"They can tell your height just by looking at you," said the nurse.

"But not weight?"

"There's a lot we girls can hide," whispered the nurse.

Lorraine thought of the peculiarity that she was hiding. Rather than say anything, she just nodded and smiled. The nurse gave her a confidential wink making Lorraine feel she was a bonafide member of the sisterhood.

"Now we just need blood," said the nurse as she directed Lorraine to sit down. Lorraine did so, then turned her head away and braced herself.

"How do!" Called a voice.

Just as the nurse jabbed her, Lorraine turned her head and saw Purvis Twankey bounding into the room.

"Pur... OW...vis," said Lorraine. The nurse apologized and proceeded with her phlebotomic duties.

Purvis looked down at Lorraine's arm.

"Eee, Miss Lorraine, you got blood comin' out yer arm," he said, as the same liquid began to drain from his face.

"I know, Purvis," she said, "it's just a routine exam."

"I hope you pass, I hope... ooh 'eck!" Purvis, who could have been the poster boy for anemia, began to buckle at the knees. Mike sprang up to catch him and steer him to a seat.

"Are you all right, Purvis?" asked Lorraine.

Purvis removed his Stetson and fanned his brow. "Oh, aye, I just..." he looked at Lorraine but turned away again at the sight of the small tube filling with her blood. "Only I don't like blood. I mean, I like it fine, in its place, like inside folks' bodies, an' all."

Mike patted him on the shoulder. "We won't have to worry about Purvis becoming a vampire."

"No fear, there, Mr. Mike. I even went all wobbly drinking a raspberry-aide once. I twar' on the promenade at Blackpool. I remember asking for lemon, but man was all out o' lemon, so he said…"

"Purvis," interrupted Lorraine, "as fond as I am of your Blackpool memories, I'm sure that isn't why you came running in here."

"Pardon?" Purvis scratched his head. "Oh, aye, Miss Lorraine, Mr. Mike," he nodded towards the nurse, "ma'am. I didn't mean to bust in, but it's exciting. It's going to be a big success. I was telling Miss Patsy, well, actually, I didn't tell her, but she was there when I first thought of it. We were eating crisps…"

"Crisps?" said Mike.

"Potato chips," said Lorraine.

"Aye, an' that's what give me the idea, for you, for a product, for an invention that you can make, an' everyone will buy, and the money will go to the charity. It'll be smashing."

Lorraine winced as the needle was pulled from her arm. "Purvis, what are you talking about?"

"It'll give every woman the chance to be just like you," he gushed.

"Purvis, that doesn't make sense. I rarely eat potato chips."

"No, it's the smell," said Purvis, as if that made it crystal clear.

"You want me to smell like a potato chip?" asked Lorraine.

"Lorraine-flavored chips?" said Mike dubiously.

Purvis stared at Mike. He turned to Lorraine. "Why would you want to smell like a crisp that tasted like you?" he asked.

"I think we're all a little confused," said Lorraine. "Purvis, what are you talking about?"

"Perfume," said Purvis, as if it were self-evident.

"Perfume?"

"Aye," said Purvis, "what else would I be talking about?"

"You said something about potato chips," said Mike.

"I got the idea while I was thinking about crisps," said Purvis.

"You want to market a perfume with Mrs. Innis' name?" asked Mike.

"No," said Purvis, "you all can do that. I just want to invent it. It'll be proper champion, like nothing ever what's been done a'fore."

"What would make it so special?" asked Mike.

Purvis leaned forward. "Ever hear a fairy moan?"

Mike Valvano looked at him sideways. If he hadn't been a former priest, Lorraine suspected Mike would have taken a poke at Purvis, especially as Purvis was now grinning inanely.

A light went off in Lorraine's head. "Purvis, do you mean: pheromones?"

Purvis smiled. "Aye! That's it, fairy moans." He then nodded at Mike. "See? Miss Lorraine understands."

Lorraine smirked. "Well, yes, sort of, Purvis. Mike, he's talking about pheromones. Basically, the chemical that one member of a species uses to attract another member of the species."

"You mean like sex?"

Lorraine blushed. "That's one type of pheromone. Purvis, I don't quite understand, and I don't think I like where this is going."

Purvis described his potato chip theory and the slight chemical difference that makes chips of different flavors unique and popular.

"And I just figgered," he concluded, "that if you could make a chip popular by boiling it down to its essential... uh... whatchacallit..."

"Essence?" offered Lorraine.

"Aye," smiled Purvis, "essence. Well, if you could do that with a potato, you could do it with a person."

Lorraine and Mike just stared at him.

"I'd buy it," said a voice breaking the silence. Lorraine turned and noticed the nurse who had been quietly packing up her implements.

"You would?" said Lorraine.

The nurse blushed and lowered her eyes.

"Sorry, I didn't mean to butt in, I mean, it's none of my business, but I'd buy just about anything if you were promoting it, Mrs. Innis. I mean, I already use a lot of the products you advertise, and of course..." She touched the small Cross of Lorraine pin on her sweater.

"And you'd buy a perfume that smelled like Mrs. Innis," asked Mike.

"It wouldn't smell like 'er," corrected Purvis, "it would *be* like 'er."

"I already use a lot of Mrs. Innis' make-up. It's good quality, and very tasteful, without being flashy."

"But what about, well, whatever Mr. Twankey was describing?" asked Mike.

"...Essential essence," chirped Purvis.

The nurse smiled, speaking to Mike but gazing at Lorraine. "Oh, yes. I don't know about essences or how any of it would work. Still, I know if Mrs. Innis' name is on it, it will be a good product, and I've read that so much of everything you do here goes to help other people. And while I doubt that anything would make me like Mrs. Innis, I don't know, I think I would just feel a little more like Mrs. Innis."

"Well, there you have it," said Mike to Lorraine, "an unsolicited endorsement. What do you call that? A focus group study?"

"More like a focus individual," said Lorraine.

"Still, I imagine that this lovely woman represents thousands of women just like her all around the world. And this is the man who thought of it." Mike clapped his arm around Purvis' shoulder. "That was an inspired idea, Purvis."

"Just shows what can come of eatin' crisps," said Purvis with a bashful grin. "Then I can go ahead with the mixin', I mean, the makin', o 'eck, I mean the whatcha call it?"

"The R & D," said Mike.

"Do what?"

"Research and development," said Lorraine.

Purvis chuckled. "To me, them letters is likely to mean 'rest and dinner.' But I'll go to working on it if'n it's all okay."

"Absolutely," said Mike, "that is if Mrs. Innis approves."

Lorraine sighed. The thought of her essence being imitated and sold was a little overwhelming. She almost would have preferred a Lorraine flavored potato chip. But glancing at the hopeful faces around her, Lorraine reluctantly agreed. "I suppose it's okay to pursue the idea further."

"Champion," said Purvis. "It'll be me greatest invention since that See-Me, Feel-Me, Hear-Me."

"The what?" asked Mike.

Lorraine rubbed her hip. "The idea that started it all." She thought back to the incident that catapulted her to fame. Certainly, this latest brainstorm from the mind of Purvis Twankey wouldn't have the same effect. What could possibly be the harm in a fragrance based on Lorraine's individuality? Besides, she had more pressing matters to face.

"Champion, then it's a go," said Purvis beaming.

"Yes, I suppose it is," said Lorraine. "I'm going to leave it in Mr. Valvano's capable hands, Purvis. He'll give you whatever help and guidance you need. I'll be traveling, to your homeland, actually."

"Eee! You're going to Lancashire, smashing! Be sure to go up Blackpool Tower and have some black puddin' and a stick of rock for me."

"Sorry, I'm only going to London," she said.

"Oh," Purvis' enthusiasm dampened. "Well, you can't get black puddin', not even a decent toad-in-the-hole there. But I'm sure you'll be fine. Well, I've got to be on me bike," said Purvis, holding the door for the nurse. "Lots to do now. Have a good trip, Miss Lorraine. Oh, wait, Miss Lorraine, what should I call this perfume essence stuff?"

Lorraine stared at his toothy grin. "I don't know, Purvis," she said, shaking her head. "That's a quandary."

"Quandary," he said, his brow lowering.

"Yes," said Lorraine.

"Okay," said Purvis, the smile returning to his face. "Have a nice trip. See you when you get back from Blighty."

Lorraine watched Purvis disappear around the corner and then looked at Mike.

"He's really very sweet," said Lorraine.

"Oh, absolutely," said Mike, "and that idea of his has real potential."

"You will look out for Purvis, I mean, oversee this project while I'm away, won't you please, Michael?"

"Keep him out of trouble," said Mike.

"Yes, please," said Lorraine.

"And watch yourself in London, too."

"Me? What could possibly happen to me in London?"

– 13 –
Dear Peignoir Pal

T his is Miss Fierro, in the Penthouse suite. Please, send up some fresh coffee."

Valerie rested the receiver back in its cradle and stretched beneath the linen sheets. She felt: what was the word? Languid. Yes, that was the word. It would be hard not to be languid as the gentle Mediterranean breezes played with the curtains leading to the balcony. A balcony overlooking the sea! Valerie imagined herself, holding her coffee in a fine china cup, standing on the terrace. The folds of her peignoir fluttering with the curtains in the breeze, atop the best hotel in Gibraltar, looking down on the azure sea, with only the Rock itself enjoying a more commanding view.

She wasn't just some girl from Delaware anymore. Now she was Valerie Fierro, the closest friend and confidant of Lorraine Innis. Wherever she went, Valerie was treated like royalty, perhaps even better than royalty. Valerie smiled. Dear Lorraine. Valerie was proud of her new charitable attitude towards her "cousin." Let Lorraine be Lorraine. If Chesney wanted to submerge himself in Lorraine, that was fine with Valerie. He could go drown himself in Lorraine. Lorraine was a better person just by being a woman. Valerie wondered why she had panicked when Chesney disappeared inside of his alter ego. She was on this tandem bike with Lorraine. Valerie could struggle with Chesney for control, or she could let Lorraine do all the pedaling while she put her feet up and coasted along for the ride.

Valerie stretched beneath the sheets. It was a good ride.

A fresh breeze wafted in from the sea, and Valerie made the conscious effort to get out of bed to take advantage of it. She could languish in bed at home. The coffee would be here any minute. She would go from being languid to statuesque and elegant.

Valerie slid out of bed, slipped her new lace peignoir over her silk ecru gown, and stepped into her three-inch mules. She ran a brush through her hair, arranging her brunette tresses around her shoulders. Walking into the living room, she crossed to the open French doors leading to the balcony, where she struck a pose. The sunlight streaming in the doorway gave her gown a translucent quality. Looking across the room, she could see that the outline of her figure was just visible in the mirror. She hoped the waiter was virile enough to appreciate the presentation.

As if on cue, there was a knock on the door. Valerie tilted her head upward and pointed her chin towards the Mediterranean, and bade the person enter.

The door opened, creating a cross-breeze that stirred the curtains and her peignoir around her thighs.

"Thank you," she said in a sultry voice that she used whenever she wanted to sound elegant, "just put it on the table."

Valerie kept her focus on the cerulean sea. She waited for the sound of a tray being placed on the table or the rattle of the china. Instead, all she heard was the breeze.

"You look like you're waiting for a bus!" said a familiar voice.

Valerie jerked her head toward the suite door. There stood Albrecht Eckner.

"You!" she spat. "I thought you were the waiter with the coffee."

Albrecht nodded at her with his familiar porcine smile. "Giving a little floor show with breakfast?"

Valerie looked down at her revealing silhouette and hurried out of the light, gathering her gown about her.

"You don't have to be so modest," he said. "I have seen you naked, well, practically; prom night?"

"Once, a long time ago, and it will NEVER happen again in this lifetime!"

He shrugged. "Makes one hope for reincarnation."

"You can hope for whatever disgusting little trolls like you hope for," said Valerie as she stormed into the bedroom and slammed the door. She emerged thirty minutes later, showered, and dressed. Albrecht Eckner was sitting on her sofa, sipping her coffee.

"Oh, I'm sorry, all gone," he said, raising the cup. "Shall I call from a fresh pot?"

"Call for a fresh urn and have yourself cremated," she snapped.

Albrecht smiled and drained the last of the coffee from his cup with a loud slurp. "Thank you," he said, "that was lovely. Almost as lovely as the sight that greeted me."

"Shut up. What are you doing here?"

Albrecht looked around as if he had been born in the room, and it was his natural habitat.

"Who else did you expect?"

"I expected you," she said, "just not this early, and certainly not in my hotel room."

"Hotel suite," Albrecht corrected. "The best in Gibraltar, too, I imagine. Am I paying for this, or is it your cousin? By the way, you never told me you had a cousin. All the time we were in school, you never mentioned a cousin."

"Lorraine is from New Jersey," said Valerie. "She didn't come down to Delaware much. And she is paying for my accommodations because she's a very generous woman and she happens to be devoted to her best friend and dearest relative. Besides which, you're not here to pry into my personal business. I'm here to investigate you."

If Albrecht was ruffled by her rebuff, he didn't show it. Instead, he seemed pleased with himself.

"Yes, that will be fun," he said with a crinkle of his nose. "Have you ever been to Gibraltar before?" He asked before answering himself. "No, you haven't. I'm surprised you being a Med Girl."

"What?"

"Mediterranean, you know, Spanish, Italian, Greek, Sicilian..." he squeezed extra sibilance from that last word. "I would have thought your family would have taken you on a trip to your ancestral homeland."

Valerie dug her fingernails into her palms.

"I never got the opportunity," she said curtly.

"Well, now you do," he said with a wave towards the French doors.

"Maybe someday," she said. "I'm here to work."

Albrecht smiled, pulled a manila envelope from his portfolio, tossed it on the coffee table, and extended his hand as if he just completed a feat of prestidigitation.

"What's that?" she asked.

"That is your ticket to enjoying yourself for the next two weeks," he said. "No need to thank me, but that is your audit, all wrapped up nice and neat."

"You mean that's your audit," she said. She almost reached for the envelope but instead folded her arms across her chest. "I'm here to go over your accounts."

Albrecht sighed. "Oh, how boring. May I tell you what you'll find? The books of our little financial institution will show you a lot of naughtiness by Peter Liverot, may he rest in peace. There's even more naughtiness by his friends; and, modesty forbids, even a little naughtiness by yours truly."

"Only a little, huh?"

"Oh, please, Valerie," he said, "I'm not in their league. They want power. I'm happy with the little comforts the position should afford me, the perks that should go with my hard labor. I'm just a minor player, a petty thief if we're grading on the curve. I'm too lazy to be any more than that."

She eyed the envelope. "And that's what that tells me?"

"No, that's what I'm telling you, my dear. That one paints the story of a small bank subsidiary that is essentially on the level. I threw in some small infractions you rooted out through your diligent work: sloppy procedures, that sort of thing, to make it look like you did a thorough job."

He sat there with an innocent expression. It was the most sincere Valerie had ever seen Albrecht Eckner. For a second, she believed him. Then she reminded herself with whom she was dealing. He was as twisted as rotini pasta. Was he admitting to lesser infractions to put her off the trail of even greater crimes? She suspected that Liverot had confessed his own crimes on his deathbed. That's why Lorraine hadn't accused Valerie of anything. Probably Lorraine knew something wasn't right, and she was trying to protect Valerie. She thought of Lorraine and Mike, both of whom were so honest, both of whom were only out for Valerie's good. A pang of conscience struck at her heart, and she felt grateful. She looked at the envelope on the table and then up at Albrecht Eckner. He was smiling, nodding, urging her to accept his audit.

"Well," he said with a coaxing lilt to his voice.

She stared at the envelope on the glass-topped coffee table. Eckner's faint reflection could be seen beside it. His face was upside down and distorted, much as he was inside. Perhaps it was the curtains blowing in the breeze or the reflection of the light. But for a brief moment, Valerie thought she could see other faces awaiting her response. There were Lorraine and Michael, and it must have been the light, but it seemed like her father. It was as if they were there, rooting for her to make the right decision.

She looked up at Albrecht and smiled. He smiled back. Then she picked up the envelope. Beaming her loveliest princess smile, Valerie ripped the phony audit in half in one swift, defiant gesture. Then she flung the two halves into the stunned face of Albrecht Eckner.

It felt so good. Valerie had been waiting to do that since high school. The look on Albrecht's face was short-lived but priceless all the same. He was shocked. He was stunned. His usually squinty eyes were wide in disbelief. Unfortunately, this only lasted a moment. In less time than Valerie had to savor her victory, Albrecht recovered his composure. He brushed the torn bits of the document from his shoulder and reinstituted his pursed smile.

"Oh, my," he said, "never mind. I have other copies."

"Yeah, well," she began defiantly, "you know what you can…"

"I also have plenty of copies of this," he said, "and he drew a smaller envelope from his jacket pocket.

– 14 –
The Hibernian Lasagna

Micheletto!" The old woman extended her hands.

Mike Valvano leaned over to kiss her on the cheek.

"Nonnia," he said and then sat down on her left at the table. "I'm sorry I'm late. I was delayed at the office."

"Eat your *zuppa*, Micheletto, before it gets cold," said Nonnia. She scowled at the man on her right. "You keep your brother working too hard, Roberto."

Robert Valvano smirked. "He's president of a bank. He's his own boss."

"*Manga*, it's your favorite, *scarola*," she said and then turned back to Robert. "He's not his boss. I know who he works for."

"Me," said Robert.

"Me," she said, asserting her place as the head of the family. Nonnia Valvano turned back to her other grandson. "Is it hot enough, Mikey?"

"Just right, Nonnia," he said. Mike glanced up. His brother's icy stare was cold enough to chill the soup. Robert was his grandmother's favorite, but the old woman fawned over Michael to make Robert jealous. Mike figured that out when he was still a child, but he doubted that Robert ever caught on. She was a cagy woman. She had to be.

"How is business," asked Robert.

"Not at the table," chided Nonnia. "Let me enjoy a family meal without all your business."

Robert rolled his eyes. Michael suppressed a laugh. In her day, she could have outdone either of them in business. Nonnia probably still could give them a run for their money. She was the toughest person he knew. She had to be.

"I hope everybody's hungry," said a redhead, as she entered the dining room carrying a casserole dish. "Hello, Michael."

"Hi, Meghan," said Michael.

Meghan Valvano placed the dish on the table and removed the cover. Steam rose from the mélange within.

"Lasagna," Meghan announced.

"That's what it's supposed to be," muttered Robert.

His wife scowled at her husband and then smiled at Michael. "It's your grandmother's recipe."

Nonnia evinced no reaction. Robert said nothing.

"I'm sure it'll be great," said Michael. "It smells delicious."

Meghan smiled at Michael, grateful for at least one ally.

"It's wonderful to see you, Michael," said Meghan as she served up the lasagna. "I was saying to Robert the other night: 'we don't see your brother enough.'"

"Yeah," said Robert after an awkward silence. "She said that. It was the other night. So, now you got him."

Everyone began to eat. It wasn't terrible, but it wasn't Nonnia's cooking, so it was pretty bad by comparison. Michael praising the effort. No one believed him.

It wasn't Meghan's fault. She was Irish and couldn't cook. In Robert's mind, those two flaws went hand in hand. But it was his flaw that initiated the marriage. Robert was colorblind and mistook the Irish flag pin Meghan wore for that of the Italian tricolor. By the time he realized it, Meghan was pregnant with their first daughter. Robert did the honorable thing and married her. She repaid the favor with every meal she cooked.

With business talk banned, Michael asked numerous questions about his two nieces and one nephew. Robert answered concerning the boy and Meghan, the girls. Guido, the youngest, was three. The girls were both dark-haired Italian beauties. Their brother had the same red hair and freckled complexion as his mother: not exactly consistent with the name "Guido." Still, he was a boy, and despite his tender years, Robert was raising him to overcome his Hibernian genes.

As dessert was being served, Meghan wandered onto a topic Michael hoped to avoid.

"So, Michael," she said as she sliced into the cake, "Robert tells me you have a girlfriend."

Michael looked across at his brother. He then looked over at Nonnia.

"Michael, do you think no one knows?" said the old woman.

"No," said Michael, "I knew some people knew. I just didn't know everyone knew." He shot an accusatory look at his brother. Robert smirked.

"It just came up in conversation," said Robert.

"I wanted to know why my grandson suddenly leaves the priesthood," said Nonnia. "I wasn't born yesterday, Michael. A priest leaves his vocation for one of two reasons. Either he no longer believes, or he has found a girl. I know you didn't lose your faith. You were raised too well for that. But you're not immune to the other. It is better to give in to the desire if you cannot overcome them and keep your vows."

Michael nodded. "That's just what happened."

"I know that's just what happened," said the old woman. "Didn't I just tell you as much? I don't sit up in my room all day, saying my rosary, Michael. I may be old, but I'm not dead yet."

"No, of course not, Nonnia," said Michael, "*mi scusi.*" Not dead? No one knew her age, but Nonnia had to be in her eighties, and she was sharper than people half her age.

"*Questo è risolta,*" she nodded before the faint smile returned to her lips. "Now, tell me about this girl."

"She's beautiful," he said.

"*Bella,*" said his grandmother. "And is she..." She glanced at Meghan.

Michael understood. "Her name is Valerie... Valerie Fierro."

Nonnia's face beamed. "Ah, a beautiful name...Valerie. Yes, a wonderful name." She then gave a brief, almost imperceptible look to Robert, who had not chosen as well.

"You will have to bring your young lady here to meet me," said Nonnia.

"Yes, I will," agreed Michael.

"After she returns from her business trip," she added.

Michael looked at his grandmother and then at Robert. He hadn't told his brother that Valerie was going to Gibraltar for an audit but was sure Robert knew. Robert always knew. Robert nodded at his brother, confirming that he was indeed in control of the matter.

Well, thought Michael, as he finished his dinner, at least they didn't know about his personal plans. They might suspect, but they didn't know what he hadn't told anyone. He was going to ask Valerie Fierro to be his bride.

– 15 –
A Selection from the Dead Letter Office

Albrecht Eckner dangled the paper between his thumb and forefinger. With his other hand, he slid his index finger along the crease of the thrice-folded document.

Valerie looked at him with disdain. Albrecht was probably bluffing. She may have fallen for his tricks in the past, but not anymore.

"Get out," she ordered and turned her back on him. "Inform your staff that I will begin my audit later this morning."

She strode towards the bedroom. It felt so good. She would shut the door, not in anger, but with authority and finality. It would signify their relationship was officially at an end. She had Michael and Lorraine behind her. Albrecht Eckner held no power over her, none whatsoever.

Valerie took the first step across the threshold when Albrecht began to read.

"'Dearest Valerie, Although I've already thanked you for the shower and the thoughtful gift, I wanted to write to you about that day. I didn't know when to bring this up, if ever, and I only do so now to hopefully ease your pain.'"

He paused, apparently as he saw Valerie freeze in the doorway. Did he know he had hit a nerve? Is that why he stopped reading? Valerie stood motionless. He couldn't have that letter, could he?

He continued reading.

"'The clinic called me a few days after your procedure. They said I had put down the wrong phone number, but they had looked up my number. Before I could explain that it hadn't been me, it became clear what procedure had been done, and that it had been carried out in my name.'"

"Stop," said Valerie, without turning around. It was the letter from Martina, the one that had gone missing, the one she had tried to share with Chesney. Now she knew it had been stolen from her handbag by...

"I'll jump to the end," said Albrecht as casually as if he were reading from a grocery list.

"'P.S.: I have not mentioned this to anyone, least of all, Chesney. He thinks of you and loves you like a sister, and I don't know if he would fully understand. This is our secret. Love. M.C.F.'"

"Very touching. M.C.F. Martina C. Fergus."

Valerie wheeled around and pointed her finger at Albrecht. She only wished it had been a gun. "Give me that."

He smiled, folded the letter, and placed it on the coffee table. "You can keep that," he said. "If you need any more, I can get you as many as you want. Don't worry. I've got the original in a very secure place."

Valerie snarled: "You stole that! That letter was personal. That letter is mine. You stole it from me."

Albrecht raised his hand. "Guilty as charged."

"You admit it!"

His eyebrows shot up. "I've got it, haven't I? Who else would I blame? Patsy? Peter Liverot?" He paused and snorted a laugh. "Chesney Potts? Oh, no, that's right, Chesney loved you like a sister, didn't he, Sis?"

Valerie's eyes widened. If she could have shown Chesney the letter that day, everything would have been okay. It would have been very uncomfortable, but it would prove that Martina's death had been an accident. Martina forgave her. Chesney would have to.

But now it was too late. Too much had happened. Chesney had clutched for answers and mistakenly blamed Peter Liverot. And as she didn't have the letter to prove otherwise, Valerie let him believe that. It was easier. Liverot was a crook and a lecher. It fit. Valerie hadn't meant for anything bad to happen to Martina. Valerie didn't know that Chesney would go to such lengths to get Liverot. How could she know that he would create Lorraine Innis just to...

Lorraine! How Lorraine would react? After all that Chesney went through to create Lorraine; Lorraine would be furious. And just as Valerie was really getting to appreciate having Lorraine around.

Chesney? Lorraine? The thought occurred to Valerie that Chesney wasn't around anymore. Albrecht Eckner couldn't show the letter to Chesney Potts because he hadn't seen Chesney for over a year; no one had. There was no Chesney. There was only Lorraine. Inwardly, Valerie breathed a sigh of relief. So what if Albrecht had Martina's letter? The relief must have been palpable on her face, for Albrecht's smug expression turned into one of confusion.

"Go ahead," she said, "you little thief. Show that letter to Chesney Potts. I don't care. I haven't seen Chesney for years. I don't know who has. Besides, Martina forgave me, so it doesn't really matter. Do you even know where Chesney is? Maybe he's married. Maybe he found another nice girl and settled down. So, go and call him up. Show him that letter. But I can honestly say I have no idea how to reach him."

She smiled and sat down.

"Oh, and, as I said before, do tell your staff that I will be starting that audit. It will be very interesting, especially since I now know what exactly I'm looking for. Thank you very much."

"Your very welcome," said Albrecht. The bravado edged back into his voice. "You know, that's an interesting idea: finding old Chamber Potts and showing him your little letter. It hadn't even occurred to me because I know you never cared what that fat little slug thought. Oh, maybe a little, maybe… that much." He held his thumb and index finger a quarter of an inch apart.

"Then what…"

"What was I going to do with the letter?" Albrecht waved his hand. "Really, I wasn't thinking about the great love affair of Miss Fergus and Mr. Potts. Too much of that couple would make me go diabetic. No, the real star of that letter is you, dear Valerie. But then I've always found you an interesting girl, even when we were back in high school, and you were romping naked on the bed with the family dog."

Valerie clenched her fists.

"For example," he continued, "while Martina doesn't say what your little procedure was – she was too much of a lady to come right out and say it – it's clear what it was. Our little Valerie was going to become our big Valerie. You were going to be a mommy. And you decided against having the baby. But so as not to sully your reputation, you had the 'procedure' under someone else's name, and without their knowledge." He pursed his lips, in his impression of a nurse, and lisped: "Your little problem is all over with. You can go home now, Miss Fergus."

"You bast…" Valerie caught herself. Albrecht couldn't tell Chesney. She regained her composure. "So what? Like I said, you're free to go tell Chesney Potts. Be my guest."

Albrecht Eckner looked as if he had smelled something unpleasant. "No, thank you. I'd rather let him fester away wherever it is that little nonentities go to fester."

"Well, then…" said Valerie. She won. Albrecht overplayed his hand. He was bluffing, and…

"But then," said Albrecht, "Why go digging up the past, when there are so many interesting things in the present? I don't know whether your former cubicle mate, Mr. Potts, would care about what you did to his dear, departed fiancée. That's all in the past. There is someone else, however."

Valerie wracked her brain. Who would care from back then? Who did she still associate with from back then?

"Patsy?" she said to herself, but it came out audibly.

Albrecht rolled his eyes. "Do I have to explain everything?" he said, in mock aggravation. "The revelation that the sweet, pure Valerie Fierro had aborted her own child wouldn't be very pleasant news to your mother or sister, would it?"

Valerie hadn't thought of them, but still, it wasn't anything she couldn't overcome in time.

"Of course," said Albrecht, examining his manicured fingernails, if a certain ex-priest found out about it..." He clicked his tongue in feigned embarrassment for her.

Valerie felt her face glow red hot.

"You f**kin' bastard," she growled. Albrecht just smiled.

"How did you know about..."

"You and Father Mikey?" He shrugged his shoulders.

It didn't matter how Albrecht Eckner knew. He knew. That was bad enough.

"You wouldn't dare," she said.

He raised one eyebrow as if to ask if this was a challenge.

Of course, he would dare, thought Valerie. Albrecht Eckner was capable of anything for almost any reason as long as it served his own twisted urges. And now he would threaten to ruin her life just for the sake of his rotten little audit. Then the thought occurred to her.

"Wait a minute..." she said.

He smiled. "My time is your time."

"There was someone else that got pregnant..." Valerie almost said, "the same night," but she caught herself. He already had too much information as it was. "...around the same time. Are you forgetting Patsy?"

"Patsy? Dear Patsy Einfalt," he chuckled at her new name. "How could I forget the mother of, well, of the seed of my loins?"

"So you admit it? You're the father of Patsy's baby!"

Another Eckner shrug ensued. "My dear Valerie, there are no secrets between you and me. The question is: I am more concerned about Patsy learning of my indiscretion, or are you more concerned about Father Mikey learning yours? We really are kindred spirits, Valerie. After all, though we're just good friends now, we were each the first for the other. We'll always have that, my dear."

Valerie extended her index finger rigidly and then curled it downward in a droop in imitation of his sexual failure on prom night.

"That wasn't my fault," he said, momentarily deflated. "Besides, I've since proved my virility, just as your proven your fertility. But we don't want to brag about our exploits, do we? Not unless we have to."

Damn, Albrect had no shame, and because of that, he still had the upper hand.

90

Albrecht must have sensed he had won. He nodded down at the torn version of the audit report.

Valerie stared at the papers strew about him. If she turned in his report, what would it matter? She wouldn't be lying, not really. Albrecht Eckner would be lying. She would just be passing it along. It wasn't the same. Was it? All she was really doing was overlooking Albrecht's petty pilfering, the padding of his expenses, his lavish lifestyle. Besides, she wasn't that sharp, not as an auditor, at least. If they wanted to know the real truth, why would they send her? They got what they deserved by not sending a trained accountant. Besides, it wouldn't hurt Michael, would it? Most of what had gone on had been done by Liverot and his cronies. None of it would fall on Michael. Michael loved her, and she loved him. What she did was years ago. Why ruin the future of two people in love for any of this?

So that only left Lorraine to consider. Lorraine had sent her to Gibraltar, but Lorraine was only worried about the charity.

"One question," said Valerie after several minutes of pondering.

Albrecht Eckner's face lit up like an angler who sees a fish dancing on the end of his line. "Yes?"

"Are you stealing from the charity? Are you stealing anything from my cousin, from Lorraine?"

Albrecht Eckner crossed his heart and swore he didn't even have access to the charity's accounts. "All those decisions come from headquarters."

"You weren't doing anything on Liverot's say so?"

Eckner's mouth opened as if he were hearing that notion for the first time. Valerie didn't believe he was that innocent, but still, she believed him enough.

Valerie bit her lip as she watched Albrecht leaning forward on the edge of his seat. As long as it didn't hurt Michael or Lorraine, she could live with Albrecht's arrangement. She sighed and nodded her head. "Okay, I'll use your audit… after I review it."

"Oh, of course, of course," said Albrecht patronizingly. "I wouldn't dream of it any other way. You won't regret this, partner."

– 16 –
A Lady in Waiting

J ust another minute, Mrs. Innis," said the woman.

"Thank you," said Lorraine. She smoothed the knee-length skirt of her suit and looked around the room. It was all very elegant.

Though she had been in many opulent surroundings over the past year, this was somehow different.

Lorraine couldn't help but feel nervous, or was it excitement or anticipation? She had the disquieting feeling that her life was about to change on the other side of that door. It must be her feminine intuition.

She twisted her necklace around her finger and then caught herself and stopped. It wouldn't do to fidget like a kid outside the principal's office, would it? She was an international figure, wasn't she? Lorraine shook her head. The media might think she was a celebrity, and the public might agree. However, Lorraine still felt like an ordinary person from New Jersey. She was nothing special. Or at least she hoped she wasn't.

She didn't feel special. The décor of the room was more impressive than she was. It made her feel that much more ordinary. She also felt like she needed to visit the ladies' room. She didn't actually have to, she told herself. She always got the phantom urge when she was nervous. If she thought of something else, it would go away.

Lorraine thought about Valerie. She had talked to her several times over the last few days. Valerie's plans had changed. They were both traveling. Apparently, the audit was going well, though Valerie was evasive on that subject, or perhaps it was just caution. Valerie couldn't give a full report over the phone. They would see each other soon enough.

Mike Valvano's reaction to this meeting also heightened Lorraine's feeling of foreboding. With Valerie away, Mike had volunteered to come along, but Lorraine insisted on going it alone. After all, what could happen to her? It was a meeting. That's how Lorraine looked upon it, and nothing…

"Mrs. Innis?"

Lorraine looked up. The administrative assistant had returned. "Yes?"

"You can go in now."

Lorraine stood up, pulled down on the hem of her jacket, took a deep breath, and walked toward the door.

– 17 –
Another Lady In Waiting

Verity Goodhue's palms were sweating. Her breathing was shallow. She almost asked for a paper bag to breathe into so she wouldn't hyperventilate.

"It will be fine." Li Gao placed his hand on her own.

"I know," said Verity, "it's just the anticipation. I've dreamed of this day ever since I knew he was alive. Maybe that's the problem. I've rehearsed it so often in my mind."

"And how did the situation resolve itself, in your imagination?"

Verity exhaled. "Oh, every time it was wonderful. I just, well, I…"

"It will be wonderful," assured Li Gao.

Verity nodded. Gao looked so different in a three-piece suit. She wished they were doing this someplace else, someplace less formal. At least this board room was private.

Verity rose from the chair at the head of the conference table and walked over to the lighting panel. For the tenth time in the last five minutes, she adjusted the dimmer and then turned to Li Gao.

"Too dark?"

"No," he said.

"Too light?"

"It is fine."

"I just want it to be right," she said. "I don't want it so dark that he can't see me, but I don't want it too bright either. This may come as a shock to him. I want to make it as easy on him as I can."

"I know, my dear," said Gao.

"Do you think…"

"I believe that no matter what happens, your beloved will experience some surprise. But even if it is a shock, it will ultimately be as great a joy to him, as it was to you."

Verity nodded. "I suppose so, yes. I hope so, yes..." she began to adjust the chairs around the large table. Li Gao beckoned to her.

"It will just be the two of you," he said.

"Yes, of course," said Verity. "I'll sit there," she said, pointing to the head of the table. "Or should I be standing?"

Before he could reply, she continued.

"Do I look all right? I tried to wear something familiar to him. I used to wear this quite a lot. I was wearing something very similar when he first saw me." Verity indicated her white silk blouse and her straight black skirt. "He thought, I was in service," she laughed, but then her face turned serious. "I've forgotten it."

"Forgotten what?"

"The beret. I was wearing a beret. He liked me in that beret."

Li Gao shook his head. "No, he liked that beret on you. I doubt he sought you out because of your headwear, but rather admired the beret for the person who adorned it."

"Thank you," she said. "I don't need the beret, do I?"

He smiled and shook his head.

There was a knock on the door, and a middle-aged assistant entered.

"Your appointment is here," she said.

"Is he?" Verity blurted before catching herself. "I mean, is she?"

The secretary gave her a puzzled look.

"Sorry, sorry," said Verity struggling to regain her composure. "It's just, well, I've never negotiated such an important agreement for my father, and I'm a little nervous."

The woman gave her an indulgent smile and started for the door.

"Wait," said Verity, "what is she wearing?"

"Wearing?"

"My... Mrs... my guest..."

"A dress," said the woman.

"Rather plain and dignified, then?" asked Verity.

The woman smirked. "Actually, Miss Goodhue, since you asked, rather flash."

"Oh?"

A deepening look of disapproval spread over her face. "Yes, I suppose it's the American style, but..." She stopped.

"No, go ahead, it's all right," said Verity.

The secretary lowered her head and her voice. "It's just a bit... tarty."

"Oh," said Verity, crestfallen.

"I'm sorry, Miss Goodhue," said the woman.

"No, no, it's not you, it's just, well, never mind. Please, show her in."

The assistant excused herself and closed the door behind her.

Verity looked at Li Gao. "Oh, Mr. Li," she moaned, "It's bad enough that my beloved has felt compelled to do whatever he's had to do, for whatever reason. But I hate to see him look tawdry."

"That is just one person's opinion. We have seen our Mrs. Innis repeatedly over the last months, in the news and on the television," he reminded her. "In all that time, she has been the very model of decorum, befitting the memory of our dear Elinor."

"Yes, that's true," said Verity wiping away the beginning of tears. "Sorry, I don't want... Mrs. Innis to see me this way, do I?"

Standing up straight, Verity smiled and turned toward the door. Li Gao took a step into the background.

The handle turned, and the door opened.

It was an expensive outfit she wore, but the secretary wasn't far wrong. It was flashy, suggestively tailored, blood red in color with a slit skirt and a large ruffle up the slit. She wore matching blood red stiletto heels. Indeed, the ensemble verged on the tarty.

"Hello," said Verity, "welcome to..."

She stopped. There was a moment of relief that Chesney, or Lorraine, or whoever's taste hadn't departed from them, then a more profound disappointment.

"Hello, I'm Valerie Fierro," said the woman in the tarty outfit, as she extended her hand.

Verity stood, her mouth agape, staring down at the hand. Then she looked up and craned her neck back towards the door, wondering if Lorraine Innis was following her. Instead, the assistant reached in and closed the door behind her. She looked up into the face of Valerie Fierro, her original smile frozen in place. However, Miss Fierro's eyes betrayed a look of annoyance as she waited for Verity to shake her hand.

Dozens of scenarios began to swirl in her mind as to why she was now facing this strange woman instead of being reunited with her beloved. Had something happened to Chesney? Had he met with an accident? Had he not realized the meeting was with Verity? Had he realized it was with Verity, and that was his reason for staying away? Verity felt faint.

"Miss Fierro, it is a pleasure to meet you," said Li Gao.

Valerie shook his hand and returned his greeting. He asked her to sit down and then gave a slight nudge to Verity as an encouragement to do the same.

"You will have to excuse our Miss Goodhue," said Gao. "Despite being a top executive, she tends to be a bit awed by celebrity."

Valerie Fierro smiled. Verity felt another subtle nudge at her side.

"Oh, yes," she said, "I'm sorry, Miss Fierro, I just... well, I never expected to meet someone, well, so... glamourous as you."

Valerie insisted, though not too strongly, that she wasn't all that glamourous.

"You must understand," said Li Gao, "that we were expecting to meet Mrs. Innis. Your arrival comes as a rather pleasant surprise. We have read so much about you."

"Really, you flatter me, Mr…"

"Li. I am here in a most unofficial capacity, as a friend of Miss Goodhue. Miss Goodhue is the daughter of Lord Bagnall, the founder and chairman of the company."

Verity wanted to blurt out Chesney's name but didn't know the relationship of Valerie Fierro to it all. "Forgive me, Miss Fierro, and welcome. I'm afraid I wasn't expecting you. We had anticipated meeting Mrs. Innis."

Valerie Fierro rolled her eyes. "Yes, I know, she's so busy. She planned on coming, but she was called away at the last minute and asked me to step in for her. I was on the Foundation's business in Gibraltar. It was just a quick flight here to pinch-hit."

"Pinch-hit?" asked Verity.

"It's a baseball term," said Valerie. "It means to step in for someone else."

"Oh, yes, I see," said Verity.

"I hope it's okay," she said. "I mean, I am Lorraine's, that is, Mrs. Innis' best friend and her cousin."

Verity nodded. Chesney never mentioned any relations other than his mother, brother, and Aunt Elinor. Valerie Fierro boasted about endorsements she had negotiated with other companies. This Valerie seemed very keen on profits and percentages. Verity began to wonder if it was all just some money-making scheme. Chesney had never been motivated by money. Maybe that's why they sent Miss Fierro. Perhaps she was the business side of the Cross of Lorraine Foundation. Maybe Lorraine Innis was as sweet and kind as her true identity. Verity found momentary comfort in that thought until another darker one intruded upon her. Maybe Lorraine Innis was as altruistic as Chesney. But, perhaps she was at the mercy of greedy persons such as this woman in the blood red ensemble. Verity couldn't hurl accusations without endangering her beloved. She would have to proceed with extreme caution.

"I'm sorry," said Verity, as Valerie Fierro paused in her sale pitch. "I'm afraid I'm not very experienced at these sorts of negotiations. In fact, to be perfectly candid, this is my first time trying to craft a sponsorship agreement."

Valerie's faced dropped. "Oh? Then perhaps I should be speaking to…" She turned towards Li Gao.

"No, he's just a friend of ours, that is, of the family."

Valerie Fierro smirked as if to say: then what am I doing here?

"It's my fault, really," said Verity. "And forgive me if I've brought you here on false pretenses. I can assure you that my father does want an endorsement arrangement with Mrs. Innis. I suppose I stepped in because I, well, because I did so want to meet Mrs. Innis."

Valerie leaned back in her chair and snorted. "You and everybody else, sister."

"Pardon?"

"Don't worry about it. You're in good company. Everybody wants to meet Lorraine. It's almost enough to give someone an inferiority complex. If I didn't love Lorraine..."

"Love her?" said Verity.

"Yeah, she is my cousin. Of course, I love her, well, like a cousin," said Valerie. "It's not like, well, like my boyfriend."

"Oh," Verity smiled, "then you have a boyfriend?"

"Yes."

"And what's his name?" asked Verity, hoping it wasn't Chesney.

Valerie gave her an odd look. "His name is Michael."

"Michael," Verity laughed, "that's a lovely name for a boyfriend."

Valerie shrugged. "I guess so." She nodded at Verity's right hand. "And I see you're engaged."

"Oh, yes, yes, I am," said Verity. "To a wonderful... person. A person who is a boy, that is, he's a man. But his name isn't important. You wouldn't know him, I'm sure. He's not from around, well, from anywhere you'd know. Forgive me. You came here to discuss business, and here I am asking a lot of questions that are none of my business."

"No harm done," said Valerie. "It's just surprising. I always heard that you Brits were so reserved," said Valerie. "Go figure."

Verity took a deep breath. At least this Valerie Fierro person wasn't after Chesney romantically.

"Yes, well, I apologize if you came here on a wild goose chase," said Verity. "But you really should speak to His Lordship, that is my father. He's very keen to have Mrs. Innis come and endorse our product line."

Valerie Fierro rolled her eyes. "She'll have to try them first. Lorraine won't endorse anything that she doesn't use. So, she'll need to try out all the products. Sorry, I know it's a pain in the ass, sorry, the rear, but that's the way she is."

"Oh, no, that's quite all right. In fact, it's admirable, just what I've come to expect from Mrs. Innis' reputation. It's good to know she's as principled as she appears."

"Yeah, she is," said Valerie. "Glad you approve."

"Oh, I do, very much so," said Verity.

"That's good," said Valerie, "because that's the only way she works. The companies she turns down aren't all that happy about it."

"When do you think Mrs. Innis be coming over to sample the products?"

Valerie grimaced. "Can't you just ship them to her in America?"

Verity struggled to hide her disappointment. "Yes, of course, how silly of me. I wouldn't want to inconvenience anyone. But, if she, Mrs. Innis, likes the products, she will be coming here to sign the contracts, and meet father, and take the photos for the ads. Won't she?"

"Yeah, I suppose," said Valerie. "Can I give you a little advice?"

"Yes."

"Don't be so crazy to meet Lorraine. I mean, I love her like a cousin..."

"But you said she is your cousin."

"What? Oh, right, and that's why I love her like a cousin because she is my cousin. She's okay, nice, and all that, but it's not like it's the experience of a lifetime."

Verity felt her anger rising. "Well, I think that she is, that is, she seems a lovely person, and..."

"...And one that Miss Goodhue very much admires and wants to represent her father's quality paper products." Verity felt Li Gao's hand upon her shoulder. She realized that no matter what Valerie Fierro was up to or her relationship to Chesney, this was not the time or place to find out.

"Yes, precisely," said Verity with a soft exhale. "Again, I'm sorry if we've wasted your time, taking you so far from your work."

Valerie Fierro waved her hand dismissively. "Not a problem. I mean, I like sun and warm weather, but face it, after a few days Gibraltar is just a big rock covered with a lot of monkeys. I was glad to get away for a little shopping."

"That is a relief," said Verity dryly. "As I said, the person you really should negotiate with is my father, Lord Bagnall. If you'll be in London a few more days, perhaps..."

Before Verity could complete the offer for Valerie to meet Lord Bagnall, his Lordship barged into the room.

"There wasn't never nothing like it, no, no, not no 'ow," bellowed his Lordship. "There you are, my dear, there you are. I wouldn't not believed it if I 'adn't 'eard it. No, not at all!"

He stopped in mid-bluster and stared at Li Gao and Valerie Fierro.

"Oo are these two?" He asked, waving his index finger back and forth between them.

"Father, this is my friend, Mr. Li," said Verity. "And this is Valerie Fierro, from the Cross of Lorraine Foundation."

His Lordship sneered at Li Gao before bestowing a beatific smile on Valerie.

"Cross of Lorraine," he beamed and took her hand. "Miss Farrow, I am charmed."

"Fierro," said Li Gao.

"Not nobody asked you, clever dick," muttered Bagnall. He turned back to Valerie. "I am so glad you've come here like this. We do so admire Lorraine In... uh... Lorraine."

"Thank you," said Valerie. "She's my cousin."

His lordly eyebrows rose. "Is she then? Well, well, then I'm all the pinker tickled. Tell me, 'ave you gotten everything you wanted? That is, 'ave we, uh, negotiated everything to your liking?"

Valerie smiled. "Actually, I just got here. We haven't negotiated anything yet."

Lord Bagnall seemed upset at this news, though he did his best to hide it. "Oh, well, I'm sure we can work something out that's very h'advantageous to you. You are fully h'authorized to make a deal for your cousin, are you?"

"Yes, for the most part."

"Most part, eh?" said Bagnall. His stiff smile was growing creakier by the second. He turned to his daughter. "Verity, dear, may I see you for a moment, in private?" He gestured towards a side room, lifted Verity by the elbow, and began escorting her from the room.

"Uh, you there, Oriental chap," said Bagnall as he hurried from the room, "get Miss Fellow some tea or something, and whatever you wants for yourself. Just press one of those buttons, over there…"

"Father, what…" asked Verity, but before she could complete her question, she was in the next room behind a closed door.

"What did you do?" asked Lord Bagnall.

"What? Nothing," said Verity. "We hardly began to speak. Mrs. Innis was supposed to come, but instead, we got…"

"Yes, yes, I know ooh you got," said Bagnall. "Does she know anything?"

"Aside from the fact I've got a barmy father?"

"This h'aint no time for levitation," he said. "Is she ready to deal right now?"

"I suppose. That's why she's here…"

"Good, good, then she don't not know," he said, rubbing his hands together. "Then, we can make a good deal before she's any the wiser."

"Father, please stop acting like a villain in a Victorian melodrama, and tell me what you're talking about. Too late for what?"

"Too late to sign up Lorraine Innis before…"

A wave of panic swept over Verity, and she clutched her father's arm. "Too late before what? Has anything happened to Lorraine Innis?"

"'Appened? I'll say so!" He laughed. "Lorraine Innis has just been nobbinated Vice President of the whole blasted United States!"

– 18 –
The Lure of a
Quart of Saliva

It's so good to see you again, Mrs. Innis."

"It's good to see you, Mr. President," said Lorraine as she entered the Oval Office. "How are your grandchildren?"

"They're great," said President Ottinger, shaking her hand. "You know my grandson cherishes that baseball glove you gave him at the World Series. He sleeps with it under his pillow."

Ottinger introduced Lorraine to his Chief of Staff, Frank Wesson, and invited her to sit on the sofa. Wesson sat on another sofa facing Lorraine while the President took a wing chair between them.

"So is this your first visit to the White House?" asked the President.

"Yes," said Lorraine. "I was supposed to come here in April, but, oh, I'm sorry, how stupid of me."

Lorraine was to have received the Presidential Medal of Freedom from Quinton Merton. Instead, she was in a car accident, and Merton was blown to bits by a crazed old lady.

"Yes," said Ottinger, "that was a terrible day. Between you and I, Lorraine, I never wanted to be president. And more than anything, I didn't want to become it that way."

Lorraine lowered her eyes and nodded.

"I… I was rather surprised to get the call the other day," said Lorraine.

"I hope it wasn't an inconvenience," said the President. "I wanted to meet with you in private. That was the reason for all the secrecy."

"I didn't tell anyone," said Lorraine.

Ottinger laughed. "Of course, you didn't. I wasn't worried about that. Still, this was best kept private."

Lorraine nodded. "I didn't have to come at all. You could have just sent me the award. For that matter, it's not that important. I mean, it's a great honor, but you must have more important people to meet."

Ottinger turned to Wesson. "You see, Frank," he said, "that's why everyone loves her. She's so genuine."

"Yes, sir," agreed Wesson with a smile, "an excellent choice."

"Thank you," said Lorraine before doing a double-take. "Choice? "

President Ottinger leaned forward. "Mrs. Innis, I'd like you to be the vice-president for this administration."

Lorraine stared at him for what felt like two or three minutes. She kept waiting for him to laugh or give some indication that it was a joke. Instead, he just kept looking at her. Finally, she looked over at Frank Wesson. He, too, had a serious expression.

"I'm sorry," said Lorraine shaking her head, "it's just that it sounded like you wanted me to..." She tailed off, daring not to repeat what she thought she had heard.

"Be my vice-president," said Ottinger.

"Are you kidding?" said Lorraine, and then she clapped her fingers over her mouth. "Sorry, sorry, I just didn't expect... it's just that... I'm only a girl from New Jersey... That is... may I have a drink of water?"

Frank Wesson got Lorraine a glass of water. She sipped it carefully, lest she spill anything on the presidential sofa in the middle of the Oval Office. After several sips, she took a deep breath.

"Better?" asked the President.

"Yes, thank you," said Lorraine.

"So, what do you think?"

Lorraine almost asked "about what," but knew she couldn't avoid the question. She just shook her head. "Why me?"

"Can you think of anyone better suited for the task?"

Lorraine grimaced. "Have you got a phone book?"

"That's why," he said. "Because you're not wrapped up in yourself. Mrs. Innis, Lorraine, I was a Marine. Colonel Wesson was, too. Do you know what the Marine motto is?"

"*Semper Fidelis,*" she said, "always faithful."

"I know you weren't in the service," he continued, "but I sense that motto applies to you, too."

"But, I'm sure that you could find any number of people in Washington that would fit that description."

"Perhaps," said the President, "most politicians are faithful, but they're faithful first and foremost to themselves."

"But I'm not a politician."

"That's precisely why you'd be perfect for the job," said Ottinger. "I've seen what Washington can do to a person. This town tends to seep into a person, changing them, I dare say, even poisoning them to a degree..."

"A large degree," muttered Frank Wesson, "sorry, sir."

Ottinger nodded towards his chief of staff. "Frank has a low threshold for political bullshine. That's why he's been invaluable to me throughout my career: in the Corps, in the Congress, and especially now."

"Then, couldn't you nominate Mr. Wesson to be vice president?"

"Not a bad suggestion," said the President, "and one I'd gladly act upon if I could. But, Lorraine, any nominee that I put forward not only has to be suited for the job, but they have to be able to pass the confirmation process. As a lifelong aide to me, he'd never pass muster. You, on the other hand, my dear, would sail through."

"I would?"

"You're the most popular person in the world, Mrs. Innis," said Wesson.

"And you've got integrity." The President's expression grew solemn. "Lorraine, I'm not a young man and don't mean to frighten you. My doctors assure me that I'm in good health. But if history tells us anything, it's that presidents can die at any time from natural or unnatural causes. I've approached every job that I've had seriously. This latest job is the most serious of them all. And this decision might be the most crucial one I'm called upon to make. I'm very comfortable you're that choice."

Lorraine sat there, unable to speak. A dozen scenarios ran through her mind, each more frightening than the one before, and all unthinkable just a few minutes ago. Finally, she shook her head.

"I'm sorry," she said, "but I don't think I could do it."

"Mrs. Innis," said Wesson, "the vice presidency is mainly a ceremonial position, much like what you do now with your charity. You make appearances and speeches."

"And preside over the Senate," added Lorraine.

"Yes," conceded Frank, "but that certainly isn't a full-time job. I believe one of our vice presidents said the job wasn't worth a bucket of spit."

"Actually it was John Nance Garner, Franklin Roosevelt's first vice president, and he said the office wasn't worth a quart of warm spit. He said it in 1932 when the second spot was offered to him. Forgive me. You didn't ask me here to receive a pedantic lesson in historical anecdotes."

"Even so, Mrs. Innis," continued Frank Wesson, "less than two years remain on President Ottinger's term."

"I would ask if the President is going to run for another term," said Lorraine, "but that's none of my business. But if he is, then I'd assume that I would be called upon to continue as his vice president, which would mean another four years. And it's not the time; it's the knowledge the longer I serve, the greater the odds that I might be expected to assume his position, isn't that so?"

President Ottinger nodded. "You can't out-think her, Frank. After all, I was brought on as the old head to balance Quinton Merton's youth. No one ever expected that I'd outlive a younger man. Anyone who doesn't approach the vice presidency as soberly as Mrs. Innis doesn't deserve the job. It is the most unimportant job in the country until something happens to the top dog, and then it's the most important."

"And if the President doesn't run again," said Lorraine, "There would be pressure on me to run for president, wouldn't there?"

Both Ottinger and Wesson conceded as much.

"And I'm not even a member of any party," said Lorraine.

"Which is why no one will oppose you," said Wesson.

"And why they shouldn't support me, either," said Lorraine.

"Are you afraid of losing half your popularity," said Wesson.

Lorraine looked at him a moment. "I would be lying, Mr. Wesson, if I said that part of me didn't enjoy that public esteem. But such adulation is a drug if I allow it to motivate my actions rather than doing what is right. I don't want to become an addict."

"Yes, but..." began Wesson.

"Frank," said the President, raising his hand, "you won't be able to argue your way past Mrs. Innis. Mrs. Innis, I respect and admire you even more after chatting with you these few minutes. I appreciate your concerns. Still, I want you to seriously consider my proposal. I agree that by accepting this chore, you'd be opening yourself up for more trouble than you've ever imagined. But at the same time, I believe it would be for the good of the country. Will you consider it?"

Lorraine swallowed hard. "Yes, sir, I will."

The President thanked her. Frank Wesson escorted Lorraine out the side door. As they left, Lorraine looked back at the Oval Office. For a moment, she felt the lure of a drug far more seductive than public adulation. She turned away and exhaled a sigh of relief when the door shut, and she was outside those walls of power.

"Well, thank you, Mr. Wesson," said Lorraine. "This is all so very unexpected. I have a lot to think about, but I'll try and have an answer for the President as soon as possible."

"Thank you, Mrs. Innis, and it was a pleasure meeting you."

Lorraine turned and then stopped. "The President's nomination hasn't been made public, has it? Mr. Ottinger has been so nice, I wouldn't want to embarrass him by turning down his nomination."

"No, ma'am," said Wesson. "It won't be announced until you accept it."

Lorraine thought as much. She had been brought in discreetly, in a limo with tinted windows. She started back towards the entrance, believing she would leave the same way, when Frank Wesson stopped her.

"Pardon me, Mrs. Innis," he said, "but before you go, there is someone who wants to meet you."

"Of course," said Lorraine. There was always someone who wanted to meet her. She didn't fully understand why.

Frank Wesson led her down a hallway and stopped in front of one door.

"In here, Mrs. Innis."

Lorraine smiled. "I'm always happy to meet new people."

"Oh, I believe you've met this person before," he said as he turned the knob.

– 19 –
Today's Top Stories:
Anxiety, Relief, and Consternation

Lorruska!" boomed the familiar voice.

There in the corner of the small lounge, was Nikolai Kropotkin.

"President Kropotkin, what are…" began Lorraine before being engulfed in his embrace.

Frank Wesson coughed. "If you're okay, Mrs. Innis, I'll leave you here… for now," he said.

"She is fine, she is fine, go, go, go," said Kropotkin.

Only after the door closed was Lorraine let up for air. Even then, she was held tightly by her shoulders.

"Let me look at you, Lorruska!" Kropotkin's face beamed, then dropped into a scowl. "What do you mean, President Kropotkin? Am I no longer your Nikki, Lorruska?"

Lorraine smiled nervously. "You'll always be my Uncle Nikki."

Kropotkin looked hurt. "Just 'Uncle' Nikki?"

It was what he had first told her to call him, but apparently, that was no longer enough. "It's marvelous to see you, Nikki," she said, trying to sound warmer. "It's really good to see you, Nikki," she repeated as she sat on the settee. "I'm sorry if I seem a bit out of sorts, but you were the last person I expected to see here."

"I couldn't tell you I was coming," said Kropotkin sitting beside her. I'm having secret consultations with President Ottinger. It is thanks to you and the Lorraine Accord. I was finally getting through to that Merton, and then he was killed. Such a pity. Now I am here to talk to his successor."

"Successor," murmured Lorraine. The word reminded her of the president's offer.

"I had hoped to see you, Lorruska," he said, "but I didn't know you'd be here, too."

"Yes, well, that's something of a secret, too," she said. "How is your daughter?"

"Oh, yes, she is fine. She is at home. As I was saying when I arranged for this trip, I had hoped..."

"And Yuri?"

"Yuri? Yuri is Yuri," he said impatiently.

"That's good," said Lorraine.

Kropotkin looked into her eyes and took her hands in his.

"Lorruska," he said softly, "I have missed you so..."

"Oh?" Lorraine shifted uncomfortably in her seat. Someone's palms were beginning to sweat, but she couldn't tell whose.

"You do not know how much, my Lorruska," he continued.

"It's good to see you, too, Nikki." Lorraine looked away from his gaze. She wracked her brain for a less personal topic. "Oh, look," she said, pointing at a painting on the wall. Kropotkin relaxed his grip, and Lorraine retrieved her hand. She stood and crossed to the picture. "This is from the War of 1812. See, that's the British burning Washington, the city, not the president. He was already dead by then."

Lorraine felt Kropotkin standing behind her. She tensed slightly as he cradled her elbow in his hand.

"You know," she croaked as her throat became dry, "uh, many people in the United States think *The 1812 Overture* has something to do with the War of 1812. That is our War of 1812. But of course, it was written many years later, uh, in 1880, by Tchaikovsky, to, uh, commemorate Russia's victory over Napoleon." Lorraine laughed nervously. "That's what a lot of people think."

"I cannot stop thinking about you," he whispered in her ear.

Lorraine took a step away.

"You are nervous," he said.

Lorraine smiled and exhaled. "Yes, yes, I am. I don't know why." She had the strangest feelings. Part of her was attracted to him, while another part of her repelled with an equal force. It was as if she were two people struggling over an urge that only one would enjoy.

"I know why," said Kropotkin. He took a step away, returned his voice to a less sensuous tone, and sat down.

"You do?"

"Of course, it is only natural. I have faced the same feelings myself."

"Really?" How could he know what she was feeling? She sat down opposite the Russian.

"What a mess," sighed Kropotkin. "It complicates life so."

Lorraine knew her life's complications but didn't think Nikki had any knowledge of them. She certainly hoped he didn't.

He looked at her and smiled. "But, it is good to see you again... as you."

Lorraine looked over her shoulder and then back at Kropotkin. "Who else would I be?"

Nikki laughed and wagged his index finger at her. "That is just what I mean. You are Lorruska again. You are the Lorruska who saved my life. You are the charming, wise, open, warm Lorruska of last October. You are the Lorruska who captured my heart."

Lorraine shrugged. "Haven't I always been me?"

"No," he said, "you came to visit me in Moscow, and you were different. Not bad, but not Lorruska."

Lorraine thought about her visit to Moscow. For some reason, it was cloudy in her memory. She recalled the events, but her feelings seemed blocked. "You fell off the parapet into the snow," she said. "Actually, I suppose that I pushed you..."

"I did not blame you," he said. "It was an accident. But that wasn't it."

"Maybe it was being in a foreign country, or maybe it was because my cousin was there."

Kropotkin shook his head. "No, I do not understand, but it doesn't matter because once again, you are the real you."

"Thank you, I guess..."

He smiled, took her hand, and then let go of it again and sadly sighed. "You are the woman once more who I love..."

"Whom you... "

"The woman whom I would marry."

"Marry?"

"Da," he sighed, "but now that has all changed, hasn't it? Marriage is impossible, if not difficult."

"Is it?" This is the first time Nikolai Kropotkin formally mentioned marriage. And even now, it was less of a proposal than a retraction of one. Did he know about Lorraine's physical difficulties? Did it show? She glanced down at her lap.

"I would have been the happiest man in the world if you, my dear Lorruska, consented to become my bride and become the first lady of Russia. But... phht!"

"But why," said Lorraine, "I mean, why not? That is how do you know?"

"How do I know? It is on the news."

"The news?" Lorraine gasped. "How did they find out? They had no business. What about doctor-patient confidentiality? What about medical ethics?" She wasn't ashamed of her body, peculiarities notwithstanding. It was her body. She was neither embarrassed nor proud. It just was what it was. Still, it wasn't anyone else's business.

"What do you mean how did they find out?" he said. "That sort of thing is impossible to keep secret."

"Is it?"

"Of course."

Lorraine shook her head. "I had no idea. This is rather upsetting."

Kropotkin shrugged and smiled. "Do not be too upset, Lorruska. I love you."

"Still?" said Lorraine, "even knowing about that?"

"Why should that make any difference?"

Lorraine just stared at him. She knew why her physical condition would make a difference but couldn't answer for anyone else on the subject.

"Still, Lorruska," said Kropotkin taking her hand, "we do not know what the future holds. Things may change."

"I suppose," she said skeptically.

"Do you not think so?"

"I don't want to dash your hopes, Nikki," said Lorraine, "but I just have to assume I'll stay this way the rest of my life."

"The rest of your life? You do not understand your own Constitution."

"I think it goes a little deeper than my constitution," said Lorraine, retrieving her hand.

"But surely," he said, "it won't last longer than eight years, at the most."

"Eight years?"

"At the most."

"But I've been this way as long as I can remember," said Lorraine.

"You've not even been formally sworn in."

"What are you talking about?"

"You becoming Vice President."

"What? How did you know?"

"I told you," he said, "I saw it on the news."

Lorraine leaped to her feet. "It's on the news?"

"That's what I've said, twice."

"Oh, yes..." She didn't know whether to laugh or cry. It was a great relief that her physical condition was not broadcast to the world. She had no choice about her bodily anomalies. But she had had a choice about becoming vice president.

"But," she muttered, "how could he tell them?"

"You seem confused, Lorruska. What is wrong?"

"I just left the president. He seemed like such an honorable man. But he must have told the media before he even asked me. Was I the last to know? How could he have?"

"He didn't tell them," proclaimed a voice from the doorway, "I did!"

Lorraine looked up. Standing there was a short, trim figure. It took a moment, but she recognized the face. She had only seen it on a television monitor the previous year: Davis Flemming.

"You?" said Lorraine.

"Don't thank me," said Flemming with the breezy confidence of a used car salesman. "Not yet, at least. And don't worry, I've got it all arranged. Your political rocket awaits! You just have to step in and take off!"

– 20 –
The Other Daughter He Never Had

"It's good tea," said Valerie Fierro. "I mean it, really good."

The Asian man nodded. She already commented on the stupid tea two times, trying to pull some conversation out of the guy. But he just sat there, sipping tea, usually in response to Valerie taking a sip.

Where had that girl gone? First, that Verity chick acts all weird because she didn't get to meet Lorraine. Then, she tells Valerie that she can't really negotiate the endorsement deal; that it's up to her father, Lord Windbag. Then Windbag barges in, grabs his daughter, and off they go leaving Valerie with this tea-drinking statue.

She took another sip of tea and forced a smile. "This is really good. You Brits sure know your tea... oh, sorry."

Mr. Lee smiled. "No apology is necessary, Miss Fierro. Though I do not look so by your standards, I am a subject of Her Majesty."

"Really," said Valerie, "have you met the Queen?"

"I have not had that pleasure."

"Oh. I guess that was kind of silly of me," she said. "I mean, I would say, on average, practically no one gets to meet the Queen."

"Quite so, of course, Lord Bagnall has met Her Majesty."

"And his daughter, too, I suppose."

"That I could neither confirm nor deny."

"Oh," said Valerie as Mr. Lee sat back in his chair and took another sip of tea. She couldn't picture Bagnall's daughter at the palace. Verity Goodhue struck her as plain, not ugly plain, just plain plain. She had nice features, but she didn't do anything with them. She wore light make-up. Her hair just sort of was, nice hair, well-kept, but just there, like the rest of her. And she certainly didn't squander the family fortune on clothes. They were plain, too: A white blouse, a black skirt. Plain, plain, plain. No wonder she wanted to meet Lorraine. She probably saw Lorraine as a role model.

Valerie finished her tea and sat in silence for another two minutes. She was just about to leave when the door opened, and His Lordship returned.

"Miss Fierro," he said with a smile up to and including his molars. At least, he finally got her name right. "Sorry to 'ave kept you waiting. Oh, good, I sees that you 'ave 'ad some tea. I just 'ad to have a little conflagration with my daughter. Uh, personal matters, you know. I 'ope I h'ain't not inconvenienced you none."

"Well..."

"Good, good," he said, rubbing his hands as if he were rolling a snake out of Playdoh. He looked around at the boardroom and then made a sour expression. "No, no, this won't not do, no, no, no. Why don't you comes into my private office? It's more, uh, private. Come this way."

For the first time since Bagnall returned, Mr. Lee caught his attention.

"Thank you," said Bagnall dismissively, as if he were speaking to a peddler. "That will be all."

The gentleman tilted his head to one side.

"I said, that's it," snapped Bagnall. He jerked his thumb towards the other door. "C'mon Mr. Wu, sling yer hook, on yer bike!"

Lee bowed and then turned to Valerie. "It was a pleasure meeting you, Miss Fierro." When he reached the doorway, he turned. "Not having brought my bicycle, I shall depart via the bus. As for hooks, unfortunately, I do not possess any for the purposes of slinging." He bowed again and exited.

"Funny birds, them chinks," muttered Bagnall staring at the door. Then he looked at Valerie. "Oh, pardon me, that's just a little crudité from my days in Her Majesty's service. I didn't not mean nothing by it. Some of my best customers is h'oriental."

"Then he doesn't work for you?" asked Valerie, following Lord Bagnall.

"Oo knows," said Bagnall, "'E might. I employs thousands of people. Though I don't recall none looking like 'im, least not in a three-piece suite."

"I was under the impression he was a friend of the family," said Valerie. "At least, that's what he said."

"Little yellow devils," growled Bagnall before catching himself and smiling. "That is to say, perhaps 'e knows my daughter. But sayin' 'e's a friend of us all, well, that's takin' liberties where none are there for the takin'. Still, my daughter's a kind girl. She's picked up all sorts of strays and misfits over the years; a lot of old baggage. Betweens you and me, some of it 'as been a damned nuisance to get shot of. Worse than drownin' cats, but still, like I says, she's got a 'eart that's too big for anyone's good."

Valerie nodded. No wonder his daughter wanted to meet Lorraine. She was probably another starry-eyed optimist.

Lord Bagnall led her into a large office that, like its owner, was rich but not necessarily tasteful. Verity Goodhue sat in one of the chairs in front of the oversized, ornate desk, looking as if the room had swallowed her whole. A look of disappointment marred her face.

"Where is..." she began.

Her father cut her short with a jerk of his thumb. "I sent that one packing..."

"But he was..."

"...Completely unnecessary," said Bagnold taking his place behind the desk. "We've got business to discuss, and it best be done quickly."

"Yes, Father," said Verity, "especially since..."

"...yes, especially since we've wasted enough of Miss Fierro's time. She's swilled enough tea with Chinamen for, well, all the tea in China. So, we'd better get down to brass monkeys." He gestured for Valerie to take a seat. Then, His Lordship pulled out a sheath of papers.

"Miss Fierro," said Bagnall as he sorted through the papers, "to cut to the point, I wants your cousin, Mrs. Innis, to be the face of my full range of products..."

"But Father," interrupted Verity, "what about the vice..."

Lord Bagnall cleared his throat loud enough to drown out the flights taking off at Heathrow. As he coughed, he shot a sharp look at this daughter.

"Vice?" asked Valerie.

Bagnall smiled. "My daughter, she's always lookin' out for my repudiation. Verity, my dear, I don't not think we needs to worry about vice, not with Mrs. Innis. H'ain't that so, Miss Fierro?"

"Vice? With Lorraine?" she laughed. "Not hardly."

"See there," said Bagnall. Verity started to speak again, and he cut her off. "No, no, I don't not want to 'ear not another word about, uh... vice... leave that to me."

Verity twisted her mouth closed and glowered at him.

"As I was saying," continued Bagnall, "about your cousin. She is a dignified, respected personage, and my complete product line is respected and top-hole all the way." He walked to a side table that held a display of paper products. "This is my family," he said proudly, and then glancing at his daughter, he coughed. "Uh, that is to say, my family of paper goods, that is, my products for the family."

He stood beside the array of paper goods with his arm outstretched like some model on a TV game show.

"Yes, I'm sure they're all excellent quality," agreed Valerie.

"Splendid, fantastic," said Bagnall scurrying back to his desk and snatching a document from the top of a pile. "I've got then this 'ere contract, an agreement to make Lorraine Innis the official, exclusive spokeswoman for all my goods. You are h'authorized to sign for the business, h'ain't you?"

Valerie threw back her shoulders. "Of course, I'm authorized." At least she was pretty sure she was authorized. Even if she wasn't completely authorized, Valerie was reasonably sure she could convince Lorraine, after the fact.

"What about the testing," interjected Verity Goodhue. "Father, Miss Fierro said that Lorraine Innis will not endorse any product without personally verifying the quality. Isn't that correct, Miss Fierro."

"Um, right," said Valerie, sorry she had mentioned it.

"Ha, ha, ha." Lord Bagnall laughed nervously. "I'm sure Mrs. Innis will appreciate the quality of our products."

"Will she come here to do it?" asked Verity. Her father shot her another censorious glance.

"That's not necessary," said Valerie.

Bagnall's face lit up. "There! You see, that h'ain't not necessary, not no 'ow."

"You can ship a bundle of the stuff to Delaware, and Lorraine will test it out. I'm sure she will like it all as much as I do."

"So you've used my father's products?" asked Verity.

"No," said Valerie. "I mean, I probably will later." She was starting to develop a dislike of this chick. Imagine asking someone you just met what they used in the toilet and if they liked it. Ewww!

"But," said Lord Bagnall, "you is h'authorized to sign, that is, we can work out the basic endorsement h'agreement only contingent on your cousin approving of the products."

Valerie looked at Verity, smiled smugly, and then turned to Bagnall. "I would say most definitely, your Lordship."

"Well, then," said Bagnall pulling a pen from his breast pocket, "we can close this all up now."

"We haven't negotiated yet," said Valerie. "In fact, you haven't even given me an offer."

Bagnall looked at his watch and then smiled. "Oh, absolutely, but that h'ain't not more than a formality. I mean, you're in the business of endorsing, and I've got something 'ere what needs endorsement." He looked down at the contract in his hand. "This h'agreement would give you, that is, your organization ten-percent of all net proceeds of any products what Lorraine Innis endorses for me."

"Lorraine routinely gets fifteen percent," said Valerie.

"Fifteen percent?" said Verity.

"Sometimes twenty," said Valerie, "and we've had some companies who have gone as high as thirty percent. Oh, and we usually negotiate on gross, not net."

Lord Bagnall's face reddened. "Thirty gross? I'll say it's gross! It's robbery!"

"Hold on a minute, Your Lordship," said Valerie sweetly. "Those aren't demands. My cousin, Lorraine, has never held up anyone. She's never asked for more than fifteen percent on any endorsement. Anything above that has been voluntary." She shrugged. "I frankly don't understand it, either."

Lord Bagnall's daughter looked skeptical.

"Uh, yes," continued Valerie. "But when people meet Lorraine and see what she's all about, they wind up giving her an even greater percentage and sweeter deals."

Bagnall tugged at the end of his thin mustache. "Good thing they sent you instead of your cousin, elseways I would 'ave given up the 'ole business to 'er. So, then," said Bagnall slapping his hands together, "we're talking fifteen percent then?"

"Excuse me," said Verity Goodhue. "I'm just a little confused. You mean people meet with Mrs. Innis and just volunteer to give her more money?"

Valerie shrugged. "Yeah, that's basically what happens."

"Ooh, I wouldn't not 'alf like to meet this Mrs. Innis," said Lord Bagnall, "after we sign up, that is. It sounds like she's a shrewd one, a real business brain after me own wallet!"

Valerie snorted. "Lorraine a shrewd business brain? Pull-eze! Your Lordship, I mean, she's my cousin, but Lorraine doesn't have a business brain. Not even one cell of it," said Valerie raising her thumb and forefinger. "Not even that much. I don't like to brag. I like to think I'm beyond pride…"

"It h'aint proud or boastin' if it's the truth, my dear," he said.

"But family ties aside, the main reason Lorraine keeps me around is for my business sense. If it had been up to her, she'd have given the business away."

"Big 'earted, eh?" said Bagnall.

"Exactly. I take care of the money."

"But," interrupted Verity, "you apparently are doing very well for Mrs. Innis. Thanks to you, she must be a very wealthy, uh, woman."

"She would be," said Valerie, "thanks to me. But she treats her organization like a charity…"

"But it is a charity," said Verity.

"Daughter," said Lord Bagnall condescendingly, "all charity is a business." He looked at Valerie and nodded. Then he glanced back at his daughter and then at Valerie as much as to say: I told you so, about her.

"That's rather cynical, Father, even for you."

"Not really," said Bagnall, "what I means is that charity 'as to be run with a 'ead, not just a 'eart. If Mrs. Innis didn't 'ave her charmin' cousin 'ere to keep track of the finances 'er train probably would 'ave gone off the rails."

"He's right," said Valerie, "Lorraine doesn't make a dime off any of it."

"Nothing?"

Valerie blew a puff of air between her lips. "She draws a stipend, and that's hardly enough to keep her in, well, in the necessities of life. I keep telling her she's earned it and that she deserves a decent salary, but she won't hear of it. That's my idealistic cousin."

"Oh," said Verity. She seemed quite pleased with this revelation.

Figures, thought Valerie, another idealistic do-gooder. Where would she be without her father's money? For that matter, reasoned Valerie, where would Lorraine be without Valerie's business sense?

"Well, then," said Lord Bagnall, "now that I understands the lay of the land, I thinks we can get down to serious negotiation." He glanced at his daughter. A slight look of concern crossed his face. "Uh, Verity, my dear, I'm…well, I'm feeling that I treated your little friend…"

"Who?"

"The yellow-scourge, that Chinese, I may 'ave treated 'im less than kindly. Why don't you goes and make sure 'e's all right."

"But Father, he's probably gone by now."

"Still, I don't not know what come over me," he said. "I may have been a tad rude to the poor old chink. Go, and see."

"But," Verity looked at Valerie.

"Don't worry about me," said Valerie. "Your father and I will be fine."

Bagnall nodded. "Right as rain, girl, right as rain. Now it's just a lot of old boring business talk. Nothing not what would interest you, dear."

Verity rose from her chair and started for the door. She stopped halfway and turned back.

"You will be fair, Father, won't you? I really do want to… that is, I really think Lorraine Innis would be a wonderful representative for the company."

Lord Bagnall smiled. "Oh, I think that's a forlorn conclusion. Miss Fierro and I will work it all out."

"And Lorraine Innis will be coming here soon?" said Verity.

Valerie was struck with the anticipation in her voice. It was like a kid waiting to see Santa Claus. She chuckled inwardly. If Verity Goodhue only knew the truth about Lorraine!

"As soon as possible," said Lord Bagnall. "Don't you worry about that. Now, go, make sure your friend is gone, uh, okay."

Verity forced a smile onto her lips and excused herself.

Both Valerie and His Lordship seemed to stare at the door several seconds after Verity left.

"Me daughter," said Bagnall with a jerk of his head towards the door, "I loves 'er, but she h'aint, well, she h'ain't not very… well…"

"Savvy?" offered Valerie.

He snapped his fingers. "Spot on. Oh, I likes you more and more h'every minute, Miss Fierro. If you was an h'orphan, I think I'd adopt you."

They both laughed at the suggestion, though apart from the money, Valerie found the idea revolting.

"So, fifteen percent, eh?" said Bagnall.

Valerie smiled. "I believe I said that was the bottom figure."

"So you did," he said, his eyes narrowing. "I likes you, Miss Fierro, ooh, I do."

Valerie assured him the feeling was mutual, though it wasn't.

"I likes you, and I don't wants you to go back to your dear cousin looking like you made a bad deal." He turned his back on her and gazed out the window. "How about thirty-five percent?"

"Thirty-five," she said, trying to remain calm.

"Not enough," he said, turning around. "Well, then, how about forty?"

"Forty!"

"Good, then we're agreed on that," he said. "Forty percent, net."

"Net?"

"Well, you certainly don't think I could do forty gross," he said.

Valerie nodded. "You don't want my cousin to think I'm some sucker," she said, "but I'd hate if you thought I was some kind of sap, too, Lord Bagnall. You didn't get to be a business tycoon and a Lord by being stupid," she said. "I've been around enough shady accountants to know that a net figure can be whittled down to practically nothing with some clever bookkeeping."

He smiled as if to validate her accusation. "Yes, I likes you even more. If it warn't for the h'American h'accent I'd think you were the fruit of me own sirloins, my dear. Of course, when I said forty percent net, that's for the charity. You said yourself your cousin isn't in it for the money, so it won't not mean nothing to 'er. Forty percent for the charity, net, and five-percent for you as a negotiation bonus... gross."

"Ten-percent," said Valerie.

"Seven an' a 'alf," countered Bagnall.

"Done!" said Valerie.

"Done!" said Bagnall.

Valerie rose to her feet. "Well, it's been a pleasure, Your Lordship. And I have time to get in some shopping. If you have your legal folks draw up the agreement to sign, I'll come back in a day or two before I have to leave London."

Bagnall smiled, raised one hand, and fished through a pile of papers on his desk. He extracted one and held it up.

"See?" He picked up a pen. "We just fill in the percentages... net for the charity. All done, Miss Fierro."

He handed it to her. Valerie looked down at the document in her hands. It did seem simple, straightforward, and correct.

"What about my..." she almost said "cut," but stopped herself.

"That's there, in clause three, listed as 'negotiation fee.'" He held up an ancillary paper that detailed a fee would be given in a separate, confidential account. "We just write in your name 'ere, and Bob's your uncle!"

"You certainly are thorough," she admitted.

"One 'as to be in business," he said, handing her a pen.

As Valerie signed the agreement, she added: "And you won't tell anyone about that other clause?"

"I won'ts if you won'ts," he said. "And I certainly won'ts."

– 21 –
The Set-Up Upset

W hat is this, a sneak inspection?" asked Mike Valvano.

His visitor crossed to an armchair in Mike's office and sat down. The sunlight shimmered off the threads in his silk suit.

"I was in town and thought I'd drop in on my kid brother," said Robert Valvano. "Surprised, huh?"

"I've just never seen you at the bank before," said Michael.

"Well, I do have a small interest in your little bank."

"A very minor one," said Michael, "that is, officially, on paper, legally."

"I always like to keep things legal," said Robert with a humorless smile.

The two brothers stared at each other. Mike wondered how much time they'd spent staring down each other. When they were boys, the contests only lasted until one of them (usually Robert) threw a punch. Their physical combat ceased years ago, but their mental struggle continued. It was one of the things that drove Michael into the priesthood. Now, he was back in the thick of it all for the sake of his girlfriend.

Robert looked around the office and nodded. "Yeah, this is a good set-up you got, Mikey. And we don't want that set-up upset."

"Set-up, upset," repeated Michael.

"What?"

"That's just an interesting juxtaposition: set-up and upset."

"Yeah, whatever," said Robert, "so let's not."

"Let's not what?"

"Upset this set-up," said Robert.

Michael paused. "You mean the bank?" He was deliberately obtuse, knowing it annoyed Robert.

"Don't be cute," snapped Robert. "I mean the bank, the charity, the whole works. This isn't a social call."

"I didn't think so," admitted Mike.

"Someone's nosing around."

"I'm assuming that you're referring to Miss Fierro's trip to Gibraltar."

"Miss Fierro?" Robert laughed. "Is that what you call her in bed?"

Michael leaned forward. "I haven't taken a swing at you since I was nine, but make another remark along those lines, and I'll lay you out right here."

Robert raised his hands. "Okay, okay, I didn't come here to spar with you."

"And I've got legitimate work to do for this bank you've pushed on me. You're concerned that Miss Fierro, in her routine duties for the charity, is going to uncover some less than routine transactions running through the bank's European subsidiary. And I suppose you're coming here to tell me that I'm supposed to catch your shit before it comes in contact with any fans. Right?"

Robert laughed, and not in his usual sardonic manner, but as if he was genuinely amused.

"You know, you're priceless," said Robert, "you really think I'd come to you for something like that. I love you, Bro. You're a clean guy. And I'm not just saying that because of your former profession. You were like that before you took your collar for a spin. Yeah, you're here looking out for the family concerns. Nonnia trusts you. She knows, hell, we all know, you'd look out for everything. But we didn't put you here because we thought you could be crooked. Hell, if that's what we expected of you, we'd all be up shit's creek. You're like a referee, but one with a rooting interest. We don't think you'd rig any calls for us, but at the same time, we know you wouldn't purposely drop us in it, either. So, no, I'm not expecting you to fix any audit."

Michael squinted at his brother. "So, what are you here for?"

"I'm giving you the courtesy of not having to act surprised when your girl, sorry, Miss Fierro gets back from Gibraltar and hands in her report."

"What do you know about it?"

"She's not finding anything crooked," said Robert.

"That would be surprising."

"That's what I'm trying to tell you. I didn't want you to be surprised by what she didn't find."

Mike shook his head. "No, I'm sorry, I don't follow you."

"You're not stupid. You're just too honest. Miss Fierro's coming back with a report that isn't going to be surprising, not to me, not to anyone, not even to you."

"How do you know," asked Mike.

Robert reached into his breast pocket, pulled out a sheath of papers, and tossed to his brother. "Because there it is, or at least the executive summary."

Mike picked up the papers and began to read. After the first few paragraphs, he looked up at his brother.

"Valerie wrote this?"

Robert shrugged. "Maybe she did, maybe she didn't, but that's what she's handing in."

Mike read on. On the second page, he stopped again. "Minor infractions?"

Robert shook his head in mock disappointment. "Sloppy work by the staff in Gibraltar. Good thing we caught it internally. I'm sure you want a good clean bank."

Clean as a laundry, thought Mike.

"And don't worry," said Robert, "I'm keeping her out of it."

"Valerie?"

"Okay, her too," said Robert. "I meant her cousin. Nonnia's a big fan of Lorraine Innis. She's proud that a nice Italian girl made good."

"She only part Italian," said Mike.

"Still, she didn't get that beak from a box of macaroni. Nonnia really likes her."

"I wonder if Nonnia would like it if she knew you were laundering through Lorraine's charity."

"The charity that we bankrolled," said Robert. "And you forget, we're talking about Nonnia. Of course, she knows."

"And she's okay with that?"

"It's business with her. She likes Lorraine, like a granddaughter, but she's not asking her to do anything she wouldn't ask a family member to do. She only said: 'Robbie, don't do nothing to land that nice girl in da *merda*.' So, don't worry about either of them."

"And Valerie went along with this?"

Robert shrugged. "All I know is that little kraut shit in Gibraltar told me the report was 'accepted as written.' Those were his words. I hate that chubby little prick. And he's stealing from us."

"And you let him get away with that?"

"Nickel and dime stuff," dismissed Robert. "Nothing that nobody else wouldn't do. As long as that's all he tries, and I don't have to look at his sorry ass, he's useful enough. So, there's your audit. Don't worry about it, Mikey. I want my bank to have a clean face, but I don't want you to be blindsided."

"Yeah, thanks," muttered Michael. He wondered about the degree of Valerie's complicity, but not enough to ask his brother.

Robert rose and slapped Michael on the shoulder. "Don't worry, Michael."

"I didn't say anything."

"You had a look," said Robert. "Nothing's gonna happen to your girls, your Miss Fierro and her cousin, especially not her cousin. She's too valuable just the way she is."

"Yes, she's quite a lady," said Michael. "I can introduce you sometime."

"Yeah, well, that's not a good idea, is it? No, Mikey, you just keep the ladies happy and look out for them. I like the way things are. Let's keep them like this."

Michael escorted his brother to the door. When he opened it, he saw the staff buzzing around chattering about some news. Mike grabbed one of them by the elbow.

"Patsy, what's going on?" asked Mike.

"Oh, sorry, Mr. Valvano," she panted, "I know I work for the charity now, but I just had to come up and tell the others when I heard the news. But of course, when I got here, they'd already heard the news. It's just so exciting: to think of it. To think we actually know her. I mean, she always was an amazing woman, ever since I met her. Well, maybe she wasn't too amazing, not the first few hours I knew her, of course, but since then she's been very amazing, and now, well, it's even more amazing, especially since we know her. Isn't it exciting?"

"Patsy," he said, taking her by the shoulders, "slow down, okay?"

She nodded and tightly pursed her lips.

"Now, I assume you're talking about Mrs. Innis..."

Patsy nodded excitedly.

"Good, now, I know you're very excited, Patsy," he continued in a calm voice, "but tell me what happened to Mrs. Innis? Go ahead."

Patsy took a deep breath and started slowly but steadily accelerated.

"Lorraine... Mrs. Innis... she had to go to Washington... D.C.... it was all very quiet... that's why she couldn't go to England... but Valerie... Miss Fierro... she took that meeting for her... but we didn't know why Lorraine... Mrs. Innis... had to go to Washington... D.C.... or who she was meeting with... but now we know... because it was just on the news. AndLorrainehasbeennominatedtobethenewVicePresident...of the United States! Isn't that exciting?!"

"Did she say Vice President?" asked Robert Valvano.

"Lorraine?" asked Mike.

"Lorraine Innis, Vice President of the whole country," said Patsy. "And we know her!"

Stunned, Mike Valvano released Patsy before she exploded in his hands. Patsy scurried off. Mike turned to his brother.

"So much," muttered Mike, "for keeping things the way they are."

– 22 –
The Necessity of
Half-a-Dozen Florentine Scarves

I just love your city," Valerie said to the posh sales assistant ringing up her purchase.

"And we love having you, Miss Fierro," said the girl. She was a few years younger than Valerie, and her nose was cute and upturned, and she had that super British accent. But, Valerie thought, as she handed the girl her company credit card, this girl was waiting on her. She would probably ride home on the smelly Tube to a shabby little flat, while Valerie would take one of those big London cabs to her suite at the Dorchester.

"But then just about any city is great," noted Valerie, "when you have the resources to enjoy it with."

"...With which to enjoy it," said the girl unconsciously.

"Shut up, Lorr..." Valerie placed her hand over her mouth. "Oh, I'm terribly sorry. I just, that is, that made me think of someone else. I'm real sorry, that is, really sorry."

The shop assistant smiled and assured Valerie she had not taken offense. But now Valerie could tell the girl thought she was better than her... uh, than she...oh, Lorraine and her damned grammar.

"Oh, I'll take one of those scarves, as well," said Valerie, pointing to a nearby display. She wasn't going to let some snooty sale girl act superior to her. "How much are they?"

"These, ma'am," said the girl sliding the scarf over her fingertips, "are the finest Italian silk, from Florence. They're one-hundred pounds sterling."

Inwardly, Valerie gasped. That was around two-hundred dollars. But she wasn't going to let the girl see her react. Instead, she lifted her head and said: "Is that all? Okay, give me three... no, five more!"

The girl just said: "very good," in that refined tone. Valerie reminded her she wanted them wrapped... individually. The girl also agreed without flinching. Damn, these assistants in these high-class stores were worse than those guards outside Buckingham Palace. At least the guards didn't say anything when you tried to ruffle them. This girl was annoying with her "yes, ma'ams," and "very goods." If Valerie had told her to "go shit in your hat," she'd probably politely agree, without actually doing it.

The girl seemed to take smug satisfaction as she swiped Valerie's credit card again. It occurred to Valerie that the girl probably got a commission. She just couldn't win, Valerie thought, until she consoled herself with the realization that she had just bought over a thousand dollars' worth of scarves. Oh, well, she could always give one to Lorraine. It would make a nice present. Still, with her ordinary tastes, Lorraine might not appreciate such a gift. Maybe she'd just keep them all for herself.

Valerie settled that thought when another followed on its heels: a thousand dollars' worth of scarves! How would she justify that on her company credit card? One expensive scarf, maybe, but a half a dozen? She might have to pay for it herself. She couldn't afford... Wait: she reminded herself of her sweet deal with the Duke of toilet paper, or whatever they called him. With Lorraine pitching the stuff and Bagnall churning it out, Valerie could buy all the silk scarves in London and make a good dent in the cashmere, to boot! Then she thought, but why should she pay? Valerie was on company business. She needed to look her best. She would submit the bills and not give it another thought. Besides, if Michael or Lorraine saw how that girl was acting, all snotty and superior, they would have told Valerie to buy ten scarves. So, actually, she had upheld the company's image while saving them money.

"Thank you, Miss Fierro," said the girl, handing Valerie her card.

"Thank you," said Valerie smiling twice as sweetly before adding, "and have those things sent... to the Dorchester."

And before the girl could register a reaction, Valerie turned on her four-inch stiletto heels and walked away. As she walked, more than one person turned and noticed her. Being an attractive woman earned her the first look. The second look came when they recognized her. She could hear her name being whispered in hushed tones as she passed. It happened everywhere she went. She was quite used to it by now, but it sounded even better with a British accent. Maybe she could get Michael to adopt a British accent. Not all the time, of course, that would be silly, just during sex.

"Miss Fierro," said the doorman. She loved shops that were exclusive enough to have a doorman. He wore white gloves and tipped his hat towards her. "May I call you a cab?"

Valerie nodded. She felt terribly regal.

"I've made it, Daddy," she muttered under her breath, as her heels clicked on the pavement. Holding her head high, she approached the waiting cab. The doorman held the door open for her, just like for a real princess.

"The Dorchester, isn't it, Miss Fierro?" said the doorman.

"How observant of you," she smiled.

The doorman guided her into the back of the cab. He was relaying instructions to the driver when Valerie heard a commotion. She looked to her side, where passersby were snatching up copies of *The Evening Standard*. From the reaction of the crowd, something had happened beyond the ordinary.

"Oh, you, uh, mister," she said to the doorman.

"Yes, Miss Fierro?"

"Could you grab, I mean, could you obtain me a copy of the paper, please?"

The doorman instructed the cabbie to wait and hustled off, returning a moment later with the paper and a final tip of his hat.

Valerie thanked him with the last breath she would enjoy for at least a minute. The headline that filled the front of the tabloid knocked the wind out of her.

LORRAINE: PICKED FOR U.S. VP!

A dozen thoughts raced through her mind, but as she read the story's details, particularly the time of the announcement, one thought came to the forefront.

"Hey, you, driver!"

"Yes, ma'am?"

"Turn around!"

"I got to keep me eyes on the road, ma'am," he said.

"No, I mean, turn the cab around; I've got to go back."

"To the store?"

"No, not to the damned store," she snapped. "Take me back to Lord Bagnall's place!"

"I don't know where he lives, Miss."

"Not his home, to his offices, Cardboard Box, or something."

"Paper 'Ouse?" suggest the cabbie.

"That's it, Paper House, take me there, and step on it! I've just been swindled!"

– 23 –
Blinding Morality
and the Greaseless Machine

orruska, are you alright? Say something, it's Nikki, that is, Nikolai…"
Lorraine Innis sat in stony silence on the setee. She was just too angry
at the moment to speak. Least said, soonest mended, the old saying
went. But the way she felt at this moment, she might never speak again.

"I knew I had a brainstorm with her," beamed Flemming.

"You?" said Kropotkin. "What do you mean, storming brains?"

"She was my idea. Not entirely; I've got to give her parents some credit,"
Flemming chuckled, "But making her Vice President, that was my idea."

Kropotkin glowered at the former presidential aide.

"Ask Ottinger," continued Flemming, "he'd tell you it was my idea.
And what a little gem it was, eh? I mean, look at her, just sitting there,
totally floored. That's a genuine reaction. You take all the senators, all the
representatives, all the cabinet officers, and all the governors, all of them.
Hand any of those motley politicos the vice presidency on a silver platter.
And they'd be doing handsprings, patting themselves on the back, and
wondering how they were going to parlay that number two spot into the
big enchilada."

"Enchilada?" said Kropotkin.

"They're all the same, those politicians; no offense. That's why when I
told the President: 'Mr. President, it's got to be Lorraine,' well, he saw my
advice for what it was: sheer brilliance. Look at her; that's genuine humility.
She's a real person. I should have realized that the first time we went at it."

"Went at it?" Kropotkin towered over the puny Flemming.

"Uh, you know, debated, on TV, last fall," sputtered Flemming.

Kropotkin grunted and turned back to Lorraine.

"Lorruska, please…"

Lorraine blinked and focused on Kropotkin, offering him a weak smile.
Then she looked past him at Davis Flemming.

"Mr. Flemming," she said, trying to restrain herself. "What was it that you said: All I've got to do is sit back and let you do the driving?"

"Yes, that's right," said Flemming, "I'm just here to serve you. That's all I want to be, your humble servant."

Lorraine nodded and rose to her feet. She was surprised at how she towered over the presidential aide. She was wearing heels, but they were only two inches. Still, she could see the top of his trendy, tousled hairstyle.

"My humble servant?" she said.

Flemming executed a mock bow, accompanied by the most genuine fake smile she'd ever seen.

They stood there for a moment, their expressions frozen. Lorraine blinked first. As she did, she noticed a small upturn to the corner of Flemming's lips, as if he had somehow scored a victory over her.

"Oh, what the heck," muttered Lorraine. She pulled back her hand and delivered a sharp slap across Flemming's grinning face. The blow almost knocked him to the floor. Even Kropotkin flinched at the force of the slap.

"I would say I'm sorry, Mr. Flemming," said Lorraine, rubbing her hand, "but I only regret that I had to do that, not that I actually did so."

Flemming pulled back his hand from his cheek and then recoiled. "Blood!" He held up his palm. "Blood!"

"Your fingernails, Lorruska," observed Kropotkin, "they have scratched his cheek."

"You drew blood," said Flemming.

Kropotkin took Flemming's chin in his hand and examined the aide's face. "Pah! Hardly a scratch; be a man! You would get less blood cutting yourself while shaving."

Flemming pushed Kropotkin's hand aside. "That's beside the point, and anyway, I use an electric razor."

Lorraine looked down at her fingers, though they betrayed no sign of the confrontation.

"What did you do that for?" asked Flemming rubbing his face.

Lorraine almost admonished him for ending his sentence with a preposition. She was too angry even to defend English grammar. "I'll tell you why," she said. "It is because you are a presumptuous person who has taken liberties with the prerogatives of others."

"What do you mean?" said Flemming.

"You said that it was your suggestion that President Ottinger nominate me to the vice presidency."

"Yes, I did."

"Did you also leak that information to the media?"

Flemming nodded. "Sure, I did."

"President Kropotkin," she continued, "informed me that he heard about the nomination on the news. Given that I had just emerged from the meeting with President Ottinger, that news must have been made public either before, or at the same time, I was receiving it."

"I would ascribe a certain amount of truthfulness to that statement."

"And you're responsible, Mr. Flemming?"

He paused a minute before puffing out his chest. "Yes, I am!"

Lorraine shifted her weight forward, and Flemming jumped back.

"Ha," laughed Kropotkin, "look at the weasel. Afraid of a lovely little woman!"

"So? So, what?" said Flemming. "Why shouldn't I tell the press about it? They have a right to know."

"Before I was asked?"

Flemming glanced at his watch. "No, probably not. I, uh, I was very careful to wait until I thought you had been offered it. And why shouldn't I tell the media? Why not? It's a big story. It's important news. They knew someone was going to be nominated, so it wasn't a complete surprise."

"It was a complete surprise to me," said Lorraine. "I wasn't told why the President wanted to see me. I was brought into the White House in complete secrecy. Even my cousin didn't know where I was."

"Well, that's not my fault," he said. "What difference does it make if they find out when you're in with the President or right after you come out?"

"The difference, Mr. Flemming," said Lorraine, "is that I have not accepted President Ottinger's nomination."

"You turned him down?"

"I didn't say that, either," said Lorraine. "I told him I was hesitant. I don't want to be vice president. I especially do not want to be the president."

"You wouldn't have to be president," said Flemming, "not necessarily."

Lorraine shook her head. "You, more than anyone, should know that choice isn't always left to the person who should make it. One deranged individual can overrule the most careful of plans."

Davis Flemming shrugged. "So? Don't be president, just be vice president and if something happens to the old man, resign and drop it on the Speaker of the House."

"No, Mr. Flemming, that would be accepting the position under false pretenses. That wouldn't be honest, and it wouldn't be fair."

"But if you took the job, it would be fair to you," said Flemming, "even if you only did it for a little while. It would be more than fair to you."

Lorraine suspected that accepting the nomination would be more than fair to Davis Flemming. Rather than answer him, Lorraine sat down again and turned to Kropotkin.

"Nikki," she began before glancing at Flemming from the corner of her eye, "President Kropotkin. I won't ask your opinion, because, well, I don't think it proper that you should advise an American citizen on an internal affair of the United States. But, as a trusted friend, please listen as I sort through my thoughts. Please, don't respond."

"Of course, Lorruska, I mean, yes, Mrs. Innis."

"As I've said, I don't want to be vice-president. I don't want to be president. I don't want to be a politician. I don't want to move to Washington or deal with Congress. I don't want any of it. I told President Ottinger as much," she continued, "but I also promised him I would think about it. And I meant that. I doubted whether any argument could convince me to accept that nomination, at least, none that I could foresee."

Kropotkin's mouth remained closed, though she could detect the beginnings of a smile around his lips. Out of the corner of her eye, she saw a deflated Davis Flemming. It was a picture Lorraine wished she could preserve: a happy friend and a frustrated adversary. Then, with a heavy sigh, she took Kropotkin's hand.

"My dear friend," she said, "I have no other course than to do what I think is right. A half-hour ago, that would have been to quietly turn down President Ottinger's nomination. Unfortunately, I can no longer do that without it being interpreted as a snub of man and an office that I respect more than my own personal preferences."

Kropotkin's face drooped.

"That is why," she continued, "I have no other choice than to accept his nomination for vice…"

"YES!" Davis Flemming jumped up and pumped his fists.

It was only after he noticed Lorraine glowering at him that Flemming restrained himself.

"Sorry, sorry," said Flemming, trying to restrain his glee. "It's just that, well, for a minute there, I thought you were going to turn it down. I mean, it was pretty close there, wasn't it? But…" he noticed Lorraine's sober expression. "Uh, but…" said Flemming, reigning in his joy, "I'm just delighted, uh, for the country, of course. It's a great day for the country. You will make an excellent president, I mean, vice president."

Lorraine stared at him.

"Mr. Flemming," she began, "your enthusiasm notwithstanding, this is only the beginning of what a long, tiring process that will demand all of my time and devotion. The confirmation process alone…"

Flemming held up his hand. "Allow me to interrupt, Mrs. Innis. That's the beauty of nominating you. You'll sail through the confirmation."

"Yes, but…"

"No buts about it," he said. "You're on my turf now. You're playing in my ballpark. Don't worry. I meant what I said: I'll drive you through all the obstacles, I'll steer your nomination to its safe destination. You're in good hands, Mrs. Innis."

Lorraine looked at Flemming's confident smile and then glanced at Nikolai Kropotkin, who wore a dubious expression. She was sure his thoughts concurred with hers.

"Mr. Flemming," said Lorraine, purposely so as not to be misunderstood, "you are the last person in the world with whom I would wish to be associated, no matter what promises and benefits you may offer."

Flemming laughed. "Sure, okay, I'm a spin doctor, a political hack…"

"I know many political hacks," said Kropotkin, "and you are being too generous with yourself, Flemming."

Flemming sneered and then turned to Lorraine. "Okay, whatever you want to call me, that's okay. I'm slimy, I'm oily, but you have to be oily and slimy to grease the wheels of power. Why do you think they call us spin doctors?"

"Because you manipulate the truth to your advantage," said Lorraine.

"Because we keep the wheels spinning," said Flemming. "If it wasn't for professionals like me, this country would come to a grinding halt. Face it, Mrs. Innis, without me doing the unpleasant jobs, nice people like you wouldn't have the luxury of appearing lofty and idealistic. As someone once said: politics makes strange bedfellows."

"It was Charles Dudley Warner," said Lorraine, "and I doubt he was ever asked to climb in bed with you, Mr. Flemming. And as for your altruistic offers to steer and grease, my political career, I must decline."

Flemming laughed. "I don't think you understand..."

"I understand far too well, Mr. Flemming," she said.

"But I can make things much easier."

Lorraine looked intently at him. "Easy or difficult is not a consideration. Due to your machinations, I have been forced into this position. I will inform President Ottinger that I will accept his nomination. I will not divulge your efforts to maneuver me into that decision. But I will inform him that you and I do not work in concert, nor will we. As far as the President is concerned, he nominated me at your suggestion, and that is where your participation ends."

Flemming winked. "I get you; keep it under the radar."

Lorraine shook her head. "No, Mr. Flemming, you do not 'get me' in two ways. You do not understand me. Nor will you and I have any relationship public, clandestine, or otherwise. I do not know how to make it clearer, but this is the last contact I wish to have with you. You will not work with me or for me. There is no common purpose between us. Do you understand?"

Flemming's face went through a series of contortions as if he were trying to reinterpret Lorraine's words, to more positive meaning for himself. But no matter how he spun them, Dlavis Flemming could find no other meaning than the one she intended. This conclusion registered upon his face in one final, malevolent look.

"So that's your decision," he said.

"Yes," said Lorraine. "Is that clear to you?"

"Quite clear," snorted Flemming. "You don't get it. Your type never does. Don't worry, you will. You're not stupid. And that's the greatest waste of all. I've guided idiots to power. The pity is that you're no idiot. You could have had it all, more than any of them. But I guess there's something that disqualifies a person more than sheer stupidity, and that's blinding morality. Together we could have had..."

Flemming raised his hand to the sky.

"No, Mr. Flemming," said Lorraine, "you don't understand. Together we could never."

Flemming looked at her and opened his mouth to reply but then just shrugged, threw a dismissive wave in Lorraine's direction, and walked out the door. As he left, she heard him mutter: "You'll find out."

– 24 –
The Anglo-American Girls' Night Out

Verity Goodhue was putting on her coat when she heard the shouting down the hall of the executive suite. It had been a disappointing day. She had awoken that morning, expecting to see her beloved. They would be together, and Chesney would know she was alive. The morning was so sunny. Clouds gathered around noon, reminding her that days that begin so brightly often end in storms. Verity could see the clouds lowering and hear the wind against the glass as she looked out the window of the skyscraper.

The first raindrops were hitting the window as the woman's voice down the hall grew louder. It was as if that woman was blown in by the storm. Or perhaps she had brought it with her. Verity recognized the voice and sighed. It was Valerie Fierro.

Verity longed to pull Valerie aside and speak in confidential tones.

"You know who Lorraine Innis really is, don't you?"

"Why is he doing all this?"

"Does he ever speak of the girl who died?"

"Does he still love her?"

Those were the questions that swirled around her mind, but they didn't dare approach her lips. Verity didn't know enough about Valerie Fierro. She didn't know if she could trust her.

"Lord Bagnall has left for the evening, Miss Fierro; you just missed him," said the receptionist.

"Yeah, when I see him, I won't miss him," snarled Valerie Fierro.

"Perhaps you'd like to leave a message."

Verity went towards the reception area.

"Look, he's a no-good, two-bit chiseler," raved Valerie. The receptionist was furiously trying to transcribe the American's invective.

"...two-bit...oh, my, the point of my pencil broke," the woman said, reaching for a replacement. "I beg your pardon, I was at 'two-bit.'"

"Chiseler, chiseler," snapped Valerie, leaning over the desk.

"Oh, yes, chiseler, how colorful."

"Yeah, if you like that, I've got the full 64-pack of Crayolas... a double-crossing weasel, dirty no-good, son of a bitch..."

"I appreciate your ire, Miss Fierro," said Verity stepping out of the shadows, "but now you're casting aspersions on my grandmother. No matter what your complaint against my father, I'd appreciate you confining your remarks to him."

Valerie scanned Verity from head to toe and smirked. "Okay, you'll do."

"Pardon me? What will I do?" asked Verity.

"Just like back home," continued Valerie, "you've got to yell your head off to get to the person in charge."

"Not to disappoint you, Miss Fierro, but I can assure you that I am not in charge of my father's affairs. As I explained earlier today, I have very little connection to his business dealings and consequently, very little authority."

Valerie rolled her eyes. "Yeah, whatever," she snorted, "but you were there in that meeting, well, for most of it..."

"Excuse me," said Verity raising her hand. She turned to the receptionist. "I'm sure we're imposing on your time, Mrs. Wilson. Thank you, I'll finish with Miss Fierro."

Mrs. Wilson gathered her handbag and her coat and hurried out. After she disappeared into the lift, Verity turned to her guest.

"As I said, Miss Fierro," said Verity. "I'm really not a business person."

"I figured that out the first time I laid eyes on you," said Valerie.

Verity nodded. "I commend your perception. Would you like to come in, or shall we go somewhere more comfortable?"

Valerie stared at her for a moment. "Are you sure your father isn't here somewhere, hiding?"

"I can ascribe many attributes to my father," said Verity, "but cowardice is not among them. If he were here, he would not hesitate to meet with you, and he certainly would never hide behind his daughter's skirts."

Valerie scrutinized Verity's face for a moment and shrugged. "Okay, what the hell," said Valerie. "I sure could use a drink."

"I was thinking more of a chat over dinner," said Verity. "I didn't think you wanted to air your grievances in a noisy pub."

"Okay, it's your country," said Valerie. "As long as I can get a drink, I don't care where we go."

Minutes later, they were seated in one of the exclusive restaurants in the area.

"Can I get a Cosmo?" asked Valerie as the maître de handed her the menu.

"Pardon?" said the maître de.

"The drink," said Valerie, "a Cosmo?"

The maître de thought for a moment. "Oh, a Cosmopolitan."

"Yeah, a Cosmo," she repeated.

"Very good, and for you, Miss?"

"Just a glass of your house white wine," said Verity. She wanted to keep a clear head. She also hoped that a few drinks might cause Valerie Fierro to disclose some of the missing pieces of the mystery.

After their orders were placed and their drinks arrived, the two women sat facing each other in silence. Verity took a sip of her white wine as Valerie Fierro took a healthy quaff of her Cosmopolitan and then sighed.

Verity smiled. "I guess this is what you in the States call 'a girls' night out.'"

Valerie attempted a smile, but it looked more like a smirk by the time it had crossed the table. "No, not really," said Valerie.

"Oh," said Verity. "I should apologize. I didn't mean to make light of the situation. I know you must be frightfully upset about something."

Valerie caught the waiter's eye, pointed to her empty cocktail glass, and signaled she needed a refill. Then she looked up at Verity.

"Upset about something?" said Valerie. "Yeah, I'd say I'm upset about something. What did you say? Frightfully upset? Frightfully!"

This second delivery of the word sounded like an imitation of Verity's British accent.

"Yes, well..." said Verity.

"Frightfully upset," repeated Valerie mimicking her. "I really love how you Brits underplay everything. Frightfully!"

The reinforcing Cosmo arrived.

Verity tried again. "Forgive my clumsy attempts at ameliorating the situation, but..."

"There's a good word," said Valerie.

"Ameliorate?"

"Mmm," she said in mid-sip. "I got to hand it to your country. You really packed the language with a load of posh-sounding words."

"I only meant that I wanted to help you," said Verity.

"I know that," said Valerie, "I am a university graduate. At least we're on the same page now. Great. You want to help?"

"Yes, that's what I said, and I mean it."

"Sure, sure," said Valerie with a wave of her hand, "you know what I want, and I know what you want."

"What I want?"

A grin spread across Valerie Fierro's face enhanced by two stiff drinks in rapid succession.

"You want to meet Lorraine Innis," said Valerie. Like her attempts at a British accent, this, too, was delivered in a condescending tone.

Verity sat there for a moment, unsure of what to say. She took another sip of wine.

Valerie nodded her head, confirming she was right.

Their salad course arrived, and Valerie ordered a third cosmopolitan.

"Don't worry," said Valerie, "don't... what do you Brits say? Don't get your nipples in a twist..."

"It's knickers, actually," said Verity.

"Yeah, knickers," agreed Valerie. "Anyway, I knew what you wanted as soon as I met you."

"Did you?"

Valerie smiled. "You seem like a very nice lady. Are you a lady?"

"I always try to comport myself as one."

Valerie laughed. "No, not that kind of lady, not a lady lady, a lady lady."

"Lady, lady?"

"You know the, one of those ones, you know lords and ladies and knights and varlets, and all that stuff. You're not one of those, are you? I mean, your father..."

"Father is a life peer," explained Verity. "He received his honor for services to the nation in the area of industry. But the honor is not hereditary. I'm not of noble lineage, though my grandfather did receive an OBE."

"Yeah, what's that?"

"Order of the British Empire," said Verity. "It's a very great honor."

"Is it as big as a lord?"

"Well, not quite..."

"What did your grandfather sell?"

"He was an entertainer, but you were saying..."

Valerie took another drink of her cocktail and, for a moment, seemed to blank out. "About what? Oh, yeah, right, I was saying you seem like a nice girl." Here Valerie paused and looked over Verity. "You're nice, but maybe a little too..." Valerie waved her head back and forth as if angling for just the right word.

"...too earnest?" Offered Verity.

"No, naïve," said Valerie. "Oh, no offense."

"None taken," muttered Verity.

"No, really," assured Valerie, "some of my closest friends are naïve."

Verity thought a moment and then jumped in with both feet. "You mean Lorraine Innis."

A wide grin spread across Valerie's lips, followed by the running of her tongue over the same. She concluded with a wink. "Maybe you're not so naïve after all."

"So, you see similarities between Lorraine Innis and me?"

Valerie squinted slightly and tilted her head first this way and then that. "You could almost be bookends, except he, I mean, she's an American, an American woman, and you're not, I mean American. You're a woman. Not a lady, I mean not a lady, lady, but you're a British woman. You two could be bookends… in some respects; not all of them. Style, you've got similar styles. And manners, not just politeness…"

"Deportment?" offered Verity.

Valerie laughed and pointed directly at her. "You see, that's just the word he, I mean, Lorraine would use: deportment. Except she doesn't have an accent."

"Not even an American accent?"

Valerie sat up, soberly. "We don't have accents."

"Oh, no, of course not, pardon me."

Perhaps it was just the effect of Cosmopolitans that confused Valerie Fierro's use of pronouns, or maybe it was the alcohol dislodging the truth. But Verity couldn't help notice that her dinner companion had twice said "he" before correcting herself.

"You're just a little star-struck, huh?" continued Valerie.

"Star-struck?"

"About Lorraine; I mean, nice girls need role models, too."

Verity suppressed a giggle at the notion that she would choose her own fiancée as a model of femininity.

"It's okay," said Valerie misinterpreting Verity's reaction. "I mean, you could do worse, and Lorraine's safe. Pure as the driven," she looked down at her salad, "grated cheese. I mean, she won't even do lingerie shoots."

"Lingerie shoots? What are those?"

Valerie lifted her hands and mimed a camera, "you know, photoshoots for lingerie ads."

"And Mrs. Innis was asked to do that?"

Valerie leaned over. The alcohol on her breath cut through the table's floral arrangement. "Between you and me…" she raised her finger to her lips. "That girl could have sold a shitload of underwear."

"Really?"

"You think your father was hot to sign up Lorraine? Well, that's nothing, nothing, compared to all the American lingerie malfunctioners, uh, manufacturers. Like I said, women love Lorraine. She's safe. I mean, I could sell some hot underwear, but a girl like you wouldn't rush out on my say so. I've got my own line of clothing coming out, you know."

"How very nice for you," said Verity.

"Yeah, but a girl like you wouldn't wear a bra because I wore it. I mean, yeah, you'd wear one, I mean, you're pretty well set there yourself…" Valerie nodded towards Verity's bust.

"Thank you," said Verity as she felt the blush rise in her cheeks. "I believe I understand what you're saying: a woman like me wouldn't necessarily purchase… a product… on your endorsement."

"Zactly!" said Valerie with a point and a wink. "But…" Valerie raised her hands, "…Lorraine wouldn't do it. He said it didn't fit her public image. It was too intimate. Hell, yeah, it's intimate apparel. But she wouldn't do it."

Verity almost said "quite right" but didn't want to interrupt the flow of information.

"Yep," said Valerie, "she's got scruples... yeah, scruples out of every office in her body."

"Orifice?"

"Yeah, okay..."

The waiter brought their entrees. There was a brief silence as Verity began to eat. Valerie prodded the food as if she were uncertain why it was there or what its purpose was. After a tentative poke, Valerie took a bite. After that, momentum took over, and Valerie devoured her entire meal before Verity was half-finished. The introduction of solid food to her system seemed to assuage the effect of the Cosmopolitans, and some of the focus returned to Valerie's eyes.

"That was... lovely," said Valerie, daintily wiping the corner of her mouth on the linen napkin.

Though she hadn't finished, Verity laid aside her utensils. The waiter came by, and Verity ordered coffee for them both and the check.

"I'm delighted you could join me," said Verity.

"Join you? Oh, no," said Valerie, "this is my party."

"I wouldn't dream of it; after all, I invited you..."

Valerie winked. "You got an expense account?"

"Well, not as such..."

"Well, I do," said Valerie. "Besides, I've got to get something out of this trip, even if it's just a free meal.

"We all must bear our disappointments," said Verity. "Wait: something out of this trip? But, surely, you concluded your agreement with Father. I saw him leave, and he seemed quite pleased."

Valerie Fierro snorted. "Yeah, he would be pleased... quite pleased." Again she attempted a British accent. "He got what he wanted, the rat."

"But I don't..."

"You don't understand? Well, kiddo, if your daddy got his lordship..."

"Knighthood..."

"Whatever, if he got a knighthood, it sure wasn't a good knighthood. Your father suckered me."

"Oh, my..." said Verity. She was more concerned about the repercussions for her and Chesney. At the moment, their reunion was blocked at one end by Lord Bagnall and the other end by Valerie Fierro.

"Oh, my exactly," said Valerie. "Do you know what that snake pulled on me?"

"No, I'm sorry," said Verity. "I'm not privy to his business dealings. I take it that you're disgruntled."

"Disgruntled? That's just the tip of the iceberg. I bet you could look all over your little country here, and you'd be hard-pressed to find anyone less gruntled than me. Your dear old daddy made me sign an endorsement deal when he had more information on it than I did."

Despite her inexperience, Verity imagined this was standard business practice. She knew from personal experience that her father was a terrible bounder and rotter. Despite that, it wasn't Lord Bagnall's responsibility to educate Valerie Fierro.

"You're referring to Lorraine Innis being nominated vice president," Verity finally said.

The fire in Valerie's eyes that had been dampened by the Cosmopolitans flared afresh.

"You're damn right; that's what I'm talking about!" said Valerie.

Other patrons in the restaurant turned their heads, and Valerie lowered her voice.

"Yes, that's what I'm talking about," said Valerie. "And you knew it, too, didn't you?"

Verity nodded. "Yes, I did. Father told me. That's what he came in to announce when first we met."

"But he didn't think he should tell me?" said Valerie.

"If it's any consolation, Miss Fierro, I thought he should have."

"Well, thanks, but no," said Valerie. "Your sympathy does me a fat lot of good."

"I'm sorry for that," said Verity. Valerie Fierro was her closest connection to Chesney, but any help from her seemed unlikely in Valerie's present mood. Verity felt tears welling up in her eyes. She lifted her napkin, ostensibly to wipe her mouth, but actually to staunch her tears.

"Hey, you really are broken up about this, aren't you?" said Valerie.

"F-forgive me," said Verity, composing herself. "It's just a slight allergy to…" She glanced around the room. "Those gloxinias, over there."

Valerie looked towards the far corner where the offending flowers were and then studied Verity.

"Gloxinias? Yeah, sure," said Valerie. "Whatever you say. You Brits are a funny bunch."

"Oh? Are we," asked Verity taking out a handkerchief to properly control her tears.

"You act all reserved, and then you crack up. I guess it's my fault, sort of," Valerie shrugged. "I mean, your Dad didn't get his knighthood from being outsmarted by a chick from Delaware. I guess I should chalk it up to experience and be happy with what I got out of him."

"For the charity?" said Verity.

Valerie just stared at her for a good ten seconds before blinking. "Oh, yeah, for the charity. Sure."

She then drained the last drop from her cocktail glass, leaving Verity to conclude that Valerie had already begun profiting from her lesson.

- 25 -
Another Daughter
Someone Never Had

In the twenty-four hours since she accepted the vice-presidential nomination, Lorraine Innis had discovered a new appreciation for bathrooms. She was especially grateful for the locks on bathroom doors. It was only that little piece of hardware and those little enclosed rooms that afforded her any privacy.

Outside of the bathroom, she belonged to the cadre of Secret Service agents that surrounded her. They were nice people, but they were so smothering.

As she sat fully clothed on the edge of the bathtub, Lorraine's mind wandered back a few days. If only she hadn't answered the phone. If only she had gone to London a day earlier. After ten months of being a celebrity, Lorraine thought she could face any challenge that fame offered. But now it was much worse. In addition to public adulation, now she had the cocoon of the Secret Service and the President's expectations engulfing her.

"Maybe you should check if she's okay," Lorraine heard a man's voice just outside the door. It belonged to Agent Hambright.

"Maybe you should," said a woman's voice belonging to Agent MacKay.

"I can't," whispered Hambright.

"Why not?"

There was a pause, then an un-professional whine. "Because... she's, you know...."

"In the bathroom?" said Agent MacKay.

"Yeah..."

"You're married," said Ms. MacKay.

"So?"

"So, what do you do when your wife is in the bathroom?"

"I leave her alone," said Hambright. "I'm not there to protect her."

"You're her husband," said Agent MacKay.

"Yeah, well, I'd protect her if someone burst into the house. I just wouldn't disturb her when she was in the bathroom. If I did, I'd be the one who'd need protecting."

"I weep for your marriage," said Agent MacKay.

"Only 'cause you're not married."

"If you're an example of an average husband, I rejoice in that fact," muttered the woman. "If you're not going to protect Mrs. Innis…"

"I didn't say that. I just don't want to disturb her."

Lorraine shook her head, rose to her feet, and turned on the water in the sink. After letting it run for ten seconds, she turned it off and opened the door.

"All done," said Lorraine trying to be cheerful. Agent Hambright's face turned red. Agent MacKay shook her head at Hambright.

"Why don't you go check the perimeter," said Agent MacKay.

Lorraine chortled. Her home was a townhouse on a sliver of property. It hardly had a "perimeter." Still, Agent Hambright hurried from the room.

Lorraine and Agent MacKay exchanged knowing looks.

"Men," said Agent MacKay.

"I heard it all through the door," confessed Lorraine.

"Agent Hambright has been trained for every contingency," said MacKay, "except how to handle a woman in the bathroom."

"That's partially my fault."

"Not at all, Mrs. Innis. You do have to use the facilities."

"Yes, well, I suppose so, but I didn't have to right now," said Lorraine.

Agent MacKay nodded. "It can all be overwhelming."

"Then you do understand," said Lorraine, "I mean, about just trying to be alone for a moment. I do appreciate what you're doing and your dedication to your job. But I'm starting to feel like a delicate piece of porcelain."

"I can imagine," said Agent MacKay. "If there's anything Agent Hambright or I can do…"

"Yes, you can tell me your first name," said Lorraine. "I'm sure your parents didn't christen you 'Agent.'"

Agent MacKay shifted uncomfortably. "It's, uh, it's Margaret."

"And is that what your friends call you?"

Margaret MacKay pulled at a lock of her red hair. "Actually, they call me 'Margie.'"

Lorraine studied the tall, fit woman. "Yes, that fits, Margie. May I call you Margie?"

Margie MacKay looked around as if she were being monitored. She cleared her throat. "It's rather unorthodox."

"But then so is this whole situation," said Lorraine, "and I would appreciate it unless it would get you into trouble."

Agent MacKay fidgeted. It was the first time Lorraine had seen Agent MacKay appear out of sorts.

"I promise," said Lorraine, touching Agent MacKay on the arm, "I won't abuse the privilege. Okay, Margie?"

Agent Margie MacKay blushed and then nodded.

"Thank you, Mrs. Innis…"

"…Lorraine…"

"Lorraine," said MacKay, "only it will avoid trouble if you don't use first names when the Chief is around."

Lorraine nodded towards the door. "You mean Agent Hambright?"

Margie MacKay laughed. "Hambright's not the Chief. I outrank him. No, you haven't met the Chief yet. He's coming up from Washington this morning. When he gets here, drop the Margies and the Margarets."

"It'll be just between us girls." Lorraine stopped and thought of her own physical challenges that might contradict that designation. As quickly as she thought about it, the thought was pushed automatically from her mind.

"Margie MacKay," she muttered several times. "Margie MacKay: A Key Magic Arm."

"Pardon?"

"A Key Magic Arm," said Lorraine, "that's the anagram of your name, just a little habit of mine. What's Agent Hambright's Christian name?"

"It's Ed."

Lorraine thought a moment and then frowned. "No, I don't think we'll share that anagram."

"Why? What is it?"

Lorraine glanced towards the doorway to confirm they were alone. "Bite Me Hard."

Margie MacKay burst out in laughter.

"Shh! You won't tell him," whispered Lorraine. "I would hate if Agent Hambright thought I was making fun of him."

"No, I won't tell, I promise," said MacKay reigning in her giggles. She wiped a tear from her eye. "Sorry, sorry…"

"For what?"

"Laughing like that," she said. "It's not very professional."

Lorraine shrugged. "Aren't you allowed to smile? In the day and a half we've been together, that's the first time I've seen you smile."

Margie MacKay bit her lip. "Smiles are frowned upon. When you're protecting an important person, a good hard scowl can almost be as intimidating as your service weapon."

"I'd dispute that there's anything important about me."

"I think you're very important," said Margie MacKay. She let her professional demeanor slip a bit further.

"Thank you, and I think you're just as important," said Lorraine as she started to put away her laundry.

"They told me at the training academy that I smiled too much," said Margie.

"Tops in the class in marksmanship and smiling," said Lorraine as she hung up a blouse.

"Yes, well, by the time I graduated, I was scowling with the best of them." Margie put on a severe frown.

"Very intimidating," said Lorraine. "But I'm glad I know there's a Margie underneath all that. But don't worry. You're only Margie when we're alone. I won't let the boss…"

"The Chief…"

"Yes, the Chief," said Lorraine, "I won't let him even know that I know you have a first name or lovely teeth."

"Thanks… Lorraine," whispered Margie.

"Anyway," said Lorraine, "who is this Chief that has been given the responsibility of protecting me from all enemies, foreign and domestic?"

A stern look crossed Margie's face transforming her back to Agent MacKay. "We take our assignments very seriously, Mrs. Innis. I know you don't think anyone would want to harm you, but the world isn't as rosy a place as you might perceive it to be. But there are a wide range of profiles that would harm a public figure for an assortment of reasons."

Lorraine felt her face redden. "Sorry, I guess this is all still so very new to me. I didn't mean to…"

A soft knock was heard upon the open door, and Agent Hambright stuck in his head.

"Excuse me, Mrs. Innis," he said to Lorraine and then looked at Agent MacKay. "The Chief is here." Then, he disappeared.

"I guess I should go downstairs and welcome him to my home," said Lorraine. As she passed by Agent MacKay, she stopped and placed her hand on the woman's forearm. "I didn't mean to make light of your duty. I'm very grateful for your protection and your dedication, Agent MacKay. Now let's meet the Chief, whoever he may be."

"Actually, he's new to our team," whispered MacKay as they descended the stairs. He's a very senior person. He specifically asked for this assignment."

"That's him," said MacKay, as they entered the living room. She pointed to a man standing with his back to them. The man turned around.

"Mr. Rocher," said Lorraine.

"You know him?" said Agent MacKay.

"Mrs. Innis," said Rocher, "you have a good memory."

"Not at all, Mr. Rocher," said Lorraine, "a woman always remembers her first…"

She heard Margie MacKay emit a gasp.

"…her first interrogation, Agent MacKay," said Lorraine.

"I was on the detail during the Kropotkin attempt in Wilmington, MacKay," said Rocher. "I met Mrs. Innis there. Excuse us, Agent MacKay. I'd like to brief Mrs. Innis in private."

Agent MacKay excused herself, leaving Rocher alone with Lorraine. She couldn't help feeling that he was scrutinizing her.

"I'm forgetting my manners," said Lorraine in an attempt to distract his gaze. "You're a guest in my home. Would you like something to drink?"

"I never drink on duty."

"I meant tea," said Lorraine.

"Oh," said Rocher, "yes, please, tea would be nice."

Lorraine smiled and put the kettle on. With her back turned toward him, she could still feel him staring at her. She busied herself with the cups and continued talking.

"How have you been, Mr. Rocher," she asked, "since that night in Wilmington?"

"Uh, fine, I guess," he said. "I won't have to ask how you've been. It's obvious what you've been up to, Mrs. Innis," he said.

"What is reported so extensively in the media isn't necessarily an indication of how I may be in reality."

"No, I suppose it isn't," said Rocher. "So, how are you?"

Lorraine shrugged. "As well as can be expected when one goes from being a book editor, to a heroine, to the head of a charity, and now the nominee for vice president, all in less than twelve months."

"Well, you've handled it well."

Lorraine smiled through closed lips. "Again, you're making assumptions on news reports, Agent Rocher."

"Yes, sorry, I am." He paused. A thought appeared to be forming when the kettle began to whistle.

Lorraine made the tea and brought the tray to the table where Rocher was sitting.

"Milk?" she asked, offering a small pitcher.

"Milk?"

"Sorry," she said, pulling back the pitcher and adding some to her own tea. "It's an English habit."

"You're not English, are you?" he asked.

"Not by birth," she said. "If I wasn't born in the United States, I couldn't be nominated for vice president. I was born in New Jersey."

"Yes, I know, Morristown Memorial Hospital," he said.

Lorraine was surprised. "I had no idea the Secret Service went into such a detailed study of their charges. Where was President Ottinger born?"

"Hmm?" said Rocher looking up from his tea. "I have no idea."

Lorraine looked at him sideways. "But you know where I was born."

"Oh, uh, yes," he said, "I, uh, I never actually was detailed to President Ottinger, not personally."

"I see," said Lorraine, "need to know basis, and all that?"

"Yes, something like that," said Rocher.

They sat in silence for a moment sipping their tea.

"So, any vice presidents come from New Jersey, before you, I mean?" he asked.

"I'm not vice president yet. Only one vice president has come from New Jersey: Garret Hobart. William McKinley's first vice president."

"Is that so? Who was his second?"

Lorraine stared at him a moment. She wrongly assumed that senior Secret Service agents knew their history. "That was Theodore Roosevelt."

"Oh, really?" said Rocher. "Ol' Teddy shoved him aside, huh?"

"He didn't have to do much shoving," said Lorraine. "Garret Hobart died in office; natural causes. No fault of the Secret Service."

"That was a few years before I signed on," said Rocher with a smile.

Lorraine wondered if this all was leading somewhere when a motive began to materialize.

"You know a lot about New Jersey..."

"I suppose," said Lorraine. "I've lived there all my life."

"But I doubt many other people from Jersey know about ol' Garret Hubbard..."

"Hobart."

"Um, right," said Rocher. "So, does your family all come from New Jersey, I mean going way back?"

Now it was getting somewhere, thought Lorraine. "I'm sure you know all about my background, Agent Rocher. After all, you know where I was born. I'm sure you know all about my family history."

Rocher smiled bashfully. "I can't fool you, Mrs. Innis."

"Were you trying to fool me, Mr. Rocher?"

Rather than answer, he launched a fresh line of conversation. "May I ask you a personal question? Not about you, really; it's more of a personal matter on my part. It's just that since the first night I met you, I couldn't help but be struck by... well, that you reminded me of someone."

"Really, who would that be?"

"A girl."

"Well, so far, I'm flattered, or at least I'm not insulted."

"Yes, well..." Rocher looked down into his cup. A look of melancholy overhung his brow.

"I can conclude then that this person, the one of whom I remind you, wasn't just a girl."

Rocher sighed.

"So," said Lorraine, "she was a very special girl."

Rocher kept his head down and then forced a laugh and looked up. "Yeah, well, that was a long, long time ago."

"And I remind you of this girl?"

"Mrs. Innis, if I didn't know that was forty years ago, and if I didn't have this old achy body on the verge of retirement..." He sighed. "I'd swear you were her."

"They say that each of us has a double," said Lorraine. "Perhaps mine is just a few years ahead of me."

"A relative perhaps?" said Rocher.

"Agent Rocher, if you know everything about me, down to where I was born, I'm sure you've researched my family tree, haven't you?"

Rocher just stared at her.

"You have researched my family tree, haven't you?"

"What? Oh, yes," said Rocher, "what there was of it."

Lorraine thought that was an awfully vague response. After all, her life was an open book.

"And you're not adopted, are you?" said Rocher.

"You know I'm not," said Lorraine.

Rocher just gave a noncommittal grunt.

"If you're still infatuated with this girl..."

"Who said I was infatuated," he said. "I'm a happily married man."

"I beg your pardon."

"No, I'm sorry," he said. "It's just that when you get to be my age, you tend to look back. I never dwelt on the past. I never even thought about this girl, hardly ever, once a year at the most. I thought I'd put it all behind me."

"Then you saw someone who reminded you of her," said Lorraine.

"Reminded me? Mrs. Innis, it's like she came back to life. It's just that when I saw you, looking exactly like her, well, it took me back. And all the years, and all the relationships, and the life I've built since her, well, it just melted away, and I was back there, the last day I saw here. And it made me think 'what if?'"

Lorraine patted Rocher's hand.

"I knew you weren't her," he whispered, "and I researched it all and was almost certain you weren't related."

"Almost certain?" said Lorraine. "But, you know my complete background."

Rocher opened his mouth but paused. "I guess I saw her in you, and it made me think you'd have been the daughter we would have had if, well, if things had worked out differently."

"I understand," she said. "And I'm afraid it must all be a coincidence. I can assure you my parents were my parents." Lorraine stopped. She could recall her parents, of course, but they seemed one-dimensional. "That is, I wasn't adopted or left on their doorstep."

Rocher nodded ambiguously.

"You said something about the girl," she said, "you spoke of her when she was alive. Is she..."

"Dead," he nodded. "Yes, I never tried to find out what happened to her, not until last October... after I saw you."

"I'm sorry for dredging up unwanted memories."

"She died a few years ago," he said. "She had moved to England."

"I'm very sorry…" The mention of England and this girl dying there brought a chill to Lorraine's heart.

"Are you okay, Mrs. Innis? Mrs. Innis?"

"What? Oh, yes, I'm sorry. I don't know what came over me."

"I'm starting to understand why everyone loves you," said Rocher.

Lorraine looked at him as if she were only half understanding his words. The mention of the girl in England hung over her like a mist.

"Pardon?" She said, shaking her head.

"Why everyone loves you," he repeated. "You're so empathetic. I mention my loss, and it's almost as if you've made it your own."

Was that it, Lorraine wondered?

"But enough about my past," said Rocher. "Let's look to your future, more specifically your schedule."

"Yes, my schedule," said Lorraine. "I'm quite a creature of habit. I rise each day at five-thirty…"

Rocher explained that he wasn't referring to Lorraine's personal schedule but her official schedule.

"Oh, yes, of course," said Lorraine. "This is all very new to me. I'm completely at your disposal. Just tell me where to be and when."

"Yes, ma'am," he said. "that isn't the duty of the Service. Your schedule is given to us so we can arrange for your security. I'm sure the White House will liaise with your chief of staff."

"My chief of staff," Lorraine laughed. "I don't have a chief of staff."

Rocher nodded. "No, of course, you don't. That's another reason you're so genuine. Everyone in Washington has a chief of staff, and that's one of the problems with the whole damn place. Do you have any sort of staff?"

"There are my cousin and our assistant," said Lorraine, "but they work for the charity. I couldn't pull them away from those jobs. Those are very important. Oh, I didn't mean that this…"

"No need to apologize, Mrs. Innis," said Rocher. "I'm sure you can work out the details of your schedule with the White House, as it develops. Here's a preliminary schedule. Until the confirmation hearing begins, the only meetings you have are courtesy calls on key congressmen and senators. They also have you scheduled for a round of policy briefings."

Lorraine looked at the schedule. It was all so overwhelming, but at the same time, she couldn't back out now. "I suppose I'll get used to it." Scanning the sheet, one date just a few days hence jumped out at her.

"Oh, this one, I can't do anything that day," said Lorraine. "That's the day I have to see my accountant."

– 26 –
The Failure of Bulbs: Three-Way and Dim

She thinks she's so clever," said Davis Flemming, "but she doesn't know how much I know about her."

He arched his fingers for a menacing effect, but when he looked up, his audience of one had his head up a desk lamp.

Flemming cleared his throat.

"Do you know how these things work?" said the man, fiddling with the lamp switch.

"What?" said Flemming.

"These do-hickies," said the man.

"It's a lamp," said Flemming, slowly enunciating each syllable.

"Yeah, I know it's a lamp," said the man, looking up the shade. "But it's got one of those three-way bulbs, you know, 50, 100, and 150-watts."

Flemming sighed. Why was he always saddled with simpletons? "You flip the switch, and it gets brighter until you come back to the beginning, and it turns off again."

"I know that," said the man, who was now looking down into the lamp. "That's how they all work."

Flemming rolled his eyes. This idiot was incapable of taking offense, even when he was spoken to as a slow child.

"No, what I wanted to know," continued the man, "oh, wait..."

"What?"

The man smiled triumphantly. "I was wrong. It's not a 50, 100, 150," said the man. "It's a 30, 70, 100-watt bulb. It's printed on the top. It wasn't as bright as I thought."

"I can relate to your feeling of disappointment," muttered Flemming.

"No, that's not it," said the man sitting down behind the desk, "I was just wondering why these three-way bulbs never burn out together. One always goes first. Why do you suppose that is?"

"It's probably because the different filaments inside the bulb are used for different lengths of time."

The man put his index finger upon his chin. He nodded as if he were pondering a profound mystery of the universe. Much as he hated to, Flemming had to admit that the pose made his host almost look wise.

"Hmm, yes, that's a very interesting theory you have there," he said with a sage tilting of his head.

"Why don't you sponsor a bill to have a government study done on the subject?" Flemming suggested.

Instead of being insulted by the sarcastic suggestion, Senator Lambert Pugh picked up a gold pen. After scratching out a reminder to turn the matter of three-way light bulbs over to a select committee, Lambert Pugh looked up and smiled.

It was all such a shame, Flemming thought. He had a winning, sincere smile, did Lambert Pugh. He had a full head of salt and pepper hair. He had deep blue eyes and broad shoulders. He was the very image of what a leader should look like, was Bert Pugh. But he was, without reservation, the biggest numbskull Davis Flemming had ever encountered in a city with the greatest per capita concentration of nitwits in North America. Poor Bert was so fencepost-dumb that even his fellow idiots in government recognized his singularity in the field.

"Now, what were you saying?" asked Pugh.

Flemming took a sharp intake of breath. "I was commenting on the upcoming confirmation hearings."

"Um, yes, yes, of course," said Pugh with severe intonations and matching head nods. Then he stopped. "Um, which ones were those?"

"Lorraine Innis... the vice presidency?"

Pugh's face brightened. "Will I get to meet her?"

"Of course you will," said Flemming. "I'm hoping you'll do more than just meet her."

"More?" His brow lowered and then shot up again. "You mean like..." A naughty grin overspread his face.

"No, Senator, I don't mean that," said Flemming. Like many politicians, for Bert Pugh, vote-getting was akin to a sexual conquest. Both wound up with him being gratified and the other person being screwed. "You're talking about the vice presidential nominee. You wouldn't have done that with Tom Ottinger when he was Veep."

"One: I don't swing that way, though I'm not necessarily condemning that lifestyle," said Pugh as if he were responding to a debate question. "Two: Ottinger could beat me up. And lastly, that Lorraine Innis has a hot body."

Flemming clenched his teeth. "Senator, you a member of the committee conducting the hearing on the nomination. Of course, you'll meet Mrs. Innis..."

"Good!" He said, sitting up a bit straighter in anticipation. "Oh, wait, what do I say to her?"

"I'll have questions for you..."

"For me?"

"For you to ask Mrs. Innis... as if they were from you... out of your own mind."

"Oh." A look of concern crossed his face.

"I'll give you the questions in advance," said Flemming, "and of course, I'll coach you on them."

Pugh relaxed. "Oh, that's okay then. So then it will be smooth sailing."

"Yes, you'll do fine."

"No, I mean for Mrs. Innis," said Pugh.

Flemming grinned. The dullard Pugh hadn't caught a word of what Flemming had said. It was probably just as well, he thought. The less Bert Pugh knew until absolutely necessary, the less chance he would put his foot through it. When the time came, it would be smooth sailing, though not for Lorraine Innis, unless her sailing over the cliff of history could be called "smooth."

"It will be okay, won't it?" asked Pugh in response to Flemming's silence.

"Everything will be fine," assured Flemming. Right now, that's all Pugh needed to know. "The builder doesn't explain the blueprints to the hammer, does he?"

"I guess not," said Pugh before doing a confused double-take. "Huh?"

"Never mind."

"Okay!"

– 27 –
Ms. Clott Goes to Washington

P lease sit here, Mrs. Innis."

"You have a lovely home," said Lorraine. "I feel as if I've been here before. It's the oddest feeling, a bit like déjà vu. I've been in a place very similar to this, only I could swear it was my doctor's office. Do you know my doctor? Perhaps the two of you have the same decorator."

"It will all be clear to you in a moment. I want you to remain calm. I am going to say two words to you, and I don't want you to get upset."

Lorraine squirmed in her seat. Two words? What two words would be most upsetting in an account's office? Rampant fraud? Fiscal Maleficence?

"Verity Goodhue…"

Lorraine blinked twice and then smiled sheepishly.

"Clo! I must look like a complete twit when I come in here. Last time you were my doctor and I wanted to take off my clothes. This time you're my accountant. It's a testimony to the effectiveness of your spell or your trance."

Clodagh Clott smirked. "I'd prefer you call it a suggestion. Spell or trance sounds evil. So, how is everything?"

"It's a mess, Clo," said Lorraine.

"It certainly is, Ches."

Lorraine sighed.

Clodagh looked at her old friend and shook her head. "Good old Chesney Potts. Will I ever see him again?"

Lorraine began to nod and then stopped. "What do you mean? Will you ever see him again?" Lorraine raised her index finger in rebuttal and then let it drop. "Sorry, your right, Clo. I'm in up to my neck. Now I've got to be Lorraine Innis, at least until President Ottinger finishes out his term. After that, who knows?"

"I'd hope you'd know," said Clodagh, "or at least have some say in your own future. I shouldn't have agreed to make you all Lorraine. If you had some awareness of Chesney, you'd never have agreed to be nominated vice president."

"I didn't agree," said Lorraine. "Do you think I'm some idiot in either mode? If anything, he'd have allowed himself to step into this mess before she would."

"You're talking about yourself in the third person."

"Lorraine's got more sense about these things than Chesney does," said Lorraine ignoring the observation. "Someone leaked the news to the media before she had the chance to turn it down. Before she knew it, it was too late, and I didn't want to embarrass President Ottinger."

Clodagh nodded. "You're a good person, whoever you are."

"Thank you, I think," said Lorraine. "But there's no use crying over the situation. I've committed to this course of action, and so I have to see it through."

Clodagh nodded and studied her friend's face. There were traces of concern, but overall a resolute expression. "I admire your dedication, dear, but how are you going to see it through, or more specifically, as who?"

"As whom?" corrected Lorraine.

Clodagh smiled. "Shut up. I'm glad to see that the depth of your predicament hasn't dulled your grammatical resolve."

"I think it's obvious, I've got to do it as Lorraine."

"Hasn't Lorraine Innis gotten you into enough trouble?" said Clodagh.

"Lorraine Innis may have gotten me into this latest difficulty," said Lorraine, "but it was through her deep sense of duty and honor. She wouldn't be in any trouble; she wouldn't even exist if it weren't for Chesney Potts. If you want to blame anyone, blame him."

"Listen to yourself," said Clodagh. "You're talking about both sides of this two-headed creature as if you were neither."

"So?"

"So, you're both, Chesney or Lorraine, or Chesney and Lorraine. I'm worried about all four of you."

Lorraine looked down. After a long silence, she spoke softly and calmly. "I know. When I'm aware of both sides of me, I don't feel like I'm either one. That's why I have to be Lorraine, and just Lorraine, at least for now."

Clodagh sat down beside her friend and took her hand. "But how long is 'now?'"

"I wish I knew," sighed Lorraine. "You only know about the public nomination. I had another offer the same day: to be the first lady of Russia."

"You mean President Kropotkin asked you to marry him?"

"He would have if I hadn't been nominated for..." Lorraine stopped in mid-sentence and stared into space.

"Ches, Ches," said Clodagh nudging Lorraine. "Are you okay?"

"That explains it," said Lorraine. "He said he had found his Lorruska again. He said I had changed. For a time, I wasn't the woman he had first known back when I saved his life. He said the attraction, or the spark, or whatever it was, had disappeared when I went to visit him in Moscow last Christmas. That's when he got a little fresh, and I pushed him off that parapet..."

"What?"

"Parapet, it's a low protective wall along the top of..."

"I know what a parapet is," said Clodagh, "I was expressing shock that you pushed a world leader off of one."

"It's was either that or, well, never mind, I'm not drawing you a diagram. But you see, Clo, he was in love with me. Then my appeal faded, and now it's back again as strong as ever."

"Corresponding with the times when you thought you were Lorraine and no one else. Fascinating," said Clodagh.

"And then there's the head of my Secret Service detail, too."

"He's in love with you?"

"No, but he was in love with my Aunt Elinor. He must have been the boy she left behind when she ran away to Tibet."

"But only got as far as London," said Clodagh.

"How did you..."

"You told me about that when you in a trance, remember?"

Lorraine related the odd way that Paul Rocher had acted when they first met, and then his most recent confession of the girl who got away.

"No wonder he was so spooked," concluded Lorraine. "I'm the spitting image of my aunt when she was younger. That poor man, I'm a constant reminder of the love he lost. Still, I've got to be Lorraine if I want to do this right. At least, I don't have to worry about President Kropotkin. He understands we can't have a relationship. I'm not worried about him."

"Not as long as you have a parapet handy," said Clodagh.

Lorraine gave Clodagh a dirty look. "You're lucky your house doesn't have a parapet!"

"And you can't worry about that secret service agent," said Clodagh. "You said he asked to be put on your detail. If he wants to pine over lost loves, that's his problem."

A pained expression clouded Lorraine's eyes. Clodagh instantly realized her friend had more than his share of heartache over lost lovers.

"I'm sorry," said Clodagh.

Lorraine shook her head; the resolve returning to her expression.

"Anyway, I've got to keep it up a little longer. After all, Valerie's due back from Gibraltar in a few days. I'm sure she'll have found something that will shed light on Martina's death and who is responsible for sending her to Chicago."

"Hey, if you're going to be vice president," said Clodagh, "why don't you have the FBI investigate all that? I'm sure they could cut through it in a few days."

Lorraine's mouth fell open. "You're suggesting I use a federal agency for personal use?"

"I'm sure it wouldn't be the first time..."

"It would be the first time for me," said Lorraine. "You pay taxes, Clodagh Clott! How would you feel if your hard-earned tax dollars were squandered so some politician could find personal details about his girlfriend?"

Clodagh shook her head and smiled. "Same old Chesney," she said, "I'm glad to see that despite appearances to the contrary, you still haven't changed."

Lorraine arched her back and crossed her arms. "It just wouldn't be right. What would happen if executives everywhere used their staffs..." Lorraine snapped her fingers. "That's it! That's what we'll do. It will make everything simplier."

"What are you talking about?"

"I need a staff."

"Yes, so?"

"So, you'll be my staff," said Lorraine triumphantly. "Or at least my chief of staff, my top advisor."

"Me?"

Lorraine scooted to the edge of her seat. "It's perfect. They said I'd need a staff. I can't use Valerie or Patsy..."

Clodagh nodded and thought it was just as well that Valerie wouldn't be involved.

"They're needed at the charity," said Lorraine. "But I can't place myself in the hands of some Washington political operative either."

"But I don't know anything about being a political aide," said Clodagh.

"And I don't know anything about being a politician," said Lorraine. "By the state of things in Washington, I'd say that puts both of us ahead of the game. Right now, I need a friend, someone I can trust more than I need some political advisor. So, what do you say, Clo?"

"I feel like I'm leaping with you into the great unknown," she said, "but at least you'll have someone there with you wherever you might land."

Lorraine smiled. "And this way, I can be full-strength Lorraine, and you can bring me out of whenever it's necessary."

"Yes, well, that will be a definite benefit," agreed Clodagh.

"And I won't have to call you my doctor or my accountant," said Lorraine. "I think the Secret Service thought I was crazy having an accountant that wasn't actually a CPA."

"I wasn't going to mention it," said Clodagh, "but they checked me out every way to Sunday and went over my house with every electronic fine-toothed comb in their gizmo bags. I guess I passed the test."

"I'm sure you did," said Lorraine, "otherwise Agent MacKay wouldn't have agreed to wait outside."

Clodagh thought a moment. "If this is going to work, you're going to have to know me."

"Of course, I know you."

"I mean, you're going to have to know me as Lorraine."

"We'll just say that you were a childhood friend of mine," said Lorraine, "and you can add that memory to my history."

Clodagh snorted. "You forget, I have three inquisitive sisters with good memories. If we place our relationship that far back, they might start putting the clues together and figure out that you're Chesney Potoski."

"Well," said Lorraine looking at her wristwatch, "we'd better figure this out and quickly. I'm due back in Washington in a few hours."

"And I suppose I am, too," sighed Clodagh.

– 28 –
The Harve de Grace Reunion

"Another coffee and another one of those iced donuts, please," he said to the waitress, as Paul Rocher approached. "And whatever he wants."

"Just coffee, black," said Rocher sitting down.

They waited until the waitress was out of earshot from their booth in the far corner of the diner.

"I hear you're heading up the security detail for our new vice president."

Rocher didn't respond.

"Decide to do one last job before you finally retire?"

Rocher looked into the eyes of the ex-CIA operative, the man known around the Agency as Rotor-Rooter. You never could tell how much a good operative knew. Searching his eyes was futile. He could hide his thoughts behind any expression he chose. That's why he had been such an effective agent and such a dangerous one. Still, Rocher couldn't show the least bit of weakness, so he pushed back in the only way he knew.

"Cut it out... Vyvyan."

For the briefest moment, he saw the corner of Roto Rooter's right eye twitch. It was a friendly warning, but a warning just the same. If Paul Rocher had wanted to be cruel, he would have used the former spy's full name: "Vyvyan R. Lily." The middle "R" stood for "Romeo." He didn't want to brawl, not at his age, not in a diner in Harve de Grace, Maryland.

Years ago, before he met Lily, Rocher heard the chatter about a CIA field agent who had garroted an informant in Thailand. That wasn't terribly remarkable in itself until he learned that the agent had done so because the other man had used the agent's full name: Vyvyan Romeo Lily.

When they finally met, Rocher was shocked at how disarmingly average the man appeared. In time, they became acquaintances. He doubted if Lily afforded himself the luxury of friends. It was only then that Rocher surmised that most of the stories about him were true.

"Don't call me that," said Lily. The waitress returned and placed their orders on the table and then left. "You know I hate it."

Rocher apologized.

"Forget it," said Roto-Rooter. He pulled out an unfiltered Camel from his pocket and then noticed the "no smoking" sign and sighed. "I shouldn't have made that crack about retirement. Hold on as long as you can."

Rocher nodded. Lily's dismissal was shrouded in secrecy.

He glanced at his unlit cigarette, then back at the sign, and stuck it back in his pocket. "I'm living in the wrong time. If I'd been born fifty years earlier..." he paused and smiled. "Damn, I would have had some fun."

"You did alright amusing yourself in this era," observed Rocher.

Lily gave a slight shrug. "It was good while it lasted. It was fun while I was doing it for the home team. But now, doing odd jobs for tin-pot dictators and half-assed regimes, it's not the same."

"I understand."

"You're a straight shooter," said Lily. "I appreciate that job you threw my way last fall. That was fun."

Rocher looked out the window at the traffic on Route 40. "That's what I wanted to update you about."

"I thought you would," said Vyvyan. "So our little creation has gone and got herself nominated to the presidential on-deck circle."

Rocher searched his compatriot's face for a clue on Lily's feelings on the subject of Lorraine Innis and her political career.

"And being the conscientious public servant that you are," Lily continued, "you've decided to stay close to our little friend for a variety of reasons. One of which being, you're covering your tracks."

"Our tracks," interjected Rocher.

Lily shrugged. "If you like, though, I never leave any tracks to cover. Or you could be doing your patriotic duty, protecting the country against someone whom we still don't really know anything about. Or, you could have the hots for her."

Rocher gagged on his coffee at the last suggestion.

"Take it easy, pal," said Lily. "I was only kidding about that last one."

"It just went down the wrong way," said Rocher wiping his mouth.

"So, you're about as close to her as anyone, at least now," said Lily. "You didn't ask me here because you're a fan of crappy diners in towns with weird names. What can you tell me?"

"You met her," said Rocher.

"You know I met her," said Lily. "I posed as her cousin's boyfriend when I slipped her my little concoction in her lemonade."

"What do you think?"

Lily rolled his eyes. "We've been over this before. I think she's a charming, intelligent woman. I think she's sure of herself, but not in an arrogant sort of way. She's confident, and more than anyone I've ever met, she knows who she is."

"True," said Rocher.

"And of course, we both know that what she firmly believes to be true is a crock of shit."

"But you don't think she knows it's a crock."

Lily's cheek bulged out as he ran his tongue inside it. "Yeah, that's the question, isn't it? No, I believe she believes it. If it were all a front, I would have cracked it."

Rocher nodded. "But yet, it is a fabrication."

"We assume it's a fabrication."

"But there's no trail, or there wasn't one until we created it."

"And now you're worried," said Lily, "because she's been nominated?"

"I'm more concerned."

"For the country?"

Rocher bowed his head. "You'll think I've gone crazy, but I'm concerned for her."

Lily just stared at him.

"Look, RR," began Rocher, "we like her. Don't say you don't like her. That's why we originally decided to back up her story based on the information you picked from her brain. Or else why would we agree to go to all that trouble of creating such thorough documentation for a girl who otherwise had no background."

A playful grin crossed Lily's lips as he knitted his fingers together and stretched his arms. "I dunno; it was good practice."

"Don't tell me you set up a person's entire past just to see if you could do it."

"Oh, I knew I could do it," said Lily. "I never doubted that. It was still the sport of it. Here was the opportunity to create an entire history of a forty-year-old woman from thin air, knowing that it would be picked over and scrutinized by the media and others." His grin widened.

"Others?" said Paul Rocher. "You mean the government. The whole Innis project was just your practical joke against the agency and the whole damned federal government."

"Not entirely," said Lily, "but that all added to the fun. It was more satisfying than setting fire to a bag of dog crap on the front porch of the White House."

Now it was Rocher's turn to stare. "I don't believe you sometimes."

"Yeah, well, so I have a motive. Maybe it's childish, but it's a lot more constructive than a hell of a lot of other stunts I could have pulled. What we haven't established is your motive, my friend."

Rocher shifted uncomfortably in the diner booth.

"Oh, don't worry," continued Lily, "you don't have to explain your reasons because I already know them." He pulled a sheet of paper from his pocket and unfolded it to reveal a photocopy from an old college yearbook. "Elinor I.A. Potoski."

Rocher felt his mouth go dry. He should have known. He couldn't involve Lily in this sort of operation without expecting him to root out every thread of every detail of every scrap, including Rocher's involvement.

"You see, Paul, I know you were handed the assignment by that little toe rag at the White House." Lily shrugged. "Fair enough. But when we had to decide what to do with it when we found out she was as hollow as a Halloween jack-o-lantern, I wondered what you were up to."

Rocher exhaled. "So, how long did it take you to dig this up?"

Lily shrugged. "Time is relative when you've got nothing else to do. Like I said, it's good to keep in practice. Hey, don't look so worried. It's not like I'm going to tell your wife that you like a girl young enough to be your daughter because she reminds you of an old college flame."

"Then…"

"Why bring it up?" asked Lily. "It's like Mount Everest. Because it's there. To show I could do it. To prove to no one but myself that I still got it, and I'm better than ever. Just exercise."

Paul Rocher felt the muscles in his shoulder begin to relax and then suddenly tense up again. Just exercise? Vyvyan Lily may have dug into his past as a mental exercise, but he rarely let anything go to waste. Everything he collected, physical or mental, was a potential weapon for a man who could kill with anything from a paperclip to a candy bar. Now he had a weapon in his arsenal, one he would probably never use, but one labeled: "Rocher, Paul, for use against."

"Yes, of course," said Rocher forcing a smile, "Good to keep all the professional faculties in good working order."

Lily nodded without betraying if he agreed with Rocher or if he was just storing more information. He began to reach for his cigarettes, caught himself, and took another bite of his donut instead.

"Yeah, well, now that we've cleared up all that," said Lily, "what's your problem now?"

"My problem?"

"Okay, not your problem," conceded Lily. "But if it were just a case of wanting to protect a girl who looks like some old flame, you wouldn't be dragging me out to this joint, charming though Harve de Grace is this time of the year."

Rocher looked out at the passing traffic, deciding to choose his next words carefully.

"I'm just concerned about what we did on the lady's behalf."

"Yeah, and what was that?"

Rocher looked him in the eye. "We created her."

"No, she created herself. We just gave credence to her."

"Well, without our collaborative effort on her behalf," said Rocher, "her story would have fallen apart by now. Or it would fall apart when she was vetted by the Congress."

Lily shoved the last bit of donut in his mouth and licked his fingers. "And you're worried about some base I didn't cover, some seam showing, some loose end that will unravel. Well, don't. You know me better than that. That dame's life and all its backup documentation are solid." He nodded out the window to the Susquehanna River. "That bridge over that river would fall down before you'd find a crack in Lorraine Innis. I know, I put every last rivet in her myself. So stop worrying."

"I wasn't worried about that," said Rocher.

"You're worried that someone will find out what we've done? Well, don't. It's flawless, without any fingerprints on it." He licked his sticky fingers again and then laughed. "The only way anyone would find out is if we told them, and..."

Paul Rocher hoped he hadn't betrayed a thought. But then, he was sitting across from an expert at reading the tiniest scraps of intelligence.

"Who?" said Vyvyan Lily. His voice had dropped an octave.

"Who what?"

"Who did you tell?"

Rocher started to feign innocence but knew it was pointless.

"I told the president."

"Ottinger?"

"No, Merton," confessed Rocher. "I told him just a few minutes just before he was assassinated."

Lily relaxed. "Well, that's okay then. Even if that dolt wrote it down on a piece of paper, there was little chance of that surviving the explosion that got him. Clean job there. From what I've heard on the inside channels, that crazy old lady acted alone. At least you don't have to worry about Merton spilling the beans."

Rocher almost mentioned that Davis Flemming was also present. Fortunately, Lily was looking in his coffee cup, so there was no chance of Rocher betraying another thought.

Rocher forced himself to laugh. "Actually, President Merton told me to forget it. He said he didn't care. So he wouldn't have talked."

"And now he can't," said Lily. "Serendipitous, don't you think?"

Rocher cringed. "I don't know if I'd call an assassination by a deranged woman 'serendipitous.'"

"Yes, well," said Lilt, "I suppose it doesn't make your branch look very good. Still, the loony old bat didn't get through on your watch, did she? And like they say, it's an ill wind that doesn't blow somebody a bit of good."

"How did Merton's death do us any good?"

Lily looked at his friend incredulously as if he were missing the obvious. "I'd say she did both of us a favor," he said, twirling an unlit cigarette between his fingers. "She saved me the bother of killing a sitting president, and she saved you feeling guilty that you made that action necessary."

– 29 –
Confessions to a Tiny Head

He locked the office door, opened the secret panel on his desk, removed the device, and inserted the earplug in his right ear.

"Let's hope our little toy begins to provide some amusement, Grigori," he muttered to himself.

There was a shrill whistle in his ear. Teplov yanked out the earphone, jiggled his pinkie in his earhole, and then returned the device to his ear.

So far, the bug in Nikolai Kropotkin's birthday present had yielded precious little information. It wouldn't have mattered if that Lorraine Innis Pez dispenser had just been cheap plastic, but the gold plating had increased Teplov's investment considerably.

Had he overestimated Kropotkin's fascination with the woman? He had hoped the golden candy dispenser would become a lucky talisman in Kropotkin's pocket. Teplov envisioned the dispenser going around the globe with Kropotkin, relaying inside information that he could use against his rival. Instead, the object was relegated to Kropotkin's desk, where its effectiveness was limited.

Teplov hadn't heard anything useful yet. He despaired of ever hearing anything that would justify the hi-tech knickknack's expense.

Today seemed no different. Teplov only heard routine meetings with aides. Kropotkin snapped at his underlings, just like the old Kropotkin, the mercenary politician who bested Teplov throughout their careers. Teplov preferred the kinder Kropotkin that had bloomed after he met the Innis woman. For months Teplov formed plans based on this softer Kropotkin. He liked a distracted rival, one who would not see the fatal blow coming. But now, Kropotkin was acting like his old imperious, dangerous self.

Teplov heard Kropotkin dismiss the last assistant from his office. He began to remove the earpiece when suddenly the reception grew louder.

He guessed that Kropotkin was sliding open the Pez dispenser for some candy.

Teplov cringed at the sound of his rival's salivary glands sucking on a mouthful of candy. He wondered how this slob become Russia's ruler over a more cultured person, such as himself?

"Ah, my dear Lorruska," Kropotkin sighed. Kropotkin was speaking directly into the gold-plated figure. Teplov held his breath.

"Lorruska," began Kropotkin, and then repeated the name several times, each with more melancholy and regret.

"My heart aches for you, my dear Lorruska. Are we to be two ships that pass, not in the night, but in full view of each other? Seeing, but never touching? Expressing desire but never consummating that passion?"

Teplov's eyes widened. He had known Kropotkin's admiration for the American woman. She, after all, was his inspiration for his naïve peace plan. But he'd never heard Kropotkin use words such as "passion" and "consummating."

"I thought, at last, you would be mine, my dearest one," continued Kropotkin, "but then fate intervened. I cannot blame Ottinger for selecting you to be his second in command. More than anything, I wanted you for my own helpmate. But now it is not to be. You will make a wonderful leader for your country, Lorruska. There is no other woman in the world like you. If only…"

Teplov sat with his jaw agape, nodding his head as if to coax the next thought out of Kropotkin's mouth. There was dead silence for at least thirty agonizing seconds. Teplov wondered if the transmitter had stopped working, then…"

"If only you were free, Lorruska. I would endure any sacrifice to make you mine."

Teplov whipped the earphone out triumphantly. It was worth the wait. It was worth a dozen gold candy dispensers. This was something with which he could work.

It was time to make some calls.

– 30 –
The Horns of Nonnia and the Horns of a Dilemma

Julius Rosen entered the study. Robert Valvano was waiting for him. "This could get messy," said Robert.

"I take it," said Rosen unpacking his briefcase, "you're referring to the appropriation of Mrs. Innis by the federal government."

"Don't we give the government enough scratch without them reaching in and grabbing my employees?"

"Actually," said Rosen looking over the top of his reading glasses. "Thanks to prudent… management, the family interests pays very little in the way of taxes… all legally, of course."

"Yeah, and whatever we save, they get twice that back in what it costs for all their f**kin' regulations," said Robert.

Rosen raised his hands. "That's the cost of diversifying into the most heavily regulated industry in the county."

"Yeah, I know, I know," said Valvano examining the cuffs of his silk shirt. "Being legal's a bitch."

"Whatcha your mouth," said a voice from the door. They looked up to see Nonnia Valvano, standing in the doorway. "Have respect in your grandmother's 'ouse."

Rosen, deferring to the real power in the family, escorted the old woman to an easy chair.

"Thank you, Julie," she said, "you're a good boy…"

Rosen grimaced. The old lady's compliments to him always ended on a raise in pitch, indicating that there were words unspoken. He imagined the end to her praise was "…for a 'merican," or, "…for a Jew."

"Now, what's this all about," said the old woman, "I hope you're… wait… I want a drink."

Rosen pushed a button on his phone, and within moments Alphonse appeared.

"Al…"

"The usual, *Signora?*" said the hulking assistant.

"*Grazi*, Alphonse," said Nonnia, "You're a good Italian boy."

A moment later, he returned with a small cordial glass containing a shot of Sambuca. Nonnia thanked him, and Al began to leave.

"*Ashpet*, Alphonso," she said, raising a bony index finger, "you got a word for today?"

"Yes, ma'am," said Al toeing the floor like a grade school boy being quizzed. "Today's word is 'Incorrigible.'"

The old woman nodded her head in appreciation, enjoying it in the same way she savored her liqueur. "*Molto bello.*"

A huge grin broke out over Alphonse's face.

"What's it mean?" challenged Robert.

The grin slid off his face. "Uh, mean?"

"Yeah, 'incorrigible,'" said Robert, "what's it mean?"

Nonnia scowled at her grandson. "Who cares? He's doing good. That's a big word. He learned to say it. He can learn what it means later."

Robert snorted.

"You think everyone knows all the big words they use?" she said.

"It means…. uh… it's bad," said Alphonse.

"It means not being able to be corrected or improved," said Rosen.

"See, and that's bad," said Nonnia. "Thank you, Alphonse."

Alphonse exited, closing the door behind him.

"You're so smart," said Nonnia scolding Robert. "He's only trying to make himself better."

"That makes him real corrigible," said Robert.

The old woman waved her hand impatiently.

"What are you boys talking about?" she asked. Then inserted what she thought they should be talking about. "What about Michael?"

"What about Michael?" asked Robert testily.

"I see it this way," said Nonnia, pausing to take a sip of Sambuca. "Michael's getting married."

"Has he finally asked the girl?"

"Michael's getting married," she repeated. "And his wife's…"

"Future wife," interjected Rosen, as a legal disclaimer.

Nonnia sneered at him. "The girl he's going to marry, she's the cousin of this other girl, the nice Italian girl who's going to be president."

"Nominated for vice president," corrected Rosen.

Again the old woman grimaced as if that too were just a technicality.

"Hey, this Ammacapane girl is going places," she assured them.

"Her name is Innis," said Robert.

"And her maiden name is Ammacapane," said Nonnia, "and that's what really counts. You can call a *cazatte* a *calzone*, but it still comes out of a horse's ass."

"So, what?" Robert sneered. "You're relying on Lorraine Innis becoming president so Michael and his girlfriend can have a White House wedding?"

The old woman laughed, though, at her age, it wasn't unkind to call it a cackle. "Who cares where he gets married? Don't you get the bigger picture? Our Michael gets married to this girl. This girl has a cousin who becomes president. We have an in-law in the White 'Ouse."

They just stared at her.

"You mean you didn't figure that out," said Nonnia. "I know you can be a *stunade*, Robert. But this one," she pointed at Julius, "he's one smart Jew lawyer."

"Actually, Mrs. Valvano," said Julius, "what we were discussing…"

"Nonnia, I'm not some *gavone* off the street," interrupted Robert vehemently. "You've done okay by me. I took what you gave me and built it up. And we're legitimate and legal…"

"Mostly," muttered Rosen.

"So don't think we don't see possibilities and opportunities," he continued. "Oh, yeah, you imagine yourself sitting in the White House as some honored guest. Yeah, but you don't see the potholes and the ditches between here and there. Pete Liverot got invited to the White House, and look what happened to him. He went there in one piece but came out in an even dozen."

"Liverot was a *stunade*," said Nonnia.

"Yeah, maybe he was," said Robert, "but don't forget who was his ticket into the White House: Lorraine Innis. We gotta be careful, so we don't wind up like Liverot."

"*Il corna!*" screeched the old woman.

Robert rolled his eyes. "How can this one go from an intelligent, sane woman to a friggin' superstitious whack job just like that?" He snapped his fingers.

"Don't mess with *Il corna*, the horns," said Nonnia, raising her index fingers and pinkies on both hands.

Robert scoffed.

Nonnia leaned forward and slapped his face. "You think it's superstitious. You no think there no bad luck? You so smart that you think that's something just for the old country. That in America they got computers, and microwave ovens, and automatic bowling alleys, but they got no luck? Let me tell you, Mr. *Sophisticato*, the horns go everywhere. They don't need no plane or boat. They go where they want, and when they're on a person… *Il corna! Il corna!*"

"Maybe it was Liverot who wore the horns," said Robert.

The old woman shook her head while continuing to make the hex sign. She walked to the door and extended a bony finger towards them. "You do what you have to do," she said, "just remember to get the horns before they get you."

With that, she exited, closing the door behind her.

Julius Rosen and Robert looked at the door. Robert shook his head.

"Looney Tunes," said Robert, but then paused. "You don't think there's anything to that, do you?"

"I've got four walls full of case law in my office," said Rosen, "and I've yet to find legal precedence for someone wearing the horns."

"Not that, I mean about Lorraine Innis being president someday."

"Which goes to the point I was about to discuss when we were sidetracked by your dear grandmother," said Rosen. "You stated that the federal government was stealing your employee. Technically that's not true. You also wouldn't want to make that claim to the wrong person, and by the wrong person, I mean anyone outside of this room. I, more than anyone, am cognizant of the ties that bind Lorraine Innis to your organization. After all, I fashioned them by your direction. I doubt that even Mrs. Innis herself is aware of the closeness of your, shall we say, your sponsorship. That is all by design and meticulous execution."

"I know, I know," said Robert impatiently.

"Just a little legal disclaimer," said Rosen.

"What's riding up my ass is what happens to that meticulous design if she becomes vice president?"

Rosen sighed. "The 'if' is hardly in doubt," he said. "Not unless something unforeseen occurred."

Robert Valvano's face brightened. He had plenty of experience in the unforeseen.

"But," continued Rosen, "to ruin Mrs. Innis politically would serve no advantage to you. A Lorraine Innis that could not become vice president would be less than useless to you, especially in her current capacity. Bringing down Lorraine Innis would destroy the charity she is unwittingly fronting on your behalf. The demise of that could be traced back to you by a scandal-frenzied media and bring down your organization. Though your relationship is indirect by design, her almost saintly popularity has been good for your business in ways legitimate and otherwise."

Robert twisted his face in contemplation. "Okay, so what do we do?"

"We do nothing. At least in regards to Mrs. Innis."

"For how long?"

"For as long as her political career continues," said Rosen. "That could be anywhere between two and ten years."

"That long, huh?"

"Or until she is no longer an asset to the organization, and then...."

Robert Valvano nodded his head. "Don't worry, Julie. I may not have any experience with vice presidents. But I know what to do with an asset that's outlived her usefulness.

– 31 –
The Vile Rendezvous and the Vital Vial

Is there anything else I can get you, Miss Fierro?"

Valerie forced a smile and shook her head. The hostess in the VIP lounge at Heathrow Airport excused herself.

Valerie couldn't wait to get out of England. She was fed up with their crumby food and weather. But most of all, she was tired of their accents. Their upper-crust accents were all too posh and polite, while the lower-class ones were too grubby and common. She longed for a conversation with someone who talked normally, like her.

Most of all, she missed Michael. She wanted him. Oh, yes, she told herself, she had wanted him before, but now it wasn't just physical. She wanted to be with him even outside of the bedroom. She yearned to hold his hand, to caress his hair, to feel his rough five o'clock shadow upon her soft cheek, and then complain to about it while savoring the sensation.

But, before the heaven of Michael, she'd have to endure the purgatory of Albrecht Eckner. She would have to suffer the indignity of taking his phony audit and submitting it as her own. Worse than that, she anticipated Albrecht asking about her negotiations with Lord Bagnall. The agreements would go through the Gibraltar office. Eckner would probably learn of her private arrangement with Bagnall. She didn't know how he would find out, but Albrecht had a way of discovering things she'd rather he not know. Valerie caressed the silk scarf around her neck. She conceded that at least she had gotten some shopping in on this otherwise annoying trip. It was just a few more days until...

"Miss Valerie!"

She was jolted from her musing by the last voice on earth she wanted to hear. Valerie lowered her head and hoped it wasn't there.

"Miss Valerie," said the voice, "tis me!"

She raised her head slightly. In front of her was a pair of cowboy boots. One trouser leg was tucked into its boot, while the other leg hung over

163

it. She slowly raised her head further. The legs were skinny and slightly bowed, though one bowed in and the other bowed out. There couldn't be another pair like that in the world, at least not one belonging to someone who called her...

"Miss Valerie!"

She looked up all the way.

"Purvis Twankey," she muttered.

"Aye, it's me, an' all!"

"What are you doing here?"

"Everybody's got to be someplace," he said, looking around.

"I mean, what are you doing in Heathrow Airport."

She almost asked who would let him into the VIP lounge, but then she remembered that he was probably more famous than she was.

"Oh, aye," he said, sitting down next to her, "I'm going to visit me Mum." He sat silently for a moment, then added. "She lives up in Morecambe."

"Well, I didn't think she lived in Heathrow Airport," said Valerie dryly.

"Oh, no," said Purvis, "I'm waiting here for connecting flight. They don't have direct flights to there."

"To where?"

"To where I'm going," said Purvis.

"I'm surprised you're able to get there at all," said Valerie sarcastically.

Purvis shook his head. "You didn't use to be able to."

There was another uncomfortable pause as Valerie fingered the ends of her scarf, and Purvis tugged at the lapels of his bright blue suit.

"I'm glad I run into you, Miss Valerie."

Valerie sighed. Mere friendship would have been bad enough, but Purvis Twankey fostered that into unrequited love and then built that into a singing career.

"Yes, well," said Valerie rubbing her arm, "you seem to be at the impact point of many accidents."

"T'warn't an accident," he said. "It's more like, whatcha call it..."

"Fate? Kismet?" ventured Valerie.

"No, I was just going t' say it warn't accident, but just something that happened to happen."

Valerie flipped her hand into the air in resignation.

"But I'm tickled I saw you here," he said.

Valerie gritted her teeth. "So you could tell me how incredibly in love with me you are. So I could inspire another one of your inane songs and then make another basketful of money. So you could swear your undying devotion to lucky me. Is that why you're tickled?"

Purvis sat quietly for a moment. "Uh, no, ma'am. I just wanted to say I was right sorry for any embarrassment I may have caused you. I didn't mean no harm. And I didn't know you had a boyfriend, and I think Mr. Mike is a right champion fella. And I wanted to wish you all the best luck, an' all."

"Oh," she said, "well, uh, forget about it, I guess…"

Valerie felt her cheeks glow. For a moment, she was embarrassed for her outburst. She quickly got over it and replaced it with fresh animosity for Purvis Twankey. He was just a jerk. If she allowed him free reign, Purvis Twankey would keep inflicting embarrassments upon her. She was about to tell him so but paused. She was deciding between telling him to get sucked into the nearest jet engine or dying a slow death by being force-fed airline meals. Before she could speak, however, Purvis broke the silence.

"Did you hear about Miss Lorraine?" he said.

Valerie exhaled. "Of course."

"I don't just mean in general. I mean about them givin' her a government job, an' all."

"Yes, Purvis, I heard about that… an' all." She thought she was getting quite good at mocking these Brits with their silly accents.

"Sure messed me up," said Purvis.

"You and me both," said Valerie thinking about the way Lord Bagnall had put one over on her. "Wait, how did that mess you up?"

Purvis grinned. "Oh, sorry, I shouldn'ta said it like that. That was selfish of me. No, I think Miss Lorraine would make a right proper vice president. 'Eck, I almost wish I was a Yank so's I could vote for her, an' all. It's just now we won't be able to market me invention."

"What invention?"

He looked around and pulled a small padded envelope from his pocket.

"This," he said, and pulled a piece of paper and a small tube from the envelope. In the tube was a clear amber liquid.

He held it a few inches from Valerie's eyes.

"What is it?"

"That," he whispered, "is what makes Miss Lorraine, Miss Lorraine."

"It looks more like something Miss Lorraine made," said Valerie backing away from the bottle.

"Just get a whiff…" said Purvis removing the top of the vial.

"Eww, no, I don't want…" Valerie protested as he waved it under her nose. Then she stopped. It was actually a subtle, pleasant smell.

Purvis Twankey noted the change in her expression and nodded. "It's champion, isn't it?"

"Not bad," said Valerie. "It's sort of nice."

"And that's Miss Lorraine," noted Purvis putting the stopper back on the vial.

"Are you telling me that Lorraine made this?"

"Aye, well, no, that is, she did, but I did. That is, it was me own idea, based on her."

"Based on Lorraine's idea," said Valerie.

"No, the idea was mine," said Purvis, "but the, uh…"

"Inspiration?"

"More like perspiration," said Purvis with a toothy grin. "This is really the essence of Miss Lorraine. It's like based on her geriatric code."

"Do you mean genetic?"

"Aye, that's what I mean," he said. "It's based on what makes Miss Lorraine, Miss Lorraine. I got the idea from a potato crisp, uh, that is chip."

Valerie stared at him, trying to figure out the connection between Lorraine and a potato chip.

"I thought about what makes Miss Lorraine unique among women," he continued, "and how she could share it with other women."

Valerie knew what made Lorraine unique, and she better not share it, or her next problem might be a paternity suit.

"You see, it all goes down to what are called fairy moans," he said.

Valerie thought a moment. "You don't mean pheromones, do you?"

Purvis smiled. "Aye, that's what I said, fairy moans. Have you heard of them?"

"Of course!" She'd been reading Cosmo since she was ten.

He proudly raised the small vial once more before returning it to his pocket. "Well, that's them."

"What's them?"

Purvis leaned forward and whispered. "That perfume contains the essence of Miss Lorraine. We had Miss Lorraine's geriatrics analyzed right down to 'er DNA. Now any woman who wears the perfume, well, she'd be a little bit like Miss Lorraine."

Valerie's mouth dropped open. The idiot had done it again. It was like that blind squirrel not only finding an acorn but then using it to build a jet, fly to Las Vegas and win a million dollars at the crap tables. She doubted whether the concept of replicating Lorraine's pheromones into a perfume was plausible. That wasn't where the genius lay. It was the marketing angle. Half the women in the world would pay to spray raw sewage on themselves if they thought it would make them a little bit more like Lorraine Innis.

"Does Michael know about this?" she asked.

"Mr. Valvano? Sure, it t'war him what gave me the go-ahead. But, it's too bad," sighed Purvis Twankey.

"Too bad? What's too bad?"

"Can't sell it now," he said.

"What? Why not? It smells okay," she said. "It smells very nice. It's lovely. I'd wear it... almost."

Purvis shook his head. "Only we can't sell it, not now, not with Miss Lorraine going to be vice president. Mr. Mike said we shouldn't market any new products, least not in the States. Too bad, after I got the recipe here, an' all." He waved a piece of paper.

Lord Bagnall leaped into Valerie's mind. He had no qualms about using Lorraine Innis' likeness to sell his cheap products in Great Britain. The fact that she was going to be vice president only enhanced her appeal to him.

She glanced down at the paper in Purvis' hands and began to reach for it. Suddenly, he looked up, and she turned her grasp for the paper into a soft caress of his arm.

"Miss Valerie?"

"You must be terribly disappointed, Purvis," she cooed.

"Uh, I, uh, aye, I am, an' all."

"It must be frustrating to have such a good idea go unfulfilled, an idea that would bring so much personal gratification to so many women."

"Do ya really think so?"

"Of course," said Valerie, "when Lorraine and I go around and speak to all those women, I can see it in their eyes... the inspiration that she gives them. And I can almost hear them think: 'if I could be just a little bit like Lorraine, how much happier I would be.'"

She held his arm for another moment and then looked at the paper in his hands and feigned surprise. "Oh? What's that?" she squeaked.

Purvis sighed. "That's the chemical formula for the perfume." He began to fold it up. "I guess it'll just have to wait."

"I guess so," she said glumly before suddenly brightening. "Hey, wait! We can't sell it in the United States, but there are other countries in the world," said Valerie.

Slowly, Purvis' expression brightened. "Hey, I think you're right." Purvis looked around and then slapped himself on the forehead. "In fact, this is one of those other countries."

"Oh, Purvis," she squealed, "how clever of you. I've been here negotiating British contracts for Lorraine's wonderful charity. We could give them your formula and produce it in Great Britain."

Before Purvis could reply, Valerie snatched the paper with the formula from his hands.

"Oh, and you'd better give me that sample, too," she said.

Valerie unfolded the formula. It was all chemical symbols and gobbledegook, except at the top.

"What's this," she said, pointing to the header of the page.

"Oh, that's what it's got to be called," explained Purvis. "Miss Lorraine named it herself."

Valerie shrugged her shoulders, re-folded the paper, and stuck it in her purse. An idea like this would smell like money under any name, lots and lots of money.

She stood up and started toward the exit.

"Where are you going, Miss Valerie?" said Purvis running behind her. "Aren't you taking a flight?"

"I'm taking a cab," she said, not stopping to explain. She was going straight back to London for round two with a certain Lordship, and this time she held all the inside information.

– 32 –
The Subduing of the Dangerous Patsy Einfalt

It seemed as if there were almost as many well-wishers as there were bits of confetti now stuck in Lorraine Innis's hair. She had walked into the conference room, expecting her final board meeting with the charity. Instead, she was met by the Cross of Lorraine's staff. One person was noticeably absent.

"I thought Valerie was going to be here," said Lorraine to Mike Valvano.

"She was delayed in London a few days and then had to go back to Gibraltar," explained Mike.

"Yes, of course," said Lorraine. "I haven't seen her in weeks. I miss her very much."

"I'm sure she misses you, too," smiled Mike.

"Oh, did she say that?"

"Uh, no, not in so many words," said Mike.

Lorraine nodded. "I also thought she would be here to deliver her audit report," said Lorraine. "I'm anxious to read it."

Mike Valvano made a vague reply, and then, as if to change the subject, latched onto the person at Lorraine's side.

"Hi, I'm Mike Valvano," he said, extending his hand.

"I'm sorry, where are my manners," said Lorraine. "Mike, this is my Chief of Staff, Clodagh Clott. Clodagh…"

Suddenly Lorraine felt a pair of arms reach around her from behind.

"Oh, Lorraine, I'm going to… OWW! Hey, you're hurting me."

Lorraine turned around to see Patsy Einfalt restrained by the Secret Service.

"Stop, that's just Patsy," cried Lorraine.

"She grabbed you from behind," said Agent Hambright.

"She was just hugging me," said Lorraine putting her arm around Patsy.

"Sorry it sounded threatening," said Hambright. "She said, 'I'm going to…' like 'I'm going to get you,' or I'm going to 'kill you.'"

"It was: 'I'm going to miss you,'" said Patsy.

Lorraine gently rearranged Patsy's bangs and then turned to Hambright. "Does this look like a face that could hurt anyone?"

Agent Margie MacKay made a subtle gesture to Lorraine miming the explosive chest of Eugenia Bupp just a few months before. "We don't view anyone as benign," she whispered.

"Oh, yes, sorry, Margie," said Lorraine, "I mean, Agent MacKay." She turned to Mike and Patsy. "This is… oh, wait, no, they don't want to be known."

"How exciting! They must be SECRET SERVICE," Patsy squealed. " Wow, I've never been mistaken for a dangerous person before. Wait until I tell my parents! I'm going to miss you so much, Lorraine, when you go… Hey, I remember you!"

"Yes, I'm Clodagh Clott."

"Right, Ms. Clott," said Patsy, "you're the woman who came to see Lorraine that time…"

"Yes, yes, that's right," said Clodagh cutting her off.

Clodagh glanced nervously at Lorraine and smiled. Lorraine smiled back. She didn't recall Clodagh coming to see her, at least not any place where she would have met Patsy.

"It's fine," Clodagh whispered in Lorraine's ear.

"Yes, I'm sure it is," said Lorraine. And for some reason, it was.

Later, in private, Clodagh said the two words that returned Lorraine to full cognizance.

"Thanks," said Lorraine, with a deep exhale.

"Are you all right," asked Clodagh.

"Yes, I was a little confused for a moment back there," said Lorraine. "I forgot that you'd met Patsy."

"I'd forgotten that I'd met her as well," said Clodagh. "She doesn't know why we met."

"No, but she does know that you signed a confidentiality agreement. Patsy doesn't forget much, but fortunately, she is easily distracted." Lorraine paused for a moment. "I was hoping Valerie would be there with that audit. I thought that everything would be wrapped up today, so…"

"So you would find out why Martina went to Chicago?" Suggested Clodagh.

"Yes, and so I could stop being Lorraine. Of course, that's ridiculous. I'm stuck here now for as long as I have to be vice president "

"The confirmation hearings start in a few weeks," said Clodagh. "You could throw the game; start babbling at your hearing. Say that you would uphold the Constitution and follow the dictates of our Martian overlords."

"I could never do that to Lorraine," said Lorraine. "People look up to her; they rely on her. If she started going loopy, it would be like…"

"Finding out Mother Theresa was an ax-murderer? Discovering Santa Claus not only ate the cookies left for him, but also the family pets?"

"Those are fitting analogies," said Lorraine. "My public image is as saintly as Mother Theresa but as imaginary as St. Nick."

"I only wish the world could see that Chesney Potoski is every bit as fine a person as Lorraine Innis, and for my money, even better."

"Yes, well, thank you," said Lorraine, "but at the moment, we don't have time to form a Chesney Potts Appreciation Society. At least I've wrapped up my work with the charity."

"And you're comfortable with Valerie running it?"

"Why wouldn't I be?" asked Lorraine, but her question was met with a vacant silence. "Valerie's the natural choice," continued Lorraine, "and I trust her like, well, like you trust your sisters."

Clodagh snorted.

"You know what I mean," said Lorraine. "And I'm sure your sisters are very proud of you."

"They're more amazed than proud. None of them can figure out how I suddenly became the chief of staff to the next vice president."

"You don't think they've figured out who I really am, do you?"

Clodagh waved her hand. "Not at all. Ches, if I couldn't see it, and your own mother didn't recognize you, there's very little chance of anyone else figuring it out. Now we've just got to get you ready for your confirmation hearing."

"Right," said Lorraine, "I'm officially suspended from the charity. There will be no new endorsements, though the current ones will be honored. And there will be no new Lorraine Innis products. I heard Purvis Twankey was a little upset that his perfume wouldn't be marketed, but that's probably a good thing."

"That was an interesting idea, but I don't see how you could approve it."

"I didn't approve it," said Lorraine, "she did. As Chesney, I wouldn't have given it the go-ahead, but I didn't know there was a Chesney when Lorraine approved it. Still, it's a good thing that the world will be spared a Lorraine Innis perfume."

– 33 –
A Kippered Peer

"A Lorraine Innis perfume?"

"That's wot I said."

Verity Goodhue repeated the question.

"'Ave you got cloth ears," snapped Lord Bagnall, "I'll be the exclusive worldwide manufacturer and distributor of the damned stuff!"

Verity stared at her father. Despite the news of a potential goldmine, he seemed annoyed.

"Congratulations," she said quietly.

"Thank you," he said, "but it's a damned annoyance!"

"I suppose Lorraine Innis is to blame for that," said Verity.

"Lorraine Inn… no, no, no, not at t'all, not no 'ow," he said as he paced the room. "No, it's h'ain't 'er, it's 'er blasted cousin."

"Miss Fierro?"

"The very same!" he snapped. "That Fierro woman has kippered me like a…a…"

"A kipper?"

"Spot on!" he said.

"I find that hard to believe, Father," said Verity.

"You finds it 'ard to believe? 'Ow does you think I feels? To think that some little whelk of a girl, a Yank, an Eye-tie Yank, could put it over on me."

"But I thought you already negotiated with Miss Fierro and to your advantage."

"And so I 'ad," said Bagnall, "I worked out a nice little earner, for me…"

"Of course."

"And Miss Fierro got 'er cut," Lord Bagnall gestured as if he were sliding something at knee level.

"You mean Miss Fierro got something under the table? Is that in the endorsement contracts?"

He pulled at the end of his mustache. "Let's just say it was a little side clause, on a separate agreement. It's what the legal boffins call a cod icicle."

"You mean a codicil?"

Lord Bagnall shrugged. "You tell me, you're the one 'oose been to university. It don't matter what you call it, she got 'ers."

"On the side."

"On the side, a la carte, it don't matter," said Bagnall. "The upshot is she got 'ers."

"If I recall, Father," said Verity, "she signed that agreement before she knew that Lorraine Innis was nominated for vice president."

"That's 'er tough luck," he said. "That don't mean that she can come back and 'old me up over a barrel of..."

"Perfume?"

"I bet she 'ad that all the time," he said, resuming his pacing. "She probably 'ad that perfume formula in her 'andbag all the time."

"Do you really think that Valerie Fierro is craftier than you, Father?"

Lord Bagnall's face underwent a series of convulsions as he pondered that question. Whatever his reply, he would come out on the short end of the proposition. Finally, he just threw up his hand, poured himself a stiff drink, and sat down.

"Wot does it matter? I ask you, wot's the difference? It don't not make no difference, no 'ow. Whether she planned it that way or whether it just fell into 'er lap."

"You didn't have to accept Miss Fierro's proposal on the perfume."

Bagnall choked on his drink. "Wot? Verity, your old dad may be the chump of the week for being backed into a corner on that deal, but let me tells you a thing or two. I'd 'ave been the chump of the century for passing it up! Me competition would 'ave jumped at the chance to sell that stuff. They'd 'ave paid 'er for the h'opportunity. No, I've been done on this deal like wot I've never been done before, but it's better than not being done. Yes, that's the way I've got to think on it. 'Alf a loaf is better than, no loaf, and even the 'eel end of the bread is better than nothing, which is wot all me competitors is left with when we start selling *Quandary*."

Verity did a double-take. "Did you say '*Quandary*?'"

Lord Bagnall gave her a concerned look. "You 'as got to 'ave your 'earin' checked, me girl. You keeps h'askin' me to repeat meself. Yes, I said '*Quandary*.'" He pulled out a piece of paper and handed it to Verity.

She took it and wondered what word he had mangled now. But when she unfolded the paper, she read aloud: "*Lorraine Innis' Quandary*." She looked up at her father.

"Wot? You're lookin' at me as if I goes around naming perfume. You knows I don't name nothing no more. Remember 'Happy Crappies'?"

Verity nodded. Fortunately, that toilet tissue hadn't gotten past the test marketing stage. She was also grateful that her mother named her, overriding her father's choice of the name "Leticia Mafawny."

"But *Quandary*," said Verity, "that means a predicament."

Lord Bagnall shrugged. "I don't care wot it means other than it means moola." He rubbed his thumb and forefinger together.

"Apparently," muttered Verity, "but why would they name it '*Quandry*?'"

"Again, I repeats meself: 'oo cares?"

Obviously not her father, she thought. As long as he could turn a profit on an item, Lord Bagnall didn't care under what name it was sold. But Verity couldn't help but wonder if this were some cry for help from Chesney.

"Oh, Chesney," she thought and then realized she had spoken aloud.

"Wot? Chesney?" said Lord Bagnall, turning around. It was an odd reaction unless he knew that Chesney Potts was still alive, which of course he did.

"Sorry, Father," said Verity, "I was just thinking about him."

"Thinking about? Oh, yes, well, I, uh, I suppose you're apt to do that from time to time, thinking about 'im. But, of course, 'e's not 'ere, cause, uh, 'e's dead."

Verity took a sharp intake of breath. "Yes, Father, I know."

"Wot? Oh, yes, of course, you knows that," he fumbled. "I just mean, well, you know, the way you said that just now, I almost thought you'd seen some sort of ghostly h'appropriation."

"No, I was just thinking about him."

"Oh, good, I mean, of course, you'll always feel for the lad," he said, then quickly added, "as will I, e's a... that is, 'e was a fine fellow."

"I know you loved him, too, Father. Didn't you?"

Lord Bagnall forced a grin. "Love 'im? Me emotions for the dearly departed go much deeper than that."

"I know, Father," she said, patting his hand. "If only he were with us now. He could be such a big help to you in your business."

Lord Bagnall's grin became more sincere. "Oh, my dear Verity, no disrespect to the dearly departed, but when you've got Lorraine Innis, you don't needs nobody else."

– 34 –
An Evening for Declarations

"Do you have anything to declare?"

Valerie Fierro stared at the customs agent. "How long have you got?"

He looked down at her customs form and then back at Valerie.

"Sorry," she said, "nothing."

Valerie had a long list of declarations. She'd start with England and Gibraltar. England had good shops but a crappy climate, while Gibraltar had warm sun, but all those stupid apes. And both England and Gibraltar had their resident chimps: Lord Bagnall and Albrecht Eckner. If nothing else, Valerie would declare she was glad to be away from both of those baboons.

At least she had gotten the better of Bagnall. She congratulated herself on that perfume deal. Even with just a paltry cut of the profits, the old chiseler would make millions from *Lorraine Innis' Quandry*. Maybe he'd make enough so his dull daughter would go out and get herself a makeover. Never mind, thought Valerie. The girl's fashion challenges were her problem. Yes, Valerie was glad to be rid of that dysfunctional little family.

Valerie only wished she could get rid of Albrecht Eckner. She didn't appreciate Albrecht's veiled threat about letting Michael know about that procedure she'd had. The little creep! Albrecht Eckner would get his someday, and if there was any justice in the world, Valerie would be in on the revenge.

As she arrived at the baggage claim area, she saw a smartly dressed limo driver holding a sign with her name on it. Valerie had expected Michael to meet her, but just before leaving London, she was informed he was called away to an important meeting. What, she thought, could be more important than meeting her at the airport after being away for weeks?

"Miss Fierro?" asked the limo driver.

She handed him her baggage checks and told her there were five suitcases. He tipped his cap and went off to fetch her luggage.

At least the driver was well mannered and appropriately dressed. If Patsy had arranged it, you never could tell. Still, she hadn't seen the car yet. Knowing Patsy, the vehicle could be a Yugo.

The driver returned with her luggage, then escorted her through the automatic doors. She waited at the curbside while he retrieved the car. Less than a minute later, the driver returned behind the wheel of a limousine, and not just a limousine, but a Rolls Royce.

The driver jumped out and came around to open the door for Valerie. It was evening, and the limo had heavily tinted windows. She couldn't see the interior. Once the chauffeur closed the door behind her, she couldn't see at all. That was when she felt a pair of hands grab her shoulders and pull her forward.

"Hey, what's going..."

Before she could complete her question, Valerie found a pair of lips pressing against hers. Valerie struggled for a moment before yielding to her assailant. A moment later, she yielded further, allowing his tongue access to her mouth. At that point, though she had suspected it from the first, she knew who it was, and she surrendered her entire body to his touch.

Only after the Rolls Royce glided away from the terminal did he come up for air.

"Oh, Michael," she panted in his ear.

"*Cara mia*," he whispered in reply as he buried his nose in her hair. "You don't know how I've missed you."

She only purred in response. She understood why cats purred. A well-placed purr could say so much. It could mean "me too," or "I'm enjoying myself," or "I'm having too much pleasure to bother talking about it." Right now, all three applied. It worked. He kissed her again, this time even more passionately.

After several more sensual episodes, Valerie came up for air and looked out the window.

"Michael, we're going the wrong way."

"No, we're not."

"But we're going towards Philly..."

He enclosed her in another embrace. He didn't release her until the car came to a stop on a city street. Valerie recognized the area immediately. Her heart began to beat faster, but she didn't dare betray her thoughts in case she was mistaken.

"Where are we?" she asked, though she knew damned well.

He smiled at her. "Haven't you ever been here before? This is Jeweler's Row?"

"Jeweler's Row?" She repeated, playing dumb. She looked around at the numerous jewelry stores set around the intersection and then back at Michael. She opened her eyes wide and tried to look mystified. "But…"

"What are we doing here?" He said. "I thought this would be the best place to pick out a ring."

"A ring?" The anticipation was beginning to strain her ability to play dumb.

"An engagement ring," he repeated. Michael took both of her hands in his and looked into her eyes. "Valerie, will you marry me?"

– 35 –
The Amorous Curriculum Vitae of Purvis Twankey

W hat's wrong, lad?"

Purvis Twankey looked up from his plate. His mother was standing over him. She was a little grayer, her wrinkles a bit deeper, but the love that shone from her eyes was as true as ever.

"Wrong, Mum? Nowt, nowt a'tall."

Mrs. Twankey wiped her hands on her apron and then sat down at the kitchen table across from her only child.

"I suppose it's being a fancy singing star that has changed my boy."

"Changed? Me? How'dya mean?"

"I'm sure that now you're top o' the pops you go to all types of fancy do's where they serve fish eggs and cheese from a squirt can, and all that sort of thing."

"Mum?"

"Well, what else would have made you lose your taste for all your favorites? You've been home three whole days now, and you've hardly touched any of it: black pudding, tripe, hotpot, an' all. You've gone all fancy, 'ave ye."

Purvis looked down at his plate and, to his surprise, found that his mother was right. He had hardly touched his supper. He poked at the toad in the hole with his fork and sighed.

"You've gone all Yankee, lad."

He looked at his mother and then down at his western-style suit with the Naugahyde trim. He shook his head. "I know must look all flash to you, Mum," said Purvis, "but that's not it."

Mrs. Twankey studied him. A frown deepened across her features. Then, like the sun emerging from behind a cloud, her face brightened into a beaming smile. She jumped from her seat and ran around the table.

"Oh, my lad's in love," she said and buried his head in her bosom.

He tried to respond but was prevented by the mass of mother engulfing his face.

"Oh, I must have been blind not to see it right from the start," she said as she rocked his head back and forth.

"Mum, Mum," he said when finally released from the maternal tilt-a-whirl, "there's nowt to be so happy 'bout."

A serious look crossed Mrs. Twankey's brow. "'ow coom?"

Purvis beckoned his mother to sit down.

"Mum, our Mum," said Purvis, "there's nothing would give me greater happiness than to tell you I'd met a nice lass and was aiming to settle down."

"And have grandchildren," she interrupted.

"Aye, kids an' all," he said. "But it's not going to happen."

He cast his eyes downward.

Mrs. Twankey followed his gaze. "You've not hurt yourself, Purvis," she said, nodding towards his groin, "down there? Like your Uncle Normy?"

Purvis scratched his head and then caught her inference. "What? Aye, I mean, no... oh, no. No, Mum, I'm fine down there."

His mother breathed a sigh of relief. "Then that's okay, then. So you're all set."

"Aye, all set," he said forlornly, "all except for the lass."

"You've nowt got the girl?"

"That's the problem, Mum," he said. "I've fallen in love, but..."

"The girl won't have you?" Motherly indignation began to rise in the voice of Mrs. Twankey at the notion that any girl would reject her boy. "Why she's not good enough for you, lad!"

"If that t'was all," said Purvis.

"Oh, my," said Mrs. Twankey rising, "I'd better put the kettle on."

Purvis agreed that his was a tale so woeful that a good strong brew was essential.

"It started with Miss Lorraine," he said.

"Her that's famous?"

"Aye, you knew that I knew her, Mum," he said. "That's what me first song was all 'bout. Miss Lorraine is champion, Mum. I fell for her the first moment I saw her, right before she punched me..." He felt his face go red. "That is, I liked her from the start. Well, almost from the start. The first time I saw her, it was but a minute. I got me first good look at her in hospital."

"What was she doing in hospital?"

"Uh, that was my fault," he said, looking down. Then he recalled that first meeting, and a smile burst upon his face. "Oh, but she was wonderful. That first time there in the hospital was like magic, it was."

"But then she punched you?"

"Well, yes, but only on the jaw," he said, "and then I was only knocked cold a minute."

"Purvis, what did you do that a woman would feel the need to punch you on the jaw?"

"Nowt, Mum," he pleaded, "Miss Lorraine was mad because I hit her cousin's car. That's why we were in hospital. We were both only visiting."

"Oh."

"I fell in love with her the moment she put me on the floor, and I loved her even more the second time."

"Purvis, she punched you again?"

Purvis frowned. "No, mum, the second time she kicked me…" He felt his face redden. "Well, she kicked me someplace."

Mrs. Twankey nodded her head. Before she was a mother, she was a girl. She knew all about girls' knees and which parts of boys' anatomies they sometimes were forced to assault.

"Joost like Uncle Normy," noted Mrs. Twankey. "And you say you loved this girl?"

"Aye, Mum."

"Daft lump!"

"It was magic, Mum," he said dreamily. "Then the three of us went out to dinner."

"Three?"

"Aye, Miss Lorraine, and Miss Patsy, and me."

"Who's this Miss Patsy, when she's at home?"

"She's a friend of Miss Lorraine," he said. "She helps out Miss Lorraine. She's a big help to me an' all. She was there when we had dinner, the three of us. And then we went to the hotel."

"Hotel? Purvis, I raised you to be a good lad. I didn't raise you to brawl in hospitals or to go to hotels for, for…"

"For what, Mum?"

"Well, I'm not going to say it, but the French call it a menagerie trio. Imagine, a son of mine taking two women into a hotel."

"We didn't go inside, Mum." Purvis scratched his head. "We waited outside with the crowd. You must have read about it in the paper. That's the night Miss Lorraine saved the Russian fella."

"Oh, yes, of course," she said, "you were there."

"Yes, me and Miss Lorraine and Miss Patsy." Purvis paused for a dreamy interlude. "That night, I thought I'd met me dream, Mum. But the next morning, I found out she was married."

"She told you that?"

"No, I saw it on telly in hospital."

"So you were sick?"

"No, Mum, I was visiting Miss Valerie…"

"Who's that?"

He grinned broadly and shook his head sadly. "Oh, Miss Valerie is even more wonderful than Miss Lorraine."

"Really? Where did she kick you?"

"No, Mum, Miss Valerie was in the hospital from the accident. I saw her there lying all passed out an' all, and I fell right on the spot."

"Lot of falling going on for it being a hospital," said Mrs. Twankey.

"Oh, don't tease me, our Mum," said Purvis. "Miss Valerie is the girl what I wrote the song about, and then the album. I remember the first time I sang the song…"

"To this Valerie…"

"No, Mum, to Miss Patsy," he said.

"You sang one girl's song to another girl? And what did this Miss Patsy say when you sang her another girl's song?"

Purvis scratched his head again. He wasn't sure who was more confused: him or his mother. "Miss Patsy said nowt. She just put her foot through her telly screen."

Mrs. Twankey shook her head. "Your father, rest his soul, used to put a pillow over his head when you sang. Thank goodness he left telly screen alone."

"No, our Mum, it was an accident," said Purvis. "Miss Patsy likes me singing. She tells me that all time. Miss Patsy says she likes me singing, and the way I invent things, and the way I eat. Miss Patsy's always making me things to eat. Oh, not like you make, Mum. Miss Patsy can't do trotters like you can, Mum. Still, she likes to cook for me."

"See Miss Patsy a lot, do you?"

"Aye, well, she likes to listen. She's a good listener, is Miss Patsy."

"Listens to your singing, does she?"

"Aye, and not just me singing," he added. "Miss Patsy listens to me ideas, an' all. She's a champion good listener, she is."

"And this Valerie, the one you wrote songs about?"

Purvis' shoulders drooped. "Miss Valerie? Not so much. I feel a right mug for doing that song and album, an' all."

"But that was number one hit."

"Aye, everyone liked it 'cept the one I wanted to like it, the one I done it all for."

Mrs. Twankey rose and put her arms around her son. "Don't worry, lad. Maybe this other one will come 'round."

"No, Mum, she's got another fella, and he's a right nice fella, an' all."

"Seems like you like almost everybody a lot, Purvis," she said, "'cept for…" The tea kettle began to whistle.

"'Cept for who, our Mum?"

"You're a bright lad; you'll figure it out," she said and then turned to make the tea. With her back turned, he couldn't be entirely certain, but he thought he heard her add: "Eventually."

– 36 –
The Phantom Encounter of Mr. Moore

I appreciate your accompanying me on this errand, Gao," said Verity Goodhue as the lorry navigated a back road through Lincolnshire.

"It is I who must express appreciation," replied Li Gao. "You have secured for me this lucrative assignment."

Verity grimaced. "I'm only sorry that it isn't more lucrative. I know my father doesn't pay the most generous rates."

"It is not only by monetary means that we are remunerated."

Verity smiled. "I confess that I'm being rather selfish. I enjoy the time I can spend with you. You're the only person to whom I can bare my soul. You're the only one who knows that my beloved is alive, aside from my father and his butler, but of course, I can't discuss Chesney with them."

"I would think that most unwise," he agreed.

"It's wonderful to share this time with you, even if we go miles without mentioning his name," she said. "It's just nice to think of him in the present tense. When I'm with Father, I have to think of him in the past tense, so I don't slip and divulge that I know the truth."

"It is an irony, is it not," said Gao. "While your father plays out the charade that Chesney is dead, his company is producing a fragrance based on the living person." He gestured towards the rear of the truck.

"*Lorraine Innis' Quandary*," said Verity, as she opened the promotional brochure and read: "'Now every woman can be a little more like Lorraine herself. *Lorraine Innis' Quandary* is formulated using a scientific breakthrough that draws on the essence of Lorraine herself. Ladies, now you can be a heroine in your own right.'"

"Quite liberal in the use of hyperbole," noted Gao.

Verity removed the cap from a sample bottle and took a sniff. "Actually, the fragrance is quite light. I'd almost say that father has reached his dream of peddling water for twenty-five pounds an ounce."

"Having not purchased perfume, I would think that price rather high."

Verity held up the bottle to the sunlight and examined the amber liquid. "That's the introductory price for the marketing test. That also why we're going to Lincolnshire. Father likes to test market new products here. He values the opinions of the regular people in Lincoln, Boston, Louth, Sleaford, and Skegness, especially Skegness. That's where my parents spent their honeymoon."

The usually stoic Li Gao grimaced over the romantic allure of Skegness.

After dropping off the displays and the supplies for a series of stores in Boston, they started for Skegness.

"I've taken a wrong turning," announced Li Gao after several miles. "Forgive me, I'm not familiar with this area. It appears we will have a slight detour."

"I don't mind taking the scenic route," said Verity. "These smaller towns are often quite charming. 'Fishtoft,'" she read from a sign on the edge of the village there were entering.

As they drove down the high street, a familiar face caught Verity's eye.

"Look," she exclaimed, "it's Grandfather! There! In that shop window!"

Li Gao stopped the lorry. Indeed, in the window of a small shop was a film poster of Hugh Goode. Above the window was the sign: "Yesterday Once Moore – Antiques and Memorabilia."

"Would you care to investigate?" asked Gao.

Verity looked at her wristwatch. "We're due in Skegness by two. But…"

"But you are the leader of the project," said Li Gao. "I'm sure your father wouldn't mind."

Verity laughed. "Actually, he probably would, which is all the more reason to have a look."

Li Gao smiled and told her to run along while he parked the truck. Like a schoolgirl released from lessons, Verity clambered out of the lorry and scurried across the street. She stopped to admire the poster, which was from the South American themed comedy *Hugh'll Rumba It*. Verity hadn't seen the film itself since she watched it on video with Chesney. She would buy the poster as a present for her beloved as a welcome back gift.

The door over the bell announced her with a merry tinkle as Verity entered the shop. There was a welcoming mustiness about the small shop, which was filled with memorabilia from bygone days.

A voice spoke from behind the counter. "Hello, hello, I'm down here. Just got the latest old copies of *Film Fun*. You might like these. Tommy Trinder's on the cover."

The man stood and faced Verity and immediately went white as a sheet. Verity's mouth dropped open and returned the man's stare. After several seconds she was the first to regain the power of speech.

"Mr. Postlewaite!" she exclaimed, for it was indeed Mr. Postlewaite. And though several years had intervened, it was the same man, wearing, it would appear the same familiar shirt, tie, and sweater.

Postlewaite looked around nervously. "P-Postlewaite? Postle… Postlewhat? No, never heard of Postlewaite. My name is Moore. It says so on the sign. Yesterday Once Moore. That's me, the Moore, not Yesterday, and not… what did you say…Pistolwhip? Ridiculous, what a silly name!"

"But it is you, Mr. Postlewaite," she said as she approached him, her arms outstretched. "I've been in your London shop dozens of times."

"No, it's not me," he said, cowering from her advance. "And don't you touch me. You're not you, either, you're just… just… a ghost, or something like that; a septic, I mean a specter! You know, because you are one!"

"But I'm real, Mr. Postlewaite." Verity patted her arms as a testament to her corporeal nature. "See, Mr. Postlewaite?"

"I don't see anything, Mr. Postlewaite, because I'm not me, and you're just not here either. Ha, I don't even know why I'm talking to you. I should have a sign out front: 'No Shoes, No Physical Body, No Service!'" He glanced around at his stock and moaned. "It was sure to happen sooner or later. All these ancient things; it was only a matter of time before some apparition came to claim a piece of it. I'm surprised it hadn't happened back in my London shop."

"There," cried Verity, "that proves it, you are Mr. Postlewaite, and you did have a shop just like this in London."

"It doesn't prove a thing," he said. "For one thing, my London shop was a little larger, and I had different stock, and, and it wasn't me, so no more of your spirit tricks. If it gets back that I've broken my part of the agreement…" Postlewaite's eyes grew wide, and he clamped his palms over his mouth.

"Agreement, what…"

Before Verity could complete her question, the shop bell rang, and Li Gao entered.

"Postlewaite!" cried Gao upon seeing his old friend.

"I'm glad you're here," said Postlewaite brushing past Verity, taking care not to actually touch her, and grabbing Li Gao by the shoulders. "You tell this, this… apparition that I'm not me."

"Not you? But Postlewaite…"

"Ah, ah," said Postlewaite wagging his finger, "I'm not me, that is I'm not him. My name is, uh, it's…"

"Moore?" offered Verity.

"Moore? Oh, yes, Moore, that's him, I mean, that's me, Moore. Yesterday Once Moore, and I'm the Moore."

"If you prefer," said Gao with a sideways glance at Verity. She shrugged.

"It's not what I prefer," said Mr. Postlewaite-Moore, "I just don't want to get in trouble. I don't want to violate the agreement and lose all this." He glanced around at his shop.

"I see," said Li Gao, "yes, you have a very nice establishment here. It brings to mind a similar store once encountered in London. That's was a marvelous shop."

"It was more than a shop," agreed Verity. "It was an emporium of effluvia Britannica."

"Quite so," said Gao. "And even more precious than the contents of the store was its kindly owner; a little quirky, but a true English gentleman. How I miss that, fellow."

Li Gao stood wistfully staring into space for a moment and then raised his hands. "Oh, well, we must be moving on; we have places to go. Don't we, my dear?"

"What? Oh, yes, yes we do," said Verity.

They took a few steps toward the door.

"No, wait, don't go," he said, scurrying everywhere at once but not getting anywhere. "You must stay. You can't leave. We have some wonderful items."

"No, we don't want to take up any more of your time, Mr. Moore," said Gao. "It was a pleasure meeting you. Perhaps we'll stop in again, in a few years, or so."

"A few years?" Postlewaite stopped and looked around as if his course of action were written on the walls or the ceiling. He began to twist the end of his cardigan.

The bell on the door tinkled as Li Gao held it open for Verity.

By now, the cardigan was nearly twisted into a ball about Postlewaite's fist when he shouted: "STOP!"

They glanced back at the agitated shopkeeper.

Postlewaite gritted his teeth as if he had just stuck his toe into a hot bath. He wiggled his outstretched fingers and then waved them in opposite directions.

"Come in, close the door, close it tight. Pull down the shade. Throw the bolt. Come in, please." He whispered with the utmost urgency.

He ushered them into a cluttered back room. Postlewaite cleared off one chair, then looked at Verity before addressing Li Gao.

"Can she, uh, you know…" he squatted.

"Can she sit? Of course, the young lady can," said Gao.

Postlewaite offered the chair to Verity, taking care not to come within a foot of her while doing so. Then he cleared the edge of the desk and offered it to Li Gao. They both sat down and looked up at Postlewaite in anticipation.

He pursed his lips, ducked his head back into the shop to confirm they were alone.

"What I'm going to tell you must not leave this room," he said. "Is that understood?"

They agreed.

"It must not leave this room, by any means," he said, focusing his attention on Verity. "By any means." He then made a waving motion with his right hand.

"I wouldn't dream of it," she said.

He nodded and then said in a low voice: "I am... Postlewaite!"

Verity suppressed a giggle. Li Gao reached out and put his hand on his friend's shoulder.

"We never doubted that fact, my dear friend," said Gao.

Postlewaite seemed surprised by this admission. "Really? Even though I was acting a bit oddly?"

"Especially because of that," said Gao affectionately. "It is one of your hallmarks."

"Oh," said Postlewaite, and he sat down on a stack of old magazines. He thought for a moment. "I did tell you my name is Moore, didn't I?"

They agreed that he did so.

He shook his head in bewilderment. "Most people just leave it at that. I say: 'I'm Mr. Moore,' and they say: 'Hello, Mr. Moore,' or 'Nice to meet you, Mr. Moore.'"

"Yes," said Li Gao, "but we only know Postlewaite. Now, for an explanation."

Postlewaite perked up. "Oh, yes, that would be nice."

"I meant that you provide the explanation."

"Me?" A burst of nervous laughter escaped his lips. "What explanation do you need from me? I'm not the chap bursting into other chap's places of business with, with, well... ghosts!"

Verity's ability to control her giggles was finally breached. She laughed out loud and reached out to touch Postlewaite's arm. He recoiled.

"Dear Mr. Postlewaite," she said, "I'm not a ghost."

After several pats on the arm, he relaxed and finally, tentatively, touched her hand.

"See?" she said.

"But you died."

"You were all led to believe that," she said, stroking his cheek.

"We were all the victims of a cruel hoax," said Li Gao.

Postlewaite sat quietly for a moment, his face going through various gyrations of thought. Finally, his expression brightened.

"Then this is a happy day," he concluded.

"Most assuredly, my friend," agreed Li Gao, "especially joyous for the rediscovery of a cherished companion."

"Yes, yes," said Postlewaite, rising to his feet. He looked around the cluttered room before finally finding an old noisemaker from a long past New Year's celebration along with a few paper hats. He tooted the horn to punctuate his happiness, placed one of the hats upon his head, and then laughed.

"Oh, this is wonderful," said Postlewaite, almost skipping in the small space, "this is marvelous. This is the best news I've heard since leaving London." His expression darkened. "Oh, it's not been too bad here, you understand. I mean, she has been very kind. I wouldn't want her to know that I was complaining."

"Who?" asked Gao.

Postlewaite's secretive mantle once more descended, and again he raised his index finger to his lips as he lowered his voice.

"Her," he said, jerking his head towards the ceiling. "My landlady, Mrs. Kaczmarek. She manages the property. She has the run of the floors above the store. That's where she lives with her daughter, Josephine. She's a widow, you know. Not the daughter, the mother. She likes me."

"Josephine?" asked Verity.

"Her mother?" said Gao.

Postlewaite shook his head. "No, both of them." He dropped down on to the bundle of magazines and forlornly removed his paper hat. "They both like me. And I both like them, that is, I like both of them. I look at Josephine as a younger sister, a rather much younger sister. Either that or an older niece. I can't quite sort that out."

"And her mother?" asked Verity.

Postlewaite threw his hands up in resignation. She's not quite like a mother to me. But not quite anything else either."

"And how do they look upon you, my friend?" asked Gao.

He grimaced. "I know how both of them would like to look upon me. One would like me to be like a son-in-law, the other like a stepfather, and both a husband. I try to spend as much time down in the shop as I can. I really don't want to offend either of them. I certainly don't want it getting back to..." He jerked his head to the side.

"To whom?" asked Gao.

Postlewaite shook his head. "No, I can't afford to tell anyone that. Not even my dearest friends. Let's just say I'm a man of my word, no matter what name I happen to have. Underneath all of them I'm me, and I'm keeping my word."

"We wouldn't want you to violate any agreements," said Gao patting him on the shoulder, "even if they meant running away from your friends without a word."

Postlewaite looked up. "That wasn't included in the agreement. I was going to write. I had every intention of doing so. But, well, I lost your address. I thought I'd written it in my book, but you can see..."

He handed him a tattered address book. Li Gao opened it.

"Here it is," he said, holding out the book, "Right where it should be."

Postlewaite did a double-take as he examined the book. "No, that's not right. It should be there under the 'G's,' what's it doing in 'L's?' And it's in your handwriting."

"I wrote it there quite a few years ago when you asked me."

"Mr. Postlewaite," said Verity, "didn't you know that in China, what we call the last name is actually their first name and vice versa?"

"Oh, this is all my fault. I'm sorry," said Postlewaite.

Li Gao clapped him on the shoulder. "It is all mended now, my dear friend. We are together."

186

Postlewaite nodded and smiled. "And Chesney?"

Verity and Gao looked at each other.

"No, Mr. Postlewaite," said Verity. "Chesney doesn't know yet, about me, or about any of it."

Postlewaite's mouth dropped open. "Well then, we must go and tell him immediately. I'm sure he will be overjoyed to know."

He grabbed his coat and started for the door. Seeing that neither of them moved, he stopped. "Oh, no, he isn't, uh, passed on?"

"No, no, nothing like that," assured Verity. "My beloved is, as far as I can tell, in the best of health."

Postlewaite looked perplexed.

"My friend," began Li Gao, "have you not heard of Lorraine Innis?"

Postlewaite scratched his head. "Innis? No, oh, wait, yes. I've heard that name. Yes, Josephine is always talking about her. She says she wants to be like her. You know how young women can be, always wanting to be like the latest pop star."

"Then you've never seen Lorraine Innis?"

"Oh, I expect she'll turn up here someday." Postlewaite picked up a handful of old music magazines. "They all show up here, sooner or later. Today's Lulu and Cilla Black are tomorrow's; what did you say her name was?"

"Lorraine Innis," said Verity. "But, I don't think you understand…"

Li Gao placed his hand on her forearm. "I think our friend can wait to experience the Lorraine Innis phenomenon. We've all had quite enough information to digest for one day."

Postlewaite smiled, content in his blissful ignorance. "I've heard them all," he assured them. "I'm sure Josephine will tell me all about it if I can't avoid it. Yes, now that I think about it, she's always going on about how wonderful this girl is. Do you like her, dear?"

Verity smirked.

Li Gao stepped in. "I can safely say that at the heart of it, our Miss Goodhue likes no one better."

"I liked Dusty Springfield, myself," said Postlewaite, "back in the day…Wishing and Hoping…"

Verity rushed out the door, returning a moment later with a small box.

"Here's a sample," she said, handing the box to Postlewaite. "It's a new Lorraine Innis scent we're test marketing."

Postlewaite opened the lid of the box and sniffed. "Thank you. I don't usually wear perfume…"

"I believe it is for your friend," said Gao.

"For Josephine," Verity agreed.

Postlewaite took another sniff. "Yes, she'd probably appreciate it more than me. She could probably use it, too."

– 37 –
The Two Carat Feral Cat

If this is the office they give you for government work, you can keep it!" The voice shattered the quiet of the room like a brick hurled through the window. Clodagh Clott jumped from her desk. Though she felt as if she knew Valerie Fierro intimately from her hypnosis sessions with Chesney, it didn't prepare her for the first encounter with the genuine article.

"Valerie," cried Lorraine as she embraced her. "I missed you so much."

Valerie seemed to bask in the attention. She was the first to break the clinch, pushing Lorraine back to arm's length. She was scrutinizing Lorraine's eyes.

"What's wrong?" asked Lorraine. "Have I got something in my eye?"

"What? Oh, no, I just, well, uh, I wanted to get a good look at you." Valerie said. "Well, how have you been... Lorraine?"

"Fine."

Though she suspected the relationship was lopsided, Clodagh was surprised at how much so it was. Oh, Ches, you poor dope, she thought. Clodagh was glad that Lorraine was in full Lorraine mode, imagining that Chesney's greeting would have been akin to that of a needy puppy. She was positive that Valerie was studying Lorraine's eyes to see which incarnation she was meeting.

"You're fine? Ha, that's an understatement," said Valerie. "Or should I say 'Mr. Vice President?'"

"That's Madam Vice President," said Lorraine, "and then not until after the confirmation hearings, the Congress voting, and the swearing-in."

"Oh, yes, right," said Valerie, with a wave of her hand, "that's a done deal. I just hope you get a better office when you're official, you know, down in Washington. This little cereal box is pretty crumby, even by Wilmington standards. I mean, look at the place..."

For the first time, Valerie noticed there was another person in the room.

"...oh..." she said, her bluster diminishing in the presence of a stranger.

"Valerie, this is Clodagh Clott," said Lorraine. "Clodagh is my chief of staff. She's really marvelous. I don't know what I do without her. We've only been together a few weeks, but I feel as if I've known her all my life."

Valerie stiffened into a formal stance, arching her back and narrowing her gaze. Clodagh had seen feral cats do the same just before attacking.

"It's a pleasure to meet you," said Clodagh.

Valerie looked her up and down. Clodagh felt as if every aspect of her: her clothing, her hairstyle, and her cosmetics were being weighed, and not on a very charitable scale. Clodagh countered with her most sincere smile.

"It's lovely to meet you," said Valerie, and continued to study her before returning her attention to Lorraine.

"I've heard that you have some exciting news," beamed Lorraine.

"Hmmm?" said Valerie, apparently still distracted by the presence of Clodagh. "Oh, yes, of course," said Valerie, "you must mean this..."

She stuck out her hand, revealing a large diamond engagement ring.

"I'm so happy for you," said Lorraine.

"Yes, it's two carats," boasted Valerie.

"Yes, that's a lovely ring, too," said Lorraine.

It took Valerie a moment to realize Lorraine was happy over the engagement, not the size of the diamond. "Oh, yes, well, I didn't... that is, Michael wanted it. He helped me select it."

"It's lovely, too," agreed Lorraine.

Valerie forced a smile then turned to Clodagh. "Michael is my fiancée," she explained. "Michael Valvano. He's a bank president. I'm sure you've heard of him."

"Mrs. Innis has told me all about him," said Clodagh.

"Has she?"

"Yes, she has," said Clodagh.

Valerie smiled sweetly and looked down at Clodagh's hands. "And are you married, dear?"

Clodagh felt the blood rise to her cheeks. "No, I'm not."

"Oh, what a shame," said Valerie with mock sympathy.

Clodagh had suspected Valerie was a genuine bitch. Until this moment, however, she hadn't realized how much pure concentrated bitchiness she possessed. She would have loved to return the attitude, but Clodagh stopped herself. It wouldn't help Chesney. She forced a smile to her lips.

"It's nice to finally meet you, Miss Fierro," said Clodagh changing the subject. "Mrs. Innis is very proud of you. And now I can see why."

Valerie did a double-take.

"You must forgive me," said Lorraine. "Clodagh's right. I can't stop bragging about my cousin. Besides, Clodagh's like a member of the family now."

"How nice," said Valerie, with artificial sincerity, "perhaps we need to start calling you 'Cousin Clodagh.' And what has Lorraine been telling you, dear?"

"Nothing embarrassing," said Lorraine, oblivious to the struggle taking place before her. Lorraine hugged Valerie again. Valerie took advantage of the moment to give Clodagh the evil eye, much like firing a shot across her bow. Clodagh didn't blink. By the time the embrace ended, Valerie's face had returned to its ersatz amiability.

"I'm sorry you had to go on that wild goose chase," said Lorraine.

"The what?" asked Valerie. "Oh, you mean going to Gibraltar. Well, it wasn't a total waste of time. Did you read the report, I mean, my report?"

"I only glanced at it," said Lorraine. "After all, I've officially resigned from the charity. But I'm leaving it in capable hands."

A worried look crossed Valerie's face. Her gaze darted over to Clodagh.

"She means you," said Clodagh.

"What? Oh, yes, of course, I knew that," said Valerie. She gave Clodagh another hostile glance.

"I won't be able to raise any new money for the organization," said Lorraine, "but all the existing endorsement agreements will remain in place. There just won't be any new ones, at least not while I'm in my official capacity with the government."

"Well, don't worry, I'll take care of the shop while you're gone," she said.

"You make it sound as if I'm going away for good," said Lorraine. "After all, it's just the business end of things. We're still cousins."

"Huh? Oh, sure, right," said Valerie. She glanced over at Clodagh. "I mean, of course, we're cousins. Sorry, it's just so much is happening so quickly." She looked back at Clodagh suspiciously.

Clodagh knew Valerie felt threatened by her. Valerie was probably wondering how much Clodagh knew and how much influence she had with Lorraine.

"And I'll be at the wedding," said Lorraine. She paused as if expecting Valerie to offer her a place in the wedding party.

Valerie looked at her blankly. "Sure, you'll be at the wedding," said Valerie, "won't you? I mean, you won't be doing some vice president thing, will you?"

"I don't have a schedule yet," said Lorraine. "When is the wedding?"

"We haven't set a firm date yet. I want it to be next spring."

"Well, then, I'll be sure to keep plenty of time around it for, you know, things…"

Lorraine awkwardly waved her hands down her body, miming something like a dress fitting, like for a maid of honor, or at the very least a bridesmaid. Valerie's eyes grew wide and darted about nervously. Clodagh pursed her lips to keep from laughing out loud as Valerie's squirmed over a man hinting for a place as a bridesmaid.

"Things?" Repeated Valerie, feigning ignorance.

"Yes, wedding things," said Lorraine.

"Oh, yes, those things. There are so many things to do, so many plans, I'm sure I'll need your help, with whatever you can help with."

Lorraine smiled. "You know you can count on me."

"As your duty and schedule permits," added Clodagh. They both looked at her. "Sorry, I suppose that's the usual chief of staff's disclaimer."

Valerie brightened. "Yes, of course." She raised her wrist as if to check her watch, but without actually looking at it. "Oh, will you look at the time. I'm due..."

"At the office?" Suggested Clodagh.

Valerie gave her a sharp glance before smiling. "Yes, of course, the office, well..."

Valerie gave Lorraine a hurried air kiss and retreated from the scene. Lorraine stared at the door for several seconds after Valerie's had gone.

"She was acting rather oddly," said Lorraine. "I suppose it must be all the excitement, all the changes, getting engaged all of that. You'll like Valerie when you can see her as she really is."

Clodagh nodded, confident she had seen Valerie Fierro precisely as she was.

– 38 –
Who Pays for a Personal Clott?

Th is is an unusually small board meeting," confessed Mike Valvano.
"We could have held it in bed," said Valerie.

A squeak was heard. Valerie looked up.

"Sorry, Patsy," said Valerie, "I forgot you were here."

Patsy smiled sheepishly. "That's okay. A good secretary should be practically invisible. After all, secretary has the word 'secret' in it."

"So you tell us, repeatedly," muttered Valerie.

"Technically, this is not a formal meeting of the board," said Mike.

"Or else you'd be wearing white tie," said Valerie under her breath. She had dreamt of being on a board. It was the seat of power. Now that she was there, it was nearly as boring as being a customer service representative. Perhaps she'd have to come up with her own little slogan: "board has the word 'boring' in it." Actually, it didn't, and that was boring, too.

"I will have to check the by-laws to see how we go about adding new members to the board."

"Do we really have to?" asked Valerie.

"Of course we have to," he said. "Right now, you represent the charity, I represent the bank, and Patsy is the board secretary. Maybe we could add Purvis Twankey."

At the mention of Purvis, Patsy sighed.

"Sorry," Patsy whispered.

"As Lorraine has removed herself from the board, we'd need more board members to conduct business. Right now we probably shouldn't even vote on resolutions."

Valerie rolled her eyes. "Yeah, okay, I get it. So what do we have to vote on that we can't vote on?"

Patsy filled through her pages of board notes. "You have to vote on adding new members to the board."

"How are we supposed to vote on new members for the friggin' board if we don't have enough old board members to vote?" Snapped Valerie.

Patsy flipped through the by-laws. "The advisory board can fill positions on the regular board if there aren't enough regular board members to do so."

"Fine," said Valerie, "who's on that board."

"I, uh, well, I've been meaning to.... I'll tell you about that later," whispered Mike. Then he looked across to Patsy. "Don't put that last bit in the minutes."

Patsy crossed out the last entry.

"Then what are we having this meeting for," asked Valerie, "if we can't have a meeting?"

Mike referred to his notes. "Well, we do have to consider the future of the charity, and how it will proceed without its founder."

"Oh," exclaimed Patsy, putting her hand to her heart, "I'm sorry, that just makes it sounds like Lorraine's, you know, dead."

Valerie couldn't help but think that Lorraine was as good as dead. At least the original Lorraine, the Chesney Potts Lorraine, was dead. She preferred the new Lorraine. Still, Valerie didn't like the way that Clott chick seemed to have Lorraine's total confidence. Was she jealous of that, Valerie wondered? Did she miss being Lorraine's best friend and closest confidant? Maybe. Valerie couldn't decide. It was often a burden, but there was power behind it all. Now Lorraine was moving up the ladder and without her. Would Washington be fun? Would they have better parties? What if Lorraine became president?

Valerie felt a hand nudge her arm. She looked up.

"What?"

"I said, are you listening?" asked Michael.

"What? Of course, I am," said Valerie. "I just...what was the last thing you said?"

"I said, we're going to face a problem if the contributions drop off."

Valerie shrugged. "We've still got all the endorsement deals. Isn't that where most of the money was coming from?"

Mike ran his finger down the spreadsheet in front of him. "Yes, but there can't be any new endorsement deals when Lorraine's in public office."

"But she isn't there yet," said Valerie. "We need to go out and scoop up what we can before she actually gets sworn in. I had a pile of offers in my office before I left for England. I'm sure there have been more since then, and we could always go back and sort through the ones that were rejected."

"That wouldn't be ethical," said Mike. "I don't think it would be right to sign up new endorsements now. It's like an engaged man cheating on his fiancée just because he hadn't technically taken the vow yet. And we can't give a product Lorraine's endorsement after we know she already rejected it. You can see that, can't you?"

Valerie reluctantly agreed. He was such an honest guy. It was one of the things about him that she found both attractive and annoying.

"So, what you're saying is our cash flow is drying up," said Valerie.

A strange look crossed Michael's face. "Yeah, well," he started, "that is, the one stream of the cash flow will be drying up, eventually. But that's not my main concern. It's…"

He glanced at Patsy, who had her head down. Michael looked at Valerie and executed a series of surreptitious movements with his eyes. He had something to say that he couldn't say in front of Patsy. That would be exciting, she thought, finding out something secret. If it was a really good secret, Valerie might even tell Michael about her little arrangement with Lord Bagnall. No, he might not approve of her bonus deal.

Patsy stopped writing and referred to her list.

"That's all that's on the agenda," she announced, "except for the approval of these items for payment." Patsy presented the bills to Valerie.

Valerie looked at the first one. It was for toilet paper. She smiled to herself. If they were in England, she knew where she could get that free.

"Pen," said Valerie, holding out her hand. Patsy supplied one, and Valerie began initialing the invoices. It was tedious but still a bit of a rush. She controlled the payments of one of the biggest charities in the world.

"Okay…okay…okay…" she said, growing more bored with each approval until she reached one that nearly jumped out and bit her. "What's this? A bill from Clodagh Clott?"

"What? Oh, wait, no, that's not for the foundation," said Patsy reaching for the invoice. "That's Lorraine's, sorry…"

Valerie pulled it back.

"Clodagh Clott," said Valerie, "isn't that the woman who's working for Lorraine as her chief of staff?"

"Yes," said Patsy, "well, yes, that is, now she is, but that's from before…"

Valerie looked down at the earliest date on the invoice. It was from right after the accident when Valerie was out of the office. So Clodagh Clott was the woman Lorraine was meeting when Valerie was recuperating. This was the woman who was meeting with Lorraine when Lorraine became so… Lorraine. And now this was the same woman that Lorraine was relying on for who knows what?

"I think I smell a rat," muttered Valerie under her breath.

"Oh, no, she's very nice," said Patsy. "You'll like her once you meet her.

I've met her, thought Valerie. Her eyes narrowed.

"And besides, that's my fault," said Patsy. "I need to send that to Lorraine. She wants to pay it from her own money."

"Really," said Valerie feigning generosity, "oh, I think we can pay it."

"Oh, no," said Patsy, "Lorraine was very clear about that. She wants to pay for that herself. It was personal."

"Personal?" repeated Valerie, fishing for more information.

Patsy reached out for the invoice. "Yes, well, at least that's what Lorraine said, that it was personal."

"Did you ask what it was about?"

Patsy's mouth dropped open. "Of course not; it was personal."

Valerie glowered at Patsy for a moment, but it was like being angry at a service dog. That's how she was trained. To expect anything else from her was beyond her abilities.

Valerie thought about Lorraine and this Clott woman. Why did she care? She didn't need Lorraine any more. She had Michael. She was getting married. He had a prestigious career. He could take good care of her. And Valerie had her deal on that perfume. Beyond that, she had an additional percentage from Bagnall's paper products.

No, Valerie realized, it didn't matter what Lorraine, or Clott, or Albrecht Eckner, or any of them did. She had finally done it. She caressed the charm her father had given her. She had clawed her way to the top. She hadn't let anyone beat her. She had looked out for herself, and with her brains and her determination, she had won.

Valerie glanced at Michael. He was very sweet, and he loved her. She loved him, too, though she suspected not nearly as much. And that was okay. In fact, she thought, that was how it should be. She would be a good wife, she told herself, but at the same time, she was secure in the fact that while she wanted him, she didn't need him. She was independent. She had made it by herself. Nothing would ever change that.

– 39 –
The King of the Sewer Requests

Paul Rocher ran his hands through his thinning hair and leaned back in the chair.

"I'm getting too old for…"

He stopped and smiled. He'd been telling himself that at the end of every work day for the past twenty years.

This day had been another long one: out the door before dawn; home again long after dark. He glanced over at the photograph of his wife. What a good woman. She never complains. She practically raised their kids by herself. She was better than he deserved.

Rocher shook his head. He knew that she loved him more than he loved her. He hadn't realized it until Lorraine Innis came along. He wasn't in love with Lorraine, of course. But she reminded him so much of Elinor. He imagined that Lorraine was just the kind of daughter he and Elinor would have had. He loved his children, all boys, all good young men. Their upbringing was the result of his wife's work, not his. But still, Lorraine was the daughter he never had, with the girl who got away.

That made these long days worthwhile. Before, it was a sense of duty, but with Lorraine, it was something more.

He started to review the security protocol for Lorraine's upcoming confirmation hearings but stopped.

"Oh, what the hell," he said to himself as he rose to his feet, "this will still be here in another twelve hours. Time to call it…"

There was a knock at his door. Rocher looked at his watch and said: "Come in."

"Hello, Agent Rocher." The man slid into the room and closed the door behind him.

"Flemming?"

"May I sit down," asked Davis Flemming after he had already taken the liberty to do so.

"Yeah, sure," said Rocher looking around for something he could offer the visitor aside from the chair. He rarely had guests. Rocher picked up a half-empty cup of long-cold coffee. "Can I get you...."

"Oh, nothing, thank you," said Flemming.

"That's good," said Rocher. "I don't have anything."

"Oh, but you do," said Flemming, gesturing Rocher to sit back down.

Rocher sat down without taking his eyes off Flemming. He never felt comfortable around the man. A year ago, he was the power behind the President of the United States. If Flemming wanted something, Rocher had to comply, within the confines of the law, of course. Now Flemming was just a political operative in a city overcrowded with that species. He was a big one, admittedly, but that was like being king of the sewer rats. Still, you didn't turn your back on a sewer rat.

"Lorraine Innis," Rocher said.

Flemming smiled and nodded. "I always liked you. I admire all the men and women of the Secret Service, and your brother agencies, the FBI, the CIA, and others. But you've always stood out from the pack in my mind."

Rocher smirked. "So I'm right," said Rocher.

"About what?"

"Our only point of contact is Lorraine Innis. You first came to me to investigate her."

Flemming shook his head. "Investigate is such a pejorative term. Sounds like she was doing something illegal, which of course, we know she wasn't. I never thought she was. Let's just say it was a fact-finding assignment."

"Look, I don't care how you want to gift wrap it. You wanted to find out anything you could about Lorraine Innis, and I did."

"With your collaborator..."

"...Yeah, sure, but now you're out of the loop, and Mrs. Innis is now a big part of that loop. And I'm the person in charge of her security detail. If there's any reason why you're here, it's Lorraine Innis."

Flemming grinned a loathsome grin. Paul Rocher guessed that his intentions were less than honorable. Hell, every intention Davis Flemming ever formed probably fell into that category. It was Rocher's assignment to protect Lorraine Innis from physical threats. Unfortunately, the menace across the desk was not a physical threat. He wished he could deliver appropriate force right now to counter whatever was fomenting in the mind of Flemming, but they only issued him a gun. Flemming's weapons had the potential for greater harm.

"You recall," said Flemming, "the briefing you gave President Merton on Mrs. Innis."

"I'm hardly likely to forget it," said Rocher, "or anything that happened that day. A few minutes after that, the crazy old lady blew him up."

Flemming nodded. "Yes, that was horrible. I might have been standing near him when the bomb went off. In some ways, I thank you for my deliverance."

"Me?"

"Yes, you gave that report on Mrs. Innis."

"The one that President Merton wanted to be destroyed."

"Yes, that's the one," said Flemming.

"So you..."

"I was attending to the report when the incident occurred," said Flemming.

"It was his last order," said Rocher. "You could say it was his dying wish."

Flemming glanced off into the corner as if he hadn't heard Rocher. Then, he looked back and spoke as if he were introducing an entirely new subject.

"I always thought it a crime to destroy documents."

"You didn't destroy that report then?" asked Rocher.

"I very nearly did," said Flemming, "but then I recalled your words."

"My words?"

"Your justification, your reason for creating the supporting documentation for Lorraine Innis' life story; remember? You said that you and your collaborator thought she would be of greater value to the government intact."

Rocher stared at him. It hadn't been his idea to create the documents to support Lorraine's backstory. He wondered what Flemming's concept of "greater value" was. For that matter, he wasn't quite sure what Lily's interpretation was either.

"So," continued Flemming, "you were quite right. Mrs. Innis is of greater value."

"Now that she's going to be vice president," said Rocher.

"By the way, did she tell you that was my idea," said Flemming. "I recommended her to President Ottinger."

"Really?"

"Of course, I'm on her side," said Flemming with such a surplus of sincerity that Rocher didn't believe him for a moment.

"Then you've destroyed that report on her."

Flemming's feigned sincerity now morphed into ersatz concern.

"Yes, that is, I will," said Flemming. "But as I explained, I don't like to destroy documents, at least not without the permission of the author."

"Good, then destroy it."

"Oh, I would, but I need the permission of both authors."

There it was. Flemming wanted the identity of Vyvyan Lily.

"So you want me to get it from him in writing, is that it?" Rocher didn't think it was.

"I'd rather meet the person," said Flemming. "In fact, I insist on it."

"You insist?" laughed Rocher. "I might remind you that you have no authority any longer."

"Very true," agreed Flemming, "but I do have that report. I don't need to tell you that could mean a messy scandal. Of course, scandal isn't an occupational hazard in my business. It's a standard contingency. We plan for it, just like other businesses order paperclips. But for someone who is a lifelong government employee, especially one approaching his well-deserved pension, a scandal…"

He stopped there as if he had completed the thought. It was much worse for Rocher to fill in the blank, which, no doubt, is why Flemming did it that way.

"It's not that easy," said Rocher. "I can't just give you his name or his number. We're talking about someone with black ops background."

"I understand," said Flemming, "and I expected as much. After all, it was a professional, even masterful job. But I'm sure you can arrange a meeting."

Rocher looked at him. "Yeah, okay, give me a day or two. Will that be okay?"

Flemming smiled. "That will be perfect. And, of course, you don't want to mention any of this to Mrs. Innis. She has enough on her plate."

"No, of course," said Rocher.

"And you won't have to be there," said Flemming.

"No, I won't," said Rocher. A meeting between Flemming and Lily? It would be interesting, to say the least. It was also the last place Paul Rocher ever wanted to be.

– 40 –
A Disappointing Appraisal of Antique Baked Goods

I never thought I'd say this," she said, "but it's good to be back in Fishtoft."

Li Gao helped Verity out of the lorry with one hand while balancing a box in his other hand.

"It is an interesting locale," agreed Gao looking around, "that our dear Postlewaite has found himself. I hope he will be at home."

"I told him we were coming," said Verity as they neared the door to the shop, "though I didn't tell him why."

Li Gao nodded. "He is as reliable as the weather, and I say that kindly. In nearly forty years of experience, I am no surer of predicting the movements of dear Postlewaite as the meteorological office is of the chance of rain in the next forty-eight hours. Under the current conditions, I would venture a seventy percent probability of Postlewaite today."

Moments later, the odds proved favorable.

"My friends, my friends," cried Postlewaite as the tinkle of the shop bell announced their arrival. "Come in, come in, this is a wonderful surprise."

"But I told you we were coming," said Verity.

A puzzled look crossed Postlewaite's face. "You did?"

"Yes."

"But surely you said you were coming on Friday."

"This is Friday," said Gao.

Postlewaite thought a moment and then brightened. "Well, that explains it. I didn't think it was Friday. So then I am surprised, but not by you, but by Friday!"

"And we have another surprise," said Verity lifting the lid of the box Li Gao was holding. "Happy Birthday."

"Happy birthday," said Postlewaite reading the iced message. He shook his head. "It's all wrong."

"But…"

Mr. Postlewaite looked to the left and the right and then whispered. "It's not my birthday. That is, yes, it is my birthday, but it's not my birthday."

Verity looked confused.

"Apparently, it is Postlewaite's birthday," Gao explained to Verity in a low voice, "but not the birthday of Mr. Moore."

"Exactly," said Postlewaite.

"But why would Mr. Moore have a different birthday from Mr. Postlewaite," asked Verity.

"Who wouldn't want two birthdays," said Postlewaite taking the cake box and setting it on the counter. "Let's just close the lid. I wouldn't want anyone asking embarrassing questions."

Then, as if on cue, a pair of footsteps clambered down the back staircase. Postlewaite flurried around at the sound. There was a knock on the door. Before he could answer it, the door swung open, and a small woman with a sizeable determined look imposed herself into the room.

"Mr. Moore," began the woman, "I was wondering…" She stopped when she saw Gao and Verity and eyed them suspiciously. "Oh, forgive me. I didn't know you had company."

"Mrs. Kaczmarck," said Postlewaite looking like a criminal might during a police raid, "I, uh, no, these aren't company. Well, not quite…."

"Then customers," said Mrs. Kaczmarck.

"No, they're, wait, yes, that's it, they're customers," said Postlewaite. "In fact, I don't even know that they're customers. At the moment, they're just complete strangers. They could be customers. Are you a customer, Miss Goodhue?"

Mrs. Kaczmarck's right eye shot up with suspicion. Her left eye squinted in an accusatory fashion. "I thought you said they were strangers."

"Of course I did," fumbled Postlewaite. "In fact, I'm certain of it. Isn't that right, Gao?"

Li Gao shut his eyes and shook his head.

"Awfully familiar with strangers," said the landlady, crossing her arms across her bosom, which was a testament to the length of those limbs.

"We introduced ourselves when we first came in," said Verity.

"What's that?" said Mrs. Kaczmarck, nodding towards the cake box.

"What's what?" said Postlewaite, first trying to ignore the item. After two seconds, he saw this too was a futile ploy. "Oh, this is a box."

"I can see it's a box," she said, "what's in it?"

"In it?" said Postlewaite innocently, as if this were the first box in history not to be empty. He looked first at Verity and then at Gao. "I suppose they brought it in. In fact, yes, I can truthfully say that they brought it in. Wait, let me recall." He closed his eyes, put his index finger to his temple for a moment, and then opened them again. "Oh, yes, I remember precisely. Miss Goodhue, that's this one here. She brought it in."

"Oh?"

"Yes, I...I imagine she wants to sell it. In fact, why else would she bring it in here? She probably wants me to give an appraisal of its worth."

Mrs. Kaczmarck flipped back the lid of the box to reveal the cake. She cast a jaundiced eye at her lodger.

"Well, Mr. Moore?"

"Hmm, yes, oh, yes," said Postlewaite moving back and forth around the cake and then bobbing in and out at it. "Oh, yes, well, I'd say... hmm...yes, it's a.... a cake?"

Verity nodded, trying to be supportive. Mrs. Kaczmarck exhaled.

"I thought so," continued Postlewaite, "and, hmm, one has to be careful not to jump to conclusions, but upon closer examination, I'd venture to say... a birthday cake? Is it a birthday cake, Miss?"

Verity agreed that it was indeed. Mrs. Kaczmarck rolled her eyes.

"Ah, yes," said Postlewaite confirming his expertise at evaluating baked goods. "Now, then, this is only half of the riddle. Once you identify an item, the next step is to establish its authenticity of the item and then its date."

"It's a birthday cake," said the landlady with exasperation, "and from the looks of it, I would guess it's fairly fresh."

"Hmm, yes... from the last ten or twenty years..."

"From the last ten or twenty hours," said Mrs. Kaczmarck. "Who's birthday is it?"

"Well, it certainly isn't mine," said Postlewaite. "We celebrated that in December..."

"November," corrected Mrs. K.

"Oh, yes, November, that's Moore's, I mean, my birthday." Postlewaite threw up his hands. "Well, that's settled. And I must bow to the expertise of my dear landlady. What a pity, I was hoping this might have been a birthday cake belonging to someone famous, like Norman Wisdom, or perhaps even Will Hay. Still, with such a late dating on it, I must concur with dear Mrs. Kaczmarck. It's probably an ordinary cake, and consequently would not be of much interest to a collector. Sorry." He flipped the box closed and raised his hands in apology.

Mrs. Kaczmarck shook her head as if her boarder had scaled new heights of idiocy.

"Thank you for your help, Mrs. Kaczmarck," said Postlewaite. "I suspect I'll see you later on, at dinner."

"I didn't come down here to watch you rate cakes, Mr. Moore," she said with steely determination. "It's Josephine."

"Josephine, you remember, that's Mrs. Kaczmarck's daughter," said Postlewaite to Gao and Verity. "Oh, wait, no, you don't know her. I mean, I couldn't have told you about her since we just met and have only barely exchanged names. Isn't that correct?"

"Oh, yes, Mr., um, Moore," said Verity.

Mrs. Kaczmarck cast a mean eye at Verity before returning to her boarder. "I don't know what nonsense you're up to now, Mr. Moore, but I've come down about Josephine."

"I haven't seen her for several days," said Postlewaite.

"And with good reason! My Josephine is a sensitive girl. She has..." Mrs. Kaczmarck came up short. She stood there gumming her lower lip while the rest of her face grimaced.

"Perhaps we should leave," offered Li Gao as he gently guided Verity towards the door.

"No, don't go, Li, uh, I mean, stranger," said Postlewaite.

"I think that might be best," said Mrs. Kaczmarck.

"You can't leave," said Postlewaite, his disappointment nearly childlike. "You haven't even cut my cake, that is, your cake, I mean, this cake..."

"We'll be back soon, I'm sure," said Verity trying to sound like a first-time customer. "You have such a charming shop, Mr. Moore."

Postlewaite looked back and forth between his mobile friends and his stationary landlady. Before he could say anything to either, the shop's back door flew open with a bang and a moan.

"Mummy," cried the voice.

The intruder froze in place once seeing others present. The person was mostly female. That is, their clothes tended towards the feminine. Likewise, the person's hair was cut and styled in a woman's style. Neither was the person's height nor their build overly generous with clues. Verity would have concluded the person was a woman, save for a short but thick beard and mustache. As beard's went, it was lush and on its way to being positively luxurious.

"Josephine," snapped Mrs. Kaczmarck, resolving the mystery, "I told you to wait upstairs. Do you want the whole world to see..." She mimed the rest of her sentence with several strokes of her chin.

For her part, Josephine Kaczmarck looked at Gao, then Verity, and finally Postlewaite. It was upon meeting Postlewaite's eyes that her own burst into tears, and she fled as quickly as she had entered.

There followed the pounding of footsteps up the stairs, and then a slamming of a door.

"That wasn't Josephine," said Postlewaite pointing at the doorway, his mouth agape.

"Of course it was," snapped Mrs. Kaczmarck.

"No, Josephine doesn't have a beard," he argued.

"She does now," asserted her mother.

Postlewaite stared at the door for a moment and then shook his head. "She wasn't exactly fetching before," he said out of the corner of his mouth, "but now..."

"She didn't do that on purpose, you idiot," barked Mrs. Kaczmarck.

"Then it was accidental?" said Postlewaite.

"Of course, it was accidental!"

Postlewaite ruminated on this for a moment before asking: "What caused it?"

Mrs. Kaczmarck threw up her hands. "How should I know? Maybe she was frightened by an Armenian!"

Postlewaite, missing the sarcasm, nodded. "Yes, well, the Armenians are a fairly hirsute people..."

"Excuse me, dear lady," said Gao, "I know we are mere patrons of this shop, but may I ask if your daughter has changed her routines at all."

"Routines? How?" asked Mrs. Kaczmarck.

"It could be any number of things," he continued. "A new brand of soap, an unusual food, an unfamiliar detergent, any number of consumer products could trigger a reaction. Admittedly, this seems a rather extreme case. Still, I have read of rare instances such the one your lovely daughter is now suffering under."

One could almost see Mrs. Kaczmarck ticking off a list of household products in her mind. After a minute, she shook her head. "No, she's used the same shampoo since she was a girl, and we've used the same detergent and such for even longer."

A thought came to Verity, and she let out a sharp gasp.

"What's your problem, dearie," said Mrs. Kaczmarck looking at her. I doubt it's contagious." She then stroked her own chin. "Least I hope it's not."

Li Gao signaled to Verity that he was nearing the same conclusion.

"A veritable conundrum," said Gao with a bow. "Best of luck to you and your lovely daughter."

Mrs. Kaczmarck rolled her eyes and started for the door, muttering as she went. "Lovely daughter! She keeps it up, and she'll be more like a pretty son!"

Only after the landlady had gone back upstairs and the door closed behind her did Verity dare speak.

"Gao, do you think?" she said.

He nodded. "I fear so."

Postlewaite looked back and forth between them. "Think what? Fear what?"

"Postlewaite," said Gao, "do you recall the last time we were here? We gave you a gift for Miss Kaczmarck?"

Postlewaite thought carefully and then nodded his head: "no."

Verity grabbed his forearm. "Mr. Postlewaite, I'm afraid Josephine's condition is my fault. We gave you the sample of *Lorraine Innis' Quandry*."

"Oh?"

"But it was tested, repeatedly," said Verity. "Hundreds of women tried it, and they sprayed it on white mice, but none of them grew beards."

Li Gao nodded. "Perhaps it's just coincidence; perhaps there is another explanation."

"I don't know what to do," said Verity. "Father prepared a nationwide advertising campaign for the stuff. It's scheduled to go on sale all across the country in a few days."

Postlewaite laughed. They looked at him. "Sorry," said Postlewaite, "it's just that's an awfully odd name for perfume: *Quandry*."

"I only hope *Lorraine Innis' Quandry* isn't Josephine Kaczmarck's as well," said Verity.

– 41 –
The Pigeon More Valuable Than Two Sparrows

D o you want to go over the questions again?"
Lorraine stared blankly at Clodagh as they sat in Lorraine's living room.

"Are you paying attention, Lorraine? Ches!"

"Sorry, Clo, were you talking to me?"

Clodagh sighed. "Do you want to go back into Lorraine world for this?"

"Do you know they wanted to build a theme park based on me in Japan? I suppose they would have called it 'Lorraine World.' I turned them down. I wouldn't recommend Lorraine world to anyone. No, I don't want to go into Lorraine mode. I need to be there some time, but I suppose it's like a job. I need my downtime to, a little time for Chesney Potts to come up for air."

Clodagh looked at Lorraine for a moment and parted her lips to speak. Lorraine raised her hand.

"Don't say it," said Lorraine. "I know, I know. I'm talking about both sides of myself as if I was neither. I know you warned me. You were right. I was wrong."

"Then give it up," said Clodagh. "Turn down the appointment. They'll get someone else to be vice president. It's not like the job needs a brain surgeon or a rocket scientist."

Lorraine shook her head. "That would be quitting; quitting on the President and his confidence in me. More importantly, that would be quitting on what I set out to do. To bring the person responsible for Martina's death to justice."

"But you thought you did that already," argued Clodagh, "and you were wrong."

"Chesney was wrong," said Lorraine, "but Lorraine found out that he was wrong. I can't give up, Clo, not until I finish what I set out to do.

Otherwise, it's all been pointless. I'll just have to deal with the unexpected as best as I can."

Clodagh shook her head. "The unexpected? After all that happened, I'd say it's a little more than the unexpected, Chesney!"

Lorraine looked over her shoulder. "Quiet with that 'Chesney,' will you?" She said in a whisper. "Margie, that is, Agent MacKay's outside! Forget my other name, will you?"

"Well, one of us needs to remember it, Lorraine!"

There was a knock on the door.

"Mrs. Innis?" said Agent MacKay sticking her head inside.

"Margie, Agent MacKay," said Lorraine. She self-consciously fumbled with her hands. She had never met the woman before outside of her trance. "What can I do for you?"

"I hate to interrupt you, but the chief wanted to see you," said MacKay, "he said it was urgent."

"Of course," said Lorraine. "Yes, I'll see him right away."

Margie smiled and backed out the door.

"He probably just wants to go over the schedule before we go down to Washington," reasoned Lorraine.

Clodagh agreed, adding: "Still, I'd better put you back under. I noticed you were a little wobbly there with Agent MacKay."

"Right," said Lorraine lying back on the sofa, "he probably won't be here for at least five minutes. So, let's get me…"

Before she could complete the sentence, another rap was heard, and Paul Rocher entered.

"Mrs. Innis, sorry for the intrusion, but…" He stopped. "I'm sorry, were you lying down? Agent MacKay didn't say you were resting."

Lorraine sat up. "No, no, I wasn't. I just didn't think… that is, when she said you wanted to see me, and I said 'okay,' I just didn't think you were right outside the door."

Paul Rocher smiled. "I just didn't want to interrupt you. I've never been in charge of guarding a lady before. Oh, hell, that sounds old-fashioned or sexist, or something, doesn't it? Sorry. I just didn't want a man barging in on you, so…"

"I understand," said Lorraine. "And I don't think common courtesy is old-fashioned."

"Thank you," said Rocher, "but I needed to talk to you about something. I've been thinking about it for a few days now, and I hate to bother you with it. However, I think you should know about it, especially before you start your confirmation hearing."

Lorraine looked at Clodagh, hoping for some sort of guidance. Clodagh just shrugged her shoulders.

"Well, certainly," said Lorraine with a nervous smile. "I mean, if I can't confer with my security chief and my chief of staff, then what's the point of it all. Come and sit down, Mr. Rocher."

She slid to the end of the sofa. Rocher sat down and glanced at Clodagh.

"I'm sorry, Miss Clott, but I think it would be better if I discussed this with Mrs. Innis alone. It's rather sensitive and just a little..."

"Personal?" guess Clodagh.

Rocher grimaced. "I hate to use that word in the line of duty. But, yes, if you like, it's very personal."

Clodagh rose. "I understand."

With Rocher looking in Clodagh's direction, Lorraine frantically tried to signal that she wasn't "all Lorraine." Rocher looked back at her, and Lorraine dropped her arms.

"You don't really have to leave, Clo," said Lorraine.

"I'll be right outside," said Clodagh lifting her binder. "I'll review your agenda. Don't worry."

"Right outside," muttered Lorraine. Clodagh would be right outside, and she would be right inside under dual control. She watched nervously as Clodagh closed the door behind her.

Lorraine was flying solo again. The last time she was alone with a man in this mode, she pushed Nikolai Kropotkin off a parapet. Now she was alone with Paul Rocher, the man who had been in love with Aunt Elinor, and she didn't have a parapet handy.

Lorraine smiled at Rocher, trying to act demure but feeling horribly masculine. She fumbled with her hands. Finally, she grabbed a throw pillow and clung to it as if it were the last life preserver on the Titanic.

"I'm sorry," said Rocher, "I didn't mean to upset you."

"Me, upset? Why would you think I'm upset?"

Rocher nodded at the pillow. "You just twisted the tassel off that pillow."

"Did I?" Lorraine looked down in her hand at the mangled decoration. "Oh, yes, I did." She threw the pillow aside and tightly cross her arms across her bosom. "You said you wanted to discuss something."

Rocher looked at her for a moment and then nodded. "Yes, it's about a visitor you had last year. It was your cousin's boyfriend."

Lorraine brightened. "Oh, yes, Michael, you mean Michael Valvano. He's not in trouble, is he? You don't have to worry about Michael. I know I was wary of him when we first met, but since I've gotten to know him..."

"Not Mr. Valvano," said Rocher. "Mr. Bleistift."

Lorraine thought a moment. "Oh, yes, you mean, her old boyfriend. They broke up. I'd almost forgotten about him. What was his first name?"

"Bob."

Lorraine snapped her fingers, as Chesney would have. She looked at her hand and then made a conscious effort to let her wrists dangle. "Yes, Bob. Now I remember. I met him at the hospital. He was there when my cousin came out of her coma."

"Not that time," said Rocher.

"But that's the only time I met Bob Bleistift."

Rocher grimaced. "No, well, yes, that is the only time you met that Bob Bleistift."

"There was more than one?" laughed Lorraine before stopping in mid-chuckle. "Wait!" She pointed at Rocher. "There was that other strange person. I'd almost forgotten him."

"That's not surprising. In fact, I'm surprised you recall him at all. He doesn't usually let people remember meeting him in those situations."

Lorraine closed her eyes. "Yes, it was at Valerie's house. Valerie was still in the hospital. And he came over. No, wait, he called me first, and he was... odd, well, no, maybe odd is the wrong word."

"Intense?"

Lorraine opened her eyes. "Yes, intense, he was definitely intense, and a little bit too earnest, almost, I don't like to say it, but almost a little goofy. And I thought he wasn't at all the type of boy Valerie would be seeing. Yes, we chatted, and then he made some lemonade, and, well, this is odd, but I think I fell asleep. In fact, I'm sure that I fell asleep and woke up the next morning. Yes, then I recall when I met the other Bob, I said he wasn't Bob Bleistift, and he was. Right after that, Valerie came out of her coma. I suppose I forgot about it all in all the confusion. I have been pretty busy since then, you know."

Paul Rocher smiled. "To say the least. Like I said, I'm surprised you recall him at all."

"Wait," said Lorraine, "how did you know about that fake Bob?"

Rocher looked down. "That's what I wanted to explain."

A shiver ran up Lorraine's spine. "Who was he? Do you know him? Do you think he's going to attempt that again?"

"Attempt what?"

Lorraine threw her hands up. "I don't know because I have no idea what he was trying to do the first time."

"He didn't try," said Rocher, "he did it."

"Did what?"

"Please, Mrs. Innis," said Rocher, "I want to assure you that he did nothing to harm you. He didn't take advantage of, well, of your body."

Lorraine almost laughed. That's wasn't very likely, at least not in the way Rocher was thinking. "Go on."

"That man was an ex-government agent," said Rocher.

Lorraine thought about that Bob. "He looked too young to be retired."

"Let's just say he was persuaded to retire."

"You mean they kicked him out? I was visited by some rogue agent?"

"He wasn't exactly a rogue..."

"Wait, he hypnotized me," said Lorraine, "didn't he?"

"Yes, he did. That's very perceptive of you to figure that out."

Lorraine shrugged her shoulders. "Not really. If he didn't have his way with me, and I was essentially knocked out, there aren't many other things a former government agent can do to a girl." She looked down at her hands. "I woke up with the same manicure, so he didn't give me a spa treatment."

"More like a spy treatment," said Rocher.

"So he was CIA, then?"

"Something like that."

"Need to know basis and all that, huh?" said Lorraine. "Apparently, you think I need to know now. And at the moment, I would like to know what he did and why?"

"You were being investigated."

"By the government?" she asked.

"Not officially by the government. Let's just say certain people well-placed within the government."

"Hence the use of a former operative."

"He was, and still is, the best at what he does," said Rocher.

"It's nice to know when you're being brainwashed that you're not getting the second string," observed Lorraine.

"It wasn't brainwashing," said Rocher. "Even he couldn't do that so quickly. That would have taken…"

"Flemming!" exclaimed Lorraine.

"Pardon."

"Davis Flemming," said Lorraine. "He was behind all this, wasn't he?"

A look of admiration shone in Paul Rocher's eyes. "You are good, Mrs. Innis. You're more than a match for that crowd."

"There's a crowd?"

"Well, no, actually, it really was just Flemming."

"It's simple deduction," she said. "Who else would want my brains picked? It was after our joint appearance on that news program, wasn't it?"

"I suppose."

"And being a true political weasel, he wouldn't go through official channels."

"Much as I have a natural antipathy towards the man," said Rocher, "let me provide a bit of justification for it all. Last October, the government was faced with a foreign head of state being assassinated on American soil. Fortunately, you were there and foiled that attempt."

"And they thank me by slipping me a psychological mickey?"

Rocher raised his hand. "So, President Kropotkin's life is saved by a mysterious woman, an average citizen, or so it was thought at the time. Then, this woman not only saves Kropotkin but accomplishes more in one short meeting with him than the State Department was able to do in years of concerted effort."

Lorraine shrugged. "I just talked to him, like a normal person."

"Yes, perhaps there's the secret of your success and the reason for their failure. Still, when an individual such as yourself makes such an impact so quickly, it gets noticed, not only in the media but in official circles."

"But why didn't they just come and see me if they want to know more about me?" asked Lorraine.

Rocher smiled at her with fatherly kindness. "You really are two people, aren't you?"

Lorraine could feel tiny beads of perspiration forming on her forehead. So this rogue agent, this loose cannon that visited her last year, knew it all. Well, at least the game was up, she thought.

"Two people? How do you mean?" she said.

"Well, you can be so savvy one moment and so innocent the next. It's like you're a wise woman and a little girl wrapped up in one person."

Lorraine laughed in a sharp burst of relief. "Oh, am I?"

"I didn't mean any offense by that," said Rocher.

"Oh, none taken, I assure you," she said. "So sending someone to pick my brain without my knowledge is the normal operating procedure in a case such as mine?"

Rocher thought for a moment. "I doubt there are many cases such as yours, Mrs. Innis. You're the history buff. Has there ever been anyone in your situation?"

"Oh, I hope not," said Lorraine.

"Combine your unique circumstances with the paranoia that inhabits the corridors of power, and I suppose this is the outcome."

"So Davis Flemming had me hypnotized so he could rummage through my head," she said.

Rocher looked surprised. "Oh, no, that wasn't his idea."

Now it was Lorraine's turn to be surprised. "Yours then?"

"No, that sort of operation isn't in my repertoire. I was asked to conduct a covert operation to gather information about you. Flemming wanted to know who you were and what you were up to."

"I wasn't up to anything," said Lorraine.

"Again, most people accepted that, but the political animal doesn't think that way."

"They all have agendas," noted Lorraine, "so they think everyone else has one."

"Precisely," said Rocher, "so he asked me to find out more about you, and I enlisted the help of the best man I knew for the job." Rocher laughed. "You really ought to see how he works…"

Lorraine rolled her eyes. "I did, first hand."

Rocher waved his hand dismissively. "Oh, that was just part of it. He went to your employer…"

Lorraine had to recall her own cover story. "Marlton Press?"

"Yeah, he went there with a whole disguise and nearly scared their HR director to death."

"Dennis Ullmer?"

"He nearly peed himself," laughed Rocher. "If you'll pardon my crudeness."

"Don't worry, I've heard the word before," said Lorraine.

"By the time he'd seen Ullmer, our friend had determined there was no public record of your life. That's when he decided to go straight to the world's number one authority on Lorraine Innis."

"Me."

"Right," continued Rocher. "He couldn't very well go to you and ask you what you were doing. Remember, at this point, we were trying to figure out what, if anything, you were up to."

"So the best way is to do that is to put me under and wander through my mind?"

Rocher shrugged. "At least it solved one mystery."

"Which was?"

"That you were exactly who you said you were. The Rooter, that is, the agent, said you couldn't fake it, not under the influence of the cocktail he gave you. You see, Mrs. Innis, he didn't exactly hypnotize you. He slipped you his own special version of what you might call 'truth serum.'"

"The lemonade!" exclaimed Lorraine.

"Lemonade, huh?" said Rocher. "That's a new wrinkle in his arsenal."

"Please, don't mix your metaphors."

"Oh, yes, sorry. Anyway, you passed with flying colors. You gave him every detail of your life, everything he'd want to know. The next mystery was who had erased you from every public record? As I said, we couldn't find birth certificates, school transcripts, tax returns, or anything. Even he was impressed. He said whoever wiped you out, in every way but physically, had done a great job. To tell you the truth, Mrs. Innis, I think he was quite envious."

That explained how the detailed documentation of her life had suddenly appeared, thought Lorraine.

"Well, they couldn't have done that good a job," she said innocently. "Because I know all my records are there now."

A sly grin crossed Rocher's face as if he were finally a step ahead of her. "He didn't put them back."

"But they're there now," said Lorraine.

"He didn't put them back. He created them fresh, from scratch, from the information he got from you."

Lorraine nodded. "But why did you replace all that information? Why did you go to all that trouble?"

Rocher gave her a quizzical look. "I thought you would be more concerned with who destroyed it all in the first place?"

"Oh, yes, well, last autumn, I did try to look up some personal information but found it was gone. I was concerned, but then it reappeared a day or so later. I didn't think it was anything more than a momentary hiccup of technology. Consequently, I didn't give it any more thought."

"I don't see a reason for destroying your records," he said, "at least not when you were an ordinary citizen, a face in the crowd. But whoever erased it, my colleague said, did an impressive job."

"But you still didn't say why you went to all that trouble to replace my official life."

"My associate did it because, well, that's the sort of thing he does for fun. He gets his kicks playing with reality. I suppose he's like a computer hacker or a mountain climber. He does it for the personal challenge."

"And why did you do it?"

Rocher looked down and seemed flustered.

"Never mind," said Lorraine, "I think I know." Rocher did it for the memory of Aunt Elinor and for the girl that looks just like her. "Thank you for explaining all that, Mr. Rocher," she said as she started to rise. "I appreciate you taking the time…"

Rocher remained seated and looked up at her. "That's not what I came here to say. That was just the background of it. It's what we did with the information."

"But you said you replaced it," said Lorraine.

"And we reported back to President Merton. It was the day he was killed."

"And how did President Merton react to what you had done?"

"That was the strange thing," said Rocher. "I expected him to fire me on the spot, but instead, he told me to forget it. He didn't want me to mention it again. Aside from short conversations with my associate, I've followed that order until today. Unfortunately, President Merton wasn't alone when he received my report."

"Davis Flemming, again," said Lorraine.

"I hate to tell you this, Mrs. Innis, but I have reason to believe that Flemming may attempt to use what he knows against you."

Lorraine nodded. "Yes, I can see that he would. You see, it was Flemming's idea that I be nominated. Apparently, he hoped to guide my political career to the top of the ladder, not very difficult since he was starting me on the second rung from the top. When he offered his services, I refused."

The look in Paul Rocher's eyes nearly broke her heart. It was fatherly and warm, but at the same time filled with melancholy. Had she been in full Lorraine mode, she would have given him a reassuring hug.

"I suppose I did the principled thing, but not necessarily the politically astute thing," said Lorraine softly.

Rocher smiled. "You're probably right. Of course, had you made the politically savvy move, you would have been smart, but not necessarily wise. And I think you would have disappointed a lot of people who truly admire you, me included."

"Thank you," she said, "that means a lot, but please, don't worry about me."

"I'm sorry, but I do worry when I think about men like Flemming."

"I'll confess that when I think of men like Mr. Flemming, I'm afraid," she said. She was silent for a moment and thought of Aunt Elinor. "But then I remember that two sparrows are sold for a penny, and I'm more valuable than many sparrows."

– 42 –
A Dope and a Slut
Out For a Ride

So you didn't tell me how I look."

"Are you trying to make me have an accident, *Cara Mia?*"

Valerie Fierro smiled to herself as Mike Valvano kept his eyes on the road, the lights of oncoming cars illuminating his profile every few seconds.

"So I look like a wreck?" she said.

He laughed. "You're the most beautiful wreck I ever saw."

"Good enough to meet your family?"

That was a rhetorical question. She was good enough to meet anyone's family. The last time she'd met prospective in-laws, it was those stuck up Dornings. This time would be different. The Valvanos were her people.

She'd also matured a lot since Bucky Dorning. She was a woman of the world, the type of woman any family would be lucky to receive.

Valerie's self-affirming reverie was broken by Michael clearing his throat.

"Valerie, I've been meaning to talk to you about… tonight."

"You said I looked beautiful. You're not going back on that, are you?"

"No, this isn't about you…"

"Excuse me?" That was not something a man said to his fiancée. If she was there, it was always about her.

"Of course, it concerns you, but there are some things you need to know about my family."

"What's there to know," she said. "We're going to meet your brother, his wife, and your old grandmother. What are they a circus act? Do they live in a treehouse? Are they dwarves?"

"Cut it out, Valerie," he snapped. "It's not a joke."

"Sorry."

"Yeah, well, I've tried to distance myself from them."

Valerie shrugged her shoulders. "So, I'll smile at them. Be polite, and aside from the wedding, we'll never see them again. If you want, we don't even have to invite them to the wedding."

"It's not that easy," he said. "You know how I got my job."

"You told me that when you took the job. Your brother is the head of the group of silent partners that controls the bank. So what's the problem with your brother?"

"Robert? I love my brother," said Mike. "I just don't like him so much."

"So, I got a sister I can do without," said Valerie. "Okay, so I'm not in business with her. But your brother leaves you alone. I've been around the bank longer than you, and I've never met him."

He steered up a winding country road.

"Why do you think I went into the priesthood?"

"I know why you left it," she said. Valerie reached over and squeezed his thigh.

"Well, yes, you're right about that," he said. "I hate to say it, but my main motivation for becoming a priest was to get away from my family. More specifically, my family's business."

"Banking?" said Valerie.

Michael laughed, but without any amusement. "You could say it was banking, on the surface, in the most generic form of the word. They deal with money. They take money from people. They give money to people. They get paid for their services."

Valerie knew from the day she'd met Peter Liverot that the bank was kind of shady. It had to be just for the simple fact that Albrecht Eckner was in a position of responsibility. Still, she didn't want Michael to think she approved of their unethical behavior.

"You mean," said Valerie, "they're crooked?"

Michael sighed. "That's a nice way to put it. Why do you think Peter Liverot gave all that money to set up the Cross of Lorraine charity?"

Valerie recalled when Lorraine had told her about it and how she had told her that wasn't good. Again, she couldn't admit that now. "I don't know. I was in a coma at the time. Remember? That's when you fell in love with me."

"Yeah, well, but Liverot must have given you some reason afterward."

"He said it was investing in the community," said Valerie. So Michael didn't think she was a total ditz, she added: "I thought that was a little bit out of character for a person like Liverot."

"It was," he said, then took a deep breath. "Among other things, my family is in the laundry business, the money laundering business."

"From drugs?"

"From whatever illicit funds need to be cleaned up. Who knows, they may even do pressing and 24-hour Martinizing."

"So they're the mob?"

Michael shook his head. "You've seen too many gangster movies. Let's say they're a service industry for criminals. They're not out robbing supermarkets or pedaling hot goods. Their dishonesty is on the back end. I suppose my family thinks that's better. They don't get dirty in the actual work, but they clean up after those who do."

"Just like a laundry," said Valerie. "But what does that have to do with…"

"With me?" asked Mike.

Valerie was actually going to ask what it had to do with her, but she figured he'd get there soon enough.

"Initially, they used the bank to make loans to small businesses, guys that were just a little desperate, but with a good thing going. Then they would call the loans, take over the businesses, and use it to filter the cash. But Liverot mixed the bank's business with his personal affairs. He was fooling around with the wife of one of the clients. That guy snapped and tried to shoot Kropotkin."

"And Lorraine stopped him," said Valerie.

"No, actually, that was the other gunman she stopped. The husband of the Liverot's girlfriend was actually a terrible shot. But that's what almost got Liverot killed. You see, my brother found out, and they couldn't afford to have the bank's front exposed. So, he had Peter taken out into the Pine Barrens in Jersey."

"They do hits, too?"

"Not normally," said Michael, "but sometimes they've done removal of individuals."

"It sounds like taking out the trash."

"I'm sure that's the way Robert thinks of it," he continued. "He keeps a man on just for that sort of clean-up work."

"Sounds like a charming person."

Michael laughed. "Actually, in many ways, he's a big teddy bear, and he even studies vocabulary words for self-improvement."

"And this teddy bear was the one they sent to kill Liverot."

"Yeah," said Michael, "from what I hear, he had the gun to Liverot's head and was ready to fire. It was only a last-minute appeal that made my brother change his mind."

Valerie snorted. "What dope would save Peter Liverot's life?"

"Actually, I was that dope," said Mike.

"You? Oh, well, I mean…why?"

"I was still a priest…"

"Oh, yeah, it was the Christian thing to do, huh?"

Michael laughed. "Actually, it was more a case of lust for a woman than the love of my fellow man."

"But you were a priest," said Valerie. "Who was this slut?"

He paused a moment. "It was you."

"Oh."

"I saw you in the hospital. I knew your cousin had saved the Russian's life. Then I read the card by your bedside, and I saw you worked for Liverot. I called my brother and let him know, but I didn't know how it all fit together. As it turns out, I saved Liverot's life. Robert, my brother, spared Liverot thinking that he could use him to get to Lorraine through you."

"Wasn't he counting on a lot of things going right?"

Michael shrugged his shoulders. "Robert's a gambler, but he's also someone who figures the odds and angles as easily as most of us breathe. So, he has the family lawyer buy off the husband of the guy that Liverot had cheated, and they went after Lorraine."

"Lorraine," muttered Valerie. Lorraine walked right into it. "So they're laundering money through the charity."

"By the bucketful," said Mike. "The charity angle worked out beyond Robert's most hopeful expectations. You see, the more money the charity was raking in legitimately..."

"...the more illegitimate money they could launder through it without raising suspicion," said Valerie.

"Exactly," said Michael, "but what I don't understand is why you didn't already know all this? Why you needed me to tell you."

"I told you that I always thought Liverot was a crook," she snapped. "I'm not Patsy Einfalt, you know."

"I meant why didn't you figure any of this out from the audit you did in Gibraltar?"

Fortunately, Michael couldn't see the anxiety on her face. How come whenever things were going good in her life, they were always upset by Albrecht Eckner? She could tell Michael that she had gone there with every intention of getting to the bottom of whatever was happening. She could even tell him that she tore up Eckner's version of the audit. She could, but she'd have to explain how Eckner was blackmailing her.

"Well," she said. Her mouth went dry, "I started to do the audit..."

That was true. She hadn't actually seen any balance sheets, but she had brought her pads and pencils. It wasn't her fault. If it weren't for...

"Stupid Lorraine," she muttered, completing her thought aloud.

"Lorraine? What did she have to do with it?"

Valerie looked at him. Yes, of course. "I started the audit, but then I had to go to London for Lorraine. She was supposed to negotiate with that British Lord, but that's when she got the call to Washington. So I had to go. By the time I got back, Eckner had told me they'd already done the audit. That is, he had an outside firm do it. I normally would have double-checked it all, but, well, I wanted to get home. I missed you."

"I missed you, too, Babe," he said.

He bought it, she thought. And why not? It was basically true, sort of. Valerie smiled and reached over to ruffle his hair. "Besides, someone had an engagement ring burning a hole in their pocket, didn't they? If I had known that, I would have run all the way home."

"Over the ocean," he laughed.

"Absolutely," she cooed.

Michael smiled. It was all good again, she thought. Suddenly his brow furrowed. Now what, she thought.

"It worked out for Robert, too," he said grimly. "What they gave you was his phony audit. He was betting that Eckner would bribe you."

"Oh!" Valerie said indignantly. "Does your brother think I'd betray you or Lorraine like that?"

Michael shook his head. "I trust you, *cara mia*, but you haven't met my brother."

– 43 –
Free Razor with Every Victim!

Verity Goodhue had dinner with her father at Bagnall Hall at least once a week. An evening with Lord Bagnall was like a ride on a poorly designed rollercoaster: long stretches of boredom interrupted by violent jerks. Right now was one of the dull bits.

They were in the library. Lord Bagnall stood in the corner puffing on a Cuban cigar and belching while he studied the spines of leather-bound volumes that he hadn't read and likely never would.

"*Martin*... urp... *Chuzzlewitt*..." he said without turning around. "Ever read it?"

"Long time ago," said Verity from an overstuffed wing chair. She turned the page in the magazine slowly, hoping that doing so would make it last longer.

"Puff...any good...burp...."

"Yes, I suppose," she said, "I don't quite recall most..."

Verity stopped short. There in the magazine was an article on Lorraine Innis. Beneath all the feminine accouterments shone the eyes of her beloved, albeit through a luxurious application of mascara.

"'Don't recall most' what... urp..." Suddenly her father's voice came from behind her. "Oh, it's 'er!"

Verity closed the magazine as if her father was intruding on a personal moment.

"I doubt we'll see the likes of that one," said Bagnall turning back to the books.

"No?" said Verity.

"Why should we? And why should we care?"

"Shouldn't we?"

Bagnall turned back towards his daughter. "It h'ain't no never mind to me, either way."

"It isn't?"

Bagnall made a face that reminded her of a cod she'd seen in the fish market. "We gots what we wanted, and just in the nick of time, too!"

Verity sighed. "I would have liked to meet... her."

His Lordship shrugged. "You meet one of them, you meet 'em all."

"One of what?"

"Muckity mucks, famous people, them types. But likes I said, it don't matter no 'ow. You'll find when you're as old as your old Dad that the only difference between anybody is this...." He pulled a wad of banknotes from his pocket. "You take away their bank balance, and they're not no difference between any of 'em. You take away the outward trappings, and there h'ain't no difference between me and, well, this Lorraine Innis you're so keen to meet."

"Well," she said, "I'd still like to meet her someday. She seems very nice."

"Probably an act," he said nonchalantly. "They're all the same, 'ceptin' Her Majesty, of course."

"As you've said."

"Cor! But that woman could 'ave moved some product," said Bagnall, a wistful look in his eyes. "But, I got second best to the Queen with this Innis woman, at least far as the public is concerned."

"Well, I like her," said Verity, "I mean Lorraine Innis."

Her father smiled at her condescendingly. "It's understandable. This Innis bird is the first celebrity you've come in contact with..."

"But I haven't met her," said Verity, before adding hopefully, "not yet, at least."

Another shrug. "Still, you've been 'andling 'er product. As good as meeting 'er."

No, it's not, Verity thought, not by a long shot.

"And a fine job you've done," he continued, "'specially for the first time out of the gate. That perfume is selling like gangbusters all around the country."

"I'm glad it's making you a lot of money, Father," she said dryly.

He winced. "Don't remind me of that. It could have been making me a lot more, but that cousin, that Furrow woman..."

"Fierro."

"She took more than 'er cream off the top," he said.

"Just as you would have done, had you been in her position."

"True! That'll be a lesson to me. Still, I'll make me bit off of it. And if it keeps selling the way it 'as, that little bit will be a lot bit more. And the thing is, it don't not 'ardly smell."

"It's based on Lorraine's pheromones," said Verity.

Bagnall waved dismissively. "I know, I know, it's all 'er compost, or whatever you call it..."

His Lordship's dissertation on human composition was interrupted by the phone ringing. A moment later, Towson appeared at the door.

"Wot is it, Splatterguard?" asked Bagnall.

"A phone call for you, m'Lord," said Towson.

"I can 'ear, Splatterguard," he said, "Oo is it?"

"Your solicitor, m'Lord."

Bagnall glanced at the mantle clock. "At this time of an evening?"

"Apparently, so, m'Lord," said the butler with Olympic obsequiousness.

"Wonder wot 'e wants," said Bagnall.

"May one assume that is a rhetorical question, m'Lord," said Towson.

"Shut up," said the life peer as he walked to the phone. "Probably telling me that someone is suing me," he said to Verity as he picked up the receiver.

"Oh, Father, how horrible."

He waved his hand. "Not at t'all. 'Appens several times a week. This brief built 'is 'ole firm dealing with ones that 'ave tried to sue me. But, 'e's worth every last farthing! Still, bit odd for 'im to call me this time of night." Lord Bagnall put the receiver to his ear and then noticed Towson still standing there. "Beat it!"

Towson bowed and backed out of the room.

"Wot?" said Bagnall, "Wotcher want? Oo's suing me now?"

Verity watched as her father's eyebrows knit in consternation.

"Wotcher mean nobody? Then why is you intruding on my connubial bliss of an evening?"

The look of concern deepened across his face as Lord Bagnall listened.

"Wot? Norfolk, Sussex, Essex, Nottingham? All? … I see, I see… Figure out what? A settlement? Ha! Fat chance? Settle? I'd sooner… Wot? How many? Well, the best defense is always offensive. No, I'll let you know in the morning…. Wot? You're the legal beagle, wot does you think? Never mind, I'll tell you tomorrow wot you thinks."

Without even a goodbye, Lord Bagnall put down the receiver. His eyes darting back and forth as if he were playing both ends of a ping pong match inside his head. Verity had seen the expression before. Competitors had commented on it. Magazines had written about it. They said it was part of his business genius. It was how he had gone from a supply sergeant to one of the titans of British industry. In the space of minutes, Bagnall would play out a business scenario in his mind, not just once but multiple times, before deciding on a course of action. Though she was in his range of vision, Verity doubted whether her father could even see her as his eyes blinked, his mustache twitched, and his facial muscles went through a series of rapid tics. Towards the end, apparently, as he was nearing his solution, Bagnall would start licking his thick lips. It was as if he could sense the answer, actually smell the roasting flesh of his adversaries.

Not wanting to either disturb the process or witness any more of it, Verity rose and edged towards the door. She had nearly gotten out of the room when a devious grin parted Lord Bagnall's lips.

"That's it," he shouted. Verity froze in her tracts.

"I don't want to interrupt your business planning," she said.

"Planning? Ha! Planning's done. Now's the time for action!"

"Then, I don't want to interrupt your action."

"It's that stuff," he said, ignoring her. "That perfume you've been pedaling."

"*Quandry?*" Said Verity. She had been wondering if there was another shoe out there. And, if so, would it be inclined to drop?

"Yes, of course, that stuff."

Verity gave him a sideways look, afraid of what she was almost certain she would tell him and hoping against hope she was wrong. "What about it?"

"It's gone haywire," said Lord Bagnall. "It's doing things to women."

The picture of the bearded Josephine Kaczmarck popped into Verity's mind. "What sort of things?"

His Lordship seemed amused. Verity wasn't quite sure, as she rarely saw her father amused.

"They're growing hair."

"Hair?" Verity touched her own tresses. "Most women grow hair, Father."

"Not on their faces they don't," he guffawed.

"Mustaches?" asked Verity, trying to play innocent.

"Mustaches, beards, goatees, Van Dykes, Mutton Chops," he said, illustrating each type with a florid gesture. "From what I've just been told, these women can style it any way they damned well choose. They got the raw material now."

"But they tested it," she said. "They tested it on animals, they tested it on people...."

Bagnall shrugged his shoulders. "If it grew a tasch on a terrier 'oo would notice? As for women..." He shrugged again.

"But as I recall, over one hundred women participated in the test. None of them grew any facial hair."

Another shrug.

"And now you're saying that every woman..."

"Ah, no!" Lord Bagnall pointed his finger. "I didn't not say every woman, not no 'ow."

"How many women, Father?"

The odd look returned to his face. "I don't not know the exact number, but I'm sure it's just enough."

Verity dropped into the chair. She and Li Gao had suspected it after Josephine Kaczmarek, but now it was confirmed. Women with the exact genetic ancestry as Chesney - Polish, English, and who knows what else - were experiencing masculine secondary sex characteristics from applying the perfume based on his hormonal chemistry.

Verity studied Lord Bagnall's face. "Father, I don't know how to put it any other way. You seem positively merry."

"Merry? I should jolly well say so, or rather: merry well say so!"

"But if all these women are becoming hirsute, and they can trace it back to your product, doesn't that mean they're apt to sue you?"

The look of amusement spread across Bagnall's face in pleased-as-punch proportions. "That's what I'd do if I was them. In fact, that's what I'm going to encourage them to do?"

"You want them to sue you?"

"Don't be daft, girl," he said. "I wants them to sue. In fact, I'm going to organize the suit."

"You're going to sue yourself?"

"No, no, no, wot I'm going to do is organize these poor 'airy women in their rightful case against the person responsible." He paused for dramatic effect, no doubt enjoying himself immensely. "Valerie Fierro."

"What?"

"After all, she brought the formula to me. She made the deal. She's the one that took the lion's share of the pie. Now the greedy little slip is going to 'ave to pay up for the damage done." He twirled his own mustache. "My legal buzzards will do her up like wot she done me."

"But the women with the beards?"

He pursed his lips. "Oh, them. They'll get something after the legal fees. Once we're done with that American slag, she won't not have nothing left."

"But you will?"

"Fortunes of war…"

"And the women on whose behalf you're so kindly bringing this action?"

He thought a moment, then clapped his hands together. "We'll give 'em free razors and shaving cream."

"Free razors?"

"Why not? After all, one of my subsidiaries makes it. Not for life, no, no, not life. Let's say for a year…six months. Then once they see the superior product wot it is…"

"…You'll have a new flock of customers."

Lord Bagnall smiled, and his merriness reverted to his usual devious form.

– 44 –
Blessings on Your Spinsterhood

Yeah, I can see why my droopy-assed brother gave up the funny collar for you. If he hadn't, I woulda gotten him a guide dog." A raspy laugh followed that matched Robert Valvano's gravelly voice.

"Valerie, this is my brother, Robert," said Michael.

"You say that like it's an apology," said Robert. "Oh, what's this?" He leaned forward, looking down her blouse. "Interesting necklace; it almost looks like..."

"It's a sort of like a tooth," said Valerie.

"A tooth, eh?" Robert chuckled. "Well, be careful. You wouldn't want it taking a bite out of anything juicy."

"You're terrible," said the redhead at Robert's side. She punched him, but he ignored it. "Hello, I'm Meghan, the wife of..." she jerked her head at Robert.

"It's nice to be here," said Valerie, "You have a lovely home."

"Hey, if you like the hallway," said Robert, "wait until we let you into the rest of the joint."

Valerie could see the family resemblance, though Michael was the better looking of the brothers. Robert was thinner with more angular features. He was also a few inches shorter than Michael, though he tried to compensate with a stance like a cocky flyweight posturing in the boxing ring.

She glanced at Megan Valvano. She wasn't Italian. Not bad looking, thought Valerie, but she looked like she needed a week at a spa... without her husband.

Robert herded them into a large living room. The main focus of the room were two large velour sofas around which were matching chairs. Robert plopped down in the most prominent chair like a king at court.

Michael sat on the sofa at his brother's left with Valerie at his side. Meghan sat across from them.

"Where's Nonnia?" asked Mike.

Robert jerked his head. "You know she had to supervise the gravy. She doesn't trust..."

His eyes darted in his wife's direction. Meghan bared her teeth at her husband before forcing a smile.

Michael looked at Valerie. "Let's go see what she's up to."

"I wouldn't," said Meghan to Valerie. "She's pretty territorial in the kitchen."

"Yeah," agreed Robert with a vague cackle, "you don't want to meet her like that. Mickey, you go see if she needs anything. She's been asking for you all day."

Michael rose tentatively.

"Go ahead," urged Robert, "it'll give me a chance to get to know what Val is like on her own."

"Valerie," corrected Valerie.

"You see," said Robert. "I learned something already."

Reluctantly, Michael excused himself. Robert stared at him until he was out of sight.

"Good guy," said Robert nodding after his brother.

"The best," agreed Valerie.

"Yeah," said Robert, though with scant enthusiasm. "So, what are..."

"So how did you two meet?" Meghan interrupted.

"I was in a coma," said Valerie, "and Michael was the visiting priest. He said it was love at first sight."

"How romantic," said Meghan, "to be lying there like Sleeping Beauty, unaware of your surroundings."

Robert snorted. "Oh, yeah? You were pretty much out of it the first time we met."

Meghan glowered at him. "You got me tipsy."

"Tipsy," laughed Robert, "you were more plastered than the ceiling of the Sistine Chapel."

Valerie tried not to look at either of them.

"Val, sorry, Valerie doesn't want to know about you," said Robert. "I understand you've worked your way up to the top at the bank."

"Until I assumed my present role at the charity," said Valerie.

"It must be so exciting to have a cousin that's as amazing as Lorraine Innis," blurted out Meghan.

Robert glared at his wife as he ran his top teeth against his bottom lip. "Hey, Beep, why don't you see how dinner's coming?"

"Me? In her kitchen?"

"Then, go, make sure the table's set right," he growled.

Meghan returned her husband's dirty look and then stood. "We'll have plenty of time to talk later," she said.

Valerie smiled and wondered if she'd enjoy getting to know her future sister-in-law. She couldn't help feeling sorry for her and annoyed that she didn't stick up for herself. Maybe she had, but what chance did an Irish girl have against this miniature Mussolini?

"My wife," he said after she left.

"She seems very nice," said Valerie. "It can't be easy for her."

Robert's brow furrowed. "What'd ya mean by that?"

Valerie shrugged.

"No, what was that crack?" He snapped.

"Look, Robert, don't bullshit me," she said, pointing at him. "It's bad enough for an Italian girl to marry an Italian guy. We've got some kind of built-in immunity, but a 'Merican girl, well, she's got her work cut out for her."

He stared at her for a moment. Valerie made a concerted effort to return his stare without blinking. Finally, just as she thought she'd have to look away, he burst out laughing.

"Yeah," he snorted, "you're it."

"I'm what?" she said curtly.

"The real deal. You're all right. You'll be okay."

"I already am!"

He raised his hands in surrender. "Hey, you got me wrong. You're more than we ever thought Mikey would bring home."

"I doubt he brought home many girls when he was a priest."

"Yeah, you're right, he didn't," said Robert. "But still, hey, I love my brother...."

"But you think he's soft?"

"As a soggy bag of donuts."

"Well, Michael's certainly not the man his brother is."

"Thanks," said Robert Valvano leaning back in his chair.

"I thought you'd think that was a compliment," she said.

He studied her face for a moment and then nodded.

"Yeah, okay, there's room in a family for two strong arms, just as long as they're not married to one another."

"You think I'm stronger than Michael?" asked Valerie. Now it was her turn to decide how to interpret the compliment, or was it a slur?

"I know you are," said Robert. "Oh, not like you're a nag. You could be the weaker one and be a nag." He glanced in his wife's direction. "And he's no sissy, either. No, but, well, I don't mean this as a knock, but you're more...more..."

"Like you?" she said dryly.

"I wasn't going to say it like that, but, yeah, that's what I meant."

"That is a compliment," said Valerie.

He laughed. "You know, that's what I would say if I thought a rat was saying that to me. You think I'm a rat."

Valerie smiled insincerely.

"Yeah, you're a lady too," he said, "or you would have said it. You're not exactly like me, but we're, what do they say?"

"Kindred spirits?"

"Yeah, that's good," Robert nodded his head. "Maybe not cut from exactly the same cloth, but the pattern's almost identical. That's good."

"You think so, huh?"

"Hey, drop the hostility," he said. "I got it, I got it. I'm going to be your brother-in-law. I can do a lot for you."

"And?"

He smiled. "And of course, you can do things for me, too. Together we'll get things done. I'm glad you're here. You've not only got brains, you know how to use them."

Valerie relaxed a little. "I like to think so."

"And you're a looker, too," he said. She started to scowl, and he retreated. "What? No, I didn't mean nothing by that. I'd have said it, maybe more, in front of my brother. All I'm trying to say is I'm glad you're in the family. You're an asset, and I like assets."

Valerie recalled what Michael said about his brother. She could see why he avoided him. But then sweet Michael didn't have what was needed to go toe to toe with Robert. Michael was probably smarter than his brother. But what Robert lacked in brains he more than made up for with cunning. Together, however, she and Michael were more than a match for this cocky guinea.

"Yes, this could work," she heard herself muttering aloud her last thought.

"I'm glad you think so," said Robert rising to his feet. He leaned over and took her hand. "*Sorella*," he said and kissed her hand.

"I'm not gone two minutes, and I catch you kissing my girl," Michael's voice echoed from the end of the room.

"Only her hand," he pleaded in mock innocence. "He can't grudge me that, can he, Nonnia?"

Valerie turned and saw Michael escorting a tiny little woman in a long black dress. She looked ancient. Her silver hair was wrapped atop her head in a bun that almost looked like a crown. She must be a million years old, thought Valerie. She stood and awaited the woman's arrival, like awaiting a queen in a receiving line. As Michael guided her, Nonnia's eyes remained fixed on Valerie. Her steps were short but determined, and soon the small woman was practically peering up Valerie's nose.

"Nonnia, this is Valerie Fierro, my future wife," said Michael proudly. "Valerie, this is my grandmother."

"How do you do," said Valerie, "It's a pleasure to meet you."

Nonnia grunted tacit acknowledgment of the introduction while she struggled to study the face before her. Finally, she spoke.

"Oh, *merde*," said the old woman, and then grasped a chain around her neck, her boney fingers following it down to a pair of eyeglasses. Once clutched, she put them on. "There, that's better, now I can…"

She stopped short, and her mouth dropped open. Then she reached up and started feeling Valerie's chin and cheeks.

If Robert Valvano had made Valerie feel like an asset of the bank, his grandmother made her feel like a horse at an auction. Valerie almost showed the old crone her teeth.

Then Nonnia studied Valerie's pendant.

"It's a tooth," said Valerie nervously.

The old woman looked up. "A tooth?"

"Well, yes, it's an abstract tooth," said Valerie.

Nonnia looked at Michael. "Abstract?" She made a yanking motion away from her mouth.

"Not an extraction, Nonnia," explained Michael. "She means it's supposed to remind you of a tooth."

The woman shrugged.

"My father gave it to me," said Valerie. "He gave it to me so I would remember."

"And what does your father want you to remember?" asked the old woman.

Valerie swallowed hard and hoped her Italian would pass muster. "My father used to say to me: *"Prima I dente, poi I parenti..."*

Nonnia flinched. *"Prima I dente, poi I parenti?"*

"Didn't I say it right?" asked Valerie.

"No, *bene*, that's good." She said, nodding her head. Still, Nonnia seemed distracted, almost unsettled. After a moment, she looked up. *"Sigilian?"*

"What?" said Valerie, "oh, you mean, Sicilian? Yes, I am; that is my father was."

"Was? He's dead?"

"Yes."

"But his name was Fierro?"

"That's right, Giorgio Fierro."

Nonnia seemed to be mentally chewing on something, much as a dog will gnaw at a gristly bone searching for a worthwhile morsel.

"What's the matter, Nonnia?" asked Michael.

The old woman waved and shushed him. Valerie felt as if she were on trial without knowing the charge.

"Giorgio... Fierro?" the woman asked again. Valerie nodded. "When was he born?"

"1940 or 41, I think," said Valerie.

"Nonnia," said Robert impatiently, "what's all this..."

"Shaddap," snapped the old woman. She looked back at Valerie kindly. "And your grandparents; tell me about them."

"Well, my mother's parents...."

"No, no," said Nonnia, "your father's parents."

Valerie shrugged. "I never knew them. My father was a war orphan. He was raised in Germany and came to America after the war."

"Mmm," said Nonnia. She closed her eyes for a moment and then opened them again and studied Valerie's face afresh.

"I don't understand what this is all about, Nonnia," protested Michael.

"Yeah, you didn't grill Meghan like this when I brought her home," laughed Robert.

"So, what's going on," asked Michael. "Don't you like Valerie?"

The Nonnia's expression suddenly lifted as if emerging from a cloud.

"Like her?" said the old woman reaching up and taking Valerie's face in her hands. "Michael, I love this girl."

Michael relaxed into a beaming smile. Valerie tried to smile as best she could with her face captured in a wrinkled vise.

"*Ah, bella, bella,*" said Nonnia, releasing Valerie's cheeks only to saturate them with a series of kisses. "*Bella! Bellissima!*"

"For a minute there," said Michael, "I thought you didn't approve. I thought you were going to say you wouldn't give us your blessing."

The old woman stopped kissing Valerie and then hugged her. Finally, when she released her, Nonnia turned to her grandson.

"Michael, I approve of this beautiful young lady, and she is a great blessing on this old woman." She turned back at Valerie, her eyes shining. Then her countenance grew serious, and she turned toward Michael. "But you will never, never marry her!"

– 45 –
Half an Eavesdrop is Enough

I just wanted to wish you the best of luck," Nikolai Kropotkin's voice was ripe with emotion. "Perhaps luck was the wrong word. I just meant that I wished for you the very best of everything. I know you do not believe in luck, but if ever there was such a thing, I would say your country has it all, for it has you. And I am lucky to be counted as… your friend."

Kropotkin was making a fool of himself with this American, thought Teplov. Though he could not hear the other end of the conversation, he doubted whether Lorraine Innis' words were as impotent as those being spoken to her.

"I will be thinking about you tomorrow when you start your confirmation hearing," continued Kropotkin. "I will be watching on the satellite news."

He sounds like a schoolboy with his first crush. And this is the man who had bested him politically at every turn?

Kropotkin's voice grew louder as he picked up his bugged Pez dispenser. A harsh scraping sound followed as Kropotkin opened the top for another candy brick.

Teplov needed a little more information to activate his plan. He rolled his eyes as Kropotkin continued his fawning talk to the American woman. Thankfully, the call ended after a few more minutes. From the sound of it, the Innis woman was probably excusing herself. Kropotkin was talking in circles as if he were yearning to advance his love talk to the next level. Teplov thanked his own good sense never to have fallen in love.

The sound of the telephone receiver returning to its cradle was followed by a heavy sigh. Poor stupid Nikolai, thought Teplov. He reached up to pull the earphones from his ears but stopped when he heard a knock over the microphone. The door opened.

"Papa, may I come in?"

It was Kropotkin's daughter, Katryna. He had assumed that Kropotkin was at the office. Now he understood Kropotkin's more intimate tone with the Innis woman. He was at home.

"Candy?" said Kropotkin. The voices becoming louder as Teplov imagined his holding the Pez dispenser between them.

"Papa, I'm not a baby any longer," protested Katryna.

"I know, I know," he said. "You are growing up so quickly. You are already quite the young lady."

"Who were you speaking with, Papa? I heard you talking," she said. "I wasn't eavesdropping. I know that isn't polite."

Teplov smirked. He wasn't polite.

"I know, you weren't," said Kropotkin. "I was talking to a friend."

"Oh, I thought maybe it was Lorraine."

"Lorraine? You mean Mrs. Innis. You still aren't that grown-up."

"She let me call her Lorraine when she visited at Christmas, and I was younger then."

"Oh, did she? Then I apologize."

"So were you talking to her."

"Do you like Mrs. Innis?" he asked.

"Yes, she very nice," said Katryna. "But that isn't the important question."

"Oh, isn't it?" said Kropotkin, a ring of amusement in his voice.

"No, the question is whether you like her."

"Have you gone from a girl to a woman so quickly," laughed Kropotkin.

"You didn't answer my question, Papa."

There was a pause. "I like her very much."

"Very, very much?"

"Yes, my dear, even that much."

"The way you liked, Mama?"

"Are you sure you don't have any homework problems you wanted me to help you with? Perhaps some trigonometry?"

"You're terrible at math, Papa."

"Perhaps," said Kropotkin, "but it's easier than these questions."

"You still haven't answered me, Papa."

He heard Kropotkin sigh. "I will never love a woman the way I loved your mother, my dear. For one thing, she loved me so much, she gave me you."

"Is Lorraine too old to have a baby?"

"I don't need more children. I have you."

"But you still like her, don't you?"

"She is a very special friend," said Kropotkin. "If for no other reason than she saved your life."

"Will you marry her?" asked Katryna with the directness that rarely survives puberty.

"My dear, and this is just between you and I, understand?"

"I can keep a secret, Papa."

"I know you can," said Kropotkin.

Teplov held his breath.

"Between you and I," said Kropotkin, "it would please me very much to marry her. She would be a very good companion for both of us."

"Then ask her," said Katryna insistently.

"I have," said Kropotkin.

Teplov whetted his lips.

"I practically asked her last month when I was in Washington."

"And you didn't tell me?"

"There was nothing to tell," said Kropotkin. "She had already been asked by President Ottinger to be vice president."

"And she'd rather do that?"

Kropotkin fumbled for his words. "It gets much more complicated, my dearest, when people have positions of responsibility. It's difficult enough when one person does, but when two.... well, it's just not possible now."

"Maybe later?"

"I don't know, dearest." There was a pause, and Teplov could imagine Kropotkin hugging his daughter. How very touching. "Still, you'll find that events often work out quite differently. Sometimes we cannot do the things we'd like to do."

"But sometimes we can," said Katryna.

"Yes, sometimes." There was the sound of the candy dispenser being placed on a table. Then their voices grew fainter as he heard Kropotkin say: "Now, enough talk. It's time for dinner..."

Teplov held his breath as he heard the door click shut. Then he hurriedly checked the time.

"Still early afternoon there," he muttered to himself. He picked up his cell phone and entered a short text message:

INFORMATION. CALL. SECURE.

He hit "send" and sat back in his chair and laughed.

– 46 –
Lambert Pugh's Limited
Need to Know

"You will have the questions for me, won't you, Davis? Right?"

Davis Flemming was jotting down thoughts on his yellow legal pad. He glanced up at Lambert Pugh pacing in front of his desk. The man was acting more like an eight-year-old than a United States Senator.

"What? Yes, I'll have your questions," said Flemming.

"You'll have them for me before I go into the hearing, won't you?"

Flemming looked down again at his writing. "Now, what good would it be to give them to you after the hearing? What are we going to do, wait for her to be confirmed and then ask the hard questions?"

Pugh stopped pacing. "Confirmed? I thought you said she wouldn't be confirmed. Did you change your mind? Are we rooting for her now?"

"She's a woman, not a football team," muttered Flemming without looking up. "We're not rooting for her, neither do we want her to be confirmed, but she will be confirmed if you don't let me finish what I'm working on. Don't you have some bill to review or a comic book to study?"

"Hey, now..." protested Pugh.

"Sit down and be quiet," snapped Flemming before adding: "Senator."

Bert Pugh sat down in the chair opposite Flemming. He was quiet enough for a few minutes, but then Flemming could hear Pugh drumming his fingers on the arm of the chair. In another moment, this was joined by the sound of humming. The humming, which started out low and almost melodious, quickly devolved into an insipid chorus of: "dum de dum-dums."

Finally, Davis Flemming threw down his pencil.

"Look, you... Senator," he said, drawing on every reserve of patience he possessed, "you might as well go home. Go home and get a good night's sleep. You don't want bags under your eyes on television."

"It will be televised, won't it?" said Pugh fingering the skin under his eyes. "I mean, the big networks, not just C-SPAN."

"Yes, I'm sure they'll all be there," said Flemming. He smiled. "In fact, I'm counting on it."

Pugh started reaching for the papers in front of Flemming. "But can I see..."

Flemming pulled them out of his reach. "They'd only confuse you at this point."

"What?"

"I mean, you probably couldn't read my handwriting," said Flemming. "Don't worry, I'll have them all organized in a neat, logical progression. You'll just have to read them."

"I'm very good at reading," said Pugh sitting up straight.

"My dear Senator, you are marvelous at reading."

"But what about follow-up questions? What if she says something I can't come back on?"

Flemming grinned. "That's why I'm doing all this. I'm writing down the responses I think Innis will give you. But it doesn't really matter. By the time you read the final questions, I doubt she'll have anything to say."

"Why not?"

"Because, if I'm any judge of human nature and the political process, by the time you finish your questions, Lorraine Innis will either be running from the hearing room or will be reduced to a sobbing mass of jelly on national TV."

"Wow."

"Exactly," said Flemming.

"And that's all there?"

"It will be," assured Flemming. "I have one more piece to add. I'll have it for you tomorrow evening."

"But the hearing starts tomorrow."

Flemming waved his hand to calm the Senator. "That's just the opening. It will all be very polite and lovely. In fact, that's what everyone is expecting the entire process to be. Don't worry. If they get to you, just yield your time until the day after tomorrow. By then, the last piece will be in place."

"The last piece?"

Flemming nodded, "Yes, or, if you prefer, the final nail in the coffin."

– 47 –
Valerie and the Pre-Fab Family

I knew the moment I saw you," said the old woman as she rooted through a drawer in her bedroom. Despite being immaculately clean, the room had a musty feeling thanks to its old furniture, its old photos, and most of all, its old inhabitant.

Valerie sat on the edge of the bed, trying to absorb it all.

"Here it is," said Nonnia Valvano. She pulled a battered photo album from the dresser drawer and shuffled to Valerie's side.

Valerie looked into the old woman's eyes and smiled weakly. This was her grandmother. This was her father's mother. The war orphan hadn't been an orphan after all. Valerie grappled with it all in her mind. She had come there to meet Michael's family only to learn they were her family, as well.

"See, see," said Nonnia, pointing a gnarled finger at a faded photograph. "See, it's you. It's me. It's us."

Valerie stared at the photo. It must be sixty-years-old. A woman was standing with a small boy. Except for the absence of make-up and a different hairstyle, the woman looked just like Valerie.

"See, I knew. You look just like I did at that age."

Valerie stared at the little boy in short pants. He must have been around two or three.

"Is that…".

Nonnia nodded. Her joyful grin was only marred by her yellowed teeth. "That's your Papa. That's my Giorgio. But how did he come to be called 'Fierro?'"

Valerie recounted her father's story as best as she could recall it.

"That was the war," Nonnia concluded. "I thought Giorgio was dead. Our village was a shambles. He wasn't the only person who was never found. Besides, I went into labor the day the battle came to our town."

"He never knew he had a…"

"A brother, then a sister, and then another brother; it was a very busy time, between the war the babies, and finally coming to America. And I've outlived them all. But I never forgot my Giorgio. And now it's like I have him back, almost," she said, grabbing Valerie's face. "I have my beautiful granddaughter."

Valerie tried to smile through the mixed emotions. Sure, it was great to find out she was meeting the grandmother she never knew. It was creepy, though, seeing a woman who had looked so much like her in her youth, but now was a wizened old thing. Was Valerie looking at herself in fifty years? What sort of skin regime had Nonnia followed? Was it just a lack of moisturizer or bad genes? She tried to stir up some emotion for Nonnia. She had been handed all this as a done deal, without any warning. But there was one overarching concern on her mind.

"Mrs. Valvano," she began.

The woman scowled.

"I mean, Nonnia," said Valerie sheepishly. "I'm still getting used to all this."

"That's okay, dear."

"Nonnia, I wanted to talk to you about Michael."

"Yes, of course, your cousin," said Nonnia.

Valerie rolled her eyes. "Yes, well, I think you should know that we're more than that."

The old woman raised her index finger. "You were going to be more than that."

Valerie took a deep breath. "We still are. We love each other."

Nonnia shook her head. "You will learn to love each other in a new way."

"Yes, as husband and wife," said Valerie firmly. "I'm going to marry him."

The headshaking grew more violent as if Nonnia's head would fly off her neck. "No, no, no! No granddaughter of mine is going to marry any grandson of mine. It would be an *infamia!* A disgrace!"

"Look," said Valerie standing and leaning into the old woman's face, "we wouldn't have even known about it if it wasn't for you!"

"Then it's lucky I stopped you before it was too late."

"Lucky? You don't seem to understand. It doesn't matter to me, and it doesn't matter to Michael. You should be thanking us. Your precious Valvano blood is going to make you some spectacular great-grandchildren."

Nonnia clapped her hands over her ears and cried for Valerie to stop.

"It doesn't matter what you think. Michael loves me; more than he loves you or any of the rest of your family."

"It's your family," insisted the old lady.

"No, it's not! We're going to have our own family," said Valerie, "without any interference from anyone else, and certainly not from you."

Nonnia started waving her hands as if she were grasping the air for a reply. Then she looked over Valerie's shoulder and pointed.

"*Infamia! Infamia!* Tell her, tell her, Michael!"

Valerie spun around. Michael was standing behind her. How long had he been there? Still, it didn't matter. She was certain she was speaking for them both.

"Michael," said Valerie plaintively.

"I came in when I heard all the shouting," he said.

"I'm sorry if I was shouting," said Valerie. "I didn't realize it, sorry..."

"Don't apologize to me," he said. "You weren't shouting at me."

She turned back to Nonnia. "Okay, sorry if I got a little upset."

Nonnia was muttering in Italian now, quicker than Valerie could follow it. Michael steered Valerie aside. "I'll take care of this," he said. "You'd better wait downstairs."

"But Michael..."

"Downstairs," he said firmly. "I'll see you in a few minutes."

Valerie started to protest, but his eyes commanded her to obey. She walked from the room, closing the door behind her. Surely, Michael would straighten out the old woman. Perhaps she had been a bit too argumentative. Maybe she hadn't shown the respect a granddaughter was supposed to afford her grandmother. They couldn't blame her, Valerie reasoned. It was a lot they were expecting of her and in a short time.

Valerie found her way back to the living room. There Robert and Megan were waiting.

"Hey, Cuz," said Robert with a grin.

"Shut up, Robert," said Megan. Valerie nodded. It had saved her the trouble.

"Drink?" said Robert advancing to a bar along the wall.

Valerie would have loved one but thought it better to keep a clear head at the moment. The old lady would really go ballistic if Valerie showed up smashed for round two.

"You'd better learn to drink, honey," muttered Megan, herself raising a glass, "if you're marrying into this clan."

"Marry into it?" snorted Robert. "She doesn't have to marry into it. She's already a member by birth." He then turned to Valerie. "So your old man and my old man were brothers. Hot shit! No wonder you've got so much..." He thought a moment. "...of me in you."

Valerie felt the pendant around her neck. "Don't call him 'my old man.'"

Robert shrugged. "Yeah, okay, whatever. Not only do we get one cousin," he continued, "but we get two."

Valerie gave him a puzzled look. She hadn't mentioned Rose. Why would Robert want Rose in his family? She had been trying to forget Rose for as long as she could remember.

"I think that's exciting. I know she must seem awfully ordinary to you," said Megan. "You've known her all your life."

"I have," agreed Valerie.

"I'll confess," continued Megan, "that I wanted to ask you about her, but I didn't want to impose. But now, well, she's family, too."

Valerie just stared at Megan. Maybe with her pert little Irish nose and her red hair, she wanted a cousin with black hair and a big beak. "I guess if you really want to meet her. I'll call her up later."

"That would be wonderful," she said.

"Yeah, right," said Valerie looking up at the ceiling. Here they were getting excited about meeting Rose while upstairs Michael was setting his grandmother straight. She hoped he wasn't too hard on the old woman, just hard enough.

Robert turned around. "Hey, I think she's a little too busy to come for a family reunion at the moment. There will be plenty of time to meet her after the swearing in."

"Yeah, sure," said Valerie distractedly. She did a double-take. "The what?"

"The Vice Presidential swearing-in," said Robert.

Valerie stared at him for a moment before realizing who they had been talking about. "You mean Lorraine?"

"Of course, who'd you think?" said Robert taking a swig of his drink.

"I thought you meant, Rose."

"Who the f**k is Rose?"

Valerie nodded. Those were her sentiments exactly. "Rose is my sister. Your other cousin. Lorraine's not your cousin."

"Hey, you're my cousin. She's your cousin. So, she's my cousin."

Valerie almost blurted out that Lorraine was actually nobody's cousin, at least nobody she knew about. But she couldn't admit that, not to a major "investor" in Lorraine.

"No, Lorraine's, she's…"

"On your mother's side," piped in Megan.

"Right! I mean, that's it, Lorraine is on my mother's side. You're on my father's side. She's my mother's, uh, brother's daughter; yeah, that's right."

"I didn't ask for a genealogy lesson," said Robert. "You two are tight, aren't you? You hear her name on TV, and your name's not far behind. You're our cousin. She's our cousin. You want her here, she'll be here. I wasn't worried about that before, and I'm even less worried about it now."

Valerie's mind was racing. Tight with Lorraine? She'd practically created her! She just couldn't be sure about her influence with her at the moment.

"I…I don't know," said Valerie, "Lorraine is pretty busy right now."

"Oh, yeah, sure," said Robert, "she's got to nail down the job. But after that, hey, once they got the job, from what I hear, there's not a lot for a vice president to do."

Valerie turned and saw Michael at the far end of the room.

"Did you calm her down," Robert asked.

"She's fine," said Michael nodding upstairs and obviously referring to their grandmother. "Just a lot to take in in one evening."

Michael came up to Valerie and took her by the elbow.

"Come on, we'd better get going."

– 48 –
Senators are Made
Not Born

"A re you sure this line is secure," said the American. "We won't be overheard by anyone?"

Teplov laughed. They didn't speak often, but when they did, the American always asked the same question. "If there's one thing my professional experience taught me is how to secure a phone line."

"What do you want?"

"A little respect, for starters, my friend," said Teplov sharply. "Recall that you wouldn't be enjoying your current status without my help. Remember that when I first met you, you were an insignificant official of an insignificant little state sent as the delegate for a trade visit."

Teplov made some of his most fertile intelligence contacts from trade missions. Most of the participants were low-level provincial characters. Many were on their first trip out of the United States. Most had no idea that their counterparts were KGB operatives mining for current data and future contacts. It was a simple matter to place these small-town fools in compromising situations and then extricate them from the same for future favors. The number of individuals pompous and stupid enough to fall into the trap was relatively small. Some of the contacts were unfruitful. But in a rare number of cases, Teplov hit the jackpot.

"Yes, well," blustered the American, "that was then. Things change. I'm an important United States Senator now. Let's not forget that."

Teplov shook his head. "I would never forget what you are now. I also beg your kind indulgence, Mr. Senator."

"Oh?" The man's tone softened. "What for?"

"I beg you to recall some of the steps along your path to your current prestigious position. I ask your gracious forbearance to recall that you were not expected to win your Senate race. That you were pitted against a much more experienced and popular opponent. You essentially were a sacrificial lamb, a place holder for your party on the ticket. You were a useful stooge."

"How dare you, Teplov!"

"How dare I? Because, my dear Senator, I was instrumental in sabotaging the sure-fire candidacy of your opponent. That's how dare I."

There were some grunts on the other end but no rebuttal to Teplov's version of events.

"Now that we fully understand each other," continued Teplov.

"What do you want?"

"Please, let's be cordial, my friend. I want you to look on my requests as a favor to an old friend. I hope you will show me the goodwill and cordiality I afforded to you when you needed me."

The senator was quiet for a moment. "Sorry," he said, "what do you... I mean, what can I do for you?"

"Much better," said Teplov, "as it should be among friends. Actually, I have but one simple request."

"Oh?"

"Very simple. It is just one question."

"One question?" The Senator asked warily. "What do you want to know?"

Teplov laughed. "You misunderstand me. I don't want you to answer a question. I want you to ask a question, on my behalf, but of course, not on my behalf."

"And then tell you the answer?"

"I already know the answer," said Teplov. "But I need the question asked all the same. You may have to repeat the question before you get the desired response. But I assure you that you will not have to be rude or browbeat. You will not even have to be unpleasant. Just ask the question politely and with respect."

"And repeat it?"

"Yes, you may have to do that several times, but as I said, you only need to be polite."

"Okay, who do I ask?"

"Lorraine Innis."

"What?" The American's voice rose two octaves. "What am I supposed to do? Go up and ask the most important woman in the country some question out of leftfield?"

"Leftfield? Oh, that is one of your American idioms. No, you do not have to go up to her. I believe she will be sitting in front of you awaiting questions."

"At the hearing! You want me to ask her at the confirmation hearing?"

"It wouldn't be very effective anywhere else."

"But she's the most popular person in the world. If I start grilling Lorraine Innis with hard questions...."

"It is only one question, and it is not difficult. It isn't even improper."

"What is this a set-up? Lorraine Innis is working for you, too."

"If only she was," said Teplov, "it would be much simpler."

"I get it; you're trying to torpedo her."

"Bravo, you do understand."

"Do you realize what my popularity will be like after I shoot down the most popular woman in the world?"

"I am not terribly concerned with your popularity, my friend. Besides, popularity is fleeting. All figures eventually topple from their pedestals. Mrs. Innis is no different. Actually, you will be doing her a favor."

"Yeah, well, I have to run for re-election in a couple of years."

"Your voters are stupid."

"How do you know?"

"Because they're your voters," said Teplov. "Even if your popularity suffers, it will only be momentary. They will forget."

"And what if they don't?" said the Senator.

"Tsk, tsk, always so pessimistic," said the Russian. "Let me put it in rosier terms. If the worst happens, you will not be re-elected. In which case you will have had two more years in your current position and be able to leave with a fat pension. If, on the other hand, you choose not to ask the question, a scandal will be uncovered showing how you were elected with the help of a foreign government. You will be sent to prison and be forced into retirement without your nice pension. It is really quite a simple choice, my friend."

There was a long silence.

"What's this question?"

Teplov smiled. "It is quite simple. Do you have a pen and paper?"

– 49 –
The Anxiety of Happiness

Lorraine Innis looked out of her townhouse bedroom window at the ever-present ring of Secret Service protection. The last trace of light was fading from the western sky. She closed the drapes and sighed.

"I don't like the sound of that," said Clodagh Clott from her easy chair.

"Sorry," said Lorraine, "it's the only way I know how to sigh."

"Nervous about tomorrow?"

"Actually, no, I'm not nervous, and that's what worries me," said Lorraine. "If I had some sense of impending doom, if I could see the Sword of Damocles dangling over my head, I'd feel a lot better. But I feel fine, and that's the problem."

"I thought only Chesney Potoski experienced calm misery, or is it anxious happiness? Either way, it's good to know Lorraine Innis suffers from it as well."

"I'm not kidding, Clo," she said. "I've never been good at anticipating disaster. Usually, it smacks me when I'm not looking. Like when Martina died, and… England. Even experienced actors say that they're nervous before they go on stage. But me?"

"Let me understand," said Clodagh, "you're nervous because you're not nervous?"

Lorraine nodded.

"I'd try to talk you out of all this," said Clodagh, "but my first hundred attempts haven't gotten through."

Lorraine smiled feebly. "Could you try it just once more?"

"One-hundred and one, huh? Okay, I'm a sport. Lorraine, Chesney, both of you, don't go through with this. Please, don't do this. You don't have to do it. And remember, if you fail, it will be bad enough, but it will be even worse if you succeed. So, don't do it."

Lorraine bit her lower lip. "Sorry, I've got to do it, but thanks for the pep talk. I don't mean to kick you out, but I like to turn in early."

Clodagh stood up. "Probably a good idea for me, as well."

"Before you go, though, could you do me a favor? I think it's a good idea if you put me under before you go," said Lorraine, "you know, so I'm all Lorraine."

"Any particular reason why? I'll be here first thing in the morning before we go to Washington."

"I've had too many close calls recently," said Lorraine. "First there was that time with Agent Rocher, and then earlier when President Kropotkin called. You noticed when he called, I called him President Kropotkin, at first?"

"Yes, it was Chesney talking to him, wasn't it?"

"To Chesney, Kropotkin is a world leader. To Lorraine, he's her friend Nikki. It's probably for the best if I'm all Lorraine for the time being unless you really need Chesney."

Clodagh studied her from head to toe and stroked her chin. "Yeah, you're probably right. At this point, you'd better be ready for anything."

"And I need to be ready as Lorraine."

- 50 -
Back Over the River
and Through the Woods

I'm very proud of you," said Valerie, breaking the uncomfortable silence that permeated the car.

"Really?" said Michael keeping his eyes on the road. "I didn't do anything."

"Don't be modest. It couldn't have been easy."

"None of this is easy," he said. "Finding out that you've been sleeping with your cousin."

"Is that how you think of me?" said Valerie.

"How am I supposed to think of you? Our fathers were brothers."

"But they never even knew each other," she reasoned.

"They were sons of the same parents," said Michael.

"Okay, whatever, maybe we're cousins now," she said, "but we were lovers first."

"Technically, we were cousins first. Ignorance of the fact doesn't change it. We didn't know we were cousins, but we were, and we are."

"Okay, if you want to get technical. We were cousins first. But we're lovers now."

The ensuing silence was more than uncomfortable; it was painful.

Finally, Michael spoke. "We were lovers."

The words struck Valerie like a slap across the face, taking her breath away. She inhaled as quietly as possible before her next statement. "Yes, we were lovers, but I hope after we're married, we'll still be lovers." She reached over and stroked the inside of his thigh.

He jerked his leg away from her touch.

"Don't," he said. "Valerie, that isn't making it any easier."

"I know, Michael... Mikey," she said softly. "I want you to know that I'm very proud of what you did."

"What exactly do you think I did?"

"You... you told your grandmother that she was wrong and that we were getting married no matter what she said."

He pulled the car to the side of the road and turned to face her.

"I didn't say any of that, Valerie."

"Because you didn't want to upset her," she said, scrambling to provide him with an excuse. "She was very upset. I understand that you didn't want to disrespect your grandmother."

Michael closed his eyes and sighed. "I didn't disrespect her, and she's your grandmother, too..."

"Well, yeah, that's an idea I'm going to have to get used to, but..."

"Let me finish. Nonnia is your grandmother, and you are my cousin. And that's the way it will be."

"But we are getting married," said Valerie.

He looked at her intently. She held her breath for what seemed a lifetime.

"We can't get married," he whispered, his voice filled with anguish.

"W-what? Of course, we can," said Valerie. "Just because some old woman with old notions. That may be the way it was in Sicily, but we're not in Sicily. We... we can get married without your family. You said yourself that they didn't matter. This is your chance to make a clean break with them, Michael. We can go away. We can make a new life. We can change our names. It doesn't matter to me."

Michael shook his head and grabbed her wrists. "No, listen, listen to me. We can't do that knowing what we know."

"But a few hours ago, we didn't know," said Valerie. "Let's just pretend we never went there, that we never found out."

"You can't undo what's been done, and you can't run away from who you are."

"Yes, we can," she pleaded. "Other people have. We don't need your family."

"Don't you understand? My family is your family. And there are others to think about."

"Like who?"

"Like your cousin," he said. "What would Lorraine think?"

Valerie laughed. "Lorraine? That's a good one. I don't give a shit what Lorraine thinks."

"You're not thinking any of this through. There's the Foundation, the reputation of it all."

"The Foundation's reputation? That's rich. You just told me it's just a front for your family's money-laundering operation. Who cares about any of that? I don't give a flying f**ck about any of that!"

"You're hysterical," he said. "You just need to calm down."

Valerie took a deep breath and tried to sort out the thoughts running through her head. It was evident that Michael needed his grandmother's approval. A few hours ago, he might not have needed her blessing, but now he wouldn't go ahead under her curse. Valerie had played this all wrong. So Nonnia thinks Valerie is her spitting image? Valerie would show her that it went deeper than that. She could be just as tough as the woman who had pulled her family through a war and across an ocean. If she had to be, she'd be even tougher. Nonnia had fought her battles. She was old. Valerie was just starting to fight. This was one fight she was going to win.

"Take me back there," she said. "To your... our grandmother's house."

"Go back to the house," said Michael. "Why? What for?"

Valerie touched the pendant around her neck. "To apologize; I need to apologize to my Nonnia."

- 51 -
Two Piselli in a Baccello

Michael Valvano stopped the car at the front door of *Bella Culo*. Valerie stepped out. "Aren't you coming in, Michael?"

"No, that is, I'm going to park the car." He looked up at a second-floor window. "She's still up. You'd better hurry."

As he drove off, Valerie rang the doorbell.

Megan opened the door. She peered out into the darkness. "Valerie, come in. Where's Mike?"

"Parking the car," Valerie said curtly. "I need to see the old..."

"She's up in her room."

Valerie nodded and rushed up the stairs. She paused by the door and reminded herself not to repeat her previous mistakes with the woman. Having composed herself, Valerie knocked on the door. The voice bid her enter.

Inside she was surprised to see Nonnia fully dressed despite the late hour. She was sitting on the window seat.

"I thought you'd be in bed," said Valerie.

Nonnia smiled. "That would be rude to welcome a visitor in my nightgown."

"I'm sorry," she said, "if you're expecting someone, I'll come back."

"I mean you, child. I knew you'd return," said Nonnia beckoning her to sit.

Valerie could feel the hairs bristle on the back of her neck. She sat beside the old woman.

"I know, you're thinking 'who does this old woman think she is talking like she can read my mind." Nonnia smiled as she took Valerie's hands. "I know because that's what I'd think. You're just like me."

"Am I?"

"Yes, and you're thinking, how I know. I know a lot about you."

Valerie smirked. "Robert had me checked out and told you ..."

Nonnia waved her gnarled hands. "You don't ask anyone for what you can read yourself."

"Where did you read about me?" She thought of the numerous magazine articles written about her since Lorraine's rise to fame.

Nonnia touched Valerie over her heart. "I read it here... and here..." She pointed at Valerie's eyes. "I see the pain, and I see the fire, but above all, I see the determination. I know you got it because I have it. I got it by having to fight for everything, just like you have. Nobody ever gave you nothing."

"No, they didn't," said Valerie, "except for Daddy."

Nonnia nodded. "He was a sweet boy. I'm glad to know he was a good man. And his greatest gift to you was this..." She fingered the pendant. "You look out for your family. But first, you look out for yourself. If you don't look out for yourself, you can't look out for nobody because you won't be anywhere. *Capice?*"

Valerie agreed.

"But you know all that," continued Nonnia. "You learned it the way I did. I fought for everything, and I had no help."

"But your husband?"

"Him?" The old woman slapped at the air. "Worthless. If it were up to him, we would have stayed in Sicily in that crumby village. No, everything I had was because I did it. I did it because if I didn't, nobody would do it. And I can see the same in you. You've had to fight. You've had to use your brains. That's what we have to do to survive, and you're a survivor just like me. You're what keeps your family together."

"Yes, that's true," said Valerie.

"And this cousin, the famous one, on your mother's side."

"Lorraine?"

"I bet she'd be nothing without you, am I right?"

"You're right."

"Because you're like me!" She pressed her fist against her chest. "They'd all be lost without you."

Valerie nodded in appreciation of her grandmother but then recalled what she had come back for.

"About Michael..." Valerie began. Before she could add "and me," Nonnia cut her off.

"Him too," said Nonnia. "You'll be strong for him."

Valerie nodded. "As his wife."

The old woman made a sour face. "You don't need him. You don't need any man! I didn't, and you don't."

"But marriage..."

"...after the first month... eh!" She waved her hand as if to brush aside romantic love. "After that, you become their *Bhutan.*"

Valerie wanted to argue that a good wife wasn't just their husband's whore.

"As far as I was concerned," Nonnia continued, "after the first months, the woman is just there to satisfy his needs, whether in the kitchen or the bedroom... and believe me, as time goes by, it's all kitchen. Either room, it's not worth it. And the man is there to give you the children. That's what you get. So you got to think of your children." She pointed at Valerie's pendant. "You take care of yourself, and then your children, and after that... phht!"

Valerie thought of Michael. He wouldn't be like that.

"Michael..." she began tentatively.

"Just a man," concluded Nonnia. "I've changed his diapers."

The children? Valerie did want children. She wanted a big family. But what would marrying her cousin mean for their children. What sort of genetic complications would that create? While she pondered that, another concern pressed to the front of her mind.

"What about me?" She said.

Nonnia looked at her as if the question was absurd. "You? You're on top of it all."

"On top of what?"

Nonnia waved her arms widely. "Everything, all that I've worked for."

Valerie smiled at the thought. "But what about Robert?"

Nonnia clasped Valerie's hands. "Robert thinks too much with his *cazzo*..." She tilted her head downwards. "I was worried about dying. Robert has done okay, but he's just a man. He can't make a move without Rosen; that's his Jew lawyer. That one is smart, but he's not us."

"You mean he's not Italian."

"I mean us! You and me! They've all had it too easy, and they're men. No, you'll be in charge after I go. Robert will have no say in it. I'm going to change it all. It's not up to him or to anyone else. I built it all. It's up to me."

Valerie laughed. "I doubt Robert will like that."

Nonnia's eyes focused intently on her granddaughter. "I don't care what he likes."

"But he's your grandson. He's been running everything for you all these years."

The old woman blew a rude noise with her lips. "Only because I didn't have anyone better. Now I do. Robert is a tough guy, but he's got no head for the business. He's not stupid, but he doesn't have what it takes. That's why he has the Jew lawyer. He's like a cripple, and the Jew is his crutch. Together they get there, but they limp. *Capice?* Now, Michael..." she tapped the side of her head, "Michael's got brains to spare, but he's got no..." she made the gesture towards her crotch. "I had to make do with what I had, until now."

"But ..."

Nonnia waved her hands. "I built this family, and I'm the one who says what will happen to it. Besides, you'll be doing them a favor. Without you, they'd run it all into the ground within a few years. Robert won't like it at first, but he'll see it's the smart thing to do. The Jew will tell him that."

Valerie's mind was spinning. She came here to meet her fiancee's family, and now she was being given control of an international racket. Nonnia studied her face.

"Don't worry," said Nonnia patting Valerie's hand. "You'll get the hang of it, all of it."

"All of it?"

"Sure, the whole thing. The connections, the stuff in the background, the partners, and of course, the banks."

Valerie's mouth dropped open. She forgot about the banks. "The banks, that includes the one in Gibraltar?"

"Sure, all of it."

Valerie's eyes narrowed, and she smiled. She would finally have the upper hand over Albrecht Eckner.

The old woman cackled. "Ah, see, I knew it! I knew you were the right one. You've already got plans. I can see it in your eyes. It's the same look I get."

Valerie nodded. This deserved serious consideration. Nonnia seemed to understand as if indeed she and her granddaughter shared some psychic connection. She patted Valerie's hand.

"Good, good," she said as she rose a shuffled to the marble-topped dresser. She picked up a cameo brooch and handed it to Valerie, squeezing it into her palm. "I want you to have this. This belonged to your great great grandmother, my grandmother. She was a lot like us: strong, smart. Maybe this thing skips every generation. I don't know. You keep it now. Someday you'll give it to your granddaughter, okay?"

Valerie thanked her and then leaned over and kissed Nonnia on the cheek, more as a token of respect than affection.

Nonnia smiled, acknowledging the sign of honor due. "That's good. Now, you go, we'll talk about it tomorrow. I'm very tired. But I'm also very happy. Now you go. I'll see you in the morning."

She said goodnight and slipped from the room. Only when she was alone in the hallway did Valerie realize she hadn't settled what she came there for. The old woman was so sure of herself and had so much information. She could bring it up tomorrow.

Valerie descended the staircase into the foyer of the large house. From there, she could see into the living room where Robert sat smoking a cigar. It was nearly midnight.

"Where's Michael?" Valerie asked. Robert seemed to ignore her question for a moment, more intent on blowing smoke rings. She was about to repeat the question when he nodded at an envelope on the table.

"He left that for you," said Robert between puffs.

Valerie opened the envelope and read the handwritten letter inside.

Valerie,

I wish I could find the words to express the heaviness in my heart. I'm sure you will feel the same when I say that we cannot be married. Please don't blame Nonnia. Had I known we were cousins, I would never have strayed down the path we must now abandon. It is best that I go away to remove all the temptations it would cause. For now, and forever, I must remain,

Your cousin,
Michael

Valerie stood silently, re-reading the short note, oblivious to the presence of Robert. It was only his hands rubbing her shoulders that yanked her back to reality.

"What are you doing?" she snapped, turning around.

He threw up his hands. "What? Hey, nothing. I wasn't doing... you just, hey, you looked upset."

Valerie was suddenly aware of the tears running down her cheeks. She wiped them away.

"Bad news?" asked Robert.

"You know what it said," she said. "You probably read it. For all I know, you may have dictated it to him."

"You got me all wrong, Cuz," he laughed. "Remember, I was all for your little wedding. I hope this doesn't hurt our... relationship."

He took a step towards Valerie. She recognized the look in his eyes. She had seen it often enough. With the tears still stinging her eyes, Valerie felt a wave of fresh anger rising within her. His smug, dirty smile was all the inspiration she needed. Robert moved closer. With all her strength, Valerie delivered a teeth-rattling slap across his face. Robert staggered backward, just barely catching himself on the end of the sofa.

"You little bitch," he spat. "You'd better watch yourself."

Valerie glanced upward in the direction of Nonnia's room.

"No, you'd better watch yourself."

She turned and went upstairs to find a spare bedroom. Once inside, she locked the door and collapsed on the bed.

– 52 –
A Dream Confirmation

Patsy Einfalt scurried into the conference room. She picked up the remote control, pointed it at the credenza on the far wall, and pressed a button. A large television screen rose from the cabinet.

"Now, which one of these..." she muttered as she began flipping through the channels. She passed through all the major network news stations before realizing that all of them were airing Lorraine Innis' confirmation hearing.

Even though she was alone, Patsy chose her usual seat in the room, the small, armless dictation chair. The more officious leather chairs stood as silent sentries around the table. She had forwarded the phones.

With a mug of tea and a plastic container filled with homemade cookies, Patsy settled in and watched as the anchorman in the studio chatted with the woman reporter on location as they awaited the start of the hearing.

Then Lorraine arrived! Patsy sat up straighter and made a conscious effort to wipe any cookie crumbs from her mouth. As Lorraine entered the hearing room, everyone rose up in a spontaneous ovation.

"How wonderful," Patsy whispered.

She had never known a celebrity, and now, she was also about to know the real vice president of the whole United States of America.

Patsy almost cried. Lorraine looked so perfect. She was wearing a blue suit and a buff-colored blouse. Patsy would have thought that Lorraine had her hair and make-up done professionally, but she knew better. Lorraine always looked that good. Not flashy good. Not overly good. Not like Valerie. Just good.

Behind Lorraine was that nice Clodagh Clott. She looked the way Patsy remembered her: nice and non-descript. Lorraine sat down behind the large table with Clodagh directly behind her in the first row. The camera zoomed in on Lorraine. She was blushing as the crowd continued to applaud. Patsy hadn't seen anything like it aside from a State of the Union speech or a Donny Osmond concert. But this was even better than either of those. She was Lorraine's friend.

Across from Lorraine was a high semi-circular dais filled with Senators, most of them were men. Behind them sat younger men and women who Patsy assumed were staffers, or messengers, or maybe just the Senators' family members who wanted to see Lorraine in person.

After some procedural formalities, the chairman of the committee welcomed Lorraine.

"The Congress hasn't been called upon to confirm a vice president very often, Mrs. Innis," the chairman stated.

"Twice previously, Mr. Chairman," Lorraine noted.

"Oh?"

"Both in the 1970s," she continued. "The first was Gerald Ford, the next was Nelson Rockefeller."

"Um, er, I thought we had some vice-presidents before that who couldn't fulfill their terms," said the chairman.

"That's true," conceded Lorraine.

"Yes, I thought so," said the chairman with a confident smile.

"But until the 25th Amendment to the Constitution, there was no way to replace a vice-president."

"Oh… yes, of course…." The Chairman cleared his throat and glanced at his colleagues, and then down at his notes. "I wasn't aware that you were a constitutional scholar, Mrs. Innis."

"I'm not, Senator," she said modestly, "just a citizen."

A senator from some western state with a dull, flat voice started the questioning. Patsy's mind began to wander. The man wasn't even trying to converse with Lorraine or ask her anything. Instead, he spent most of his time making a vague speech about her as if she wasn't even there. In fact, he could have been speaking about any nice person. Lorraine sat politely, paying attention to what was obviously political dribble. Every few minutes, the windbag would actually stumble upon a statement that required a response from Lorraine. Her answers were short and respectful. The senator seemed to like that.

Despite her best efforts, Patsy found her head nodding forward. She would immediately jerk it back again and redouble her efforts to stay awake. Finally, after ten minutes, Patsy succumbed to the allure of dozing and fell into one of those odd states where reality and dreams created a third plane of existence. In this condition, she found she was there next to Lorraine, right beside her. She was on television, too, and rather than feel nervous, it was quite nice. She looked over at Lorraine and received the loveliest smile in return. Then Lorraine reached out and held her hand in a warm embrace that was almost electric.

"I'm glad I found you here," said Lorraine, though her voice was odd in tone, deeper and more masculine. "I want you to be with me always."

Patsy felt her head jerk back, and she shook her head to dispel the drowsiness. She looked at the television. Another senator was now talking, one with a less boring voice. Lorraine was where she had been.

But she still had the strange feeling that someone was holding her hand. She looked down. It was a man's hand.

"I mean it," said the same voice she had heard in the dream, "I've been a right puddin', and I hope you'll forgive me, an' all. I want you with me... always."

Patsy looked up into the moist eyes of Purvis Twankey.

– 53 –
A Full Breakfast,
But One Cup of Coffee Too Many

Davis Flemming glanced at his watch and then looked around the rest stop café. Out the window, traffic flew by on the Interstate. I knew it, thought Flemming; Rocher double-crossed me.

The waitress came by with a half-hearted smile on her lips and a half-full coffee pot dangling casually from her hand. She raised the pot towards Flemming's cup.

"No, thanks," said Flemming placing his palm over the cup. He checked his watch again. "No, I better be going." He rose and took a handful of ones from his pocket and put them on the table. Walking down the row of booths, he passed a burly man, probably a truck driver gorging himself on a jumbo breakfast. Flemming's lip curled in disgust as the man attacked the trough of bacon, eggs, sausage, fried potatoes, and toast.

The truck driver glanced up at Flemming, nodded, and smiled. His yellow teeth were made all the more so by egg yolk.

Flemming grimaced as he walked by.

Just as he passed, Flemming heard the man mutter.

"I thought you wanted to talk to me."

The comment didn't register for a second, uttered as it was by just a common laborer. Then Flemming stopped and craned his neck to look back at the man. The innocent, benign look of just a moment before was still there, but there was a difference: the eyes. Between his flat cloth cap and his bushy mustache resided a pair of eyes that were anything but benign.

Flemming's mouth dropped open as he took a step backward for a better look at the man. The man smiled again. This time, a hint of ruthlessness betrayed itself behind the scraps of food. The eyes were the same, however, cold and businesslike.

"You?" whispered Flemming.

"Hey, Mack, you look like you need a cup of coffee," said the man. His voice, like most of his appearance, advertised that he was crude and common. "Have a seat, pal."

Flemming slid into the seat opposite the man.

"Hey, honey," bellowed the man, "how's about some coffee for this guy, and I'll take a refill too while you're at it."

The waitress brought a fresh cup and eyed Flemming as if to say: "I thought you left." Instead, all she said was: "Separate checks?"

The truck driver stuck his thumb in his chest. "This is my party. Unless you're gonna order food or sumpthin."

Flemming assured him that he wasn't.

"Okay then," said the man generously, "the Java's on me."

The waitress filled Flemming's new cup and topped off the driver's before giving both of them a long look. Flemming realized that it must have been incongruous, even to a waitress. Here he was impeccable dressed, not a hair out of place sitting across from this fat slob. Still, he concluded, this had to be the man he was here to meet. This was the appointment he had asked for and which Rocher had arranged.

The husky man continued to eat in a revolting manner.

"I assume you're here to meet me," said Flemming quietly, though there was no one near to overhear.

"Yeah?" The man asked as he tore off a piece of toast and started sopping up an egg yoke.

"You are the person, aren't you? Or are you an intermediary?"

"Wotcha mean, buddy, intermediary?"

"By that, I meant, are you going to take me to see..." Flemming allowed his question to trail off suggestively.

"See who?" Compared to Flemming's sotto voce, the man's normal tone sounded like a shout.

Flemming looked over both shoulders. "Did Paul Rocher send you?"

For the first time, the man's façade slipped ever so slightly.

"Keep it down, Mr. Flemming," he said quietly and in a more polished accent. It was then that Flemming noticed that his booth mate had a slimmer face than the rest of his body. The man was wearing a disguise only discernable when he let any bit of it slide.

"Sorry," said David Flemming leaning forward, "So?"

"So what?" He said, returning to full character. "In my business, you go where the customer wants you. So whatcha want, pal?"

"Lorraine Innis," whispered Flemming.

"What about her?"

"You created her?"

"I guess you could say that I had a hand in it. I'm not her father, but you could say that I assisted in the delivery." He laughed. "Hey, that's a good one; why is an obstetrician like a truck driver? They both deliver for a charge."

Flemming bit his lip. If this was all an act, it was good enough to be annoying. "Yes, very comical, but you helped create her history, right?"

The man splashed some chocolate milk into his coffee and stirred it with the wrong end of his spoon. Then he licked it.

"Yeah, no, create? No, let's say I helped establish it, you know."

"And that woman helped you do it?"

The man shook his head. "Nah, never had the pleasure of meeting her. Oh, wait, yeah, I did meet her. That is, not me. Let's say it was another incarnation or a relative of mine. But, she never knew me, or him, or what we did for her. She's more in the dark than you are, or at least you were. So, what's that to you, bub?"

Davis Flemming bristled at an obviously intelligent person talking to him from behind such a crude façade. This man was someone who could manufacture an international celebrity practically out of thin air and yet degrade himself as a common lout. Still, Flemming couldn't antagonize the man, not yet, at least, not until he got what he came for. He forced a smile on his lips.

"My friend," said Flemming, "I'm just looking for confirmation of that fact, that Lorraine Innis is a fraud at worst, at best a complete blank."

The man looked deep in thought as he pushed a piece of sausage back and forth across his plate. After a minute, he nodded his head.

"Yeah, okay," he said, "I confirm it."

Flemming rolled his eyes. The man was toying with him. "I know that. You've already said that."

"But now I'm saying it again. I'm confirming it."

"I need proof. Do you have proof?"

The man's face brightened. "Oh, you mean written proof? You mean something like this?" He pulled a business-size envelope from his plaid coat and put it on the table between them. Flemming's eyes lit up. He grabbed for the envelope, but the man was quicker and pulled it back.

"But…"

The man smiled in such a way that his intelligent side peeked out. "Excuse me, but I need to know what you want to do with it."

Flemming was growing impatient with the game. He folded his arms across his chest and leaned back. "What do I want with it?"

"Yeah, buddy." He smiled as if he had the upper hand.

"It's very simple," said Flemming, and he nodded to a television across the room. The Lorraine Innis confirmation hearing was playing. By coincidence, Senator Lambert Pugh had just been called upon.

"Mr. Chairman, Mrs. Innis," said Pugh sounded every inch a statesman, "I yield my time, but I would reserve the right to ask Mrs. Innis a few questions at a later time."

"When would that be, Senator?" asked the Chairman.

The confident look fell from Pugh's face, replaced by anxious confusion. The last time Flemming had seen such an expression, it was on a kindergarten classman just before he wet his pants. "I, uh, I'm not sure. I mean probably, um, tomorrow?"

The Chairman stared at him then said: "Very well, thank you, Senator Pugh."

"That what I want with it, pal, buddy, mac," said Flemming tartly. "I want to keep a cipher, possibly a fraud, from rising to one of the highest offices in the land. Get me, pal?"

The man nodded in resignation. "Yeah, I get you."

Flemming held his hand out for the envelope.

"Not so fast," said the man. "I know when I'm licked, but don't we get something for our trouble?"

Flemming studied his eyes. They were no longer confident but had a pitiful, plaintive look. "Your friend, Mr. Rocher, gets to keep his job, his comfortable retirement, and his pension."

The desperation swelled in the man's eyes. "What about me?" He was almost whining.

Flemming sneered at him and shook his head. He had been so cocky just moments before. It was almost hard to believe that this was the man who had built up Lorraine Innis. "You? You got paid for what you did."

"Yeah, I guess," he admitted and then brightened. "But I haven't gotten paid for what I didn't do."

"Are you blackmailing me, my friend," said Flemming in a far from friendly tone.

"Huh? No, no, I mean, I suppose not, only, you know…"

"You know what my problem is," asked Flemming rhetorically, "I'm too kind-hearted."

The man smiled, hopefully.

Flemming glanced at Lorraine Innis on the television screen and made some quick calculations. "Okay, you've done a good job for me so far…"

"I… I even did more than you asked…"

"Yes, well, we won't go into that," said Flemming draining the last few swallows from his coffee cup. "You're obviously a useful fellow… in some areas."

"Thank you, thank you, sir," said the man, now totally humbled.

"I'm sure I can find some useful little jobs for you in the future," He looked back at Lorraine Innis, "if things go the way I'm planning."

"Whatever you say, you're the boss."

Flemming nodded. "So, that's settled. Now, let me have that little envelope."

The man blushed. "Uh, sorry, that one's just a dummy. The real one's in my truck."

Flemming sighed. A few minutes ago, this rank amateur thought he could con him. Pitiful! "Okay, well, let's go and get it."

The man tugged at the brim of his cap as a gesture of servitude and rose from the booth. Flemming followed. They stopped at the cash register, and the man handed the hostess his check, and then searched his pockets for enough to pay it. After watching him extract one-dollar bills from various parts of his ratty wardrobe, Flemming sighed and pulled out his wallet.

"I'll pay," he said. "Anything to get out of here. I'm very busy."

The man was profuse with gratitude and followed Flemming from the eatery like a whipped dog.

"I'm parked over there," said Flemming pointing towards his Lexus. As he did so, he felt light-headed.

"Okay, boss, you go over there. I'll bring you all the goods on that Mrs. Innis."

"Good, yes, right," said Flemming. His legs suddenly felt unsteady as he reached his car and unlocked the door. Once seated behind the wheel, he loosened his tie. Had the day suddenly turned humid?

In another moment, the man was knocking on his passenger side window. It was all Flemming could do to press the button to lower it.

"You feeling okay, boss?"

"I'm... I feel... is it... do you have..."

"This?" asked the man holding up a simple envelope.

"What... I don't feel..."

"Feel well?" said the man.

Flemming tried to focus. Once more, the man looked sly and confident. "No, I don't feel good..."

"Oh, my," said the man with mock concern. "I wonder if it could have been that poison I slipped in your coffee."

"Wha... when..."

"When you looked away at the television," said the man. His voice held no exultation. It was just cold and factual. "It only takes a moment. The poison is my own special blend. Quick, but not too painful."

"But..." Flemming could hardly speak.

"But why? I suppose our motivations clashed. You wanted to ruin a woman, and I wanted to keep in practice. Or perhaps you want to know how effective my little mixture is. In short, Mr. Flemming, it's fatal. But you can have this."

The man reached in the car with gloved hands, unlocked the door, opened it, raised the window, and placed the envelope on the passenger seat, along with a small vial.

The envelope no longer mattered. Lorraine Innis didn't matter. All that mattered was that little bottle. It must contain the antidote to the poison. With every ounce of strength remaining, Davis Flemming grasped for the bottle. It was only inches away from his fingertips. But suddenly, it was the most difficult thing he'd ever attempted in his life. His chest tightened with each second, the pain wracked through every sinew of his muscles, his fingers were constricting into hideous claws. But against all this, Flemming clutched the bottle. He smiled or attempted to do so. It felt more like a spastic grimace, but still, it marked his victory. As quickly as he could, Flemming unscrewed the cap of the vial only then to discover it was empty. His face contorted in horror, he looked up at his tormentor, watching him as impassively as if he had seen it all before.

His strength gone, Flemming let the bottle drop. Now every breath was an agony as it felt his body was simultaneously exploding and imploding. He looked down at the envelope on the seat next to him. It contained the information, the evidence against Lorraine Innis. All that was left now was for the man to take it back. Flemming couldn't stop him now. Instead, his murderer looked down at the envelope, nodded slightly, and then to Flemming's shock, left it there, and closed the door. It was locked. The man couldn't retrieve it. Had he mistakenly left it there? No, he seemed perfectly content with leaving it. The imitation truck driver stepped back and then turned away.

A final wrenching pain ripped through Davis Flemming's body.

– 54 –
More Coffee, But No Pie

Valerie Fierro hated wearing the same clothes two days in a row, especially if the people who saw her knew they were the same clothes. Staying overnight at *Bella Culo* gave her no choice. She was the only woman of style in the house. Her emaciated grandmother only wore long black dresses, and those were probably a size or two too small. Megan Valvano, Robert's wife, was a size or two larger than Valerie. Besides judging on what she wore last night, Megan's taste was too plain. As Valerie slipped on her outfit from the previous day, she consoled herself that at least it was haute couture. With Michael leaving her stranded, she would grab a quick cup of coffee and have someone drive her home to Delaware.

Thankfully she had all the essential cosmetics with her in her purse. Make-up was a vital part of her routine. It was fifteen minutes alone. It gave her time to think about the day ahead.

This morning, as she flawlessly blended the blush into her cheeks, Valerie couldn't help think about Michael. He dumped her. He thought he had some moral justification. Valerie always wondered if his high ethical standard would create trouble someday. She just couldn't have guessed it was because they were first cousins.

As she expertly lined her eyes, Valerie made a resolution not to dwell on Michael. If she thought too much about him, she would drive herself crazy. She glanced at her gold pendant.

"Daddy's right," she muttered, "I'm taking care of me first." She thought of the second part of the adage and shook her head. "And screw the family right now, or at least most of them."

That made her think of Nonnia and what the old woman had said to her. Valerie would be her heir. Nonnia was going to leave control of everything to her. From there, she could get any man she wanted. She glanced at her body. She could get any man now. Her new position of power would make that much easier.

A few deft strokes of mascara, a swipe of lipstick, and she was done. Opening the door a crack, Valerie paused and listened. There were voices downstairs in discussion. The most audible belonged to Robert Valvano. He didn't sound happy. Perhaps, Valerie thought, Nonnia had already explained the new family order to her headstrong grandson. For a second, she considered waiting but then remembered Nonnia's confidence in her. They were cut from the same cloth, weren't they? Valerie could handle Robert Valvano, especially with Nonnia's help.

Valerie thrust her shoulders back and strode confidently downstairs. She found them in the large kitchen. To Valerie's surprise, Nonnia wasn't there. All conversation halted when Valerie entered. Something was going on. Robert and Megan were sitting at the kitchen table. Across from them sat a well-dressed, slightly paunchy middle-aged man. Valerie guessed he was the Jewish lawyer. Smiling politely, she crossed to a coffee pot and helped herself to a cup. Valerie took her own sweet time, adding sugar and milk, making a production of the process, and being sure to loudly rattle the spoon as she stirred. She turned around and crossed to the table.

"Good morning, Megan, Robert," she sat down and then locked eyes with the stranger; after a moment, she flashed her sweetest smile. "I don't believe we've met. I'm Valerie, Valerie Fierro."

"Miss Fierro," said the man, "I'm...."

"This is Julius Rosen," interrupted Robert. "He's my lawyer."

Rosen stood and shook Valerie's hand. "I'm the family's attorney, Miss Fierro."

"Charmed, Mr. Rosen," said Valerie before taking a sip of coffee. *The family lawyer, Nonnia works fast.*

The trio sat silently for a moment. Valerie enjoyed the fact that it was obviously her presence that was upsetting them. They would have to get used to it, she thought.

Finally, Julius Rosen broke the silence. "I'll have to call Michael," he said in a low voice to Robert.

"Yeah, sure, of course," said Robert, "if you can find him."

Michael? Why did they want Michael back? Robert obviously wanted to put up a fight, and he didn't have the brains to take on Valerie alone. Valerie almost laughed aloud. *Michael may not think he could marry Valerie, but he wouldn't join his brother to fight her. The idea would be comical if it wasn't so desperate.*

"He'll want to be here, of course," said Rosen.

"Yeah, sure," said Robert. "He'll want to be here."

Rosen looked through a sheath of papers. "All the plans have already been made."

"That was quick," said Megan.

"They've been set for years," said Rosen, "down to the last detail."

"Oh," said Megan, "I didn't know."

Robert laughed sardonically at his wife. "What are you surprised, or something? She controlled everything or tried to. Why wouldn't she have it all done up in advance the way she wanted it right down to the hymns and the flowers?"

Suddenly Valerie realized what they were talking about. They weren't planning a power struggle. They were planning a funeral. A cold chill ran down her spine.

"What... when did she die?" asked Valerie.

"This morning, last night, sometime in between," said Robert, not looking up from the list Rosen handed him.

"But how..."

"She was an old lady," said Rosen respectfully. "Frankly, I always marveled at her stamina, but even she couldn't live forever."

"She damn well tried," muttered Robert.

Valerie sat in stunned silence as they discussed the funeral plans. If Nonnia died in the middle of the night, she couldn't have changed anything regarding Valerie. Unless..."

"Uh, when did you last speak to her, Mr. Rosen?" she asked.

Rosen thought a moment. "The day before yesterday."

The day before yesterday? Then there couldn't be... wait...

Robert looked up from the paperwork and stared at Valerie before turning his attention to Rosen. "Look, Julie," said Robert, "this one thinks she's entitled to some part of the inheritance."

"As Michael's spouse," said Rosen.

"They're not getting married," said Robert.

"No? This is news to me. I don't understand. Why aren't they getting married?"

Robert opened his mouth and then froze as if at a loss for the right words.

"I'll explain it, Mr. Rosen," said Valerie, "even if my cousin won't."

"Cousin?" said Rosen, his puzzlement being replaced by shock.

"Yes, that's why Michael and I can't be married. I thought we could. I mean, it doesn't make a difference to me. But Michael..."

Rosen nodded. "But when did you find out about this?"

"Last night," said Valerie, and then explained the circumstances of the situation.

When she was done, Rosen looked at Robert. "And you were going to tell me all this when?"

Robert darted a sharp look at Valerie. "Gee, I dunno, Julie, when we found Nonnia in bed this morning stiff as a plank, my first thoughts were about a funeral that had to happen, not weddings that weren't going to. As far as this one being family, that's just the opinion of an old lady who unfortunately isn't around to stand up for them anymore."

"But I am her granddaughter," insisted Valerie. "You were there. You heard it. Ask your wife; she was there."

"Keep her out of it," said Robert.

Rosen raised his hands, urging calm. "Please. Miss Fierro, you explained that the late Mrs. Valvano based her opinion on your appearance..."

"Half the guinea girls on the East coast could fit that description," protested Robert.

"Robert, please," said Rosen before turning back to Valerie. "Even based on any family resemblance and the circumstances of your father's story...."

"Circumstances, that's circumstantial," interjected Robert.

"Robert," said Rosen, "let me handle this in the proper way. Miss Fierro, is there any other proof you can offer? Perhaps your father had something connecting him with the deceased. Did he give you anything like that, anything at all?"

"All I have is this..." She held up her pendant.

Rosen leaned forward and studied the abstract piece of gold. "It looks rather modern to be an old family heirloom."

Valerie sighed. "It's not old. He had it made for me. He gave it to me along with an old Sicilian adage."

Rosen raised his eyebrows and leaned back. "Unfortunately, old Italian proverbs don't prove a connection. They might be supporting evidence if it were part of a coat of arms, but this family hasn't one."

"But you do believe the story, and you believe that Nonnia, that is, Mrs. Valvano believed it, don't you, Mr. Rosen?"

Rosen shook his head. "Whether I believe or not is not germane to the situation at hand. I believe that Mrs. Valvano believed you were her granddaughter, but that doesn't actually prove you are."

"She had pictures," remembered Valerie, "in her room; pictures of her that look just like me. And she had pictures of my father. He was only about three, but I have pictures of him later. They have computer programs that can guess how someone would age..."

"As you say, that is speculative," said Rosen. "Unfortunately for you, Miss Fierro, the law does not trade on speculation but facts, of which you seem to be bereft."

"But she...she..." Valerie almost blurted out Nonnia's plans to have Valerie command the family business. But, the lawyer was right. She had nothing to stand on, not now at least. Until she could prove her rightful place, until she could claim what was hers, any challenge to Robert could be disastrous. Nonnia had said she was the smartest. The best way she could prove that now would be by keeping her mouth shut and waiting.

"Yes?" asked Rosen, waiting for Valerie to complete her thought.

Valerie looked around the table and swallowed hard. "I guess you're right, Mr. Rosen."

The reaction was palpable. Valerie could see it in their eyes: Rosen seemed puzzled. Megan seemed disappointed, as if she were rooting for Valerie. Robert, however, went through a rapid display of emotions. First, he was surprised, which quickly ran to delight, then victory, and finally suspicion that the first three reactions had been premature.

"Then we can assume…" began Rosen.

"So you don't want a piece of the pie?" interrupted Robert.

Valerie played dumb and looked around the kitchen and then raised her cup. "No, coffee's fine for just now."

"Cute," said Robert, "I mean, you don't want money?"

"What for, Robert?"

He smirked, obviously becoming annoyed, which only made Valerie enjoy her act all the more. "You don't want some of the old lady's money? You don't want your piece of the family fortune?"

Valerie shrugged. "If you're convinced that I'm your cousin, and my father was the eldest child of your late grandmother, then I'll rely on you to do what's right…"

Megan laughed. Her husband glowered at her.

"…but if you don't think we're related, as Mr. Rosen says, I don't have a legal leg to stand on."

"What about your cousin?" said Robert. "I mean, the one who you can prove: Lorraine Innis."

Valerie kept forgetting about Lorraine. It was ironic; Lorraine was probably the only cousin who wasn't one. Obviously, Robert needed Lorraine, and by extension, that meant he needed Valerie. While Valerie didn't have the influence with Lorraine she once had, nobody else knew that. So, Robert couldn't afford to cut Valerie loose. Valerie smiled.

"Oh, yes, cousin Lorraine," said Valerie. "You know she was going to be my maid of honor."

"Will she be…" Robert searched his mind for the right word, "… interested in any of this?"

"Lorraine is interested in everything that happens to me," said Valerie. "I'm her favorite cousin." She emphasized those last two words. "And, of course, she left me in charge of the foundation."

Valerie smiled sweetly as Robert sat across from her chewing on the corner of his mouth.

Julius Rosen broke the stalemate. "You're in a curious situation, Miss Fierro. One brother won't allow you a piece of an inheritance because he doesn't believe you're related. In contrast, the other brother refuses to marry you because he believes you are related. Rather unfortunate, I'd say."

"Yeah, sucks being her," muttered Robert Valvano.

Valerie smiled. "It does…. sometimes."

But beneath her smile, Valerie had to agree with both assessments.

– 55 –
A Punt is as Good as a Pass

The whole Washington Beltway establishment was shocked. Paul Rocher was shocked, but he wasn't surprised.

Davis Flemming was dead. He was found in his locked car at a highway diner. He had taken poison. There was a suicide note. The note explained that he couldn't shake the depression that began with the assassination of Quinton Merton.

Everyone believed it. The media was playing it as a Washington tragedy, a calamity in the halls of power. Rocher knew better. Vyvyan Lily was his usual masterful self. There was no connection to anything Flemming was now doing, no mention of Lorraine Innis. It was all so neat.

The only person nearing that of a witness was a waitress at the diner. Aside from some observations about what Flemming had ordered – a few cups of coffee – the only other mention was of a fat truck driver with whom he had been chatting. Fat truck driver! Rocher knew the real identity of that man immediately. It was like a game to Lily, a deadly game, but a game none the less. Rocher was afraid this is what would happen when Flemming pushed to meet Lily.

Poor, stupid Davis Flemming. He spent his career being a Beltway god. But ultimately, it was only a charade when he came up against a true devil of the intelligence field.

Much of the conversation outside the Senate hearing room was about Flemming. It was respectful on the surface. Nobody really liked the man. The one exception came as Senator Lambert Pugh came stumbling around the corner and bumped into Rocher.

"Oh, sorry," said Pugh. Rocher looked into his eyes. They were red as if the man had been crying.

"Senator, are you okay?" asked Rocher.

Pugh searched his face for a moment, but he seemed at a loss for words without a teleprompter.

"Rocher, Secret Service," said Rocher identifying himself.

"Oh, Secret Service, right, sure ..."

"Chief of Mrs. Innis' security detail," said Rocher.

"Oh, no, don't remind me," said Pugh. "That's what I'm here for, too. I wish I wasn't. I wish I was anywhere else."

"Is there something wrong, Senator?"

Again, Pugh darted his head about as if a swarm of gnats was attacking. "I don't know..."

"You don't know if something's wrong, Senator?"

"What? No, I know something's wrong. I just don't know... I don't know what I'm going to say."

"To whom, Senator?"

"To her, in there," Pugh jerked his thumb towards the hearing room door. "I said yesterday I was going to have something to say. I was going to say something big, but now I don't know what to say. He didn't leave me anything. He went off without anything for me."

Rocher stepped back from the Senator. He was reasonably sure whom Pugh was talking about. Evidently, Flemming promised to give Pugh the dirt on Lorraine Innis.

"He left a note, but he didn't leave anything for me," whined Pugh. "Now, what am I supposed to do?"

Rocher thought a moment. "Pass."

"Pass?"

"Pass, yield your time," said Rocher.

Lambert Pugh stood there for a moment, his lips silently mouthing the word "pass." After three or four times, his face brightened. "Pass," he said aloud, "yield my time."

"That's right."

His brow lowered a moment. "But it's more like 'punt,' isn't it?"

"Okay, yes, if you like, punt, Senator."

Pugh nodded. "Yes, that's a good idea."

"Glad to be of help, Senator."

Pugh started to turn away but then looked back at Rocher. The confusion had evaporated from his countenance, replaced by an air of haughtiness.

"It was my idea," said Pugh. "Punt! You said 'pass.'" Then he wheeled on his heel and strode into the hearing room, confident in his ability to go forth and do nothing.

"Whatever," muttered Rocher, and went to escort the nominee.

– 56 –
In Which Several Items Begin to Smell

Valerie Fierro's mind raced as she watched the countryside go by from the passenger seat of Julius Rosen's SUV. With which one of the Valvano's was she angrier: Michael, Robert, or Nonnia? She had loved Michael but was stunned that he would dump her. Nonnia was the cause of the trouble, but at the same time, she did believe that the old woman was really her grandmother. And Nonnia had promised to give her control of the family business and fortune. But then she went and died before she could deliver on the promise. Then there was dear Robert, the rat. At first, he enjoyed that his brother's wedding was ruined because Valerie was their cousin. But then he denied Valerie had any relationship to them when he thought it would cost him money. Though she wasn't sure of the order, Valerie swore she would make each of them regret their actions. Michael would regret dumping her. Robert would regret, well, being Robert. She wasn't sure how she could make a dead woman regret anything, but Valerie would do her damnedest to do that, too.

"I have to admire you, Miss Fierro."

The voice of Julius Rosen jerked Valerie back to reality. He hadn't said a word up until now. She almost forgot he was there.

"What?"

"I said, I admire you," said the lawyer. "You displayed a lot of poise this morning. I know that Robert isn't the easiest person to deal with. His first impulse is usually to bully his adversary. But you didn't budge. You definitely have your grandmother's perceptiveness."

"Grandmother? Then you believe I'm part of the family?"

"Yes, I do," he said, not taking his eyes off the road.

"But you said…"

"That is my personal opinion. Legally you have very little standing. But, yes, I believe you're a Valvano, and so does everyone else."

"Even Robert?"

"Especially him," said Rosen, "but at this stage, he'd never admit it. To do so would give you an advantage, and he's not a man who relinquishes an edge when he doesn't have to do so."

"Even to a relative."

Rosen laughed. "Especially to a relative. Robert knows you're smart, as do I."

"Thank you," said Valerie, "but you've both just met me."

"But we've known all about you for some time."

Valerie nodded. "Because of my relationship with Michael, of course."

"No, before that," said Rosen. "Remember, Robert's organization provided the seed money for your cousin Lorraine's foundation. And before that, you held a key position in the bank. We've known a lot about you for quite a while. The deceased Mr. Liverot first brought you to our attention."

"He was another one who made me promises and then died on me," said Valerie. "I guess I'm just too trusting."

They rode on in silence for several miles before Rosen spoke again.

"I would offer you some advice, though I doubt you'd need it."

"Oh?"

"I wouldn't act too hastily in your position," he said. "Your cousin Robert is a hothead, so it's best not to provoke him needlessly. Your positions in the charity and the bank have afforded you opportunities to observe and understand both organizations. I'm sure Robert will see that you'd make a better ally than an adversary. In addition, if he antagonizes you, he risks antagonizing your other cousin."

"Michael."

"Lorraine Innis."

"Oh, right," said Valerie sardonically, "Madam Vice President."

Rosen glanced at Valerie. "In my position, I've had ample opportunity to observe family dynamics. Rarely do close family members give much credit to people they've known all their lives."

"Oh," said Valerie, "I didn't mean…"

Rosen raised his hand. "No need to explain or apologize. As I said, I have a lot of experience with families. But your cousin Lorraine is in a unique position."

"You don't know how unique."

"Pardon?"

"Nothing," said Valerie.

"Oh," said Rosen. By the look on his face, he was storing away Valerie's off-hand comment for future analysis. "Your other cousin, Mrs. Innis, is another reason why I say that you're in a strong position for getting what you want if you're patient," said Rosen. He paused and then quickly added: "Of course, I'm not speaking as a legal advisor…"

"But as a friend?" said Valerie with veiled sarcasm.

"Lawyers don't have friends," said Rosen returning the sarcasm. "But I do think that your interests, and those of the rest of the Valvanos, are best served in a cooperative effort. You have a lot going for you, Miss Fierro. And here you are..."

Rosen pulled up outside Valerie's townhouse. He pulled a card from his pocket.

"Here's my card. If you need anything..."

"Like friendly advice?" said Valerie taking the card.

"Anything you may need," said the lawyer. "It was a pleasure meeting you. I just wish it had been under more pleasant circumstances."

Valerie watched Rosen drive away. At first, she was surprised that the family attorney was driving her home instead of one of their flunkies. Now she realized that Rosen was hedging his bets, trying to get on the good side of both her and Robert Valvano to secure his future. Apparently, Julius Rosen saw enough in her that he thought he could use her. Perhaps she could use Mr. Rosen, as well.

After a quick shower and change of clothes, Valerie left for the office. How would she treat Michael? Should she give him the icy treatment? Or perhaps she would adopt Robert Valvano's approach and claim there was no evidence that she was a member of the family.

Did she even want Michael back? He dumped her and left her stranded. Even if she took him back, she would make him pay for that. She didn't need him or any man. When she saw Mr. Michael Valvano, she would make that clear to him. She may have been caught by surprise by the last twenty-four hours, but Valerie was back in control now. She would settle things on her terms and with no more surprises.

When she entered the office, Valerie was overpowered by the aroma of flowers. Patsy Einfalt's desk was engulfed in floral arrangements. Valerie called out the secretary's name, and her head popped up from between two vases of roses.

"I'm here..." said Patsy.

"Patsy, what's going on?"

"I know, I'm sorry," said Patsy. "He should have sent them to the house, but he did. In fact, he sent even more there."

"To what house?"

"Why, to my house, and here, too," said Patsy.

Valerie looked around. "I don't understand."

Patsy blushed. "You won't be upset? That is, I wouldn't have ever thought it would happen. Of course, I always hoped, but then, it was just a wish. Even in high school, all the way back then, I didn't think I ever had a chance. I mean, the idea is frankly ridiculous..."

"Patsy! Stop babbling," said Valerie. "What are you talking about? What's ridiculous?"

Patsy suppressed a grin. "That I'd steal a fella from you. Sorry."

"Michael?" Had he lost his mind? Had Patsy Einfalt caught Mike Valvano on the rebound?

"Mr. Valvano? I couldn't take Mr. Valvano away from you. That's silly."

"Then who are you talking about, Patsy?"

Patsy waved her arms at the flowers. "Purvis, of course."

"Twankey? What makes you think you stole him from me?"

"He did dedicate an entire album to you," said Patsy. "And it was number one!"

"More like number two," muttered Valerie.

"So many surprises happening," said Patsy, "and totally unexpectedly, but then I guess if we expected them, they wouldn't be surprises. First Lorraine, then Purvis, and then Mr. Valvano, but that one's not a surprise to you, I expect."

"What about Mr. Valvano?"

"About how he resigned."

"Resigned, from what, the board of the charity?"

"Yes, but you knew that. Didn't you?"

Not wanting to appear less informed than the densest person she knew, Valerie hid her surprise. "Oh, yes, of course, yes, I knew he was resigning from the board of the foundation."

"I suppose he had to," continued Patsy. "once he resigned from the bank, too."

"What!"

"But you knew that, too, huh?"

"Yes, of course, I knew that," said Valerie.

Patsy studied Valerie's face for a moment before her eyebrows lowered. "If you knew that, how come you're acting like you're surprised."

Valerie stood blank-faced while she wracked her brain. "Ummm, because I didn't think you knew, so I didn't want to make you feel bad because I knew and you didn't."

"But I knew," Patsy raised a letter. "He had me type out his resignation. Good thing I got in early."

"Yes, good thing," agreed Valerie wryly.

"But since we both know, it's okay, isn't it?"

"It's great."

"Really? I thought you might be upset, but then I suppose you'll see enough of him at home."

Valerie stared at Patsy's cheery expression. Obviously, she didn't know that the wedding was off. "Sure, whatever."

Patsy picked up a cardboard box and headed towards the door. "I was just about to clear out his desk. He asked me to do it."

His desk? Maybe there was something good in there, something Valerie could use against Robert.

"Wait! You have enough to do, Patsy," said Valerie snatching the box from Patsy's hands. "I'll do that."

"Uh, okay, if you're sure," said Patsy. "You know, if we planned it right, we could have a double wedding. You and Mr. Valvano, and me and my Purvis."

Valerie stood in the doorway and stared at her insipid grin. If she had been closer, and if the box had been filled, say with bricks, Valerie would have clobbered Patsy for that. As it was, she just went to Michael's office.

She began by rifling the desk drawers. There must be something to use against Robert.

"C'mon, c'mon," Valerie muttered to herself as she looked through the files in Michael's office. "There's got to be something. I'm the smartest one, your grandmother said so. Something here..."

Valerie stopped when she came upon a file marked: "Foundation Insurance." Though the title wasn't that interesting, the policy within was; in fact, it was very interesting."

"Five million bucks," said Valerie. "Well, that's good to know. A nice gesture, wish it was more." She flipped through the policy. "I wonder how she passed the medical exam."

The rest of the desk held boring stuff, the sort of things that wouldn't even stir the curiosity of the fussiest bank examiner. Valerie sat in the large swivel chair and sighed.

"Nothing," she said. Robert might not have been that clever, but he was smart enough not to leave anything incriminating in his brother's care. Figures, she thought. If Michael was handed a smoking gun, he would turn it over to the Feds. She would have to figure out another way to gain control.

The intercom buzzer went off, causing Valerie to jump. She put her fist down on the talk button.

"WHAT?"

"Oh, sorry, Valerie, but there's a call for you," said Patsy. "I thought you might want to take it. It's long-distance."

"Yeah?" Maybe it was Michael begging to come back. Valerie sat up straight. "Okay, put him through."

The line started to blink, and Valerie picked it up.

"Valerie Fierro," she said, trying to sound cool and cruel.

"Verity Goodhue, here," said the voice on the other end.

"Oh, you..." It was that limey daughter of Lord Bagnall.

"Pardon?"

"Nothing, I just thought it was... never mind. What do you want?"

There was a short pause, and Valerie could imagine that plain, fashion-challenged woman looking uncomfortably into the receiver.

"Well, actually, I wanted to do you a favor, Miss Fierro."

"What are you going to do, poison your old man?"

Another awkward pause ensued. "No, though you might very well wish for something along those lines. Actually, I was calling to warn you."

"Warn me?" Valerie laughed. She had her hands full with Robert Valvano, and this English chick was warning her about some old British toilet paper maker.

"Yes, I wanted to warn you about Father."

"Look, Miss Goodhue, you could have warned me about him when we first met, but it's a little late for that now. I've got him all figured out. He may have won the first battle, but I've won the war. I won't go into the details, but you could bet your last pound on that."

"Presumably, you're referring to the royalties on *Lorraine Innis' Quandary.*"

"That's right," said Valerie as she examined her manicure, and then turned her hand around and made a clawing motion. "I'm surprised he told you about that."

"Yes, well, you did get the better of Father in that negotiation."

"I sure did," said Valerie. "And I hear it's selling like hotcakes over there."

"Oh, you've seen the sales figures…"

"No, I just stick my head out the window, point my ear to the ocean and listen to the cha-ching-cha-chings coming over the water."

"I don't understand."

"That's the sound of the cash registers," said Valerie. No matter what happened to Michael or the rest of the Valvanos, no matter what Albrecht Eckner and the stupid bank did, Valerie still had her little perfume deal, and that was all hers.

"Oh, I see," said Verity Goodhue.

"It was sweet of you to call," said Valerie in a patronizing tone, "but I'm kind of busy…"

"Actually, I wasn't calling to warn you about father. It's the perfume…"

"Oh, yes, what's wrong? Doesn't it smell okay? I gave them the exact formula."

"No, it's been followed to the exact specifications you provided," said Verity.

"Then there's no problem. I smelled it myself. It's not something I'd wear personally, but then I'm a little different from my dear cousin Lorraine."

"Thankfully…"

"What?"

"I mean, thankfully, you didn't use it too liberally."

"Why, what's wrong with it?" Valerie leaned forward. For the first time, she had the uncomfortable feeling that this British bird knew something that Valerie didn't.

"Well…"

"Well, what? Spit it out!"

"I just wanted you to advise your cousin, Mrs. Innis."

"Never mind about her…"

"But it's her scent..."

"Yeah, but I'm the full owner of the property."

"I suspected that may be the case," said Verity. "When Father was ranting about it, yours was the only name that he referenced in the pejorative."

"The dirty dog..."

"I just wanted to be certain that you were the full and legal owner of the perfume."

"Yes, I am," insisted Valerie, "and it's just too bad for anyone else. After that fleecing your father gave me at our first meeting, I don't mind boasting that I drove a very hard deal the next time around."

"What about Lorraine Innis?"

"What about her?"

"I just wanted to know if she had a part in any of it," asked Verity.

"Aside from her name on the bottle, no," said Valerie. "I don't know what your game is. I'm not ripping off Lorraine if that's what you're insinuating."

"I wasn't insinuating anything," said Verity.

"Yeah? Well, you're sure dancing around something. I work damn hard for Lorraine Innis. She wouldn't be who she is today without me. You could say my rights to that perfume is just a little gift from Lorraine."

"I see," said Verity. Valerie couldn't read this chick. After sounding worried, then threatening, then accusatory, now she sounded relieved. "That's all I wanted to know."

"I see," said Valerie, "and since I've answered your questions, do you mind answering one for me? What are you talking about?"

There was a slight pause. "Actually, Miss Fierro, I shouldn't be saying, but as you'd certainly find out in the next few days, it probably doesn't matter."

"What doesn't matter?"

"That Father is leading the lawsuit against the owner of the fragrance known as *Lorraine Innis' Quandary*. He's doing it on behalf of himself and the women in England who have been affected through its use."

"What? He's suing me? How were they affected?"

"A significant number of women using it have, well, they've grown beards."

Valerie sat silently for a moment before hanging up without another word. She knew in an instant what she needed to do. She reached into her purse for Julius Rosen's card.

– 57 –
The Bear, the Skunk, and the Hommonculus

For the second day, Lorraine Innis sat alone facing the semi-circle of Senators. Added to this impressive gathering were banks of cameras and microphones and a host of reporters. Behind her sat a packed room of strangers. She was surrounded.

The only familiar faces belonged to Paul Rocher and agents MacKay and Hambright. And, of course, there was Clodagh Clott.

Clodagh made all the difference. Lorraine wasn't quite sure why, but a few minutes alone with Clodagh put her at peace. A few words from Clo, and she felt confident and sure of herself. She had the oddest feeling that she knew Clodagh before, though she couldn't recall where or when. Still, it didn't matter. As the Chairman banged his gavel to begin the day's proceedings, Lorraine glanced back at Clodagh. She flashed a friendly smile. That's all she needed. Lorraine was ready.

After opening remarks, the Chairman turned to Senator Lambert Pugh.

"Senator Pugh," said the Chairman, "you yielded your time yesterday."

"Um, yeah, I think so," said Pugh, "that is, yes, I did."

"…with the understanding that you'd speak today."

Pugh looked around the room and then at the papers in front of him. He seemed unnerved. The day before, he had been assured with an attitude bordering on the belligerent. Lorraine couldn't imagine why. She'd never met the man.

"Senator? Senator Pugh," the chairman said after more than a minute of this fumbling.

"What?"

"Do you have some questions for Mrs. Innis?"

Pugh looked directly at Lorraine. She smiled. He looked down and then leaned forward.

"Punt!" He said, almost swallowing the microphone.

"I beg your pardon," said the chairman.

"I punt," repeated Pugh, this time with more confidence.

A general murmuring broke out around the room. The chairman whacked his gavel sharply.

He glowered at Pugh. "Do you mean that you yield your time? The only reason I ask that in over twenty-five years of working under the procedures of this body, I have yet to come across any 'punt' rule."

"Um, yes, I mean, that is, okay, yes, I yield."

The chairman squinted at Pugh. "And do you expect to get the ball back after another series of down, Senator Pugh?"

"Downs?" asked Pugh.

"Will you be asking any more questions, or are you all done?"

Pugh shuffled quickly through the papers in front of him, the hopeless expression returning to his face. He looked up. "I can't see how... I mean... he didn't... um, no, I'm done."

With a roll of his eyes, the Chairman moved to the next Senator on the schedule. "Mr. Hutton."

"Thank you, Mr. Chairman," said a high-pitched voice from the end of the row.

Lorraine looked down at the figure seated there. She had hardly noticed him before. In a room filled with impressing looking men and women, Senator Hutton was practically invisible. He was short, stocky, and almost completely bald. He had a wide mouth with a broad, warm grin emanating above a strong jaw.

Lorraine looked at the nameplate in front of him. Lucius M. Hutton. Perhaps it was his abbreviated stature coupled with the slight point of his bald dome, but she couldn't help but rearrange the letters of his name into an uncomplimentary anagram: Homunculus Tit!

"Let me begin," said Lucius Hutton, "by saying how very honored I am to take part in these hearings." Senator Hutton droned on for at least three minutes on the Senate's duty to fulfill the dictates of the Constitution. It was closer to a high school civics lesson than a hearing. Finally, he took a deep breath, glanced down, and then bit his lip. Only his eyes betrayed slight uneasiness.

"I really only have one question, Mrs. Innis," he said, his high-pitched voice tightening.

"Yes, Senator?" said Lorraine.

"I'd like to know about your relationship with President Kropotkin."

The spectators, who had been whispering among themselves during Hutton's speech, fell silent.

"My relationship?" said Lorraine.

"...with President Kropotkin," said Hutton, "President Nikolai Kropotkin of Russia."

Lorraine just stared at him for a moment. "Well, I first met President Kropotkin last October, in the Hotel du Pont, after I inadvertently saved his life. He thanked me for that, and then we talked. Though I claim no credit, President Kropotkin went on to author his plan for peace..."

"Yes, yes," said Hutton impatiently. "We know all that. That's public record. I want to know about your personal relationship with the President of Russia."

"I'd call it friendly," said Lorraine.

Hutton rubbed the top of his nipple-like head and grimaced. He looked like a child eating broccoli against his will.

"I can appreciate that, Mrs. Innis," said the legislative homunculus, "you've always seemed such a congenial lady."

"I try to be, Senator."

"But how would President Kropotkin classify your relationship."

Lorraine shifted uncomfortably in her seat. "That's a question more appropriately posed to Mr. Kropotkin."

Hutton nodded and looked at his notes. "Mrs. Innis, do you know what a PEP is?"

Lorraine thought a moment. Pep was a slang word for energy. Pep was a comic book title in the Archie series. She doubted Hutton was referring to either of those.

"A PEP," continued Hutton, "is a Politically Exposed Person."

Lorraine unconsciously pulled the hem of her skirt over her knees. "I see, Senator," she said. Her mouth felt dry.

"The reason I feel compelled to ask you these questions, Mrs. Innis, is that I am trying to determine if you are a politically exposed person."

"Me? But I've never been disloyal to my country..."

Hutton smiled with a pained expression. "I can appreciate that, Mrs. Innis, and I believe you. But that does not mask the potential danger to national security if your relationship with the president of Russia compromised you in any way."

"But we're just friends."

"As you've said," said Hutton. He wiped a bead of perspiration from his brow and looked at the clock, much as a boxer might look for the bell to ring. No one was stopping him. Instead, the room seemed to hang on his every word. "But even if you consider him only a friend, one has to wonder how President Kropotkin views you."

"You're asking me to read his mind or put words in his mouth," said Lorraine.

"Not at all, Mrs. Innis," said Hutton. "So you're telling me that Nikolai Kropotkin has never revealed to you his feelings towards you?"

Lorraine sat in silence while her mind filled with dozens of examples of things that Nikki had said and actions he had taken, all of which gave clear evidence of his deep feelings for her.

After thirty seconds, Hutton pressed the point. "I repeat the question, Mrs. Innis, has Nikolai Kropotkin, the president of Russia, ever told you how he felt about you?"

Lorraine felt the blood rising to her cheeks. "I... I think that's a private matter, don't you, Senator?"

A sympathetic look filled Hutton's eyes as he nodded his head. "In many ways, Mrs. Innis, I believe it is a private matter. If you are a private citizen and President Kropotkin is a world leader, it would be a private matter. Or if you were vice president, and he was a private citizen, it might be a private matter. But if you were a leader of one county, and he was the leader of another nation, I would contend that it rises to the level of a very public matter. And not only a public matter, but one that calls into question matters of national security."

"But..." Lorraine wanted to contest Hutton's points, but she realized that she could not argue with his conclusion. She was a politically exposed person. She would never consider taking their relationship beyond its current level of friendship. But, Lorraine was confident that Kropotkin would if he ever had the opportunity to do so.

The packed chamber began to murmur. Lorraine turned to look at Clodagh Clott for some sign of encouragement, but Clodagh's eyes seemed to be filled with the same sense of desperation that Lorraine was feeling.

"Mrs. Innis, Mrs. Innis," Senator Hutton kept repeating until Lorraine turned back to face him. "Mrs. Innis, please, I want you to understand that I would never call into question your honesty or your patriotism. But at the same time, a woman in your position with a close personal relationship to a person of prominence could find themselves compromised."

"Compromised, but..."

"Whether they realized it or not," said Hutton. He smiled sympathetically.

Perhaps this sawed-off senator was right? She had only accepted the nomination because she had been backed into it by Davis Flemming. Was Hutton one of Flemming's operatives? But she read in the morning paper that Flemming had killed himself. Maybe Hutton was a friend of Flemming, and this was revenge. Did Hutton think that she had driven Flemming to take his own life? Did anyone believe she was complicit in Flemming's death?

No, Lorraine reasoned, she knew better. None of that mattered at the moment. She had accepted the nomination out of respect for President Ottinger. The question now was: would these charges tarnish his administration? And what about Nikolai Kropotkin? Lorraine knew he was in love with her. She could never return those feelings, but still, she regarded him as a dear friend. What would these allegations do to him?

Lorraine looked up at Hutton, who was patiently waiting on her with that phony expression all over his mammalian head. She hated to retreat, especially from a homunculus. She never wanted this job, and even though she was forced into it, she loathed to be forced from it. She wasn't a quitter, and it wasn't like her to run from a fight. But...

A quotation popped into her head: A bear may defeat a skunk, but it is not always the most prudent action.

"Li Gao..." she whispered. Where did that come from, she wondered. And who was Li Gao? Probably some old proverb she had once read.

"I'm sorry, I didn't hear what you said."

Lorraine looked up at Hutton. In the absence of a skunk, he would do.

"Mrs. Innis..." said Hutton.

Lorraine raised her hand towards him and turned to the Chairman.

"Mr. Chairman," she said.

"Yes, Mrs. Innis?"

"I would like to ask for an adjournment."

"Certainly, Mrs. Innis," he said, glancing down at his agenda. "How long would..."

But before he could complete his sentence, Lorraine was already on her way out the door.

– 58 –
The Unlikely Quitter and
The Improbable Cupid

That didn't take very long," scoffed Clodagh Clott at the television news. A pageant of pundits were weighing in on the big story of the day: Lorraine Innis had withdrawn her name from nomination for vice president.

"I never quit anything in my life," said Lorraine, staring into space.

"I can't believe this," continued Clodagh, "all they have is one fact. You've withdrawn... period. That should take all of thirty seconds to report, but look at this..." Clodagh flipped through more than a dozen channels, all of which were discussing nothing but Lorraine.

"I quit," muttered Lorraine, "I hate to quit, but I had no choice." She turned to Clodagh. "Clo, I'm not a quitter, am I?"

Clodagh took Lorraine's hand and looked into her eyes. "A quitter? You? No, in fact, I think that might be your tragic flaw."

Lorraine gave her a puzzled look.

Clodagh rolled her eyes. "Do I have to spell it out? You never let anything drop. You gnaw on everything like a dog with a bone. Oh, I'm not saying that your causes haven't been noble. But if you let a thing drop now and then..."

"What?"

Clodagh sighed. "If you weren't so obsessive, your brother might still have both his testicles. I can't vouch for everything in between then and now. I wasn't there. But if you had quit some things more often, I might be sitting here talking to a fat and happy Chesney, instead of a trim and miserable Lorraine."

"I'm not miserable, am I?"

"You're not exactly jolly at the moment," said Clodagh.

Lorraine put her head down.

"Hey, I didn't mean it like that," said Clodagh. "You did the right thing. You were forced into accepting that crazy nomination, and now you were forced to withdraw. It wasn't part of your plan. It was an unfortunate detour. You're best out of it."

Lorraine sighed. "Maybe you're right. I just hate to be seen as a quitter."

"And I hate to be seen as a violent person..." said Clodagh just before she punched Lorraine on the arm. "Now, knock it off, and let's get on with whatever is next."

◆

"What reason did she give you?" asked Frank Wesson.

"What reason could she give," said President Ottinger, "you saw that little twerp Hutton. He effectively derailed a promising career in government with just pure speculation."

"Do you think Mrs. Innis would have been compromised by her relationship with Kropotkin?"

The President peered over his eyeglasses at his aide. "Frank, do you think I would have nominated her if I thought there was anything untoward about Lorraine Innis anywhere?"

Wesson just looked at his chief.

"Okay, Frank, out with it, we both were in the service too long to know when a subordinate is holding back from saying something. Spit it out."

"Well, Sir, looking back on how the Innis nomination unfolded, wasn't it a bit like a card trick?"

The President thought a moment. "You mean like 'pick a card, any card' all the while you're being forced to take the one the magician wants?"

Frank Wesson nodded. The President stroked his chin.

"You know, when Flemming first came in here, I thought he was going to try to convince us to take one of his stable of hacks. But then he comes out of leftfield with his Lorraine suggestion."

"Yes, sir," said Wesson, "but in doing a little recon, I learned that Lorraine wouldn't have anything to do with him."

"It would have surprised me if she had," said Ottinger. "So did Flemming think he could get his hooks in her?"

Wesson shrugged. "Possibly, but this is all backward. Suppose Flemming was a jilted suitor, politically speaking, and trying to get revenge on Mrs. Innis. Why would he kill himself just before her nomination fell apart? If anything, he'd be making the rounds of all the news shows to crow about it. It doesn't make any sense. Do you think Senator Hutton was carrying Flemming's water?"

"No," said Ottinger with a dismissive wave, "a junior senator from a tiny state? He's not even Flemming's type. Flemming's candidates always are tall with a good head of hair. Hutton's short and bald. Flemming probably didn't even know the man was alive."

"Do you want the Agency or the Bureau to look into it?"

President Ottinger made a sour face. "No, it'd just be a waste of taxpayer's money. Besides, Lorraine Innis has been through enough. She wasn't a happy woman when she left me. She just kept apologizing. Frankly, Frank, I'm sorry I put her in that position. Chalk it up to a case of a person with too much integrity for the job."

◆

"A very neat job," said Paul Rocher.

Vyvyan Lily, the Rotor Rooter, sat passively as if his friend hadn't said a word.

"I knew the first one was your handiwork," continued Rocher.

Lily took a sip from his overpriced boutique coffee and looked off in the opposite direction. It was as if he were alone.

"But have to admit I was surprised by the second trick."

Finally, Lily faced Rocher.

Rocher stole a surreptitious glance to make sure they weren't being overheard. They weren't, but he still leaned forward.

"That little show this morning at the hearing," said Rocher.

Vyvyan Lily was a consummate performer, but Rocher could tell this wasn't an act.

"That wasn't me," said Lily. "I'd admitted it if it was, well, I wouldn't deny it, at least not to a trusted associate."

"If it wasn't you, then who did that?"

Lily took a swig of coffee, made a sour face, and then shrugged. "Don't know, don't really care. That's out of my pay grade."

"I thought you liked her."

The former CIA agent smiled. "Not as much as you." Rocher bared his teeth, and Lily dropped the grin. "Yeah, well, it was somebody, but it wasn't me."

"Then, who?"

"I don't..." Vyvyan Lily suddenly stopped looked over his shoulder.

"What is it?" asked Rocher.

"In my line of work, it's very unsettling to find out you've got competition. Whoever did... what you're talking about... either got lucky, or they have excellent inside information, good enough to hit a nerve in a woman who I thought had stronger nerves than that. Remember, I spent a lot of time wandering barefoot through her mind."

"And you didn't find any romantic connection between... them?"

Lily shook his head. "Nope, not even a whiff of puppy love. Of course, that all could have happened later. Or..." He shivered.

"Or what?"

"Someone got deeper than even I could," said Lily rising from his seat and glancing towards the back of the coffee bar. "I gotta go."

"To the toilet?"

"To ground," said Lily in a hushed tone. "You've got to be careful. The world's a dangerous place with a lot of loose ordnance around. And either I've been sloppy, or someone else has been a little neater. Either way, I've got to make sure things are clean."

Rocher shook his head in disbelief as Lily patted him on the back.

"How about you," said Lily, nodding at Lorraine's picture on the TV screen. "Still watching over her?"

"She's not entitled to my protection anymore."

"Oh, yes, of course," said Lily, "I forgot. See, I'm getting so careless lately. Maybe I should hang it all up, for good."

Vyvyan Lily pulled up the collar of his coat and disappeared out the door.

◆

"What now, Julie?" Robert Valvano glanced up at Julius Rosen as he entered the room. "I've been busy arranging the old lady's funeral. Anyone find Michael yet?"

"No, they're still looking," said Rosen. "But I thought you'd like to know I have heard from your cousin, Miss Fierro."

"She contacted you? What about? Don't tell me she's going to try to stake her claim on Nonnia's will." He snorted. "Fat chance."

"I'd caution you on taking Miss Fierro too lightly," said Rosen, "if indeed, that's what I thought you were doing."

"You think that I think that she's really family?" said Robert.

"It doesn't matter what I think," said Rosen. "But I think that you must think so, or you wouldn't be whistling past the graveyard."

A puzzled looked crossed Robert's face. "She wants to come to the old lady's funeral?"

Rosen shook his head. "No. That's not why she called."

"Then what did she want?"

"She wanted me to amend a contract she had."

"Who's she want to bump off," said Robert sitting up, "Not me?"

"Not that kind of contract. Miss Fierro wanted me to amend a business contract for her," said Rosen, "and before you ask, no, it doesn't have anything to do with you. Your name didn't even come up. As far as I could ascertain, it had nothing to do with anyone in the family."

"Yeah? Why'd she come to you?"

"She didn't know any other lawyers," said Rosen.

"And you did it for her?"

Rosen shrugged. "It was a simple enough transaction."

"What was it?"

"There is such a thing as attorney-client privilege."

"Did she pay you?" asked Robert.

"No."

"Well, I pay you. I'm the client, and it's my privilege to know what my attorney's up to."

"She wanted to transfer ownership of something to her cousin, the cousin who admits to being related to her. It was the rights to some Lorraine Innis perfume that she was holding."

Robert snorted. "She had the stuff, and she gave it back? She can't be part of this family, the dope."

"Actually, it was a shrewd move," said Rosen. "I can't say exactly why, but she wanted it drawn up quickly, too quickly. I think she knows something that's she's not telling her cousin Lorraine. It might be nothing, but it would appear that our Miss Fierro has a problem with other cousins aside from you."

"You mean the Innis broad? She said that?"

"Not in so many words," said Julius Rosen, "but her transference of the rights to that perfume was more urgent than trying to do something nice for a relative. I got the distinct impression that something was about to explode, and Valerie Fierro did not want to be anywhere near it when it did."

Robert bared his teeth. "I knew we couldn't trust her. I don't care what the old lady saw or thought."

"In Valerie, she probably saw herself," observed Rosen.

"Which is why we gotta take care of her. This whole thing with these two dames is getting to be more trouble than it's worth. I shoulda let Al polish off Liverot back when we had a chance."

Rosen tilted his head to one side. "You've made a good profit on them so far, but I tend to agree. Especially given another nugget of information. It seems that Lorraine Innis was at Peter Liverot's bedside when he died."

"So?"

"So, Miss Fierro let slip that Liverot divulged information to Mrs. Innis on his deathbed."

"I'd kill that shit, Liverot, if he wasn't already dead, the rat. What did he tell her?"

Rosen shrugged. "That's just what's bothering Miss Fierro. Her cousin won't tell her."

Robert stood up and banged on his desk. "That's it, get Alphonse in here. I got a twofer for him, a real doubleheader."

"May I suggest a much more economical way to deal with two birds?" said Rosen as he sat calmly.

Robert stared at him for a moment and then sat down. "I'm listening."

◆

"Wot? An entire day's production?" Lord Bagnoll bellowed into the phone. "Wot nincompoop is responsible?" continued His Lordship. "Wotcha mean: I am?!"

Bagnall looked up, saw his daughter enter, and made some flailing gesture at her. In his current agitation, he could have been directing her to do anything from taking a seat to jumping out of the window. She was too excited to sit and too happy to risk bodily injury, so Verity just stood there.

"I knows I bought the new machine," hollered Bagnall, "but I h'ain't expected to install the damned thing. You can just..."

His face turned a bright vermillion. "You deal with it. Fix the damned thing!" His Lordship slammed down the receiver and ran his hands back across his scalp.

"If I 'ad more 'air, I'd pull some out now," he said.

"Isn't it wonderful, Father?" said Verity. Usually, she trod carefully around her father's outbursts, but this was a time for rejoicing.

"Wonderful? That your Dad is sparse on top of 'is coconut? You're as barmy as the idiots down in the Bristol plant."

"Oh? Trouble, Father?"

Bagnall looked at his daughter, then down at the phone.

"Trouble? I boughts a new machine for the Bristol toilet paper plant."

"How very generous of you, Father!"

He snorted at her and continued.

"I gets them new machinery, and wot does they do with it?"

"What, Father?"

"They doesn't set the perforatin' on the blasted contraption!"

Verity smiled. "At the risk of being pedantic, Father, that's what they didn't do with it."

"You can jolly well be perpendicular," he said. "But now I'm stuck with a whole day's output of bog roll wot h'ain't got a single perforation in 'em. What am I supposed to do with that?"

"Father, it doesn't matter," she said.

"It don't, eh? You tell that to the bloke wot gets one sheet to a roll, one long sheet. It can be damn inconvenient!"

"Oh, Father," said Verity, "it doesn't matter, you can sell them all to me. I'm so happy I could use them all for streamers! We can throw a parade!"

Bagnall gave her a prolonged one-eye squint.

"'Appy?" he finally said, "Wotcher do? Buy yourself a new 'at? One of them pancake things you like?"

"Father, they're called berets; they're French."

His Lordship rolled his eyes.

"No, Father," she said, "I'm delighted, and it has nothing to do with headwear. Obviously, you haven't heard the news."

She stood there beaming at him, knowing that his curiosity would eventually get the better of him. That took all of five seconds.

"I give up, wot news is making you so blasted cheerful even in the face of me own manufacturing disasters."

Verity grinned broadly for a few more seconds to heighten the effect and then blurted it out: "Lorraine Innis is not going to be vice president."

Lord Bagnall stared at his daughter. Verity Goodhue stood with a frozen smile straining her cheeks to their bursting.

"So?" he finally said.

"So? SO?" repeated Verity. "Father, don't you know what this means? Lorraine Innis can be your spokesperson. She can do all the product endorsements you wanted. Remember, it was your idea. Don't forget that! And best of all, she can come and meet with me, that is, with us."

His Lordship shrugged. "Yeah, maybe."

"Maybe? But Father, you forget how beloved Lorraine Innis is."

"And you forget about her little viper of a cousin," he said, studying a production report. "I could always have it re-pulped."

"What re-pulped?"

"Me unperforated rolls," said Bagnall, "I 'ates to do it, but that's the most practical way. I'd like to make that imbecile line manager put the perforations in by 'and, but I h'aint not a vindictive man."

"Father, the toilet paper doesn't matter."

"Haw! Everybody says that until they need the stuff!"

"I meant that's not important right now," said Verity picking up the phone and handing the receiver to her father. "You could call right now. She could be here tomorrow."

Bagnall took the handset and placed it back in its cradle. "You is forgetting that I'm suing that Fierro woman. Wot does you expect me to say: 'Mrs. Innis, come on over and endorse me goods, and, oh, you can stay to watch me fricassee your cousin in court?'"

Verity bit her lip. In her excitement, she had forgotten about hair sprouting on the unsuspecting faces of women.

"Well," she said, "you don't have to sue Miss Fierro, do you?"

"Don't 'as to sue 'er?" said Lord Bagnall incredulously. "Oh, sure, that Fierro woman gets all the dosh, and your dear old dad gets 'is bum sued for all the damages."

Verity sat down and felt the tears well in her eyes. Would she ever get Chesney back to England? Every time she thought her hopes would be realized, those same hopes were dashed like crockery around the feet of an amateur juggler. She pulled out a handkerchief and dabbed her eyes.

She looked up at her father, who was recoiling disdainfully. At first, Verity thought it was the sight of his only child in tears. Then looking down at her hand, she saw the actual cause of his disgust. She was using a linen hankie.

◆

"Yuri, Yuri, my little Yurivitch!"

Yuri Belikov took a step backward. He had just entered his uncle's office to find the president of Russia pirouetting. Even more surprising than the dance was the realization that such a large man was so light on his feet.

"Uncle?" said Yuri scanning the room for signs of starches that would trigger Kropotkin's candida and explain his buoyant mood.

"Yuri, come in, come in!" Kropotkin pulled his nephew-in-law in and closed the door. "Is it not wonderful?"

"*Da*, Uncle, very pretty," said Yuri, "I never knew you so enjoyed the ballet. Very nice, very nice, indeed!"

For a second, Kropotkin's expression hardened. Instead, Kropotkin's frown melted into fresh rays of facial sunshine.

"Ah, I cannot be angry, not today, not even with your peculiar brand of congenital imbecility, my Yurivitch!"

"Thank you, that is good… I think?"

"It is all good. Everything is good today, Yuri," said Kropotkin crossing to his desk and picking up a television remote. "And do you know why? This is why!"

Yuri looked at the object in his hand. "You got a new remote control, Uncle, I mean, President."

Kropotkin laughed. "Uncle, please, call me: Uncle! Today I am the world's uncle, even a diddling dimwit such as yourself."

"Again, thank you, I think," said Yuri scratching his head. "It is a very nice new remote."

Kropotkin sighed and shook his head, but as before, his disapproval was overtaken by cheeriness. "Not the remote, my blubbering boy. Have you not seen the news? Look! Look!"

He pointed the controller at the television across from his desk. One of the satellite news channels appeared on the screen.

"….still buzzing over the news that has stunned Washington," said the anchor, "Lorraine Innis has withdrawn her name from nomination for vice president. Reaction is still coming in from…"

Kropotkin clicked off the TV and then playfully flipped the remote in the air, batting it with a deft backhand and sending it across the room where it shattered into plastic bits.

"You will definitely need a new remote control now, Uncle," observed Yuri.

Kropotkin waved his hand. "Pah! What care I for such things?"

Yuri gnawed on the end of his thumb, trying to interpret the snippet of news. "So Mrs. Innis won't be vice president?"

"She will not, Yuri."

"And that is happy news?"

"The happiest," said Kropotkin.

"Yes," Yuri nodded. He gave Kropotkin a frozen smile.

"Go ahead," said Kropotkin. "I can see the question, so ask it."

Yuri's grin grew crooked. "Okay... why?"

Kropotkin laughed. He ran to Yuri and pinched both of his cheeks before taking Yuri's fat face in his strong hands. "Because Yuri, because she did it for me."

"For you, President Uncle?"

"All right, maybe not for me, but definitely because of me, because of our relationship," exulted the Russian. "At the very least, she did not deny me."

"Not like the time she pushed you off the balcony..."

"Shut up, Yuri, besides that was an accident," said Kropotkin. "But that was before when she was odd, not herself. Now Lorruska is Lorruska..."

"Who else would she be?"

Kropotkin ignored the remark. "She is her glorious womanly self once more, and more importantly, she is not going to be a politician."

"What will she be, then?" asked Yuri.

Kropotkin winked. "A politician's wife?"

"Who?"

"My wife, you idiot," said Kropotkin.

"Now?"

Kropotkin grew slightly more serious. "Well, yes, eventually. Now there is nothing keeping us apart. Of course, we will have to wait a respectable time."

"And she will come here to live?"

Kropotkin put his arm around Yuri's shoulder. "It doesn't matter, my boy, I will go wherever she wants."

"But the presidency?"

"It does not matter," said Kropotkin. He picked up the gold Lorraine Innis Pez dispenser from his desk and kissed her image before tilting back her head and extracting a tiny candy brick. "She has given up the vice presidency for me. I am man enough to give up the presidency for her."

◆

Gregor Teplov chuckled to himself. "You are indeed man enough, dear Kolya."

He turned off the receiver tuned to the Pez dispenser and then closed and locked the cabinet that housed it.

And a good long life to you both thought Teplov. For an ex-KGB man, he was actually quite a sentimentalist, he told himself. The KGB had gotten a bad rap. Silly spy novels and films only saw the group as a collection of cutthroats, all wearing black, filled with evil thoughts, and continually searching for the next person to shiv. But that was fiction, he thought. They were a more practical bunch who, at their core, were a decent enough group of lads.

This whole Kropotkin-Innis affair was a perfect case in point. He could have assassinated his rival, but Teplov wasn't a brute. He used an electronic bug on the man. It was gold, and it was in a form that delighted Kropotkin. The device would soon outlive its usefulness to Teplov. After that, Kropotkin had the rest of his days to enjoy the expensive trinket.

The goal was for Teplov to grab power, of course. But in doing so, he was bringing joy to a lovely pair of human beings. Kropotkin had said so himself. He would gladly swap his political power for his love. Teplov was only working behind the scene to give Kropotkin his heart's desire. Bad? Evil? Far from it, Teplov reasoned. He was actually a modern-day cupid employing electronic listening devices instead of those old-fashioned arrows.

Employ? Oh, yes, there was another tool in his quiver. Teplov picked up the phone and dialed a secure number. After three rings, a deep, somewhat hollow voice answered.

"Hello?"

"Listen, Hristo..."

"Teplov?"

"Is there anyone else who has this number?"

"No."

"Then it must be me," said Teplov.

"That sounds logical," said Hristo.

"Is everything in place?"

"Yes, we are ready, only waiting for your command."

"Go," said Teplov.

"When?"

"At the earliest possible time. There is no need to wait. Only be certain that there is no longer the Secret Service to get in the way. That would be messy. And make sure she is out of Washington."

"I understand."

"Good," said Teplov. He hung up the phone and smiled. Yes, just like cupid... after a fashion.

– 59 –
Cousins Who Lunch

Valerie Fierro stood at the entrance of the Green Room of the Hotel du Pont and surveyed the surroundings. No one had ever done a hit at the posh restaurant, but there was a first time for everything. When she arrived, Valerie found Robert Valvano and Julius Rosen waiting. She purposely arrived ten minutes early. She wanted to welcome them. She wanted to tell them where to sit. Evidentially Robert had the same idea. He sat in the corner, his back to the wall.

"Thanks for coming, Cuz," said Robert.

Valerie eyed him suspiciously. "Is that South Philly slang, or are you acknowledging we're related?"

Robert laughed the raspy chuckle that she was growing to despise.

"Whatdya think?" he said.

"I don't know," she replied. "That's why I asked."

He waved his hand at her. "Relax, You can't expect me to learn I got a cousin and not have some sort of reaction, do ya?"

"I think what Mr. Valvano is saying…" began Julius Rosen.

"Zip it, Julie," said Robert. "I know what I'm saying. This whole arrangement came as a shock to all of us, some more than others. I spend most of my life trying to, uh…" he snapped his fingers at Rosen. "What do I call it?"

"Mitigate risk?" suggested the lawyer.

"Exactly," Robert agreed. "When you're responsible for an international organization, it's more than a little unmitigating to find out that you not only got previously unforeseen relatives, but they're already in the business with you. You know?"

Valerie merely smiled and reminded herself of Nonnia's assessment: she was the smart one in the family.

"Yeah, well, I guess you're wondering why I wanted to meet you today," said Robert.

"I didn't think it was to invite me to the next family reunion," she said, "not unless you have your lawyer plan those as well."

Robert's leaned forward, his fist clenched. Julius Rosen reached out and place his hand upon his client's forearm. Robert exchanged glances with Rosen and relaxed.

"Yeah, that proves you're a Valvano," said Robert. "Sorry, I gotta stop thinking of you as an employee."

Valerie picked up her handbag and started to stand.

"Whoa, where are you going?" asked Robert.

"I don't want to impose on you any further," said Valerie calmly. "If I'm no longer working for you, I'd prefer…"

Robert burst out laughing at a volume inappropriate for the genteel surroundings. The other patrons looked on aghast, and the maître de hurried to their table.

"Is there anything wrong?"

"Whoa, sorry," said Robert. "My cousin here just told a joke, sorry."

The maître de offered the obsequious expression that came standard with the service and returned to his station.

"Sit down, sit down," said Robert, "nobody's giving you the shove. Tell her, Julius, make yourself useful."

"Please, Miss Fierro, Valerie, sit down," said Rosen. He gave Valerie a quick wink away from his employer's notice. Valerie sat down.

"Valerie," continued the lawyer, "Mr. Valvano didn't ask you here to fire you; rather, he wants to promote you."

"Promote me?"

"Certainly, due to the unforeseen circumstances of the last few days, the bank no longer has a president. That position is yours if you'll take it."

For a split second, Valerie's eyes widened. The presidency of the bank! It had been a long climb. She thought of the embarrassments and the setbacks. She recalled the times she had been forced to submit to the indignity of working for such people as Mitchell Minear, Peter Liverot, and, worst of all, Albrecht Eckner. And now, at last, she would be in charge. She looked at Julius Rosen. He was smiling warmly. She glanced at her cousin Robert, who wore his usual smirk.

"Hold it," she said, looking at the smirk. "What's the catch?"

For a second, she thought Robert's temper was about to erupt again, but instead, he looked at her, and for the first time, a genuine smile spread across his face. He almost looked handsome.

"How about this one?" Robert said to Julius Rosen.

"Valerie, what, Mr. Valvano is trying to say…"

Robert put his hand on Rosen's arm. "No, Julie, I got this. Valerie, you want to know what the catch is?" He shrugged. "I don't know. Maybe the catch is that you're family, the family you didn't know you had until a few days ago, your family needs you. And I need you. Look, I can't run this bank. Rosen's could run it, but he's too busy with other things, and between you and me, he's a lawyer, you know?"

"But why me?" asked Valerie.

"Because it's a perfect fit," said Robert. Gone from his tone was a hard, egotistical edge. He was human, professional, almost charming. "It's a better fit than my brother. I can imagine you're devastated by the way everything with Michael turned out, and I can't blame you. But at the same time, I can't help but see a good side to it."

"Oh, really?" said Valerie skeptically.

He smiled compassionately. "I won't go into the implications of it all, the danger to any children you two might have had, or any of that. But from my purely selfish point of view, I'm glad to find a cousin, a friend, and an ally. Before you say anything, I know that's not how I first reacted to you. I was a real bastard when you first showed up at the house. That's just my front. I'm a cocky S.O.B. I guess I was jealous of my brother. Brothers can be like that. Michael's got the looks. He's got the nicer manners. I've got the face that looks like it wants to start a fight, and so that's what I do most of the time. Why do you think I gotta go around with this mouthpiece next to me all the time?" He jerked his thumb at Julius Rosen and laughed at himself. "No, when I first saw Michael bring you home, I thought: 'damn, he did it to me again. He got the most beautiful girl.'"

Valerie felt herself blush.

"Oh, I got a good wife," said Robert, "I know I should treat her better, but Michael landed the real looker. And now I know why you're such a good looker: you're the spittin' image of our dear grandmother. You got her looks, you've got her brains, and you've got her balls."

Valerie blanched at that last reference.

"Figuratively speaking," interjected Julius. "I believe Robert is referring to your internal fortitude."

Robert Valvano nodded towards his attorney. "See why I got him around? Look, Valerie, Michael's a good guy, but he's not cut out to run a business the way it oughta be run. And I'm tired of having flunkies that I can't trust."

"Like Liverot," said Valerie.

"I don't want to speak ill of the dead," said Michael, "but between you and me, that French piece of shit was a hell of a lot more trouble than he was worth." Robert leaned forward and lowered his voice. "Do you know that fat frog f**k got us into all kinds of shit? I mean illegal stuff."

Valerie stared at Robert, and then at Rosen, and then back at Robert. Both wore innocent expressions.

"You didn't know what he was doing?" asked Valerie incredulously.

Robert shook his head. "You think just because we're Italians we're the Corleone family? You've watched too many gangster movies. You're Sicilian. Are you a crook?"

"No," said Valerie.

"No, of course not," said Robert, "and neither are we. The ironic thing is that it was that Frenchie, Liverot, who dragged us into it, him and that stinkin' little German shit…"

"Albrecht Eckner," offered Valerie.

"I hate that little shit," growled Robert.

Valerie resisted the urge to shout: "me, too!"

"Between the two of them, they got us into it up to here," said Robert raising his hand over his head. "And I won't even go into what they did to your cousin."

"You or Michael?"

"No, your other cousin, Lorraine."

"Oh, right, her," said Valerie.

"It was Liverot's idea to set up your cousin's charity the way he did. Do you know what he was doing?"

Valerie knew very well, but to admit as much would make her seem like an accomplice. "No, I mean, of course, I had my suspicions. I'd have to when I was dealing with Liverot and Eckner, but I was kept in the dark about those things. But then there was Lorraine."

"What about Lorraine?" asked Robert.

Valerie hesitated. "Nothing, really, only Lorraine was with Liverot in the hospital when he died. He told her something just before he died."

"What was that, Valerie?" asked Rosen.

"That's the thing," she said, "Lorraine wouldn't tell me. I asked her repeatedly, but she would never tell me. I figured it was some sort of confession or something, but she wouldn't tell me."

"And you and Lorraine are close," said Robert.

Valerie laughed. "Believe me, no one is as close to Lorraine as me. I know things about that girl that nobody else could even imagine."

"It's nice to have a close relationship like that," said Rosen.

"But that all changed after Liverot died," said Valerie. "It's like I can't reach her."

"And you think that Liverot told her something that changed her."

Valerie thought it was more than just that, but she wasn't about to delve into her full history of Lorraine Innis at this point.

"Oh, definitely," said Valerie.

Robert Valvano and Julius Rosen exchanged nods.

"That's one of the reasons you're perfect for the job of president of the bank," said Robert. "Not only because you're the smartest person, not just because you know more about the internal workings of it, and not just because you're family and I trust you. You need to get in there and clean up all the dirty dealings that Liverot did, not just for your new cousin, but for your old cousin, Lorraine."

Valerie thought a moment. "And I'd have full control?"

"From top to bottom," assured Robert.

"You'd be accountable to the board of directors, of course," added Rosen, "but that's just standard business procedure."

Robert jerked his head towards Rosen. "Lawyers, huh, Valerie! Don't worry about the board. You do the same smart, honest job as president that you've done throughout your banking career, and the board will thank you in more ways than one." He rubbed his thumb and forefinger together.

"And does my authority also include Gibraltar?"

Robert smiled and nodded knowingly. "That can be arranged."

Valerie smiled and put her handbag down at her side. "Well, then, let's order lunch."

She couldn't wait until Albrecht Eckner found out who his new boss was.

– 60 –
Returning Your Scent

Valerie Fierro rushed back to the office following lunch. Things were moving quickly. Julius Rosen would take care of all the necessary arrangements. Being president of the bank would give her extra leverage at the Cross of Lorraine. She was essentially in charge of both operations. But first things, first: she needed Lorraine's signature on a certain document.

"Good morning, Valerie…"

Valerie flew by Patsy Einfalt's desk. Valerie made a mental note to tell Patsy to start calling her "Ms. Fierro," now that she would be president of the bank. Or maybe she would just replace Patsy altogether.

"Oh, wait," said Valerie sticking her head back around the corner, "Patsy, do you think Lorraine will be back to the office any time in the near future."

"Yes, I do."

"Yeah, okay, good," said Valerie, "let me know when she comes in."

"Do you mean to let you know if she goes out and comes back in?"

"What?"

"Because she's already here," said Patsy.

Valerie stared at Patsy for a moment, muttered: "Oh, shit," ducked into her office, and slammed the door.

It's a good thing Rosen had the papers for her today. Valerie took the document out of her handbag and then looked around the desk.

"Gotta hide this," she said and grabbed a few older contracts that had been sitting on her desk. Valerie would have negotiated for higher royalty percentages. However, at this stage, they were worth more as decoys than they would be as revenue streams. She shuffled the papers in random order and then stuffed them into a portfolio.

She wouldn't announce that she was taking over as president. Right now, she just needed that paper signed. Valerie rushed to Lorraine's office. The door was open, with Lorraine sitting behind her desk reading correspondence.

Valerie cleared her throat. Lorraine looked up and smiled. It was a warm smile, a welcoming smile, and it was totally "girl." Wherever Chesney had gone, it was clear that he hadn't come back yet.

"Valerie," said Lorraine rising to meet her, "you don't know how happy I am to see you!"

"Good to see you, too," said Valerie, as Lorraine took her arm and led her to the sofa.

"I feel as if it's been years," said Lorraine. "So much has happened. I suppose it all started back in Washington on that terrible day."

Valerie lifted her arm and smiled. "It's okay; my arm's all better now."

An uncomfortable look clouded Lorraine's face. Valerie realized that Lorraine called it a terrible day because of all the people killed at the White House, not because Valerie broke her arm.

"Yes, everything will be better now," said Lorraine squeezing Valerie's hand, "now that we're a team again."

Valerie glanced down at the portfolio in her other hand. She wanted to shove them under Lorraine's nose and get the necessary signature but she didn't want to arouse suspicion.

"I, uh, well, uh," said Valerie trying to think of some small talk.

"It's all right," said Lorraine.

"It is?"

"Dear Valerie," said Lorraine, "you want to console me about the withdrawn nomination."

"I do? Oh, yes, I mean, I do. I do very much," said Valerie adding a sorrowful edge to her voice. "I just didn't know how to say it. I checked the stores, and Hallmark still doesn't make a 'sorry you won't be vice president' card."

Lorraine laughed. "There's really no need to feel sorry for me. Still, you, more than anyone else, should know what's bothering me."

Valerie clutched the documents in her left hand and pushed them further behind her back. Lorraine had figured it out. What Chesney couldn't see in a million years, Lorraine had spotted. It proved what Valerie always knew: women are smarter than men, but at the moment, this offered her little consolation.

"I do?" said Valerie cautiously.

"Of course," said Lorraine. "I never wanted to be vice president or anything else in politics. But, I hate to be a quitter."

"Quitter," repeated Valerie. Then Lorraine hadn't figured it out. Valerie would have to work quickly.

"You know I'm not a quitter," said Lorraine.

Valerie laughed. "You? A quitter? Never! Well, that's all behind you now." She started to pull out the folder. "And you can put it all down as a bad experience and get back to work with the Foundation."

"I wouldn't call it a bad experience," said Lorraine. "After all, it introduced me to..."

Lorraine nodded over Valerie's shoulder. Valerie turned to see Clodagh Clott sitting across the room.

"Hello," said Clodagh with a nonchalant smile. It was irritating.

Valerie almost asked how long she'd been sitting there but realized she must have been there all the time.

"Visiting," said Valerie, "how nice."

"Clodagh's working with us," said Lorraine.

"Us? Like me, us?" said Valerie.

"Yes, of course, you're part of us," said Lorraine. "We're all 'us.'"

Valerie glanced back at the Clott woman and wondered what she knew. She must know a lot because she didn't say much. She looked back at Lorraine, who was beaming. Valerie forced a smile.

"Well, that's great," said Valerie as if she were taking a bite out of a moldy sandwich. "The more, the merrier."

"I heard about Michael Valvano's resignation," said Lorraine. "That was very disappointing news. I liked him very much."

"Yeah, me too," said Valerie.

Lorraine's face dropped. "Do you mean that you two...."

Valerie nodded but also saw an opportunity. "I'd...I'd like to tell you about it...." She rolled her eyes in Clodagh Clott's direction.

"Oh, yes, of course," said Lorraine. "Clodagh, could you give us a few minutes? This is a little bit personal."

"Certainly," said Clodagh rising. She gave Valerie a suspicious glance. "Are you sure you'll be okay?"

"Me?" asked Lorraine. "Of course, it's just a little cousin talk. You understand?"

Clodagh nodded. "I'm certain that I do," she said, meeting Valerie's eyes. Clodagh slowly closed the door behind her, leaving her alone with Lorraine.

"How can I help?" asked Lorraine.

Valerie almost pulled out the papers to get them signed before the Clott woman returned. But she didn't want to arouse Lorraine's suspicion. For a few minutes, Valerie poured out the sad tale of her broken engagement omitting the fact that she and Michael were related. And Lorraine, damn her, was so sympathetic Valerie almost couldn't do what she had come in there to do; almost.

"So, that's basically the story," concluded Valerie. "Michael has gone. He's even resigned from the bank. I don't know who's going to run that."

"I sure they'll find someone," said Lorraine. "If they asked me, I'd recommend Clodagh."

Hadn't it occurred to Lorraine that Valerie was the perfect choice, not some woman with a name like a blob of blood? Thankfully it was up to her new real cousin Robert and not her old fake cousin Lorraine.

"If anyone asks, I'll tell them your suggestion," said Valerie.

"I'm sure that will all sort out," said Lorraine, "these business things usually do. I'm more concerned about you. If there's anything I can do for you, you just have to ask."

"I appreciate that," said Valerie standing up and pretending to leave. Then she looked at the folder in her hand. "Oh, I almost forgot, I came in for some signatures. These were some endorsements, some renewals, that is some endorsement renewals. We couldn't do it when you were going to be in public office, but now that you're not, well, I'd like to get them wrapped up as soon as possible. The Foundation needs to get its revenue streams flowing again."

"Oh, yes, of course," said Lorraine. "If you want to leave them…"

"I'll wait," said Valerie producing a pen. "Like I said, they're all routine, and we need to get your approval as quickly as possible."

"Oh, yes, fine," said Lorraine taking the pen and the folder.

Lorraine scanned the first one, nodded, and then signed it. She did the same with the next two. Valerie held her breath as she came to the fourth item in the stack.

"Wait, what's this?" said Lorraine.

"Hmmm? What?" said Valerie innocently.

"This here," said Lorraine holding up the document. "This isn't a renewal. This is about something called '*Quandry*.'"

"*Quandry*? Oh, yes, that's your designer scent."

Lorraine looked puzzled. "I don't have a designer scent."

"Um, yes, you do," said Valerie nodding towards the paper, "and it's called *Quandry, Lorraine Innis' Quandry*."

"I've never seen it," said Lorraine.

"Oh, yes, that's because it's only been on sale in England. You remember, don't you? It was Purvis' idea."

Lorraine thought a moment. "I do recall him talking about some perfume based on my blood type or something."

"Yes, that's it. That's *Quandry*."

"What an odd name for a perfume," said Lorraine.

"That's what I thought. But Purvis insisted you said that's what it should be called."

"I said that?" Lorraine shook her head. "Oh, wait, when he told me the concept, he asked me what I would call it. I said that was a quandary. I meant that it was a tough question, not that we should call it '*Quandry*.'" Lorraine laughed.

Valerie chuckled along. "That explains it," she said. "That Purvis Twankey can get so easily confused, but I wouldn't hold it against him. He really is a sweet guy."

"Sweet?"

"Yes, don't you think so?" asked Valerie.

"Well, yes, I always thought so," said Lorraine, "but I thought you couldn't stand him."

Valerie shrugged her shoulders. "Oh, well. He means well, and he did think of that perfume. And it is selling well in England, despite the unusual name. And since you were busy in Washington, I had to sign the distribution deal. But it really doesn't belong to me, does it? It's your blood, your genetic makeup, your name on it. This just transfers the legal ownership back to you, all of it."

She smiled sweetly.

"Okay," said Lorraine, "I suppose it all makes sense," and signed her name.

"Thanks," Valerie said, taking the papers back and sticking them in the folder. "Well, I'd better get going."

"Going?"

"Yes, uh, back to work," said Valerie. "I'm sure you're busy, too."

"Yes," said Lorraine, "and thank you for keeping an eye on everything, and especially for that *Quandry* business."

"My pleasure."

"I suppose now we can bring it to the United States," said Lorraine.

"I'm sure," said Valerie opening the door.

"When do you think we'll have it here?"

"Oh, it'll probably be here before you know it," said Valerie closing the door behind her. "Before you know it."

– 61 –
The Manhandling of the Well-Mannered Englishman

Valerie Fierro patted the portfolio on the passenger seat and smiled. She had everything she needed now. Well, almost everything. She felt a pang of regret when she thought of Michael but quickly salved her bruised heart with a healthy dose of ego. Michael was the one missing out, not her. He would realize what he lost. She thought of her father and her grandmother and concluded that there was no stopping her now. Once that English girl tipped her off, Valerie got out of the way before the perfume hit the fan. Soon she would be formally announced as president of the bank. Then she would have a wonderful time making Albrecht Eckner squirm under the stylish heel of her Louboutins. After that, once she had consolidated her power base at the bank, she would see about fulfilling dear Nonnia's last wish and take control of the entire Valvano operation. Then they would all have to answer to her. Maybe even Michael would have to come to her for an allowance. Another man under her…

"Louboutins," she said aloud as she drove past the mall. Yes, she would have to do some shoe shopping soon as a reward for her success.

Valerie arrived home and poured herself a glass of wine and sipped it as she imagined which she would enjoy more: the shoes or the revenge. Valerie jumped when the doorbell rang. She made her way to the front door.

"Miss Fierro?" asked a well-dressed man with a British accent.

"Yes."

"Miss Valerie Fierro?"

"That's right, I'm Valerie Fierro."

He started reaching into the inside pocket of his double-breasted suit.

"Oh, this is good timing. I've been expecting you," said Valerie, "just not so quickly. Still, it's fine. Please won't you come inside?"

The man managed a confused smile and followed her inside.

"I was about to go shopping," said Valerie, "but I doubt our business will take very long." She retrieved her glass of wine. "I'd offer you some wine, but I don't think you'll have the time. You have something for me?"

The man looked around as if he had come to the wrong address.

"Well, yes, I do, Miss Fierro," he said, reaching into his left inside jacket pocket. He gave a start when he found it was empty.

"Other side," said Valerie, "or at least that's the side you were reaching for a minute ago." This was fun.

"Other... oh, yes, thank you," said the man, "you'll forgive me. I'm not usually so nonplussed."

"Really, how nonplussed are you, usually?"

"It's just that you not only appear to know why I'm here, but you seem to know the contents of my suit better than I do myself."

Valerie winked, "well, at least the upper half."

The man blushed and coughed.

"I represent the firm of Blaketon, Ventris, and Bellamy, Solicitors," said the man in more authoritative tones, and handed Valerie a business card.

"Solicitors," interrupted Valerie, "that's like British for lawyers, right?"

"Quite..."

"Thought so," said Valerie, "go ahead, oh, wait, just a second."

She put down her wine glass and retrieved a document from her portfolio.

"Sorry," she said. "If I knew you'd were coming this afternoon, I would have had this out for you."

"As I was saying," he continued, "I represent..."

"Right, Lord Bagshot's lawyers..."

"Bagnall, Lord Bagnall..."

"And he's suing me about that hinkey perfume..."

"Hinkey? Well, yes," he looked down at the paper in his hands, "the scent known as *Lorraine Innis' Quandry*. But it isn't just his Lordship. He's just one of the parties in a class-action suit..."

"Sure, sure, him and a flock of British babes with beards, right?"

"I wouldn't have put it so alliteratively," said the attorney, "but that's approximately..."

"Great," said Valerie presenting her own document, "this is for you. It's a copy, but it will tell you all you need to know."

The man began to read the document drafted by Julius Rosen.

"I'll save you the time," said Valerie, "it says you got the wrong woman. Lorraine Innis is the full and rightful owner of that perfume: all its rights, all its royalties, and all its, uh...." Valerie stroked her own smooth chin, "...all its residual effects."

The lawyer looked up from the document. "Then you know of..."

She shook her head. "Know? I don't know anything aside from the fact, all spelled out in that document, that I don't have anything to do with

Lorraine Innis' Quandry. Please, keep it, take it back to jolly old England with you if you like. Read over it with Ventris, Baloney, and whoever you got kicking around your office with their silly white wigs. But take my word for it. That's all nice and legal, and it all says just what I'm telling you now in simpler language: I don't own that perfume. I didn't invent it. I don't even use it. Now, if you'll excuse me, Mr..." she looked down at his card, "...Walker, I'm rather busy. Thanks for dropping by."

"Yes, thank you, I think," said Mr. Walker glancing at the writ. "This will all have to be changed now."

"Oh, well," said Valerie.

"Yes, it will take days," he suddenly looked up. "You won't divulge to Mrs. Innis about this. I would consider it a great favor if you didn't."

"Wouldn't dream of it, old bean," said Valerie as she gently pushed him out the door and locked it behind him. Valerie was struck with how easily one could manhandle a well-mannered Englishman.

– 62 –
Minnie's a Dirty Girl

"Now, there are only three of us."

"These sandwiches are really good, Hristo."

Hristo looked at his two assistants eating cheesesteaks. One had iridescent cheese stuff ringing his mouth. The other had the goo dripping down his elbows.

"I'm not hungry," said Hristo, "besides, that's your second and your third."

"So, we need to build up our strength. We have a big job ahead of us," said Anton.

"You'll have a big punch on your nose if you don't keep your mouth shut," warned Hristo. He glanced around the Minquadale, Delaware sandwich shop.

"You need to relax, boss," said Anton. "If you're not picking on me for what's going into my mouth, you're complaining about what comes out of it."

"I'd be happier if we could just have your big trap sewn shut," said Hristo.

The third member of the party wiped the cheese from his fingers with a thin paper napkin before poking his leader's elbow.

"He's right, take it easy, boss," said Mecko. "Besides, no one knows what we're saying. I doubt anyone here in Florida knows Bulgarian."

Hristo rolled his eyes.

"Florida? You idiot," laughed Anton, his mouth once more half-full of cheesesteak, "we're in Detroit!"

"We're in Delaware," growled Hristo.

His henchmen gave a collective shrug as if to say such information was beyond their pay grades.

Hristo shook his head. If he wasn't afraid of Teplov, he'd call off the whole mission. First, Mecko's brother Marco didn't even make the flight due to an expired passport. What was worse, Hristo had reckoned Marco to be his brainiest assistant. Now he was lumbered with the second- and third-class imbeciles in what was a very delicate operation.

He watched in silence as Anton and Mecko pulled napkin after napkin out of the metal dispenser on the table. They were averaging two and a half napkins per each sloppy bite of their sandwiches.

"I told you two to speak as little as possible," said Hristo in a low voice. "The idea is not to attract attention to yourselves, to blend in with your surroundings."

Mecko forced down a mouthful of meat. "That's why we're eating these. I looked it up. This is a favorite local food."

"That," added Anton, "and we got our American type shirts. Everyone will think we're average Americans."

Hristo looked at their t-shirts and nodded. They had done well in that regard. Anton wore a shirt emblazoned with Minnie Mouse, while Mecko's shirt had a picture of some people called "The Backstreet Boys." Yes, in that respect, they both had managed to blend in.

"Still, we can't be too careful. We've already lost Marco."

"He's not lost," said Mecko, his mouth bulging with meat, "he's back home. I called him earlier."

"I thought I said 'radio silence,'" said Hristo.

"I didn't use a radio. I used the phone in the Motel 6."

"I don't mean radio, radio," said their leader. "I mean no contact, especially not with home."

"Marco had the pictures," said Anton wiping his fingers on the last napkin and looking for some more.

"I have a copy," said Hristo. "You don't think I'd come all this way without it, do you? Idiot!"

Mecko took a loud slurp of soda from a styrofoam cup. "Can I see it?"

Hristo looked around furtively. The place was empty. Even the counter person was in the back talking with someone in the kitchen.

"Yeah, okay," he said and looked down. "Where is it? It's gone! We've been robbed!" He looked at Mecko, who merely shrugged as he picked a piece of gristle from between his teeth. He looked at Anton, who was innocently wiping his hands on the missing picture.

"Dope!" He said, grabbing back the crinkled photograph. It was smeared with bright orange cheesy goo. Hristo looked around for a napkin. Finding none, he used his fingers to squeegee the mess from the photo and then wiped his fingers on Anton's shirt.

"You've soiled Minnie Mouse!" cried Anton.

"Now you look even more like an American, you fool," said Hristo. He looked down at the photo. It was stained. It was creased. But it would have to do.

– 63 –
Any Friend of Peter Liverot

I would advise against it, Miss Fierro."

"You wanna watch yourself, Cuz."

The warnings of Julius Rosen and Robert Valvano ran through Valerie's mind as she drove. After they had expressed such confidence in her brains and her business acumen, they were hesitating. One of the bank's clients, an old contact of Peter Liverot, wanted to meet her. And Robert and Rosen were suddenly squeamish about her abilities.

"You don't want to meet that guy," Robert told her.

"Why not?" Valerie asked.

"He's a person with questionable ties," said Rosen.

"He a crook," said Robert. "He's filth."

"How do you know?" asked Valerie.

"Because he's a friend of Liverot, another piece of shit."

"He's the sort the bank wants to disassociate with," said Rosen.

There followed at least 30 minutes of warnings, advice, and hand wringing by the two men. She got the impression this was a test on her qualification to be the bank's new president.

"I appreciate your advice, boys," she said, "but I can handle this. If you don't think I can, well, you have my resignation. Otherwise, I may meet with this Mr. Long, or I may not, but either way, the decision will be mine."

Both men exchanged uneasy looks.

"Yeah, yeah, you're right," said Robert reluctantly. "Only be careful. You're in the big leagues now, and this guy can play rough."

"I'll look out for the bank's interests," said Valerie.

"Yeah, well, I mean, look out for yourself, too," muttered Robert. After the tempestuous start of their relationship, it was almost sweet. Big tough, swaggering Robert Valvano was worried about his cousin.

"I'll be careful," said Valerie. "I haven't even said I'd meet with him."

As soon as she left Robert, Valerie was on the phone arranging the meeting. Reports of his shady business practices were well-founded: he wanted to meet Valerie on a park bench in a secluded corner of a remote park down in Kent County.

She was sitting there, glancing at her watch, when suddenly she heard a voice behind her.

"Did you come alone?"

Valerie Fierro turned around. The speaker was short and skinny.

"I said, are you alone?"

Valerie peered over the top of her sunglasses and glared at him.

"Of course I'm alone," she said after a prolonged pause.

He sat down on the bench, taking care not to sit too close to her. "It's a good place to meet if you don't want no one to see you."

Valerie was beginning to question the wisdom of meeting this man. Maybe Robert had been right. But then, this was her chance to prove that she was up to the job. She would be a better bank president than Liverot.

The man raised a newspaper and pretended to read. "So, you're the replacement?"

"I am the president of the Fourth Fiduciary," said Valerie.

He glanced at her from behind the paper and made a slight shrug.

"Look, Mr. Long…"

"Shhh," he cautioned, "not so loud. And just call me 'Sh…' uh, 'Sheldon.'"

"Sheldon?"

"You got a problem with people named 'Sheldon?'"

"No."

"Okay then, look, I got somewhere I gotta be, so let's wrap this up," said Sheldon.

"We have nothing to wrap up."

"Sure we do…" He removed a document from his breast pocket and handed it to her. Valerie took it and glanced at it.

"I'll have to review this…"

"Review?" said Sheldon putting down his paper and looking both ways. "It's the same deal I had before."

"I wasn't the president of the bank before," said Valerie. The man's scrawny appearance coupled with the name "Sheldon" suddenly made her feel quite confident. "I'll take this with me."

The man reached out for the papers. "Don't you trust me?"

Valerie laughed.

"Yeah," whined Sheldon, "well, Liverot trusted me."

Valerie laughed even harder.

"Mr. Long…"

"Sheldon."

"Mr. Long, there's a new person at the helm."

"Who?"

"Me!" said Valerie. "And I am not going to renew any arrangements you had with my predecessor without reviewing it, along with the firm's lawyer."

"Lawyer?" Sheldon Long started squirming as if army ants were suddenly crawling up his leg. "You don't need no lawyer. You know this can be mutually beneficial… to both of us."

Valerie thought of Lord Bagnall and shook her head. "Mr. Long, I've negotiated with bigger fish than you. I don't know what arrangement you had before, but your manner, your choice of meeting place, and frankly everything about you makes me think that it won't be renewed, not at my bank."

"Can I have my proposal back?"

She handed it to him, and for some odd reason, he paused as she held it between them.

"Now, I think you've wasted enough of my time," said Valerie. She began to rise.

"Hold it," he growled. Valerie was surprised at the menacing tone of his voice. He reached back into his breast pocket. She expected him to pull out a gun. Valerie clutched the strap of her handbag, ready to swing it into his face and run. Instead, he pulled out a photograph.

"Is this really your cousin," he asked, his tone once more benign. He held out a picture of Lorraine.

"What?"

"Is this really your cousin?"

Valerie nodded.

"I really think she's terrific," said Sheldon Long.

"Oh, uh, well, thank you," she started to stand.

"Wait," he said and pulled out another photograph. This one was of a car. "My nephew is trying to sell his car."

"What?"

"Yeah, look, it's really nice, see?"

"So?" asked Valerie. She glanced at the picture. The car was probably stolen.

"You in the market for a car? It's really nice."

Valerie looked at him as if he were crazy and shook her head. "No, no, I've got a car. Thanks."

She got up and walked away.

"You have a nice day," called Sheldon Long.

Valerie walked a little faster.

– 64 –
The Slipping Halo

Lorraine expected it, sooner or later. It was inevitable. She just didn't expect to hear it from Patsy Einfalt.

"You're not a nice person," said Patsy, bursting excitedly into Lorraine's office. "And you're a spy, too!"

Lorraine looked up at Patsy and smiled. "Oh?"

"Yes," said Patsy, "oh, wait, I don't mean that's what I think. No, it's what they're saying," she said, jerking her thumb over her shoulder.

Lorraine looked past Patsy, but she was alone.

"They?" asked Lorraine.

"The TV!" said Patsy.

Lorraine looked at Patsy for a moment. The secretary's face was filled with anxiety as if the worst judgment conceivable was rendered by "them" on television.

"I see," said Lorraine. She went back to reviewing the reports on her desk. After a moment, she could feel Patsy still staring at her. "Was there anything else, Patsy?"

Patsy's eye widened. "Anything else? I don't know, I only saw two channels. Isn't that horrible enough?"

Lorraine smiled. "Is it true?"

Patsy's brow furrowed as she pondered the question. "True? Oh, I hope not! I mean, is it? No, it isn't true. Is it?"

Lorraine shook her head. "I'm not a spy. And as far as being a nice person, that's a rather subjective question that is open to a wide range of personal opinions."

"Well, I think you're a nice person!"

"Thank you," said Lorraine, "I value your opinion more than anyone on television."

"Have you seen these," asked Clodagh Clott, entering carrying a stack of newspapers.

"No," said Lorraine, "but by the look on your face, I can guess what they say."

"'Lorraine Innis: Russian Plant?'" read Clodagh from one headline. She threw it down on the desk and continued. "'Was It All a Set-Up?' 'Did Lorraine Steal Our Hearts To Stab Us in the Back?' 'Senator's Questions Throw Suspicion on Innis.'"

Lorraine picked up the last one. "Innis, eh? The headlines used to just call me 'Lorraine.' The honeymoon's definitely over when they go from first names to just last ones." She leaned back in her chair.

"You seem to be taking all this very calmly," said Clodagh.

Lorraine shrugged. "I've tried to take it all calmly. I tried not to get carried away on all the adulation when the roller coaster was going up, so I'm certainly not going to get upset on the ride down."

"But they're saying things about you that just aren't true," said Patsy, almost in tears. "It's not nice! It's not fair!"

Lorraine rose and put her arm around Patsy. "You're right, Patsy. They're saying things about me now that aren't true. But they were also saying things about me that weren't very accurate before when they were praising me to the skies. I accidentally saved Nikolai Kropotkin's life. After that, I had a normal conversation with him from which he somehow drew inspiration. I was just being myself. Other recreated me as some sort of saintly icon. Hopefully, the roller coaster will come back to the start, and I'll get off the ride the same ordinary person I was at the start."

"But what they're saying now isn't true!" repeated Patsy. "You're a wonderful person, and they can't get away with saying these things."

"Always be wary when people but a halo over your head, Patsy," said Lorraine. "It only has to slip a few inches to become a noose."

"But what will you do about it?" said Patsy.

"The same as I've always done, nothing," said Lorraine. "I can't control what other people do or say. I can control how I react to it. I have work to do here. This foundation has been entrusted to me. I will discharge my duties faithfully until the time that work is finished or I'm discharged."

Lorraine gave Patsy a hug. "Now, I suggest we all get back to work and not worry about people whose only job is to talk about others. Okay?"

Patsy nodded, wiped away a tear, forced a smile, and left, closing the door behind her.

Clodagh asked Lorraine to sit down. Then looking at her intently, said: "Verity Goodhue."

Lorraine laughed. "Clodagh, you're a bit mixed up. I'm not under now. Remember?"

"Oh," said Clodagh, scratching her head, "I forgot. It's just that your speech just now was so eloquent and mature…"

"That it couldn't come from Chesney Potts?"

"Sorry."

"I'm teasing you, Clodagh," said Lorraine. "Remember, you brought me out last night?"

"Oh, yes, that's right," she said with a shake of her head. "I'd better start writing this down or hang a sign around your neck. One side could say 'in' and the flip side 'out.'"

"Well, hopefully, it won't be necessary for much longer," said Lorraine picking up a newspaper. "Actually, if public opinion is turning, it will make it that easier for Lorraine Innis to fade back into obscurity and disappear for good. It's all been a terrible distraction to finding out the truth about Martina."

"I have a theory about that," said Clodagh. "I don't have any evidence, but perhaps it may open up a new avenue of investigation."

"That's great!" Lorraine delivered a masculine slap to Clodagh's shoulder. "Oh, sorry, Clo, but at this stage, I'm open to any suggestions. Now, sit down, let's hear your theory…"

The phone rang, the light indicating that it was Patsy. Lorraine answered it.

"Okay, give me a few minutes, I'll come out…" she said and then hung up. "You'd better put me under."

"Why? What's wrong?" asked Clodagh.

"I don't know, but I have a funny feeling. There's a lawyer waiting to see me."

Clodagh shrugged. "You've seen lawyers before. It's probably something to do with a donor or a sponsor."

Lorraine shook her head. "No, I could tell by Patsy's tone. She's always professional with visitors, but this one gave her pause."

"Pause?"

"Patsy probably would have called it 'the willies,'" clarified Lorraine, "but the end result is the same. Whoever this visitor is, there's something different about him."

"Like what?"

"For one thing, he's not from around here. Patsy said he had a British accent."

"Maybe it's something to do with… you know. Maybe she's left you something."

"I don't know, perhaps, but that's why I want Lorraine to handle this, so, if you'll do the honors…."

– 65 –
Puttin' on the Writs

The visitor looked distinguished. He wore an impeccably tailored suit complete with what could be described as an "old school tie." He seemed oddly familiar to Lorraine.

"Mrs. Innis, it's an honor," said the man.

It may have been an honor, but nothing on the man's face indicated that it was also a pleasure.

"My name is Walker," he said, handing Lorraine a card.

"Blaketon, Ventris and Bellamy, Solicitors," read Lorraine aloud. She glanced back at Clodagh. "Won't you come in, Mr. Walker? Would you like some tea?"

"Regrettably, this is not a social call.."

"I didn't think it was," said Lorraine. She smiled at Walker, but his businesslike expression soon drove away that pleasantry.

"Neither is it a particularly agreeable task," he said. "I would say that I have the greatest admiration for you, but my professional duty precludes that personal observation."

"Oh, well, what can I do for you, Mr. Walker," she said. "Hopefully, nothing tragic has brought you here all the way from London."

"That remains to be determined by individuals and parties aside from myself, Mrs. Innis," said Walker. He looked at Patsy and then Clodagh as if to verify that they were watching. "It is my duty, unpleasant or otherwise, to present you with this."

The attorney handed Lorraine a document.

"Thank you," she said, "what is it?"

Clodagh glanced over Lorraine's shoulder. "I think you're being sued."

Lorraine scanned the paper. "*Quandry*? But that's the perfume…"

"Precisely," said Mr. Walker.

She flipped through the document. There was a long list of names going on for several pages. "There are an awful lot of people here," said Lorraine, "and it seems like they're all women."

"Yes," said the lawyer.

"No one's been hurt, have they?" asked Lorraine. "I mean, what could perfume do?"

"It's all there, Mrs. Innis," said Walker taciturnly. "I'm not at liberty to comment."

Clodagh reached over Lorraine's arm and grabbed the edge of the document. "Beards?"

"What?" said Lorraine.

"It says here that the perfume caused these women to grow beards... and mustaches, too!"

Lorraine looked up at the attorney. "Is this true?"

"It is not my duty to ascertain the merits of the case," said Mr. Walker. "It is only for me to serve the writ."

"I meant is it true that women in England are growing beards because of this product?" said Lorraine.

The man rolled his eyes slowly around as if trying to detect some hidden camera or microphone. "I don't believe I'm disclosing anything not in the writ, but, yes, Mrs. Innis, the claim is that the fragrance known as *Lorraine Innis' Quandary* has led to an unusual amount of hirsuteness on part of the half of the population not usually given to such follically produced appendages on those parts of their persons, vis a vis their faces."

Lorraine and Clodagh stared at each other for a moment.

"I think he means 'yes,'" said Clodagh.

"I appreciate your understanding," said Mr. Walker with a polite nod. "And now, my charge having been discharged, I bid you ladies..."

"Hold it," said Clodagh, "I think you're making a mistake. It's only her name on the bottle," said Clodagh. "She didn't invent the stuff. I don't care if it grew hair on the Queen's bottom..."

"Have a care!" gasped the lawyer.

"Lorraine Innis has nothing to do with it," continued Clodagh flipping through the document. "She wasn't even in charge of anything when this all happened. She was nominated for vice president at the time. She had relinquished all control."

Mr. Walker nodded. "I refer you to the document at the end. The one in which Mrs. Innis asserted her full ownership of the product, including all rights, benefits, and liabilities."

"That can't be," said Clodagh flipping through the pages.

"Yes, it can, Clo," said Lorraine softly.

"Yes, it can," repeated Clodagh as she read the page in question. She looked at Lorraine. "When did you do this?" Before Lorraine could answer, Clodagh looked down at the bottom of the paper at the date. "But that was just a few days ago when...who..."

Clodagh stopped in mid-sentence. She clenched her fists and gritted her teeth.

"Well, my duty is discharge, thank you," Mr. Walker started backing towards the door without taking his eyes off the enraged Clodagh Clott. "I'll bid you…" He reached to tip his hat and then realized he hadn't worn one. "…yes, well, goodbye…"

With that, the attorney exited.

"I'm sorry, Clo, please don't be angry with me," said Lorraine.

Clodagh looked at Lorraine and tried to smile. The attempt was brief and unsuccessful. She stroked Lorraine's arm.

"I'm not mad at you, Ches."

"Who?"

"What? Oh, right, never mind. I mean, I'm not mad at you, Lorraine, but I smell a rat in this perfume."

"Eau de Rodent, how revolting!" said Lorraine.

"Come on," said Clodagh grabbing Lorraine's hand.

"Where? Where are we going?"

"To talk to your dear cousin," said Clodagh through gritted teeth.

"Do you think Valerie knows who did this," said Lorraine.

Clodagh stopped and stared at Lorraine. "How can someone be so smart and so naïve in the same day?"

Before she could reply, Clodagh was pulling Lorraine down the hall.

"I assumed that was a rhetorical question," said Lorraine tottering behind her on her heels. "Yes, it was, wasn't it?"

Clodagh pulled Lorraine into Valerie's office. She wasn't there.

"Okay," huffed Clodagh, and whipped out of the room again, still with a tight grip on Lorraine's hand.

She led her out to the reception area where Patsy sat.

"That English lawyer talked awfully nice," said Patsy. "Purvis is English, but he doesn't talk like that. Posh, I think they call it. I'm glad Purvis doesn't talk like that. I couldn't relax around a man who talked like that all over the house."

"Patsy," said Clodagh, "where's Miss Fierro?"

"Valerie? She left," said Patsy glancing at her wristwatch. "She left right after Mr. Walker came in. She saw him, and she said she had an appointment."

"Did she say when she'd be back?" asked Clodagh.

"No, no, she didn't, not exactly. She said she had an out of town speaking engagement on behalf of the Foundation."

"Out of town?" said Lorraine.

"Yes, she said she was booked in to speak to a Brownie troop this afternoon in Scranton."

"Scranton?"

"That's in Pennsylvania," said Patsy.

"Yes, I know," said Lorraine. "It just seems odd."

"That's where it's always been," said Patsy.

"That's it," said Clodagh. She ran back towards Lorraine's office and quickly returned with her handbag. "I've got to go out."

"Are you speaking somewhere, too?" asked Patsy.

"Where are you going, Clo?" asked Lorraine.

"I'll tell you when I get back," said Clodagh, "and I expect to come back with the answers to some of your biggest questions."

Clodagh hurried out. Lorraine looked at Patsy, but before she could say anything, Clodagh returned.

"Damn!" said Clodagh.

"What?" asked Lorraine.

"Did you get the answers already?" asked Patsy.

"They picked up my car from the lot this morning for an oil change," said Clodagh. "Can I borrow your car?"

"Of course you can," said Lorraine.

She retrieved her keys and handed them to Clodagh.

"It's in my parking space," said Lorraine. "The gray..."

Before she could finish her sentence, Clodagh had thanked her and was out the door.

– 66 –
Boom, My Honda Went Boom

Lorraine Innis stared at the writ.

"This has certainly been an eventful morning," said Lorraine.

"It's been kind of exciting," said Patsy. "I'd even say it was fun, except for everyone suddenly not liking you and you getting sued."

"I suppose I'll have to get a lawyer," said Lorraine. "Maybe Valerie knows of one."

"Purvis will be upset," said Patsy.

"Why?"

"It was his invention," said Patsy.

"Oh, yes, that's right. I'd almost forgotten."

A look of horror crossed Patsy's face. She reached in her desk drawer, pulled out a small mirror, and examined her face. After scrutiny of her chin, she sighed a sigh of relief.

"What's wrong?" asked Lorraine.

"I used that perfume, too," said Patsy. "Thankfully, I'm not growing a beard."

"Yes, odd that," said Lorraine. "Oh, I don't mean that you should have grown a beard. I wouldn't want that. I meant it's odd that these other women grew beards."

"It was supposed to make them feel more like you," said Patsy.

Lorraine winced. "Well, I certainly can't grow a beard. I don't even have one of those light peach fuzz mustaches."

"You're lucky," said Patsy fingering her own upper lip. "Was your mother like that, too?"

Lorraine opened her mouth to answer but suddenly realized she couldn't picture her own mother. "I... I don't know.... I suppose..."

Her confusion was short-lived as a familiar face entered the office.

"Margie!" said Lorraine and embraced Agent MacKay. "What are you doing here?"

"We're just closing up our satellite branch," said Margie MacKay, "now that you don't need our protection. I just wanted to stop by and say goodbye before I head back to Washington."

"It must be so exciting to be a real Secret Service lady," said Patsy. "Just like in the movies."

Margie smiled. "Actually, most of the work is fairly routine. We never perceived any credible threats against Mrs. Innis. But all the same, we had to follow…"

Margie MacKay's explanation was cut short by the sound of a muffled thud, and a tremor shook the building.

"What was that?" said Patsy. "Did you feel that? What was it?"

"It almost felt like an earthquake," said Margie.

"Earthquakes are rare in Delaware," said Lorraine, "at least ones that can be felt so…"

A second later, the sound of alarms could be heard in the distance.

"Maybe it was a car crash down on the street," said Patsy. "Maybe one of those big dump trucks hit the building. I suppose if…"

Patsy's phone rang.

"Hello, Cross of… What? Yes…yes…"

Patsy put her hand over the mouthpiece and looked up at Lorraine.

"Your car is a silver Honda?"

"I always thought it was just gray," said Lorraine.

"And do you park it in your assigned parking space?"

"Yes," said Lorraine.

"Yes, that's Mrs. Innis' car," said Patsy into the phone. "Okay, thanks. Well, that explains the noise," said Patsy as she hung up the receiver.

"Someone hit my car?" said Lorraine.

"It would have to have been a tank to shake the building like that," said Margie MacKay.

Patsy shook her head. "No, they didn't hit your car. It just blew up."

– 67 –
Recollection of Another Burnt Shell

Lorraine Innis hurried down the stairs. Agent Margie MacKay advised it in case the power went out as a result of the blast. Lorraine negotiated the concrete steps as quickly as she could in heels. Margie was ahead of her, wearing much more practical rubber-soled shoes.

"I still think you should have stayed upstairs," said Margie pausing on a landing, waiting for Lorraine to catch up.

"It's my car," said Lorraine. "At least I…" She froze for a moment.

"What?"

"Good heavens," cried Lorraine, "Clodagh, I gave the keys to Clodagh…."

Heels be damned; with a burst of adrenaline, Lorraine shot past Margie. By the time they had reached the level of the garage, she was at least half a flight ahead of the Secret Service agent.

"Wait…" shouted Margie, but Lorraine was already through the steel door leading to the parking area. The burning automobile was in an isolated spot, about twenty yards down the garage. Margie caught up with her and put her arms around her.

"Clodagh…" cried Lorraine.

"Stop, let the fire crew do it," said Margie. She turned Lorraine around and shielded her as best she could.

Firemen were putting out the fire in what remained of Lorraine's car. It was indistinguishable, except as a charred, blackened metal frame.

Suddenly, Lorraine started to pant for breath, and the scene in front of her faded away, replaced by another burnt car, this one a convertible in a ravine.

"Mrs. Innis, Lorraine," she heard a voice say.

Lorraine looked to her left, and the face of Margie MacKay came back into focus.

"You had the oddest expression," said Margie.

"It was a convertible," whispered Lorraine.

Margie looked at the car and then back at Lorraine. "It's a sedan."

Lorraine looked at the car in front of them. "Yes, of course, a sedan," said Lorraine.

"Fire's out," said the head of the fire crew. "Just have to wait for the coroner."

"For a car?" said Lorraine.

Margie looked at the fireman, then back at Lorraine. She put her arm tightly around Lorraine's shoulder.

"There was someone in the driver's seat."

Lorraine stared at the man.

"The body, or what's left of it, is burnt beyond any recognition," said the fireman. "We can't even tell if it was a man or a woman."

Lorraine looked at the car.

"It's a woman," said Lorraine softly. "That is, it was a woman."

Margie MacKay flashed her Secret Service credentials. "Are the police here? I want this area sealed off. I don't want anyone touching that car."

She looked off to the side. Two building security guards were there.

"Surveillance cameras?" said MacKay to the guards. They looked at each other for a moment.

"Uh, yeah, cameras, they're right..." the guard turned and pointed toward a bare bracket and tangle of wires. "Well, they were there."

"Great," muttered Margie.

"Who would want to hurt Clodagh," muttered Lorraine.

"No one," said Margie.

"But then..."

"It's your car," she said softly. "You were the probable target."

– 68 –
I Buy a New Dress, but I'd Better Make It Black

When the going gets tough, the tough go shopping. At least that was Valerie Fierro's solution when that English lawyer arrived to serve the papers on that hinky perfume. Fortunately, Valerie had just enough time to give Patsy a lame excuse and get out of the building before Lorraine was served.

She hated to dump that whole perfume mess on Lorraine or Chesney, or either of them, but it was ultimately all their fault after all. Valerie wasn't going to sit idly by while a bunch of bearded women sued her. She wondered whether Lorraine would be smart enough to figure out why Valerie had re-assigned the rights to the perfume back to her. Probably not, thought Valerie, but then that posh-talking English lawyer might fill her in. Or, that smart-ass Clodagh Clott would probably figure it all out. Either way, Valerie knew her only move at the moment was to get out of the office. She couldn't very well go home. That would be the first place someone would look for her. That just left shopping.

She was ensconced in a dressing cubicle, trying on a little cocktail dress, when she heard the commotion outside in the shop. The noise was curious. After all, she was in Greenville, in an upscale shop. Outbursts and hubbubs were to be expected in the mall, but here she was among the moneyed classes. Perhaps someone saw a spider, or a middle-class woman wandered in and saw the prices. That would have made sense if the uproar had died down. But it continued and was accompanied by a buzz of discussion and even the sound of sobbing.

"It's horrible," said one woman.

"Those sort of things don't happen in Delaware," said another.

"There's more to that one," said a third, "I've always said so."

"But she was so nice. I saw her once in the grocery store "

"What's happened," asked Valerie, emerging from the dressing room.

321

"It was just on the radio," said one of the shop assistants, "and then..."

All the women turned and looked at Valerie.

"It's her," one whispered to another, "that's the cousin."

Valerie smiled and nodded. She had been on enough magazine covers to be recognized in public. It was a bore. She'd have to sign autographs. Instead of asking for autographs, however, they stood there staring at her.

Finally, one spoke. "Someone should tell her."

They exchanged uncomfortable glances.

"Tell me what?" asked Valerie.

More uneasy looks were swapped.

"It's your store, you tell her," said a saleswoman.

"Come with me, dear," said an older, impeccably dressed woman.

"Is there something wrong?" asked Valerie.

The woman smiled sympathetically and led Valerie by the arm into a back room. There, she sat Valerie down, pulled a bottle of whiskey from a desk drawer, and poured Valerie a glass.

"It's a little early for the hard stuff," said Valerie. "What's going on?"

The woman closed the door and sat next to Valerie. She held Valerie's hand.

"You're Valerie Fierro, aren't you?"

"Yes, of course..."

"Lorraine Innis' cousin?"

"Yeah, okay..."

The woman bit her lower lip, eyed the liquor as if she might need the drink, and then looked Valerie in the eye.

"Your cousin, Mrs. Innis," said the woman, "has just been blown up."

Valerie stared at the woman for a minute, as if somehow the words might change, but she just stared at her. Finally, Valerie nodded slowly, picked up the whiskey, and swallowed it in one gulp.

She then took a deep breath, looked around the room, and then back at the shop owner.

"I'd like to see some black dresses," she said.

– 69 –
When I Take My Golf Clubs to Sea

The boat was waiting along the Delaware River on the New Jersey side.

"Are you our boat?" Hristo asked a scruffy fisherman type in an equally dilapidated cabin cruiser.

"You the foreign folks looking for a bit of fishing?"

"We are us," said Hristo.

"Then I'm yer captain."

Hristo looked at the boat and grimaced. "Can this takes us where we need to go?"

The captain looked fore and aft, and then back again, scratched his beard. "I reckon so. Either way, I've got your dough, and I m insured, so even if I don't come back, my old lady will be set."

Now it was Hristo's turn to scratch. Not having a beard, he had to make do with the top of his head. He didn't understand the references to dough or old women but reasoned if the man was satisfied with his own boat's seaworthiness, Hristo wasn't in a position to argue with him. Besides, they had to keep to schedule.

Hristo motioned to Anton. Anton just stood by the trunk of the car.

"I can't do it alone," he pleaded in Bulgarian.

Hristo looked at the captain, who apparently didn't understand, but also didn't seem to care what language they spoke. Hristo hustled over to the car and opened the trunk. He nodded towards the one end of the long vinyl bag and picked up the other end. They struggled to carry the zippered sack towards the boat. The captain just stared.

"It is our golf clubs," explained Hristo. "His golf clubs. He never goes anywhere without them."

"Very handy on a fishing trip," said the captian.

"Yes," agreed Hristo, not understanding the sarcasm.

"What did you say?" asked Anton in Bulgarian.

"Shut up, don't worry about it," replied Hristo.

"You didn't tell him about Mecko, did you? You didn't tell him what happened, did you?"

"Shut up," said Hristo as he lifted the weight over the edge of the boat. "Did you hear me say 'Mecko?' Mecko is the same in English as Bulgarian. Did you hear me say 'Mecko?'"

"No."

"Well, then I couldn't have said anything about the idiot. May he rest peacefully, the moron."

Anton climbed aboard and stumbled, almost dropping his end of the load.

"Be careful," shouted Hristo before turning to the captain. "He's very clumsy with his golf clubs."

The captain shrugged.

Hristo gently lowered his end against the bulwarks and motioned Anton to do the same. Then, spying a canvas tarp, covered up the bag.

"Just to keep it out of sight," explained Hristo in English, before hastily adding, "I mean, to keep them from getting wet."

The captain shook his head and walked to the boat's small enclosed cabin. After several asthmatic wheezes and several belches of smoke, the engine started, and they got underway.

"What about the car?" asked Anton.

"It doesn't matter about the car," said Hristo.

"But you bought it," he said as they watched the rusty brown Buick disappear from view.

"Look, if you want, I'll give it to you," he pulled the car keys from his pocket. "It's a present, a bonus. Once we finish the mission, you can come back here and sell it or drive it around, or use it to pick up girls, I don't care."

Anton held out his hand for the keys. Hristo rolled his eyes and then threw the keys into the river.

"Hey! That's my car!"

"If I didn't need someone to help with the… golf clubs, I'd throw you in after them."

"Golf clubs?" said Anton.

Hristo nodded towards the tarpaulin. "That what I told the captain what we had in the bag. I think he believes it."

The two shared a hearty laugh entirely in Bulgarian. After twenty seconds of unbridled jocularity, Hristo turned serious.

"Let us not get carried away," he cautioned Anton, "the mission was a success, but it was not without cost."

Anton removed his cap and lowered his head.

Their moment of silence was cut short by the sound of Hristo's cell phone beeping and blipping as he punched in a number.

"It should be okay, now," said Hristo looking around at the widening river as it grew into Delaware Bay. "And I need to give him an update while we still have a signal."

The phone rang twice before being answered by a familiar voice.

"Yes?"

"It is done."

"And you have her?" asked Teplov.

"Of course," bragged Hristo as if there was ever a doubt. "She is right here."

"What? You fool!"

"She is safely hidden in a bag. The boatman thinks it is our golf clubs. Clever, yes?"

There was a momentary silence on the other end.

"You used what I gave you?" continued Teplov.

"Yes, to knock her out. She will be out until we meet the trawler, no?"

"Yes."

"When she wakes up, should we take her out of the sack?"

"If you are safely aboard the trawler and the other boat has left, of course. I do not want her harmed."

"I understand," said Hristo.

"And no one saw you?"

"No. We took her in the parking garage, just as you suggested."

"You disabled any security camera?"

"We didn't need to," said Hristo, "they were already ripped out."

"Americans are vandals and hoodlums," noted Teplov. "Still, I am pleased it went off without any difficulties."

"Um, well..."

"What?"

"Mecko is dead."

"Dead? I thought you said no one saw you."

"No one did, Comrade Tep... uh, my friend."

"Then how did the fool die?"

"It was an accident, I think," said Hristo nervously. "We grabbed Mrs... that is, we neutralized, temporarily, of course, the package. We put her in the trunk of our car. And then we were going to move her... uh, the golf clubs' car to another location to buy time and make it look as if she had driven away on her own. That was the plan."

"I know it was the plan," said Teplov, "it was my plan. What did the idiot do, drive off a cliff?"

"It's odd that you should say that, for there are very few cliffs in this area..."

"What happened, fool?!"

"Mecko got in the car, turned the key, and the car exploded."

"Exploded? How?"

"It was like: BOOM!"

"I didn't mean what it sounded like, never mind. I thought I told you no explosives. What was that moron doing with explosives?"

"We didn't have explosives, just the chloroform. We followed the plan exactly."

"I don't recall giving orders to leave one man home because he didn't have a passport and having one blow up himself! Perhaps you should make another copy of the rest of the plan and give it to Mrs. Innis."

"Why would I do that?"

"So when she wakes up and finds that her remaining two captors have accidentally fallen overboard, she'll know to come here."

"I don't think that she…"

"Just get the woman back here safely, safely you understand, and try to survive the journey yourself, as well!"

"Yes, yes, we will," assured Hristo, but the line had gone dead. He guessed that Teplov had hung up. He looked around, half expecting to see the severed connection dangling in the air.

"Everything okay, matey?" asked the skipper coming out of his cabin.

"What? Oh, yes, uh, just talking to, um, my… mother."

"Your mom, eh," said the captain with the same degree of credulity he had shown with the golf club story, which was precious little. "That's nice. Everything okay with mom?"

"Who? Oh? Yes, mother is fine. I told him we were hurrying home. And he said: don't fall off the boat."

"Good advice," said the captain shuffling back to the wheel, "always listen to your mum; he knows best."

– 70 –
The Magnesium Maggot Wins a Wager

Lord Bagnall hung up the phone. He took a deep breath, vigorously rubbed his hands, and broke into that smile that always made his daughter nervous.

"Good news, Father?" asked Verity warily.

He tried to conceal his glee. "Oh, yes. That was Sidney. Things are just proceeding nicely, nicely indeed. Hee hee!"

Verity eyed him cautiously. "Isn't Sidney one of your lawyers."

"Wot?" He looked back at the telephone. "No, no, I mean, yes, technically 'e's a lawyer, and 'e works for me."

"This wouldn't have anything to do with that perfume, would it?"

His Lordship's face nearly bisected itself under the strain of his grin. With a Herculean effort, he dampened the expression down to a mischievous glint. "Oh, you know lawyers. They're always doing some legal wot not."

"I don't really know lawyers," said Verity, "but I know you. And I'd bet a penny to a pound that the reason you're so chuffed is that your lawyers served papers on Miss Fierro."

Bagnall's palm shot out. "You owes me a penny, smarty. Show's 'ow much you knows!"

"You're not suing Miss Fierro?"

"I h'am not! Not no 'ow!"

Verity looked at him sideways. "Why not?"

His Lordship's lips curled up, and his teeth burst forth. "Cause I got the bigger fish in me net! That's why! Now, cough up me penny!"

Bagnall stood there with his hand extended. Verity sighed under the realization that she wouldn't learn anything further until she'd paid him.

She retrieved a coin from her purse and put it in her father's waiting palm. He looked down at it in surprise.

"I said I'd bet you a penny to a pound," explained Verity nodding to the one-pound coin. "If I had won, I'd have gotten a penny. So I owe you a pound, even though it's just an expression, and I am your daughter."

"Quite right, to all of it," said Lord Bagnall as he triumphantly flipped the coin into the air before snatching it again and thrusting it into the safety of his pocket.

"Now," said Verity, "now that I've paid you, could you tell me what you're so happy about if you're not suing Miss Fierro?"

"I told you, I gots a bigger fish in me net, a much bigger one."

Verity bit her lip. There could only be one person her father would consider bigger. She kept silent, afraid of what he would say next.

"My lawyer just served papers on Lorraine Innis!"

"But Father," said Verity, "didn't you want Lorraine Innis to endorse your products? I don't think the way to ingratiate yourself with her is to drag her into court."

"Ah, that's where you's is all wet," said Bagnall. "That's why I'm a maggot of industry, and you is just a daughter of an industrial maggot."

"I can't argue with you on that assessment, Father."

"Don't you see," he said, "this not only gets me off the hook for that perfume fiasco with all them bearded birds..."

"...By leading their suit after you sold them the stuff."

"Exactly," he continued ignoring her sarcasm, "not only does it do that, but it will put that Innis woman in me debt."

"By suing her? Oh, yes, you'll be her absolute favorite person after that."

He shook his head and tapped his temple. "No, no, you don't not understand. She'll be in me debt because after me legal team scares the knickers off her, I'll be magnesium and offer her a settlement that will make her beholding to me. Then I waits a few months, and she can be the face of me products at a rock bottom price. In fact, I'll practically own her after all that!"

Verity rolled her eyes. "As much as I'm in favor of you being 'magnesium,' Father, why would you want her to be the face of your products after you rubbed that same face in the mud?"

"Mud washes off," he said. "The public's got the attention span of an 'ousefly with amnesia. They won't not recollect wot's 'appened a few months before."

"Especially when you're 'magnesium' to Mrs. Innis in public," said Verity with disgust.

"Precisely! Now you's got it. I won't not sully her too much in public, but in private..." His face twisted into a malevolent corkscrew as his fingers clutched at his imaginary prey. "...in private, that's where we'll stick it to 'er! Make 'er beg for mercy!"

It took every ounce of restraint for Verity not to part her father's thinning hair with the desk lamp. She was trying to decide on an appropriate response when the phone rang.

"Wot?" snapped Lord Bagnall into the receiver. "Oh, it's you again, well, wot…"

The face that had just moments before been aglow with malicious glee suddenly dropped.

"Wot? When? Okay, keep me posted." His Lordship hung up the phone and stared into space, mustache twitching as it did when he was pondering a tricky problem. Apparently, thought Verity, Chesney, or Lorraine Innis had already parried to her father's legal thrust. Good, she thought, good for our side!

"Bad news, Father?" asked Verity, trying to restrain her pleasure.

Lord Bagnall looked at her as if she had just appeared from nowhere. "Wot? Oh? If it h'ain't bad news, it's sure h'ain't not very good."

"Oh? Having trouble suing Mrs. Innis?"

He rubbed his chin. "I'd said so. As much as you can't not get blood from a banana, you can't not take a corpse into court."

"A corpse?"

"That was my man in the States. The Innis woman's car just blew up."

– 71 –
Margie Goes Commando

A re you sure I can't get you anything else," said Patsy Einfalt placing a cup of tea in front of Lorraine Innis.

"No, thank you," said Lorraine.

"Want anything stronger?" asked Margie MacKay.

"I dunked the bag five times," reasoned Patsy. "It's probably pretty strong as it is."

"I meant, oh, never mind," said Margie.

Lorraine looked at the tea without taking a sip. "The tea is fine, thank you."

"Poor Miss Clott," said Patsy. "Who would want to hurt her? She was so nice."

Lorraine and Margie looked at Patsy.

"Patsy, it was my car," said Lorraine. "Clodagh borrowed it because her car was being serviced."

Patsy shook her head sadly. "I wonder how they knew that."

"Patsy," said Margie, "I don't think the perpetrators knew Clodagh would be driving it."

Patsy stared at her blankly.

Lorraine patted the back of Patsy's hand. "Patsy, dear, I think what Agent MacKay is trying to say is that whoever did this thought I would be driving."

A look of consternation crossed Patsy's face. "That's ridiculous. I like you even more than I like Miss Clott. Who would want to hurt you?"

"I don't know, but I wish they had gotten me rather than Clodagh," Lorraine turned to Margie. "If someone wanted to kill me, wouldn't they have done it before this? I was a political target then, at least potentially. What could someone gain by killing me now?"

Margie MacKay paced back and forth. "Nothing I can think of, unless, of course, this wasn't politically motivated."

"Again," said Patsy, "I can't think of anyone who would even want to hurt Lorraine, let alone kill her, and that's the worst kind of hurting you can do to a person!"

Margie closed her eyes in concentration. "Whatever the motivation, we've got to make sure they don't try it again."

"That would be fine with me," said Lorraine. "I'd feel terrible if another innocent victim became collateral damage because of me."

"I doubt you'd feel very good if they succeeded and got you," noted Margie.

"Feel very well," corrected Lorraine, "But what can we do?"

"I'll ask to be re-assigned back to protecting you," said Margie. "I think the Chief would agree. And if he doesn't, the President would surely okay it. And if neither of them likes the idea, well, I'll take some time off and do it free-lance."

"But if someone's determined to kill me," said Lorraine, "I wouldn't want you to get hurt, especially not on your own time."

Patsy shook her head. "I bet the people who blew up your car are going to be pretty upset when they found out it wasn't you."

Margie MacKay stared at Patsy for a moment and then brightened. "Unless they did get her."

Patsy's mouth dropped open. "What a horrible thought!"

"I don't mean that," said Margie. "But if we let them think it was Lorraine in the car, then they wouldn't try again. They'd have no reason to make another attempt if they thought their first try succeeded."

"What am I supposed to do," said Lorraine, "put on a disguise? That's ridiculous."

"You wouldn't have to disguise yourself. You'd just have to lay low. It would buy the investigators time," said Margie. "You were just seen by a few firemen. I'm sure they'll cooperate. I'm sure the FBI is already on their way. They'll be all over your car for evidence. You probably wouldn't have to go underground for very long. And even then, I'll be with you to provide personal protection."

"Like an underarm deodorant," said Patsy. She looked up at Margie. "Oh, sorry."

"Don't worry, Patsy," said Margie, "I'll stick to her that close."

"Closely," muttered Lorraine.

"So what do you think?" asked Margie.

Lorraine sighed. "I suppose. After all, it will just be for a week."

"A week?" said Margie. "How can you be sure."

Lorraine picked up the court document from the table. "That's when I have to be in England. Don't forget, I'm being sued."

- 72 -
Hope from an Abhorrent Source

Nikolai Kropotkin's blood ran cold when he saw the news flash. "Lorraine Innis Dead in Car Explosion."

He stared at the teletype for several minutes. He recalled his Lorruska's skill at scrambling words and tried in vain to rearrange these words into a different meaning. Finding no other possible meaning, he burst into tears.

"I must be strong," he sobbed. "But my strength is gone. My strength is dead. Dear Lorruska..."

The phone rang. Kropotkin ignored it as long as he could, but the damned thing would not stop. Finally, he snatched the receiver from its cradle.

"What?" he snapped.

There was a moment of silence on the other end, followed by a familiar but abhorred voice.

"Good evening, Nikolai," said Gregor Teplov.

Kropotkin did not reply. He wished his adversary was there in person. He felt like choking someone, and Teplov would be a satisfying candidate.

"I know you are there, my friend," said Teplov. "I can hear you breathing. Your breathing is rather labored."

Kropotkin was loath to share any feelings with Teplov, least of all feelings of grief.

"I was just doing some push-ups in my office."

"Very commendable," said Teplov. "I'm glad to see that you're keeping fit. It is a good way to deal with sorrow."

"Who said I was sorrowful?" snapped Kropotkin.

"Just an educated guess. I thought you would have heard the news from America."

"What do you want, Teplov?" he said curtly.

"I have some good news for you, my dear friend."

"I doubt that," said Kropotkin. He raised the receiver in preparation for slamming it down. But then he heard.

"She is alive, Nikolai."

Kropotkin froze, his arm in the air. He stayed like that for several seconds before slowly lowering the receiver to his ear.

"What?"

"I said, your little friend is alive," said Teplov.

"Is there an updated report... was it a mistake?"

Teplov chuckled. "Don't believe everything you hear or read, my friend. They don't know what your old friend Teplov knows."

"It was not her car?"

"Oh, it was her car."

"It didn't explode?"

"In a great ball of fire," said Teplov. "But the person in the car was not your little friend."

"How do you know?"

"Because I know where she is, my dear Nikolai."

"Where? What have you done with my, with Lorr...."

Before he could complete the question, Teplov had hung up.

– 73 –
An Orphan's Confidence

L i Gao opened the door of his flat. Like its inhabitant, it was modest and clean. There stood Verity Goodhue looking as if she had just taken a shower fully clothed.

"My dear, come in," said Gao. "Please, let me make you some hot tea. Sit down; you're drenched."

"Thank you, yes, it's raining. I walked from the station. I forgot my umbrella." She reached up and felt the top of my head. "I forgot my beret, as well."

"Thankfully, you remembered your raincoat," said Gao helping her off with the garment. "Please sit here, in front of the electric fire. I'll turn it up a bar. Take off your wet shoes. I'll go into the kitchen so you can remove your wet tights, as well."

A few minutes later, he returned with a tray of tea to find Verity staring at the electric fire.

"It's not the same, is it?" said Gao rhetorically. "When I first came to England, all the fireplaces were functional with actual fires. Now they're all blocked up with these contrivances. It is hard to accomplish profound contemplation while staring at an electrical element."

He placed the tray on the table and sat down.

"But, you did not come here for my philosophy of the English fireplace. Nor, did you come here for the tea, but I would urge that upon you if only for the slight restorative effects it may provide."

Verity lifted the cup and took a sip. "So, then you've heard."

"About Lorraine Innis," he said with a solemn nod. "Yes, I heard. I tried to call you but was told you'd already left."

"I didn't know where else to go," she said and then burst into tears. "There's no one else…"

"There, my dear one," said Gao placing her head on his shoulder.

"I've lost him again," she cried. The tears flowed in a torrent for several minutes. Finally, Verity sat up and wiped her eyes with a handkerchief Gao offered her. "I'm sorry," she said, "I just need someone who understood."

"No need to apologize," he said, "for I do understand."

"No one else knows," she said.

"No one on Earth, except for our friend, Postlewaite."

She laughed. "Yes, well, he knows, but I don't know if he fully understands. I don't mean to disparage dear Mr. Postlewaite, but his sympathy is similar to that of a dog."

Li Gao nodded. "You are not casting aspersions on our friend; would that more people had the depths of caring and sympathy of a faithful dog. Yet, you are correct that Postlewaite's understanding rarely reaches the level needed for the empathy presently required."

"So, it falls to you," she said, "I'm sorry."

Li Gao bowed his head and closed his eyes. "Unfortunately, this is almost precisely the scene that your beloved Chesney experienced the day he thought you had died."

"And you were there for him as well," she said and touched his hand. "Only I was really alive."

"But he did not know that, my dear. In fact, he never rejoiced in that truth in this life."

"My poor beloved."

Gao smiled kindly. "How deep your love is for our boy. You have had to endure his passing twice, yet your heart remains fully his."

"He was lucky," said Verity. "He had you to lean on."

"Such grief is not lessened though a hundred try to share it."

Verity sighed and wiped away a stray tear. "I'm glad you appreciate that, but you're correct. It is nearly impossible to explain this horrible feeling. I hope you will never experience it."

Li Gao looked at her intently for several moments. His soft eyes, usually filled with gentleness and compassion, now displayed a pain she had never seen there before. At that moment, Verity realized that his steadfast kindness and charity must have been forged in a furnace of desperate circumstances. She reached out and touched his hand. He bowed his head and was silent for several minutes. Then, his head still bent, he spoke.

"I came to this country as a very young boy. My father and mother were converts to Christianity in China. When the communists came to power after the Second World War, my parents were persecuted and then arrested for their faith. Just before their arrest, knowing almost of a certainty their fate, they gave their only child into the care of the English missionary couple who had shepherded them to Christ. Though I was barely four years old, I remember as clearly as yesterday the moment my mother kissed me goodbye, her tears wetting my face and mingling there with my own, and my father lifting me up into the arms of his English friend. And then he pressed into my tiny hand a scrap of paper inscribed with a Scripture passage from the sixteenth chapter of the Gospel of John: 'I tell you the truth, you will weep and mourn while the world rejoices. You will grieve, but your grief will turn to joy.' My father promised me that we would be reunited soon. And then, after a long voyage, I came to England."

"And your parents eventually joined you?" asked Verity.

Li Gao looked up, his eyes moist. "My parents were killed not long after that."

"Oh," said Verity, "I'm sorry."

"But my father's words were not empty nor his promise in vain. Neither were those of the verse hollow. The promise is as true today as those many years ago. In fact, they are more certain. Their fulfillment is closer as we measure time. I will be reunited with my parents. I am surer of that than I am that the sun will rise tomorrow morning."

Verity looked at him and then sighed. "I wish I could see it all that way. It must have been terrible to lose your parents at such a young age and be taken halfway around the world. Maybe being so young helped you to accept it."

Gao smiled gently. "But I did not accept it, my dear one."

"But you said…"

"I accept it now, but wisdom rarely comes in well-digested portions that may be easily absorbed. An infant must develop teeth before he can receive nourishment from meat. As a small child, I did accept it. I had that childlike faith that readily accedes to what is told, whether they be facts or fantasies. When I grew older, I rebelled against a God who would purport to be the essence of love and yet make a small boy an orphan. And I was not the only aggrieved party. All around, I witnessed misery and suffering. I turned my back on the God of my parents and of my guardians."

Verity thought of the loss of her beloved and nodded. "How can God be loving and do those things?"

A beatific calm overspread his face. "I saw that the God who claimed to be love proved that love by not sparing his own perfect and innocent son. I saw a love much deeper because it was infused with mercy and grace. I saw a sovereign God who showed the path beyond sorrow by taking it first Himself. I realized that I did not have the proper perspective when I looked at circumstances from my insulated vantage point. Little children often want things that seem good to them but are not the best way. They often think their parents cruel or unjust by not indulging every whim. Hopefully, if they have wise parents, and they themselves grow in wisdom, they will come to realize that their parents' commands, though seemingly severe at the time, are actually greater expressions of love. When I was a child, I thought as a child, but when I was grown, I put away childish things."

"So you could see why your parents died?"

He smiled. "No, I do not yet understand that. But I trust that someday I will fully understand it and at that time rejoice in the loving wisdom that ordained it. And on that day, I will stand with my parents and join in their joy that we not only have been treated mercifully but with more grace and kindness than we ever deserved."

Verity looked into his eyes and wished she could accept his well-meaning words, though, at the moment, they offered little comfort to her broken heart.

"But what is it all for?" she finally moaned. "You lost your parents. Chesney is dead. Isn't there any reason for all the pain?"

Li Gao looked intently at the electric fire. "Scripture says that we are to count it all joy when we encounter trials. The testing of our faith produces endurance, and when that endurance is complete, we are perfect, complete, and lacking in nothing."

Verity looked at him for a moment. She had the urge to tell him to stuff all his platitudes and his sage advice. Instead, she just continued to look at him.

"I can see this is not a satisfying answer," he said.

"You're right, it's not," she admitted, and then recalling his kindness, apologized.

"That is not necessary," he said. "I have reacted much more badly in my own case. May I offer an example from childhood? A baby is a beautiful creation. It is so small and helpless. It must depend on others for the meeting of all its needs and the satisfying of all its desires. Of course, a good parent will meet those needs. But a good parent will not meet those needs forever. A mother and father will teach their child to grow, and growth involves the exercising of muscles. At the time, when it is learning to stand and then walk, the child finds it challenging. There will be falls and hurts, and tears before that child grows into maturity."

"So all this…" Verity waved futilely at the air.

"We are all growing into the creatures we will be," said Gao, "and we are not alone in this process. A child has parents to whom they must look and trust. I believe that in this journey, we have something far greater. We have an all-wise, and as importantly, an all-sovereign heavenly Father. That is what I have come to trust and believe. That brings me peace and assurance throughout the great pains and disappointments through which I pass."

Verity searched his eyes. His gaze, though tinged with sorrow, remained resolute. She tried to find words, words to either refute or embrace what Gao had said, but she found none. Instead, she picked up her coat, and without another word, went back out into the rain.

- 74 -
Shorty Long's
Short-Term Remuneration

Robert Valvano sat at his ornate hand-carved desk. Aside from a phone, it was empty. It was always that way. He didn't need papers or pens or staplers, or whatever other people used at a desk. He gave orders verbally. Nothing was ever written. Robert Valvano hadn't signed any document since his marriage license, and he often regretted doing that. Julius Rosen took care of the paperwork. His desk was filled with all kinds of paperwork, but Robert wouldn't know that. He'd never been in Rosen's office. Rosen came to him.

In the bookcase, a television played news reports, as it had for the better part of an hour. Robert picked up the remote and changed the channel to a replay of a baseball game. Julius Rosen sat across from him.

"Alphonse is waiting," said Rosen looking at his watch.

"Yeah, okay," said Robert. "Show him in."

A moment later, the hulking figure of Alphonse entered the room.

"You get all the pictures, Al?" Robert Valvano muted the sound on the television but kept his eyes on the screen.

"I obtained them," interjected Alphonse.

"Yeah, and how did you obtain them?" asked Robert.

"Uh, because I took 'em," said Alphonse. "And after personally procuring them, I delivered them to Mr. Rosen."

Robert looked at Alphonse and then at Rosen.

"They're in the safe," confirmed the lawyer.

"Good," said Robert, "nice job, Al."

"Thanks, Mr. Valvano," said the henchman. "Only..."

Robert scowled. "Only? I don't like onlys, Alphonse."

"Oh, it's ain't my 'only,' Mr. V. Only, it's Shorty's only."

Robert reached for the remote and turned off the television. "What's his problem?"

"He says he needs additional remuneration," said Alphonse.

Robert stood up. "You mean more money? He got what he always gets for that type of job. In fact, he got a little bit more. We're not unreasonable people. I'm not a slave driver. I gave him a cost-of-living adjustment."

Julius Rosen smirked. A cost-of-living adjustment for killing a person.

"I know, Mr. V.," stammered Alphonse, "I relayed your generous largess to Shorty."

"What? With every new one of them vocabulary lessons this idiot takes, I understand him less. Julie?"

"He explained to Shorty Long that you were already paying him more," translated Rosen.

"Then what's that little weasel want?"

"He said he wanted more because of the mark," said Alphonse. "He said he never decomposed so prominent a personage before. Thus, his expenses are likely to increase exponentially in case, uh, in case he's got take it on the lam."

Robert nodded. "I got that last part. Look, he's just a, uh...." Robert snapped his fingers.

"A subcontractor," offered Rosen.

"Exactly," said Robert, "if he's gotta leg it, that's his problem. He shouldn't have taken the job. You can tell him that."

Alphonse looked down at his feet. "Yes, sir, Mr. V. I told him that already. Only..."

"There's getting' to be too many onlys in this conversation," growled Robert.

"He says he can prove who hired him to do the job on that prominent personage's car."

Robert stared at Alphonse and then at Rosen. "Nah, he's blowin' smoke. I never talked to him. Besides, we got the pictures of him arranging the hit with Fierro. The only person who could finger us would be..."

Alphonse shook his head. "I would never disclose private information about you, Mr. V. My loyalty and confidentiality is, uh, saccharine."

"I think you mean sacrosanct," suggested Rosen.

"I know you'd never sing," said Robert. "Besides, even if you did, nobody'd understand you anymore."

"Thanks, Mr. V."

Robert sat down deep in thought for a moment before opening a desk drawer. "Okay, okay, here." He removed two banded stacks of hundred-dollar bills. "You give these to Shorty."

Alphonse did a double-take and then slowly reached out his hand.

"Go ahead," said Robert. "Give it to him with thanks for a job well done. And then after you give it to him. You can demonstrate to him your special talent. And then bring the money back to me. *Capice?*"

Alphonse thought a moment, and then a look of understanding spread across his face. He nodded. "I'll do a good job. Nice and neat, Mr. V."

"Good," said Robert. "You know I like it neat. And this is getting neater all the time."

– 75 –
The Assurance of
the Mink Tornado

Y ou're Lorraine Innis!"
The woman seemed shocked as she entered the conference room.

"Yes, I am," said Lorraine as Margie MacKay closed the door behind the woman. Lorraine glanced down at the information sheet prepared by Patsy. "And you must either be Ms. Friseur or Ms. Madison."

The woman stood before Lorraine, her mouth agape. Even with her mouth hanging open, Lorraine thought she was attractive. Tall, thin, and with brunette hair arranged in a short, professional bob that well- suited the image of a lawyer.

After a moment, the woman realized she was staring. "I, uh, I'm Ms. Madison, Hilda Madison."

Lorraine glanced at Patsy, sitting on her right to take notes. "I thought your partner, Ms. Friseur, would be joining us, too."

"You're Lorraine Innis..." repeated Hilda Madison before catching herself. "Sorry, it's just that..."

"You thought I was dead," said Lorraine. "Yes, that's the common misconception that we've allowed to continue, at least for a little while. My friend, Margie, Agent MacKay, thought it best for my safety."

Hilda looked up at Margie standing guard by the door. "What? Oh, yes, we've met, that is, she escorted me in."

"And I believe you've spoken to Ms. Einfalt," said Lorraine. "Please sit down."

"Yes, I spoke to Ms. Einfalt," said Hilda taking a seat. "Forgive me, but I thought this was something to do with your passing. Of course, I'm relieved that our firm can be of service to you now."

"Thank you, I hope so," said Lorraine. "Patsy, Ms. Einfalt, researched the local firms. We were looking for a smaller firm that had a good reputation in international law. That your firm is owned by women is a bonus." Lorraine looked at Patsy. "I thought you said we'd be entertaining two attorneys."

"I thought we were," said Patsy looking at her notes.

"There are two of us," said Hilda Madison glancing at her watch. "My partner, Lindsay, Ms. Friseur, will be here, at least she said she'd be here. That is to say, she never misses an appointment."

"That's good to know," said Lorraine.

"Yes, she never misses an appointment," said Hilda with an awkward smile. "She's just never quite on time for one, either."

There followed thirty seconds in which all four persons in the room exchanged glances with each other. This period came to an abrupt and violent end as the conference room door burst open, nearly knocking Margie MacKay to the floor. What could only be described as a "mink tornado" stormed into the room.

"There's no place to park in this damn town," bellowed the interloper. The woman was of imposing stature and moved with the confidence of a sleepwalker behind the controls of a Sherman tank. "I can assure you that I'll never get used to the parking in this city. Will you?"

This question was leveled like a mortar shell at Patsy Einfalt, who cringed under the assault. The speaker took no notice, for she had already steered to the windows and pushed aside the closed drapes.

"There, see, there!" She pointed. "That's where I had to park. If I could have gotten a cab from the parking garage I would have done it, I can assure you of that! It's too warm a day to be walking two blocks…" She paused here to blow a puff of air across the nape of her coat. "…in mink. The weather report last week said it was going to be cooler today." This sentence was delivered to Margie MacKay, who, despite all her Secret Service training, seemed genuinely at a loss on how to deal with this person. "I mean, would you wear mink on a day like this? If they had gotten the damned weather report right, I wouldn't have, I can assure you!"

By now, the mink was half off her shoulders. Her long chestnut hair met it just at the collar, making it hard to tell where one ended, and the other began.

"Hilda," said the woman, turning to Hilda Madison, "when are we getting going? Are we going to get started? Come on, let's get it going."

With this, she unfurled the mink, lowered it into an empty chair with the care of a furrier displaying it to a client, and then dropped herself in the seat next to it with not nearly as much caution. She stared at Hilda, who returned the look before turning to Lorraine.

"My partner in law," said Hilda, "Lindsay Friseur."

Lindsay Friseur sat there nonchalantly tossing and rearranging her long wavy hair.

Lorraine stared at Lindsay Friseur for a moment. The anagram "Assuredly in Fur" popped into her head. It was as if her name was made for her, or she had spent her life growing into it.

"Lindsay," continued Hilda, "this is Patsy Einfalt, Margie MacKay, and of course this is…"

For the first time since she steamed into the room, Lindsay Friseur gave her full attention to the others present.

"…Lorraine Innis!" Lindsay screeched.

"…Lorraine Innis," muttered Hilda.

"Lorraine Innis," repeated Lindsay, almost gleefully. "I knew it! Didn't I tell you the other day? Didn't I?"

"You did, Lindsay," agreed Hilda.

"Tell her what, Ms. Friseur?" asked Lorraine.

"I told her that you weren't dead! Didn't I tell you that, Hilly?"

"Yes, you did, Lindsay."

"How did you…" began Lorraine.

"I told her," said Lindsay, "there wasn't conclusive evidence. Just because a person's car blows up, and there's a body in that car, it doesn't prove the body belonged to the owner of the car. I told her that, and here you are to prove it."

"Right again, Lindsay," said Hilda as if she had to admit her partner's correctness quite often.

"Yes, I knew it," said Lindsay leaning back in her chair before quickly sitting bolt upright again. "Who was it?"

"One of my aides," said Lorraine grimly.

"Oh, I am sorry," said Lindsay sincerely. "Did you see it happen?"

"No, I was up here…"

"But you've gotten back forensic evidence that it was your aide?"

"No, but…"

"Then you can't conclude that it was him…"

"Her…"

"Her," said Lindsay Friseur.

"But who else could it be?" asked Patsy.

Lindsay looked at Patsy. "It could be practically anyone, Ms…"

"Einfalt, Patsy Einfalt."

"It could be almost anyone, Ms. Einfalt," concluded Lindsay. "After all, look at how many people around the world are mourning the passing of our Mrs. Innis. Yet, here she sits. I can assure you that you'd be well served not to jump to conclusions, especially in important matters like the law or even exploding automobiles."

"I wish I had your confidence about poor Clodagh," said Lorraine. "Clodagh Clott, the person in the car."

"In my profession, Mrs. Innis, I do not have the luxury of jumping to conclusions. I can assure you that in your case, as in all others, I will await the facts."

"I wish I could share your hope," said Lorraine.

"It's not hope I can assure you. It's just a lack of all the information at this time." Lindsay Friseur smiled with assurance.

Hilda Madison gave her partner a dubious glance. "Mrs. Innis, I'm sorry for your loss. Was Ms. Clott a good friend?"

Lorraine opened her mouth to reply but then found herself at odds with her own feelings. She had only known Clodagh for a short time, hadn't she? But there was something, something she could not define that was missing without Clodagh there. It was as if Clodagh held some key to an integral part of Lorraine, a part that only Clodagh could open. Lorraine realized Hilda Madison was waiting for a reply.

"Uh, no, she only worked here for a short time," said Lorraine. "That is, I think I've known her for only about a month."

"What they say about you is true, Mrs. Innis," said Hilda, "you are a remarkably compassionate person."

Lorraine shrugged.

"So this is what it's all about, huh?" Interrupted Lindsay, who was reading the suit against Lorraine. "Beards, huh? That's ridiculous."

"No, really, those women in England grew beards, and mustaches, too," said Patsy. "There are pictures."

"I don't care if they've got goatees knitted into cardigan sweaters," said Lindsay. "This looks like a nuisance suit, but then I don't go by first appearances. Don't worry, Lorraine, I can call you 'Lorraine,' can't I, Lorraine? I can assure you that this will amount to nothing, and even if it did, I can get you off."

"Off?"

"Out of it," said Lindsay. "Free as a bird."

"But what if the perfume was responsible," said Lorraine.

"What if it was? I've been through enough English courts to make sure they can't hold you responsible."

"But that's not what I want," said Lorraine. "If I'm responsible, I want to make good."

Lindsay Friseur looked at Hilda Madison as if she were suddenly about to recommend an insanity defense. "Yeah, I agree with my learned partner, Mrs. Innis. You're remarkable."

"But you do understand," said Lorraine, "I want to do the right thing."

"I understand, dear," said Lindsay trying, but not succeeding in disguising a patronizing tone. "You do the right thing, and I'll do my best to do the right thing for you."

"And hopefully," added Hilda, "they won't clash."

– 76 –
Long, You Made the Legs Too Short

I don't get it," whined Shorty Long as he dangled from the rafter of the old garage, his toes poised just inches from the floor.

"You will," said Alphonse calmly.

"But Mr. Valvano gave me an extra 10 G's, that's more than I wanted. It was really generous of him. I woulda been happy with five."

"He's generous to a fault," noted Alphonse.

"Yeah, but now it looks like it's my fault. Hey, if he wants, I'll give it back."

Alphonse looked up. "Don't worry, he'll get it all back."

"I don't understand," repeated Shorty.

Alphonse shook his head sadly. "Let's just say he changed his mind about things."

"But why?"

"That's his, uh, prerogative," said Alphonse. "You like that word? Prerogative? I learned that one last week."

"I wished you'd learned it next week," said Shorty. "Could you at least let me down? These ropes are chaffing my wrists."

"Don't worry about it. You won't feel anything in a few minutes."

Alphonse picked up the steel bar and slowly approached Shorty Long. Shorty's beady eyes grew large and then squinted tightly shut in anticipation of the first and final blow. Alphonse was about five feet away, nearly in swinging-distance, when he stopped and stood still. His head cocked to one side as if listening for something. Then suddenly, Alphonse pivoted, swinging the bar behind him in a mighty arc at shoulder level.

Had he not anticipated the move, Michael Valvano would have been the bar's victim ahead of Shorty Long. Instead, Michael ducked, causing Alphonse to swing through and stumble from his own momentum.

Michael caught the bar in his right hand the second time around while catching the Alphonse as well. Alphonse cocked his free hand, itself a lethal enough weapon. Just before he was about to strike, he recognized his adversary.

"Mikey," cried Alphonse.

"Shh, Al," cautioned Michael, his finger raised to his lip.

"Mikey, sorry, I almost perforated you; only I was not cognizant of your presence in the vicinity."

Michael patted Alphonse's arm. "No harm done," he glanced at the trussed-up Shorty Long, "especially to him."

"That? Oh, that's just a transaction I gotta actualize for your sibling."

Michael nodded. "I figured as much, and I've got a pretty good idea what's going on. That's why I came back."

"And am I glad to see you," said Al. "You been up to the house?"

"Shh, no, I didn't think that was a good idea, under the circumstances, not yet at least. I'll try to slip in later and see Nonnia, but I want to find out a few things first."

"Gee," said Alphonse scratching his head with the end of the steel bar, "I don't know how to break this to you. Only, I figured..."

"What? Something happened to Nonnia?"

Alphonse went through a series of facial contortions. "Yeah, well, I mean, sure, you could say that I guess..."

Michael put his hand on Alphonse's shoulder. "Al, just say it."

"The old lady deceased herself by entirely natural circumstances."

Michael Valvano made a sign of the cross, bowed his head for a moment, and then patted Al's shoulder a second time. "I suppose I'm not really surprised."

"She was awful old," said Alphonse sympathetically.

"When?"

Alphonse rolled his eyes upwards, calculating. "I'd say, yeah, it was the night you left."

Michael sighed and shook his head.

"Only I don't think you had any complicity in her resigning from this plane of existence," said Al.

"I wish I could be sure of that," said Michael sitting on a crate.

"Excuse me," said Shorty Long. "I don't mean to interrupt or nothing, but do you suppose you could get me down, at least until you off me?"

Michael looked up. "Shorty, isn't it?"

"Yeah, that's Shorty Long," said Alphonse.

"I thought I recognized him from the old days," said Michael.

"Can you at least let me down until you finish talking," repeated Shorty.

Michael looked at Shorty and then at Alphonse.

Alphonse lowered his head. "Yeah, you know I wanted to talk with someone about that, like a priest. Hey, are you a priest again, Mikey?"

"Close enough," said Michael. "Let him down, and let's talk. I go away for a few weeks and come back to all this. I heard the news about Lorraine Innis, and I thought I'd find out what it's all about."

Alphonse lifted Shorty off the hook but paused before setting his feet on the ground. "You ain't going to elope, or nothing, are you?"

"Al, you've still got his ankles taped together," observed Michael, "he can't run away."

Alphonse squinted at the bonds. "He could hop away."

"I won't, on my honor," pledged Shorty.

Alphonse dropped him on the floor and then sat down beside Michael.

"Now, what is it that you wanted to talk about?" asked Michael.

Alphonse rubbed his head. "I dunno, Mike. It's just what you call a conundrum."

"Impressive word."

Al brightened. "Yeah, ain't it? I learned that a few weeks ago. It means like a puzzle. Only I didn't know when I learned the word that I was gonna have one, a conundrum, I mean."

"Well, what's the problem."

Alphonse jerked his thumb toward Shorty. "There it is. Everybody's got a job to do. He had a job to do, and he did it."

"You mean Lorraine Innis?"

Alphonse sighed. "I felt real bad about that. I didn't know until afterward whose car it was that was gettin' conflagrated. That means blown up."

"Yes, I surmised as much," said Michael.

Alphonse smiled and pointed at Michael. "Surmised, yeah, that's another good one." His smile faded. "Like I said, I knew someone's car was gonna get incinerated, and most likely when that happens, the person whose car it is, is sitting inside it. But I didn't know it was Mrs. Innis' car."

"Life is life, Al," reasoned Michael. "It shouldn't make a difference if the person is someone we like or a total stranger."

Al nodded. "You're right. I knew that. But it's like I was cognizant of it here..." He tapped his forehead. "But it felt different here..." He pointed to his chest. "And like I said, Shorty did his job. But now I gotta do my job."

"No, you don't," cried Shorty.

"Shut up," snapped Alphonse, "and mind your own business. This is between me a Mike. Anyway, Mike, the thing is, I don't know if I'm good at my business."

Michael gave him a puzzled look. "But surely, Alphonse, you've been working for my brother for years."

"Yeah, but I guess you could say I was inexperienced in the actual execution of my executions."

"A virginal assassin," offered Michael.

Alphonse looked down at his crotch.

"Metaphorically speaking," added Michael. "But what you're trying to say is that you never actually killed a person."

Al's face reddened. He lowered his head and shook it. "No, I never had to, not directly anyways. When you've got an imposing appearance and a scary face, everyone just assumes you go around expiring people all over the place. Before today, I've only ever been given the assignment once, and that didn't come off."

"Peter Liverot," said Michael.

Alphonse looked surprised. "You knew about that?"

"I was the one who stopped it."

Alphonse exhaled. "I'm glad. I liked Mr. Liverot. I like everyone."

"Do you like me?" cried Shorty Long.

"I told you to shut up!" shouted Alphonse before turning to Michael. "I like him, too. I don't want to kill nobody, but when you've got my peculiar skills, people just assume that's all you're good for. That's why I'm always taking my vocabulary courses, so's maybe someday there will be the eventuality that I can do what I really want to do."

"Which is?" asked Michael.

"I figured, if I learned some education and talked good, maybe I could be," he paused and looked around, "a nursery school teacher."

Alphonse paused as if he were waiting for Michael to laugh. When he didn't, Al continued. "Anyway, that's what I'd like to do."

"I think that's fine, Al," said Michael. "But I think you shouldn't pursue that career with blood on your hands. We need to find a better solution for you and Mr. Long."

Alphonse smiled as if a great weight had been lifted from his brawny shoulders. But a moment later, it returned. "Oh, yeah, there's one more thing I better straighten out. You see, I took some pictures..."

– 77 –
Why Do They Call It
"Life Insurance?"

Valerie's Fierro's first reaction had been one of shock. Someone had blown up Lorraine. Thankfully, according to news reports, the body was so completely incinerated that no one would ever be able to realize they'd really blown up Chesney Potts.

While she was looking for the perfect black dress, Valerie remembered she was the sole beneficiary of Lorraine's life insurance policy. Valerie was suddenly a multi-millionaire. There was an initial pang of guilt, but then she reasoned that Lorraine had wanted her to have the money. Besides, no one takes out a life insurance policy thinking they're going to live forever.

Valerie wondered who had done it. She assumed everyone loved Lorraine. Still, the public thought that she and Lorraine were bosom companions. If someone hated Lorraine, they might not like Valerie very much either. She'd have to talk to Robert about a bodyguard.

For some odd reason, no one had contacted her. She had expected to get a call from Robert Valvano, or Julius Rosen, or, at the very least, Patsy Einfalt. She imagined Patsy would be in tears, looking to Valerie for support, and all that jazz. But there was nothing.

Now, the next day, Valerie was going to the office. She couldn't hide forever. Everyone was probably worried sick, wondering where she was. She would at least put their minds at ease that she was okay.

Valerie slipped into one of her new black dresses. She liked black. It was slimming, though she didn't really need to look any thinner. Still, black was flattering. And now, it wasn't just flattering; it was elegant, and it was rich: five million dollars rich.

She had carefully applied her eye makeup to look as if it were smudged. Valerie loved makeup. Usually, it was utilized to make you look better, but it was so versatile that, if you needed it to, it could make you look worse; like you'd been crying. It was wonderful: credit for tears you hadn't shed.

Valerie had cried a little bit. She did hold a place in her heart for Chesney. It had never been the place he wanted, but that wasn't her fault. Still, she was fond of him in a way that he should have appreciated. And no one deserved to be blown up in their own car. She would probably miss him.

Valerie slipped into the building by the side entrance, parking in a lot instead of the garage. She didn't want to see the site of the explosion. Besides, if they hadn't caught the person responsible, maybe her car would be next. Under her broad-brimmed hat and dark glasses, no one recognized her. The first person she met was Patsy Einfalt.

"Valerie," said Patsy rising from behind her desk.

"Oh, Patsy, Patsy, Patsy!" Valerie added just the right quiver to convey that she was terribly upset, "Isn't it horrible?"

"It sure is!" agreed Patsy.

"It's just horrible," repeated Valerie as she stepped back and made a pretense of wiping away some tears.

"Very horrible," said Patsy nodding her head and then suddenly stopping. "Which part are you talking about?"

"What?"

"I mean, which thing is horrible? Do you mean Miss Clott? Or the lawsuit? Or Miss Clott and the lawsuit?"

"Miss Clott and…"

"Of course, I'd say Miss Clott was much more horrible," continued Patsy. "I mean, the lawsuit is pretty bad, but Ms. Madison says that Ms. Friseur can straighten all that out. But no one can straighten out poor Miss Clott. Oh, how were the Brownies?"

"What brownies?" said Valerie, totally confused. She hadn't eaten any brownies. She ran her tongue across her teeth just to make sure there wasn't any food stuck there.

"The Brownies," said Patsy.

Valerie shook her head. "I haven't had any brownies."

"The Scranton Brownies," said a familiar voice from behind.

Valerie spun around to see Lorraine Innis standing there.

"Patsy said you had to go speak to a Brownie troop in Scranton."

Valerie's mouth dropped open.

"Please," said Lorraine, "don't say the obvious thing."

"Uh, no?" Valerie finally said.

"Don't say: 'I thought you were dead,' or, 'is it really you?' or any of those things."

"I won't," said Valerie as she found herself being embraced by Lorraine.

As they hugged, she was aware of Lorraine saying something; stuff about being thankful that Valerie wasn't hurt by whoever did this. Lorraine's words were drowned out by the questions in her mind.

If Lorraine wasn't blown up, who was in the car? Then she recalled what Patsy said about the Clott woman. That must have been her.

Then she recalled the mention of the lawsuit. Would Lorraine realize that Valerie dumped that on her?

One final question was preeminent in Valerie's mind: Can you collect a life insurance policy on someone who is still alive?

That question found an immediate answer: No!

– 78 –
Hope on a Mountain Pass

"Miss Verity!"

"Hello, Mr. Carstairs," said Verity Goodhue.

"You're drenched, Miss," said the butler, "quickly, come in. I'll inform Mrs. Carstairs that you're here."

Carstairs ushered Verity into the foyer of Lord Bagnall's Eaton Square home. He scanned the doorstep and the street, and finding nothing, he shut the door.

"Your automobile, Miss?"

Verity glanced over her shoulder at the back of the door and then shook her head. "I must have left it… somewhere else." Since leaving Li Gao's, she had wandered aimlessly through the rainy streets of London. It must have been hours. Some natural homing instinct must have brought her to the townhouse.

"Very good, Miss. No luggage?"

Verity looked down. "No."

"Not to worry, I'm sure Mrs. Carstairs will be able to find something not only suitable but most comfortable."

Verity smiled weakly. "Thank you."

"Your father is up at Bagnall Hall."

"Good," said Verity, "I mean, yes, I know. I'm, I'm sorry to intrude upon you this way. I'm sure you and your wife didn't expect a refugee at this time of night. It is night, isn't it?"

"Yes, Miss, it's just gone half-past ten," said Carstairs, "and I beg your pardon, but you're not a refugee. If you'll allow me to say so, there's no one the missus and I would rather welcome any time of the day or night and in whatever condition you arrived."

"Very kind," Verity whispered.

"Rupert, just what… Crikey! Miss Goodhue!"

The aforementioned Mrs. Carstairs entered the foyer rushed to Verity's side.

"Rupert, you great puddin', why didn't you call me?"

"Hello, Mrs. Carstairs," Verity muttered, "I've just arrived."

"Rupert, can't you see the state this poor child is in? I've not seen her like this since…well, we won't throw bad memories after current situations. But help me get her up to the Rose bedroom."

"I don't want to be any trouble."

"Trouble?" Mrs. Carstairs snorted as she helped Verity up the stairs. "You're like the daughter we wished we'd had, my little wren. Let's get you up into a hot bath, and then some warm tea and scones."

"What can I do?" asked Carstairs following behind.

"Go put a fresh kettle on," said his wife, "and warm the pot!"

"Yes, absolutely, my dear," he said. "And I'll call his Lordship."

"No!" said Verity loudly. "I mean, no thank you. Please don't call Father."

"No, of course not," said Mrs. Carstairs as she stroked Verity's matted hair. "Just as you wish, my wren."

An hour later, after a hot bath and warm tea and scones, Verity was being tucked into a soft bed by Mrs. Carstairs as her husband entered to retrieve the tray.

"I can't thank you enough," said Verity. "You've been more than kind."

"You don't need to thank us, my little wren," said Mrs. Carstairs.

"No, the missus is right, Miss," added Carstairs, "you just being you is like a holiday for us. It's just nice to be treated decently."

"You're referring to Father," said Verity.

"No, no, he's not," said Mrs. Carstairs, "we've been in His Lordship's employ for many years now and have no cause for complaints."

"Only it's nice to be called 'Carstairs,'" said Carstairs. "Your Dad never calls us by our proper names. It's always 'Ramp,' 'Rampy,' 'Rampo.' For the first ten years or so, I just grinned and bore it, but after that, it starts to grate." Carstairs stopped at this point and lowered his head. "Forgive me, Miss Goodhue. That was a liberty."

""I understand more than you know, dear Mr. and Mrs. Carstairs," said Verity. "And I can assure you that I shall never betray your confidence on the matter with anyone, ever."

Carstairs smiled, looked at his wife, and winked. "What have I always said? Real royalty there, a true princess."

"Yes, well, I suspect she'd like a little rest now," said Mrs. Carstairs joining her husband by the door. "If you need anything at all, my little wren, just call."

"Thank you, both."

"Oh, I almost forgot," said Carstairs, nodding to the television opposite the bed, "one of your grandfather's films is on tonight. He was a grand gent. I always watch the schedules to see when he'll be on. If you're interested, it should be starting in a few minutes."

"Thank you," said Verity, "that's very considerate. Good night."

Carstairs smiled and closed the door leaving Verity alone with her thoughts. In fact, she'd had nothing but her thoughts all day. They were about to crowd her out of her own head. Li Gao's words about some great eternal purpose, some greater joy behind suffering, were still buzzing in her head. They had been there through her hours walking in the pouring rain. At times she had been angry with Gao and his Sovereign. It must be nice to be able to swallow that pie-in-the-sky comfort. A few hours ago, as she stood on the Thames Embankment, Verity considered ultimately ending the debate, at least as far as she was concerned. Then she found herself in the kind arms of the Carstairs.

Verity looked at the remote control. If she had lost her beloved, at least she could still see her dear grandfather, if only on video. Yes, she would watch one last Hugh Goode film, then perhaps...

She turned on the telly. The film was just starting. It was one of his wartime movies. The majority of grandfather's films included his name in the title, and *Yodel Ay Hee Hugh* was no different. It was the usual cheerful silliness that made her grandfather famous. Hugh was a gormless traveling salesman stuck in Switzerland when the war broke out. He got involved in and ultimately thwarted a Nazi plot while managing several comical songs along the way.

In her wearied state, Verity nodded off into a fitful sleep. She awoke with a start about an hour later at the sound of her grandfather's voice.

"Come on now! You can't quit now, my girl!" he said.

Verity sat up and stared at the screen. It was nearing the finale of the film. Hugh Goode had sent the film's heroine up an Alpine pass while he followed, providing rear-guard protection from the pursuing villains. Hugh was guiding a donkey from behind up the mountainside. As he progressed, the path became narrower and narrower. On his left, the sheer cliff rose vertically. On his right, a 90-degree drop down into a rocky chasm. It was at this point the donkey refused to go any further.

"Please, dear, you've got to go on," said Hugh waving a switch but not applying it. "We've got to get to Mary. She waiting for us up on the other side. I expect she'll have a carrot for you, a whole bunch of carrots, no doubt!"

The donkey shook its head.

"Look, it's no use it saying no. We can't go right, and you can't go left." Just then, the sound of the pursuing villains was heard further down the mountain. "An' even if you could turn around, we surely can't go back that way. Please, won't you move?"

The donkey remained planted. Then, as only as could happen in a musical comedy, Hugh Goode reached into the donkey's pack, pulled out his trusty ukulele, and launched into song.

"Not everything that happens will seem to go all right.
To get ahead often means a scrape and even means a fight.
Even when it seems like a mess,
I'll tell you right now, it's all for the best!
So when your back is up against the wall,
Don't turn tail and run.
You won't get through by giving in,
There's a battle to be won!
There's no turning back,
So just face that fact,
And get on getting on!

When you're in a spot and get a shove
You'll find that shove is from above.
So keep your eyes ahead,
Not on what you dread,
And get on getting on!"

As her grandfather launched into a cheery syncopated uke solo, Verity dissolved into the mass of tears that she'd been fighting throughout her long walk in the pouring rain.

"I can't..." she sobbed. "It's just so hard..."

Through the blur of her tears, she watched the scene that she'd seen dozens of times, though never to this effect. It seemed as if her grandfather or someone was trying to get her "getting on." She felt more stubborn than that donkey. Finally, Hugh Goode reprised the last chorus, reminding the donkey and his granddaughter that there was a battle to be won. There was no turning back, and standing still was not an option. Then as the scene ended, a shot rang out from the pursuing villains hitting the frying pan hung on the animal's rear end, and both Hugh and the animal rushed off at double-quick time.

Verity rolled over and buried her head in the pillow, her tears still flowing. She hadn't really prayed since she was a little girl, and she wasn't exactly sure it was a prayer now, though it was as sincere a declaration as she had ever made.

"I'm stubborn, but just stop it all from hurting. I'll do whatever it takes, whatever you want. I'm just tired of fighting..."

For some reason, though she had no idea why, her heart felt strangely warmed, somehow lighter for the exercise. Maybe this was what Li Gao had been trying to say. Or perhaps it was what he had said, but she couldn't understand. It didn't matter. It was just better.

"Thank you..." she began again.

Before she could go any further, she fell into a deep, exhausted slumber.

- 79 -
Miss Glott and the Employer of Idiots

Clodagh Clott had been in a car, on a small boat, on a ship, then some kind of truck, followed by an airplane, and then another truck. It may have been days or even a whole week since she was abducted in the parking garage. With all the movement and the fitful periods of sleep, measuring time was difficult.

Except for a brief time on a boat, the only words she had heard spoken were in some Slavic-sounding language. Her mouth was kept taped shut. Her eyes blindfolded. Her hands tied behind her back. Periodically she was sat up only to have the tape yanked from her mouth. At that point, one of two things happened. Either a bottle was lifted to her lips, or a piece of bread was shoved in her mouth. Then, the tape was reapplied, and Clodagh was pushed back into isolation.

The worst was at the beginning when she had been transported in some suffocating vinyl sack.

Now Clodagh found herself being guided into a room. For the first time since the ordeal had begun, she was placed in a chair. She listened as the two voices of her captors whispered in their unfamiliar language. Clodagh detected excitement in their voices. She felt her own pulse race as she wondered where she was now and what would happen next. A series of knocks were heard on a steel door, followed by the throwing of several bolts, then a series of signs and countersigns were exchanged from either side of the door.

A third person entered. From the deferential tone, Clodagh surmised that this was their boss. Perhaps she would finally get some answers, if the boss could speak English.

After another minute of conversation, she heard two men walking away. Then, a door opened and closed. All was silent for an eerie interval. Then a single pair of footsteps walked away. She heard the door being re-bolted, and then the steps walked towards her, stopping just in front of her.

"It is an honor, my dear lady," said the voice in accented but good English. "Allow me. I will remove the bandage from your mouth."

The tape was pulled back with much greater care and less pain than her previous captors had employed. Clodagh flexed her mouth several times and then spoke.

"What do you think you're doing?"

"Doing?" The man laughed. "I am freeing your mouth, my dear. If you are well-behaved, I will remove the wrapping from your eyes."

"Aren't you afraid I'll be able to recognize you?" asked Clodagh.

"I doubt you have ever seen me, dear lady."

"Well, then, I could identify you when you're caught and brought to justice," she reasoned.

"Justice?" He snorted. "I do not think you understand the situation."

"So you're going to keep me," said Clodagh, and then swallowed hard. "Or you're going to kill me?"

"Kill you? That's absurd. And as for the first option, I'd no sooner keep you than a bad tooth."

"They pull bad teeth. You are going to have me eliminated."

The man made a clicking noise. "You have seen too many silly films."

"Oh, yes, thanks. I was just overreacting when I was kidnapped, bundled up, taken out to sea in a bag, and taken who knows where. Yes, that is just the stuff of silly melodramas. I don't know what I was thinking. I'm probably back in Delaware, instead of, well, wherever."

"You are in Russia."

"Russia?"

"You sound surprised," said the voice. "You disappoint me, dear lady. I thought you were much smarter than that."

"Smarter than what? And why should some Russian want to kidnap me?"

The footsteps began to pace. "Really, this is becoming tiresome. Do not play the fool with me. You can figure out why a rival of Kroptokin's would want to borrow you."

"Kropotkin? Borrow me for what?"

"For a bargaining piece," he said. "Do not act so stupid, Mrs. Innis."

"I'm not acting, I just..." Clodagh stopped. "Mrs. Innis? I'm not Lorraine Innis."

The pacing stopped in front of her. "Please, Mrs. Innis, you are not dealing with stupid people."

"I'm not saying anyone is stupid," insisted Clodagh, "I'm just saying I'm not Lorraine. I'm her friend. My name is Clodagh Clott."

"Please, Mrs. Innis, do not play these patronizing games," said the man. He came closer. Clodagh could feel his breath on her cheek. "You fit the description for Lorraine Innis. You are the same height as Lorraine Innis. You are the same weight as Lorraine Innis. You have the same hairstyle as Lorraine Innis. And do you know why?"

"Because I'm not Lorraine, but just happen to be the same weight and height and hairstyle? But I'm not her," said Clodagh. "And for your information, I'm a half-inch taller than him, uh, her."

"Pah! This is childish," he said.

Then Clodagh felt his hand on her head. For a moment, she thought her captor was going to strike her, but instead, he was unwinding the blindfold that had cover her eyes.

"I will prove to you what everyone in the world knows. The face that belongs to the most famous woman in the world...."

Clodagh squinted as, for the first time in days, her eyes were subject to light. She looked around. She was sitting in a concrete block room. In the corner near the door was a table with several black and white closed-circuit TV monitors. The only other piece of furniture was the chair upon which she sat. Then she looked directly ahead into the face of her captor. He had neat close-cropped hair, a pointy chin, and vibrant blue eyes. Those eyes were studying her face closely and then darted back and forth between Clodagh and a photograph in his hands. As he did so, the man's thin mouth dropped open.

"You are not her."

Clodagh smiled weakly. "Yes, I know. I'm sorry, but I told you that."

"You are NOT her!" The man turned the photograph toward her. It was, as Clodagh expected, Lorraine.

"Yes, you're right," said Clodagh.

The man covered his face with the photograph and then crumpled it while emitting an agonizing groan. "Those fools. Those idiots."

"You mean your friends? The two fellows who kidnapped me?"

The man looked up. "Two fellows. Ha! They started out as four. One didn't even get out of the country. He forgot his passport. Then the second one blew himself up in your car..."

"That's what that explosion was," said Clodagh. "Right after they put me in that trunk. They blew up Lorraine's car?"

"No, they did not blow up her car," said the man, "though given their stupidity, I'm surprised they didn't blow themselves up."

"Then who blew up Lorraine's car?"

The man stared at Clodagh in disbelief. "I don't know, and I don't care about that."

"Well, if your friends..."

"Stop calling them my friends. I do not have idiots for friends."

"No, just for employees, apparently," muttered Clodagh.

The man growled and started to pace. He seemed upset that his henchmen hadn't gotten Lorraine Innis and apparently was trying to consider his next move.

"Excuse me, excuse me," she said, "I know this all didn't work out exactly as you'd hoped…"

He stopped pacing and looked at her. "You are either the master of the understatement or an imbecile."

"Hey, hold on there, buster! There's no need to be rude. I didn't ask to be kidnapped, and it wasn't my fault that you hire people who can't tell one American from another. Besides, you might not get as much for me, but I'm sure my friends would pay something for me. I've got a pretty big family, too. They would pay something, maybe not as much as you hoped to get for Lorraine, but still, it wouldn't be a total loss."

The man rolled his eyes. "Forgive me if I was abusive, Miss Blott…"

"Clott!"

"Of course, Miss Clott. But you do not realize this was not an operation for monetary gain, hard as that may be for an American to understand. Nor do I consider this some crude kidnapping. It was my goal to borrow Mrs. Innis for political reasons."

"Political? But she's not going to be vice-president. That's old news. Don't you read the papers?"

He smiled at her patronizingly. "Indeed. But understand, not all politics take place within the boundaries of the 'good ol' USA.' This is an internal Russian matter."

Clodagh thought a moment. "Kropotkin!"

"Bravo, Miss Clott."

"You wanted to borrow Lorraine so President Kropotkin would… what?"

"Resign," he sighed. The man would have made a very poor elementary school teacher.

"Oh, I get it," said Clodagh with a smile. Then she shook her head. "No, I don't think it will work."

"Of course not. Not now!" Shouted the man.

"So can I go?"

He stared at her. "Eventually. Not yet. For some reason, the world thinks your Lorraine Innis was blown up in the car. Kropotkin knows she is alive and thinks she is in my care. I do not know why the real Lorraine Innis has not surfaced, but that is in my favor. As long as my dear friend Nikolai thinks that you are Mrs. Innis, I have, as they say, 'leverage.' I only hope for all our sakes that your friend does not reemerge in public before I can conclude the negotiations."

"You won't get away with it," snapped Clodagh.

"You watch too many detective shows on television," said the man.

"Well, you won't!"

He shook his head and then snapped off a fresh piece of duct tape and plastered it over Clodagh's mouth.

"I can still get away with that," he said, pointing at her gagged mouth.

The man returned to his pacing. A minute later the sound of muffled gunshots was heard. Her captor rushed to the television monitors.

"He got them both! The fools," he snarled. He flipped a dial changing the view of the monitors to other cameras. "But, he came alone. A real cowboy to rescue his pretty American schoolmarm." He laughed and then scanned the room. Running over to Clodagh's chair, he turned its back to the door. Clodagh tried to speak through the gag.

"There, there, dear Miss Glott, you won't have long to wait. You will have company. I'm sorry it turned out this way for all of us." He patted her on the head. "At least you look like her from behind."

Clodagh heard his footsteps retreating towards the door and then heard the locks being opened. It was less than a minute later than the door opened.

"Lorruska! My Lorrus..." The voice began. It was interrupted by the sound of metal striking skull, followed by the sounds of a body being dragged a short distance and some more duct tape being unrolled.

Then the lights went out, the door shut, the bolts were re-locked from the outside, and finally total darkness.

– 80 –
Sympathy from a Lummox

So, it was back to London. Valerie Fierro enjoyed travel when it was done right. This wouldn't be done right, or at least not as right as it could be done. She would be traveling with the new Lorraine. Valerie could convince the Chesney Potts version of Lorraine that they needed to go first-class. Now they were traveling business-class. Valerie half expected Lorraine to suggest they travel on the Underground and eat fish and chips at some corner take-away. The rest of the time, she would have to be supportive of Lorraine in that stupid court case. Valerie had to feign ignorance of the whole case. She had to say that she was just as surprised as Lorraine about all the bearded British broads. That would probably hold up unless Bagnall's daughter squealed on her. Even if she did, it was only Verity Goodhue's word against Valerie's. Who would Lorraine believe: her best friend and cousin or some English chick she'd never even met?

As she stood in her bedroom, packing, Valerie wondered why Lorraine hadn't been blown up in the car. She felt a pang of guilt. She should be happy to have Lorraine alive. But Valerie couldn't help thinking that living with five million dollars was easier than living with Lorraine. If there was any consolation in the whole mess, it was that at least that snotty Clott woman had gotten hers. And there was also the likelihood that whoever had tried to kill Lorraine might try again and this time succeed.

Valerie was staring at her half-packed suitcase, wondering what the weather was like in London. She turned on the TV, hoping to find some international weather report. Instead, there was the news. She began to reach for the remote but then stopped. They were talking about Lorraine again. They were always talking about Lorraine. Valerie was sick of the subject but couldn't turn away. Maybe they'd mention her. The anchor was Carrie Colic, a persistently cheery, persistently annoying woman.

"The world is still stunned over the violent and untimely death of the beloved Lorraine Innis." Colic paused to gently touch a black ribbon, presumably for Lorraine, pinned over her heart.

"Oh, pull-eze!" moaned Valerie shaking a blouse at the screen. "A few days ago, you were ready to burn her at the stake over that dumb senator's accusations! Now because she's dead, you're all gushing over her again. You all make me sick. You're not only phony, you're also stupid! You don't even know yet that she's not dead, damn it!"

Valerie's rant, which she was enjoying, was brought to an abrupt halt by the sound of the front doorbell. She scurried to the window and pulled back the drapes to peek. There wasn't anyone there, at least there were no cars in front of the house. She couldn't see the front door from her vantage point. Valerie held her breath. She wasn't expecting anyone, at least not anyone she wanted to see. She started for the stairs and then stopped. It was probably one of those stupid reporters to ask her how devastated she was over Lorraine's death. She'd pretend she wasn't home.

"I don't usually talk about feminine protection!" A woman's voice boomed from across the room. The news had gone into commercial, and the audio was twice as loud as the program. Valerie rushed back and grabbed the remote. In her haste, she pressed the wrong button. The volume went up to an ear-splitting level.

"WHEN I WANT TO FEEL FRESH AS A BREEZE THROUGH THE FOREST…"

Valerie fumbled with the remote. Finally, she just pulled the plug out of the wall.

There was silence, and then the sound of a brace of angry knuckles banging on her front door. Valerie heard a very gruff sounding voice. It certainly didn't sound like a reporter. A thought occurred to her. Maybe the person who thought they had killed Lorraine was now after her for some reason.

"She's not home," said the gruff voice.

"Then we'll go in and wait," said a barely audible voice.

"Oh, shit," she whispered, "they're coming in." Valerie scanned the room, looking for a place to hide or a weapon with which to defend herself. While she was debating the lethal nature of her curling iron, she heard it: The sound of scratching, like someone was picking the lock or perhaps jimmying the door.

"Oh, shit!" she repeated. Valerie grabbed the curling iron, and, brandishing it like a dagger, she inched towards the door.

She heard muffled voices and then the barely audible tread of footsteps coming up the carpeted stairs. Damned the wall-to-wall carpeting; if only she had hardwood floors, she'd know her adversary's exact location.

The doorknob turned in front of her. Her muscles tensed for action. The thought of her grandmother flashed through her mind, the little woman who had survived World War II and founded a business empire. She had Nonnia's genes; she was ready for anything. Well, almost anything…

Valerie took a step backward between the wall and the door. She would have a clear shot at the intruder's back before he knew what hit him. The first thrust with the curling iron would have to tell. She raised her arm to estimate where the interloper's shoulder blades would be.

Slowly, the hulking form leaned into the room and looked at the suitcase on the bed. "Nobody's here, but it looks like…"

"YIIIIIII!" Valerie let loose an ear-splitting scream, shut her eyes, and lunged at her adversary. She should have kept her eyes open since instead of finding the center of his back, Valerie found herself falling forward. The man, large as he was, was apparently quite agile. She hit the floor, her weapon falling from her hand. She reached for it but was stopped by the knee of her attacker planted gently but firmly in the small of her back.

"I found her," he said calmly.

Valerie twisted her head around. Her subduer smiled at her; not a menacing "Now, I've got you" kind of smile, but a "Gee, it's good to see you" smile.

"It's my pleasure to make your acquaintance, Miss Fierro," he said. "I seen you before, but we've never been introduced, formal. I m Alphonse"

Valerie squirmed futilely under his weight.

"It's okay. Let her up, Al," said a too familiar voice.

Alphonse raised his knee, and Valerie turned over.

"Michael!"

There was Michael Valvano. She knew he'd come back. Well, maybe she didn't actually know that, but she'd hoped he would.

Michael held out his hand and helped her up. Valerie opened her arms to embrace him, but he had turned away.

"Going somewhere?" he asked, looking at her suitcase.

Valerie shrugged. "Oh, you know me, always on the go."

Michael rubbed his chin. "Really? Where are you going now?"

"I'm going to London," she said, crossing to the dresser. She pulled out a particularly sexy negligee and nonchalantly placed it in the suitcase. When she looked over for a reaction, Valerie was irritated to see that only the hired goon had noticed.

"Yes," repeated Valerie, "I'm going to London. Not that it's any of your business. You so clearly removed yourself from all my affairs: both personal and business."

Michael bit his lip and looked towards Alphonse, as if he'd rather not have this conversation in front of him.

"Well, I hope you have a good trip," said Michael.

"Yes, I'm sure I will," said Valerie. "Thank you for coming to wish me bon voyage, even if you broke into my house to do it."

Michael removed a key from his fob and placed it on the nightstand. "I still had a key. Here it is."

"Thank you," she said and turned her back to him.

"Only, I came here to warn you," he said.

"Warn me?" She faced him and laughed. "I'm not interested in your threats. I can fight my own battles." She waved her hand toward Alphonse. "I don't need a big, big…"

"Lummox," offered Alphonse.

"What?" said Valerie.

"Lummox," said Alphonse proudly. "It's another new word this week. It means a clumsy person, often larger than average."

Valerie rolled her eyes. "Yes, well, no offense, but thank you." She turned back to Michael. "I don't need hired muscle to take care of me."

Michael sighed and shook his head. "I'm not warning you about me. We're trying to warn you that you've been set up."

Valerie waved at him dismissively. "Set up, that's ridiculous…"

"…And you don't even realize it," said Michael.

Valerie looked at Alphonse, who was also shaking his head. It was bad enough to be called a dope by a smart person, but when a lummox knew it as well, that was really bad.

"W-what are you talking about?" she asked.

"Robert and Julius Rosen," said Michael.

"Robert? And Mr. Rosen? No, you see, that's where you're wrong. They made me the president of the bank after you left them hanging."

"I didn't know that," said Michael.

"No, well, you wouldn't," she said. "It's not public knowledge yet. It needs board approval, but…"

Alphonse laughed and then quickly covered his mouth.

"Valerie, there is no board; Robert's the board. Whatever he says goes."

"Well, then," she fumbled, "he just wanted to see if…"

"If you could handle the job," said Michael. "And he sent you for a meeting with a Mr. Long…"

"How did you know that? Were you there?"

"No, I wasn't," said Michael. "I just heard about it."

"Robert told you…"

"Alphonse told me."

"But…."

"He was there, about a quarter of a mile away, taking pictures."

Valerie stared at Alphonse. "You pervert."

"I had my clothes on," protested Alphonse.

"He was taking pictures of you meeting with Shorty," said Michael.

"Shorty?"

"Your Mr. Long," said Michael.

"But he's a crooked businessman," said Valerie. "He wanted to make a deal. He had a crooked arrangement with Peter Liverot."

"He told you that?"

"No, Robert and Mr. Rosen did," said Valerie. "Or at least they implied as much."

Michael shook his head sadly. "Mr. Long, or Shorty Long to those in the business, is a hitman; specifically, he blows up things. Didn't you think he was a little unusual for a businessman?"

Valerie thought a moment. "Yes, I suppose I did, but then I figured he was probably the type of shady character Liverot would do business with. But then he handed me Lorraine's picture, and when I took it, he held it for a second. That struck me as odd. He did the same thing with the papers he handed to me."

"That was the set-up," said Alphonse. "That was for the photographs, to implicate you with all kinds of culpability and stuff like that."

"Implicate me in what?"

Michael and Alphonse exchanged awkward looks.

"Who do you think blew up Lorraine's car?" asked Michael.

Valerie's mouth dropped open. "Why would I want to kill Lorraine?"

"Because you're the sole beneficiary on her life insurance policy," said Michael.

Valerie almost agreed that she knew that but stopped herself. Michael didn't know that she knew about the insurance.

"Oh, yes, well, then I guess it's a good thing Lorraine's alive," she said.

"What?" said Michael.

"Yay!" said Alphonse with childlike delight.

"But Shorty blew up her car," said Michael.

"He blew up Lorraine's car, but not with Lorraine in it," explained Valerie. "They blew up some aide. Lorraine's alive. In fact, that's who I'm going to London with."

Michael sat down on the edge of the bed, deep in thought. In some ways, he seemed even more upset to learn Lorraine was alive.

Valerie laughed. "What's the matter? Did I ruin your whole rescue scene, Michael? I suppose you thought I was some helpless little female who needed your protection."

Michael looked up. "No, not at all, but this makes it more complicated and more dangerous."

Valerie leaned over him, consciously giving him a good look down her cleavage, a not-so-subtle reminder of what he'd given up. "Hello, Michael, you didn't hear me! Lorraine is alive, so they can't pin her death on me."

He shook his head. "Don't you understand? That means that Lorraine is still in danger. As soon as they learn that she escaped the attempt…"

"So she's in danger," said Valerie with a shrug. "That's her problem. With all her money, she can hire a bodyguard or hide somewhere nice."

Michael looked at Valerie as if he suddenly didn't know her. "Don't you care about your cousin?"

"About as much as my real cousins, I mean my other cousins, care about me," snorted Valerie. "You dumped me as soon as you found out, and your brother wanted to pin an assassination on me. From here on in, it's every cousin for herself, and that includes Lorraine."

"You still don't get it," he said, grabbing her shoulders. "There was a body in that car."

"Yeah, well, it was some aide of hers. Believe me, everyone's better off without her around. I didn't trust her. She had too much influence over Lorraine. Good riddance to her."

Michael shook his head. "That's even worse. Even if he didn't get Lorraine, Robert could still implicate you. He still can prove you hired Shorty Long for the hit."

"Yes, but all they have is that little creep holding up a picture of Lorraine, not the Clott."

"The Clott?"

"The woman that got blown up, her last name is, was, Clott."

"That's even worse, they'll say you hired a hitman to blow up Lorraine, but you also killed an innocent victim."

"And," offered Alphonse, "they got Shorty's confession in writing."

Valerie gave him a dirty look for his contribution.

"Just saying…" muttered Alphonse.

As they stood there silently looking at her, Valerie could see sympathy in their eyes. If there's one thing she wouldn't take from anyone, especially Michael Valvano, it was pity.

"Alright," snapped Valerie, "thanks a lot for coming, for the tackling, and interrupting my packing, but I've got a lot to do, so if you'll just show yourself out…"

Michael stared at her and then softly said: "I wanted to make sure you were okay."

"Okay?" Valerie felt the anger rising within her. "You wanted to make sure I was okay? You left me up shit's creek to fend for myself, and now you want to make sure I'm okay? Isn't it a little bit late for that? And what makes you think I need you to look after me? I don't need you or any man to make sure I'm okay."

"I suppose I deserved that," said Michael, "but you don't understand."

"I don't, huh? I understand enough. I understand I can't depend on you, Michael Valvano, or anyone to cover my ass. I'll do just fine without your help."

Michael nodded slowly. "You sound just like someone else I know."

"You mean my grandmother?" said Valerie proudly.

"Our grandmother," said Michael. "At least now you admit it."

"Why wouldn't I admit it? She was a great woman, and I'm just like her."

"Yes, I can see that, now," he said.

Valerie studied his face. "What was that supposed to mean?"

"Nothing," said Michael.

"No, it wasn't nothing. That was a dig. I thought you loved Nonnia."

"Very much," said Michael. "But I knew her much better than you."

Valerie put her hands on her hips. "Then knowing her as well as you did, and knowing that I'm my grandmother's granddaughter, it will come as no surprise that I ask you to get your sorry ass out of my house before I throw you out. And take this lunkhead…"

"Lummox," corrected Alphonse.

"Shut up," she said, "both of you get out."

"We're leaving," said Michael, "just remember, to take care…"

"Like I need…." Valerie picked up a figurine from her dresser and threw it at him. It shattered against the door as he closed it behind him.

Valerie seethed as she heard them descend the stairs and then go out the front door. It was only then that she went downstairs and poured herself a stiff drink.

– 81 –
Blonde One:
Blonde on Flight

Lorraine Innis looked out of the plane window as the dawn was breaking over Ireland. She reached up and touched her blonde tresses and turned to Valerie Fierro.

"I feel silly," she said.

Valerie rolled her eyes and exhaled.

"What?" asked Lorraine.

"You've said that at least four times an hour since we got on the plane." She glanced at her wristwatch.

"I'm sorry," said Lorraine, "but I do feel silly. This blonde wig, and these fake glasses, and this is a lot more make-up than I usually wear. It just feels so bizarre to be wearing this ridiculous disguise."

If she didn't know better, Lorraine could swear that Valerie was biting her lip.

"It's okay for you," continued Lorraine. "You can dress normally. This skirt is too short, and, well, I feel cheap."

"That's the idea. You're not supposed to be yourself. You're supposed to be what's-her-name's secretary," said Valerie nodding her head to the row in front of them. Lorraine peeked through the gap between the seats where Lindsay Friseur and Hilda Madison were pouring over legal briefs. Hilda was drinking coffee. Lindsay was sipping champagne. Both seemed to be working very intently.

"I wish I could have been, well, more like myself," said Lorraine.

Valerie gave her a cryptic look and shook her head.

"I suppose," said Lorraine, "it's better than the first disguise they suggested."

Valerie just nodded and made a non-committal hum.

"They wanted me to…" Lorraine stopped herself. She had already shared with Valerie that first suggestion. Lindsay Friseur suggested that for the sake of secrecy that Lorraine disguise herself as a man. "...well, never mind that."

"Okay," said Valerie, and buried her nose in a magazine.

Lorraine sighed and looked out at the brightening horizon. She wished the approaching daylight was an omen. At the moment, however, she felt as she was groping through a fog-shrouded landscape. It was such an odd existence. She felt both supremely confident in herself and her abilities. While at the same time, she had the uneasy sense that part of her was locked behind a door deep within her own soul. Lorraine also had the strangest feeling that Clodagh Clott held the key. To what, Lorraine didn't know, but it was as if the poor deceased girl knew more about Lorraine than Lorraine knew herself. It wasn't just the physical aspects, either. Lorraine knew that her bodily parts didn't match those of a normal woman, but somehow that didn't bother her. She thought it should bother her, but it didn't, and that too was something that Clodagh understood, even if Lorraine didn't. Even Valerie, her closest relative, didn't understand. When Lorraine would try to talk to her about it, Valerie would get angry and invoke someone named "Chesney." The name was familiar, if only through Valerie's repeated reference to it, but it wasn't a name Lorraine needed to hear.

"Are you okay, Shirley?" a voice asked.

Lorraine continued to stare out the window until she felt Valerie's elbow jab her side.

"What?"

"She asked if you're okay, *Shirley*," said Valerie.

"Huh?" Lorraine looked up. Margie Mackay was standing in the aisle.

"Shirley, that's you," muttered Valerie out of the side of her mouth. "Remember? Shirley, the secretary."

"Oh, sorry, I was a million miles away, metaphorically speaking," said Lorraine. Then she remembered her disguise. "Does someone need to dictate a letter?"

Margie smiled. "No, just wanted to make sure you're okay. Can I get you anything?"

Lorraine smiled and shook her head. "No, I'm fine."

She wasn't fine. But there wasn't any living person who had an answer to her problems.

– 82 –
Blonde Two:
Blonde in Flight

W hat a relief it was when the plane finally touched down at Heathrow. Valerie was growing bored with the full-time Lorraine. Valerie could put up with a lot, but boring was the unpardonable sin. Valerie hadn't realized how boring Lorraine had become. The seven-hour flight sitting next to her made that apparent. If Lorraine wasn't going on about the stupid court case, she was talking about her disguise. Actually, Valerie thought Lorraine had the complexion that suited being a blonde, as well as having the legs to carry off the shorter skirt. Still, that didn't matter. Lorraine was boring.

At least Lorraine didn't realize Valerie had stuck her with the legal ownership of the perfume. Thankfully both Lorraine and Chesney were endowed with that dopey naiveté that overlooked when someone had intentionally screwed them over. It really didn't matter, Valerie told herself. Even if Valerie still held the rights to *Lorraine Innis' Quandry*, Lorraine would have insisted on taking responsibility. So, Valerie actually was just cutting out the middle-man. Right now, she was only there for moral support.

"You'd better get behind us, Shirley," Hilda Madison told Lorraine as they rose to deplane. "Remember you're supposed to be our secretary, at least until the press conference."

Lorraine stepped behind her lawyers and stood aside Valerie.

"You'd better not stand too close to me either," said Valerie. "If you do, people might see through your disguise. I'll just hang back a bit."

Lorraine nodded. "Yes, you're probably right. You wouldn't be seen with a secretary."

Valerie looked at Lorraine. It was said without malice but so matter-of-fact that she wondered if Lorraine was started to see things in a way that Chesney Potts never could. Lorraine was right, of course. Valerie Fierro had a position to uphold. She was almost a bank president and an internationally known figure. True, that was due to Lorraine, but still, the public expected things of her.

Valerie stood back and allowed Agent Mackay to go ahead of her. It was easier this way.

The procession worked their way up the gantry, and quite a procession it was. Lindsay Friseur strutted at the head of the party, her mink coat waving as she moved in broad theatrical gestures. Behind her was Hilda Madison looking just like what she was: a smart, professional attorney. Lorraine tottered along at Hilda's elbow in her tight short skirt and four-inch heels. Bringing up the rear was Margie Mackay looking conspicuously inconspicuous as she scanned the area for threats real or imagined.

The column bunched up again as they reached customs. There was a brief moment of anxiety as Lorraine's true identity was revealed to the customs clerk.

"I thought you were dead," he said in a low voice.

"Most everyone thinks so," said Lorraine lowering the large framed glasses. She pulled back the edge of the blonde wig and nodded towards her passport photo. "See, it's really me."

"Is there a problem," asked Hilda Madison in a discreet tone.

"Look, I'm this woman's attorney," bellowed Lindsay. "If there's any further hold-up, I'll have the American ambassador on the phone to your boss so quick it will melt your little rubber stamps. I'm a personal friend of the ambassador, not to mention several members of Parliament.

By the time Lindsay finished, the clerk had stamped Lorraine's passport. He handed it back to her, expressed his delight that she was alive, and wished her welcome to the United Kingdom.

"Thank you," said Lorraine.

"See," noted Lindsay to no one in particular, "you have to make a stink to get action. He sure took care of that when I said something."

"Or in spite of you," said Hilda under her breath.

Once they were all through customs, they were met by a distinguished middle-aged man.

"This is my Brit associate," announced Lindsay, "Morty." She gave the man a hug and a kiss, which he returned, albeit with discomfort.

"Mortimer Bounds," said the man correcting his American associate's familiarity. "How very good to see you again, Hilda."

"Morty," said Lindsay, "this is Valerie Fierro, and this is a secret service agent. I'm sorry, hon, I forgot your name…"

"Margaret Mackay," said Margie, shaking Mr. Bounds hand.

"Right," continued Lindsay, "and Morty, this is you-know-who." She made that last introduction indicating Lorraine and accompanied by a wink.

"A singular pleasure to meet you all," said Mortimer Bounds.

"Isn't he cute? I love his little accent," said Lindsay. "Is everything ready, Morty?"

"Ah, yes," said Bounds blushing slightly at Lindsay's comment. "I've contacted the media, and they're waiting in a briefing room. I had to drop Mrs. Innis' name and promise them a major revelation from her legal representative. All the UK outlets are here, along with the major American and international press."

"Isn't he a doll?" said Lindsay beaming. "Morty, you're a doll. Now, lead me to the room. You go first, Morty, and introduce me, and then, I'll do the big build-up, and we'll spring the surprise. Is there a side room, like I asked, Morty?"

Bounds assured her there was an anteroom.

"Perfect," continued Lindsay, "Hildy, you and Val can wait back there, with our girl here. Get her presentable, you know, lose that blonde get up. Then, when I'm ready, I'll make the big announcement and bring her out. Okay, everybody?"

"I thought I'd have a chance to change," said Lorraine indicating her uncharacteristic outfit.

Lindsay studied Lorraine before concluding. "You look fine!"

"Well, then, the media is waiting," said Bounds. "If you'll just come this way."

Valerie saw her chance. "You all go ahead. I'll catch up with you. I've got to use the bathroom," she whispered in Lorraine's ear. "Don't worry. I'll be right behind you." Then, she leaned over and gave Lorraine a peck on the cheek.

Valerie turned and headed to the nearest ladies' room. Once inside, she founded an empty stall and hung her carry-on bag on the back of the door. From it, she pulled a mirror and a plastic bag containing her own blonde wig.

"She's not the only one who can go blonde," she muttered to herself.

Then, after a quick brush, a freshening of her make-up, and other necessaries, Valerie exited the convenience, made her way to the baggage claim, and then to the nearest airport exit, and hailed a cab.

"Where to Ma'am," asked the cabbie, "London?"

Valerie thought a moment. "No, the opposite direction."

"West?"

"Yes, west," she said, "what's that way?"

"A good part of the country, until you get to Wales," said the cabbie facetiously."

"Yes, that sounds good," said Valerie climbing into the cab.

The driver shrugged and pulled away.

Away from London, thought Valerie. It was her only option under the circumstances.

- 83 -
Alive, Dead, Alive

It had been a deep sleep, like the sleep of a warrior who had fought valiantly but had lost. Yet, the defeat was somehow better than a victory, vanquished by a kind and merciful adversary.

Verity Goodhue slowly stirred to the sound of voices. She kept her eyes closed as she recalled where she was and what had happened. It must be morning. Yes, it was mid-morning. She had fallen asleep with the television on, watching her grandfather's film. Now a morning chat show was on. She recognized the voices. Verity opened her eyes and sat up. It was as she recalled: she was in her bedroom in her father's Eaton Square townhouse. She reached for the remote to turn off the television when the host's words commanded her attention.

"We're going live now to Heathrow Airport for a press conference with the attorneys of the late Lorraine Innis..."

The picture switched to a podium where a middle-aged man was in the middle of an introduction.

"...to represent the defense in the upcoming civil suit precipitated over the fragrance known as *Quandary*: Ms. Lindsay Friseur."

The man stepped aside or almost seemed pushed aside as a woman commanded the stage. Everything about her was larger than life: her manner, gestures, and even her hair commanded attention. The woman put on a pair of reading glasses, which looked very expensive and trendy, and then proceeded to look over them.

"Thank you, Mr. Bounds," the woman began in a forceful tone saturated with a vibrant East Coast accent. "I also want to thank the members of the media for coming out today, and I promise you that you won't be disappointed."

Suddenly a buzz ran throughout the room. At first, Ms. Friseur seemed pleased, as if they were reacting to her promise of a scoop. But it became evident, last of all to the woman at the podium, that the excitement was generated elsewhere.

"Excuse me, excuse me," said Friseur, but the room's attention was somewhere else. "Pardon me... HEY! Come on, I've got something to... HEY!"

Friseur was banging on the microphone when the picture was switched back to the studio.

"We apologize to our viewers," said the chat host, "and we'll return to Heathrow momentarily, but we switch live to Washington, where the head of the Federal Bureau of In..."

The scene switched again to an FBI official behind yet another podium.

"...forensic evidence which confirms that the body incinerated in Lorraine Innis' automobile did not belong to Lorraine Innis..."

Verity's mouth dropped open, and tears of joy welled up in her eyes. It wasn't Lorraine in the car. That meant her beloved, her Chesney, was alive. She leaped up and, for the first time since she was a small girl, began jumping on the bed.

"He's alive! He's alive!" She cried.

Verity hopped off the bed and was about to run out to find Li Gao to share the joyous news when the flat, official tones of the FBI director intruded.

"We do not yet know who the victim was in the car, but DNA evidence indicates the person was definitely a male..."

Verity fell on the bed as if she had been shot. Of course, it was a male. They assumed that it wasn't Lorraine Innis because they didn't know Lorraine was really a man. All hope was now dashed, and Verity broke down in a torrent of tears.

"We apologize for these quick cutaways," said the chat host, "but rapidly unfolding events necessitate that we..."

Before the host could complete the segue, the picture switched back to the podium at Heathrow Airport, where the strident American lawyer was in the middle of what seemed to be a fit.

"...I know she's alive, damn it! If you'd all just listen! I don't care what the FBI says. It's nothing I couldn't have told you if you'd just shut up and...what?.... because she's right here.... that's what I'm trying to tell you stupid limeys! Hilda, bring her out! I'm done with you all!"

With that, another woman escorted Lorraine Innis to the podium. It was Chesney, or Lorraine, or both of them. The hair was matted down as if she had just taken off a hat, and the clothing was a bit down-market, but it was Lorraine Innis.

As quickly as her tears began to flow, Verity's sorrow turned back once more to joy, and a new issue of tears streamed forth.

– 84 –
A Suite Visitor Turned Away

Lorraine Innis sat in the eye of the hurricane that was her suite at the Dorchester. Thankfully it was the largest suite in the hotel.

Lindsay Friseur generated much of the activity. The parade of her London associates and contacts extended far beyond the legal realm. Each catered to Ms. Friseur's needs to ensure the primary goal: success in court.

"Do we need all these people," Lorraine asked Hilda Madison.

"They're all Lindsay's," explained Hilda.

Lindsay was busy issuing a dizzying series of commands. Lorraine was impressed by the way the attorney juggled so many different topics so rapidly and efficiently. One minute she was grilling Mortimer Bounds on a nuance of British courtroom etiquette. Next, she would be giving precise instructions to a waiter on how she wanted her lunch prepared. She even conveyed strict details for the automobiles that would transport them to court.

"It just seems so frantic," said Lorraine.

"Believe me," said Hilda, "it would be worse if we didn't have people from Mr. Bounds' office posted outside. Your friend Margie's been a big help with that as well."

"I don't know what I've done without Margie," said Lorraine. "Especially since Valerie disappeared so suddenly. At least she sent me a postcard."

Hilda shook her head. "Did your cousin ever tell you before about this uncontrollable urge to visit Wales?"

"No, I had no idea until she disappeared from the airport and sent me a postcard from Caerphilly." Lorraine scratched her head. "There seem to be too many people disappearing: Clodagh, and then Valerie."

"Still, it must be a relief to know that Ms. Clott was not the person who was killed when your car blew up."

Lorraine nodded. "Yes, I'm thankful that she's alive, or at least that she might be alive. She's such a responsible person. It's not like her to go off like that without a word."

"You've known her long, then," said Hilda.

"I...I'm not sure when we met," said Lorraine, "I just hope she's okay, if only..."

Margie Mackay came in from the suite's foyer. "Lorraine, there's someone here to see you."

Hilda Madison shook her head. "These British newspaper people..."

"She's not a reporter," said Margie. "She's been here several times. She won't go away. She says she wants to see you personally. It's very important."

"Important? Is it Clodagh? No, of course, Margie, you know Clodagh." Lorraine turned to Hilda. "Maybe it's someone with news about Clodagh. That would be very important."

"She says she's Lord Bagnall's daughter," said Margie. "Her name is..."

"WHAT?!" The mention of Bagnall shifted Lindsay Friseur's attention away from discussing the suit she would wear to court. "Bagnall? Here?"

"Uh, no, it's his daughter," said Margie. "She said her name is..."

"I don't care what her name is," said Lindsay.

"Lord Bagnall," muttered Lorraine with a shiver. "That name gives me the oddest feeling."

"It should," said Lindsay. "He's the bastard that's leading the class-action suit. He's the snake who manufactured the perfume. Then, when the army of bearded ladies, alleged, started coming after him, he double-crossed you."

"Maybe his daughter wants to apologize, or maybe they're offering to settle..." said Lorraine.

Lindsay whipped back her head, bringing her voluminous hair to its full mane-like splendor. "Not on your life, you tell little Miss Bagnall..."

"She isn't named 'Bagnall.' Her name is..." began Margie Mackay.

"I don't care if her name is Queen Elizabeth the third," insisted Lindsay. "You tell her to.... Morty, what the expression you Brits use?"

"Uh, hop it? Sling your hook? On your bike?" offered Mortimer Bounds.

"All of those work for me," said Lindsay. "Tell her if it they have anything to say, say it through their lawyers. Otherwise, hop on their hook and sling it!"

Margie Mackay rushed off to convey the message.

"It couldn't hurt to just see her, would it?" asked Lorraine.

Lindsay Friseur smiled patronizingly and smoothed her hand over Lorraine's tresses. "You're too nice, doll. But you stay that way. No need to be vicious. That's why you've got me."

– 85 –
His Lordship's Domicide

It was so frustrating," said Verity Goodhue. "They wouldn't let me see him. If I could have just seen him for a minute…"

Li Gao patted her hand. "A moment of satisfaction, but possibly at the cost of days of regret, my dear."

Verity looked into his serene expression and nodded. "Yes, of course, you're probably right. It was foolish for me to go there. I may have ruined everything for my beloved. I was wrong."

"It is not wrong to try to open a door," said Gao. "Error only comes when we attempt to force our way in after we find the way closed, even closed temporarily. Providence has kept our boy safe thus far against many dangerous and trying circumstances. And now he is back with us. We must be patient and trust that…"

The door to the sitting room flew open with a bang. As loud as the sound of the door was, it was a mere whisper compared to the voice that accompanied it.

"THERE YOU ARE!" Lord Bagnall leveled his finger at his daughter.

"Hello, Father," said Verity softly.

"Don't not give me 'ello, father,'" said Bagnall. "Does you 'ave h'any h'idea wot you done?"

"Good evening, your Lordship," said Li Gao.

"Good even…wot's 'e doin' 'ere?" said Bagnall.

"He's my guest, my friend…"

"I don't care if 'e's your chiropodist! It don't not make no difference if you invite in all the Chings from Chingford. You is confusing the point. Wot was I sayin'?"

"You asked if I knew what I had done," said Verity.

Lord Bagnall looked towards the ceiling as he mentally retraced his thoughts. "Oh, yes, right! Does you know wot you 'ave done?"

Verity bit her lip. "I suppose you're referring to my visit to the Dorchester this afternoon."

"It h'ain't the Dorchester or even the h'afternoon, which is in question, it's 'oo you went to see that's got under me nipple!"

"Lorraine Innis…"

"H'exactly! Lorraine Innis! Lorraine Bloody Innis!"

"Please don't swear, Father," she said, "not in front of guests."

"May I remind you this is still my 'ouse and if guests don't not like 'ow I behave in me own domicide they can bloody well lump it, or better yet leave."

Lord Bagnall glowered at Li Gao, who sat there as placidly as if the room were devoid of raging Lords. Seeing that his bluster was wasted in that direction, Bagnall returned it to his daughter and the matter at hand.

"Yes, right, well," said Bagnall, "it h'ain't not enough that me own daughter, me own prodigy goes to see the very woman wot I is suing. But me, muggins, I gots to find out from me own lawyers. I gets a right royal rodgerin' from the banisters wot I is payin', because she did. Now, what I gots is one question: wot was you, me own daughter, doin'?"

"I wanted to meet Lorraine Innis, Father," she said.

"H'obviously! But wot I wants to know is why?!"

Verity demurred. She couldn't very well truthfully explain what she hoped to accomplish by meeting with Lorraine Innis. Li Gao, sensing her discomfort, stepped into the breach.

"Miss Goodhue had matters of a personal nature to discuss with Mrs. Innis," said Gao.

"Personal nature?" said Bagnall cocking a suspicious eye at Li Gao and then turning the expression on his daughter. "Personal nature? Is this true?"

"Yes, Father, it's personal."

"But not at all germane to your lawsuit, your Lordship," added Li Gao.

Lord Bagnall snorted. "I didn't not h'imply that the Germans 'ad h'anything to do with it, neither does h'any Chinamen!"

"Don't be rude to Mr. Li, Father."

Bagnall's eyes opened wide in shock. "Me? Rude? I h'ain't being rude to no one, no how! I said 'Chinaman,' I wasn't not even thinking: 'Chink.'"

"I appreciate your courtesy, your Lordship," said Li Gao.

"There, you sees?" said Bagnall to Verity. "Now, if this oriental chap can extends me that respect, why can't me own daughter?"

"How have I been disrespectful to you, Father?"

"'Ow? You says you have personal reasons for seeing that Lorraine Innis and I respects your privacy. But then you keeps it a secret from your old Dad while h'obviously telling this little rice picker!"

"But, you wouldn't understand," said Verity. Or, she thought, he'd understand too well and try to ruin everything a second time.

Lord Bagnall adopted an air that was hurt, magnanimous, and patently phony. "I h'understands. You keeps your little secrets. Only you're to stay away from Lorraine Innis until this little legal fracas is done being fricasseed. That h'ain't just a fatherly omission, but it comes from me lawyers as well. I will not 'ave this case mucked up because me own daughter is star-struck by some American bird with a big beak. Do you h'understands me?"

Verity nodded. "Yes. I will not try to contact Lorraine Innis before the start of the trial."

"Nor during it," said Bagnall.

"But surely I can sit in the court in the area you've reserved," she said. "You promised."

"Promise reneged," said His Lordship.

"But..."

Lord Bagnall raised his hand. "It h'aint me, well, maybe a bit of me. But me lawyers. They don't wants you too close to Lorraine Innis. And I agrees with them."

"Do you think I'll be passing secret signals to Mrs. Innis or giving her advice on how to beat you?"

He stroked his chin. "That's what the law birds said, too. H'anyways, they don't not trust you."

"And do you agree with them?" said Verity. "Do you distrust your own daughter?"

"I trust you insipidly," assured Bagnall, "but when it comes to business, money, law cases, and things like that, I'll still keep me eye on you."

"Thank you very much, Father," said Verity with frosty sarcasm.

"You're welcome," said Bagnall, either not understanding nor caring or both. With that, he left the room.

Verity slumped into the wing chair. "Oh, Gao, at the very least, I had hoped to be in the front of the courtroom. If I could only sit close to him, he would know I'm alive, and he'd know I cared. Now, I don't know if I'll even be able to get into the gallery."

Li Gao bowed his head. "Hope deferred makes the heart sick, my dear. But when the desire comes, it is like a tree of life. Your tree will bud and bloom."

– 86 –
Trial by Awakening

L orraine Innis took the witness stand at Her Majesty's High Court of Justice, Queen's Bench division. It literally was a witness stand, unlike in the United States where a person sat. Lorraine wished she had worn more comfortable shoes.

"You look perfect," Lindsay Friseur had pronounced when Lorraine emerged from her bedroom in the suite at the Dorchester. "The suit is just right, knee-length, tailored to show your figure without flaunting it. And the color is just the right shade of blue: not too dark to be intimidating, nor too light as to be frivolous. Didn't I tell you that my people know how to dress a person for court? They're worth every penny."

Lorraine grinned sheepishly. "This is my suit. I didn't like any of the expert choices. Sorry."

Lindsay Friseur waved her hand. "What do they know? Be yourself; that's what I say. I always say be yourself, don't I, Hildy?"

"Yes, Lindsay," sighed her law partner. "Be yourself. Who else could be you?"

"Exactly," said Lindsay.

Those voices echoed through Lorraine's mind, along with a dozen others, or so it seemed. She heard the voices of Valerie, Patsy, Purvis Twankey, Nikolai Kropotkin, and others that she couldn't identify. She listened for a word or two from Clodagh, but there was none. There was the curious, nagging sense that she needed a word or two from Clodagh.

"Remember what we went over," Lindsay Friseur advised as Lorraine rose to take the stand. Lorraine nodded. She would have reminded Lindsay of her own promise, to tell the truth, and take full responsibility, but it wouldn't have done any good, not at this stage. Every time Lorraine said as much to Lindsay, she had received one of two reactions. Either the lawyer thought it was a cagy strategy to avoid culpability, or it was proof that they needed to pursue an insanity defense.

"Never mind," Lindsay Friseur would say, "I'll get you out of this despite yourself. You've got the best attorney on either side of the Atlantic."

So Lorraine took the stand at the end of the plaintiffs' case. A dozen women, all with impressive displays of facial hair, testified. Backing their testimony was a raft of doctors, family members, chemists, cosmeticians, barbers, and experts in the study of trichology. All painted the vivid picture that these women, along with many others represented in the suit, were all smooth-faced until they had begun using *Lorraine Innis' Quandry*. The lawyers for the plaintiff were careful to emphasize Lorraine's name whenever the fragrance was cited. Lindsay Friseur objected but was overruled since it was the legally trademarked name of the product.

The courtroom was packed, including the balcony area. Lorraine hadn't noticed the crowd when she was sitting facing the bench. Now, upon the stand, they were hard to ignore. Also sitting there was the plaintiffs' champion, the man who was paying for the suit, Lord Bagnall. There was something oddly familiar to Lorraine about the man. She had never met him before, but the very sight of him stirred up the strangest flood of emotions, the strongest of which was a deep, almost unbearable sorrow. She couldn't explain this. If there was anyone she should feel sorry for, it would be all those poor bearded women, not the man who was paying their legal fees. Still, there was something about Bagnall that pained Lorraine.

After she was sworn in, the questioning of Lorraine began.

"You are Lorraine Elizabeth Innis of Wilmington, Delaware, United States of America."

"Yes," said Lorraine, "well, technically, I suppose I'm still Lorraine Elizabeth Amaccappane, as my marital status proved to be invalid as my husband was already married, and, in fact, he wasn't even named 'Innis.' Still, by then I was already famous, through no desire of my own, but there you have it. And the part about Wilmington is also up for argument. I live there now, but I'm still a resident of New Jersey. I haven't voted since I moved to Delaware, and I haven't changed my voter registration. So, I'm not sure how British law regards these distinctions. I could either be Lorraine Elizabeth Innis of Delaware, or Lorraine Elizabeth Innis of New Jersey, or Lorraine Elizabeth Amaccappane of Delaware, or Lorraine Elizabeth Amaccappane of New Jersey."

The attorney who had posed the question sighed. "I believe that given your international notoriety, you are the subject in question."

"Yes, I don't think there's another person with both my name and a perfume named *Quandry*."

"Then you admit, Mrs. Innis…"

381

"You can call me 'Lorraine,' if you like. I know that part is correct."

The attorney smiled. "Thank you, I think we'll keep this on a formal basis, Mrs. Innis."

"Yes, that probably is best," admitted Lorraine.

"Thank you."

"You're welcome," she said.

Laughter broke out across the courtroom, even from behind the ladies' beards.

"Mrs. Innis," continued the attorney, "I wish to make full disclosure that I am an admirer of yours. As such, I am well acquainted with your reputation as a charming and disarming pedantic."

"Excuse me," said Lorraine, "but the correct term for a pedantic person is a 'pedant.'"

"Of course, my apologies..."

"Though I suppose it proves your point," she added.

"Just so," said the blushing attorney. "Again, we are all well acquainted with your charming and candid manner. But I caution you, despite your winning reputation, I will not allow you to use these tactics to mitigate your responsibilities to the claimants in this suit."

Lorraine looked at the attorney and then at the hairy women assembled.

"I am not here to mitigate my responsibilities. Rather I am here to satisfy them," she said. "I plan to make full restitution to all the injured parties."

A buzz ran through the courtroom, and the judge gaveled for silence. Once it was restored, Lindsay Friseur arose.

"Your honor," said Lindsay, "she doesn't know what she's saying..."

"I certainly do," said Lorraine.

"No, you don't," asserted Lindsay. "Did you invent the product in question?"

"No, but..."

Lindsay Friseur grabbed a document off the table and waved it. "The original idea for a perfume based on a person's unique essence came from one Mr. Purvis Twankey..."

"The singer?" asked the judge.

"The same," said Lindsay.

"But I consented to Purvis, that is, Mr. Twankey, pursuing the idea," said Lorraine.

"That may be so." Lindsay snapped her fingers, and Hilda Madison handed her the next document. "But did you approve the product, either in its prototype stage or approve it going into production?"

"I..."

"Again," said Lindsay waving the new document handed her, "that decision was made by your cousin, Miss Valerie Fierro..."

"Yes, but only because..."

"...made by Miss Fierro, without either your knowledge or consent, is that true?"

"Technically, yes, I suppose, but..."

"Yes, is sufficient, Mrs. Innis," said Lindsay.

"Mrs. Innis?" said Lorraine giving her attorney a confused look.

"And where is Miss Fierro right now?" asked Lindsay putting her hand above her eyes and searching the courtroom.

"I... I believe she's in Caerphilly, at least I think so..."

"Caerphilly," repeated Lindsay.

"That's in Wales," said Lorraine.

"Thank you for the geography lesson, Mrs. Innis," said Lindsay receiving the next document from Hilda. "I have here a copy of the agreement between Miss Fierro and the lead plaintiff, Lord Bagnall. Have you ever met Lord Bagnall?"

Lorraine looked over at the life peer, who was nervously fingering his collar. "There's something awfully familiar about him, but no, to the best of my knowledge, I've never met the gentleman."

"No, you never have," said Lindsay. "Agreement was reached between Miss Fierro and Lord Bagnall to produce and distribute the scent in the United Kingdom. Miss Fierro supplied the formula. Lord Bagnall provided the manufacturing, marketing, and distribution. And what did you supply, Mrs. Innis?"

Lorraine thought a moment and shrugged. "I suppose a sample of my blood and my name on the bottle..."

"Your pure blood and your good name," said Lindsay.

"Yes, but..."

"And in return, Miss Fierro and Lord Bagnall split all the proceeds of the product."

"Yes, technically, but I own it now."

"And when was the property transferred to you?" asked Lindsay.

"It was..."

"It was after the product was pulled from distribution. After the proverbial effluence hit the proverbial fan! Mrs. Innis, you were the patsy..."

"Patsy had nothing to do with... oh, sorry," said Lorraine. She hadn't expected her own attorney to start treating her as a hostile witness.

"So, Mrs. Innis," concluded Lindsay Friseur, "these events were not precipitated by you. This was not your idea. You did not authorize its manufacture or sales. You did not receive a penny of any profit. But now that it's all gone sour, the entire debacle is thrown upon you. And you hold yourself responsible, Mrs. Innis?"

Lindsay Friseur struck a dramatic stance. It was a physical exclamation point to her verbal summation, and it dared anyone to disagree with her conclusions.

Loathe as she was to fly in the face of her own lawyer's efforts, Lorraine cleared her throat and began in a timorous voice.

"I appreciate all that you've said," began Lorraine. "I know you're working for my best interests, and I thank you for that. It must not be very easy to have a client such as me, and you have executed your duties admirably on my behalf."

Lindsay Friseur nodded but looked as if she were reserving judgment for what might come next.

"You really are a fine attorney," continued Lorraine. "I couldn't ask for a better representative, even as you're countermanding my stated wishes. You're right. Most of this isn't my fault. I see all those poor ladies sitting there, and I know that they represent many more women who, because of me, don't feel quite as womanly as they once did. Certainly, none of them wanted to grow beards. I can't understand why they grew beards. I don't have a beard. I don't even have that little peach fuzz that some women have, not even a light mustache. I don't say that to brag or somehow excuse myself. It's just my first step of saying I don't understand what that perfume did, or why, or how. But even though it wasn't my idea, and it wasn't my plan, and I didn't receive any money from all this, I do know one thing. Those women bought that product and used that product because they admired me, they trusted me, and maybe they wanted to be more like me. They didn't want to grow facial hair, but that's what happened. They purchased the product because of me. If I don't take responsibility, then who will? To shirk my responsibility or wriggle out of making this right would go against the trust that those women had in me. I want to do the right thing because it's a great responsibility to be a role model. I never asked to be a role model. Still, if by some strange circumstances I've become one, then I have to fulfill that calling, especially when it's not convenient to do so. I have to confess, I don't have much money. I don't know what these ladies want or how I can make their situations right again, but I promise I'll do what I need to do."

The courtroom sat in silence, watching Lorraine. After a moment, she shrugged her shoulders. "Sorry, Ms. Friseur, Ms. Madison, but that's what we need to do. I hope you'll help me work out an equitable ending to all this. Thank you."

By now, Lindsay Friseur's brave stance had melted into one less heroic, like a wax statue left standing in the noonday sun. Finally, she just shook her head and slumped into her chair. She looked at Hilda Madison with a silent plea for help. Hilda just smiled and then looked up at Lorraine Innis and began to clap. Then she stood. Then others joined in the applause, and they stood. Within moments, the entire courtroom was giving Lorraine an ovation, except poor Lindsay Friseur, who, by now, was sitting with her head in her hands. Even Lord Bagnall gave grudging applause, though he didn't stand.

The outpouring of adulation was at first embarrassing to Lorraine and then made her feel disoriented. Like an amateur actor on stage, she didn't quite know what to do with her hands or where to look. Then she glanced up in the gallery. There in the back row, she caught a glimpse of someone, the briefest glance in the crowd. Lorraine felt herself go weak in the back of her knees, and she clutched at the rail of the witness stand. She started to look back up, but the rapping of the judge's gavel refocused her attention.

"Mrs. Innis," said the judge, once order had been restored. "Mrs. Innis, thank you for sincerely shouldering responsibility in this unfortunate matter. I take it then that you are directing your legal representatives to make an equitable settlement with the plaintiffs?"

"Yes, please," said Lorraine. She put her hand to her brow. She felt dizzy and tried to glance back towards the balcony while still paying attention to the judge.

"I commend your devotion to justice and verity..."

"Verity?" Lorraine felt the strangest stirring. It was as if there were a window in her mind, and it was being opened a crack.

"Yes," repeated the judge, "the devotion to justice and verity show the sincere good you possess..."

"Verity...good...you..." muttered Lorraine. "Verity...good...you. Verity Goodhue!"

The window flew open wide. A gust of thoughts, memories, and realizations flew into her head. In less than a moment, the gust grew into a gale as she came back to herself after weeks in a trance without respite. It was all so intense, so violent, so much had happened, and now...

"Mrs. Innis...Mrs. Innis..." The voice of the judge was calling to her, a look of concern etched in his face.

Lorraine felt herself sway...

– 87 –
The Kind of a Girl Who Still Makes the News of the World

The reporter straightened her jacket, checked her microphone, tossed back her hair, and looked at the camera.

"All right, fellows, in three… two… I'm standing outside of the Royal Courts of Justice here in London, where Lorraine Innis has been giving testimony in the civil case before the Queen's Bench. In a remarkable series of events, Mrs. Innis took the stand to claim full responsibility for any damages resulting from her signature fragrancy, *Lorraine Innis' Quandry*. After this, she was subjected to hostile questioning by her own attorney. Next, she successfully rebuffed her representative's probing, eliciting a spontaneous and prolonged ovation from the courtroom. Finally, as she was receiving the approval of the judge, Mrs. Innis, still in the witness box, fainted. Initial efforts to revive her on the scene proved fruitless, and she had been taken to an undisclosed location by private ambulance."